The 12th Disciple
Book Two
The End of Alpha
By Scott Peters

Editors
Heather Peters
Emily Peters
Joe Sharkey

Cover Artwork
Illustrated Covers By Maya Ritchie
Graphic Design Cover By Crystal Peak
Design in Colorado Springs
www.crystalpeak.com

Copyright Information

The 12th Disciple
The End of Alpha

Acknowledgements

A very special thanks to Heather, Emily, Joe, and Maya for becoming a significant part of The 12th Disciple series. Thanks to the readers and fans that have joined us for the ride. I really appreciate the feedback, reviews, and constructive criticism of the stories and writing style to help me become a better author.

A heartfelt thanks to my parents and the wonderful years we've spent together in Colorado. Thanks for the inspiration, the discipline, and the "teachable moments" to help me become a productive person and parent.

For my wife, stepsons, and son

www.12thdisciple.com

Twitter: 12DiscipleBook

To contact the author: scott@gigs-n-rigs.com

The 12th Disciple (Book One) Rewind

Disciples

Sesom Ishmael (Africa)
Amen Jordan (Israel)
Cering Kadesh (Egypt)
Ethan Mubarak (Egypt)
Dorje (Tibet)
Kimi Kei (Japan)
Lucas Tavares (Brazil)
Li Che (China)
Talan Serin (India)

The 12th Disciple: Matt Hiatt (North America)

Disciples In Memoriam

Liam (Canada)
Trevor (England)

Key Characters

President Palmer—Current President of US
Vice President Crevan—Current Vice President of US
Elisabeth—Woman found at the Western Wall
Mary Barnes—Matt's sister
Mike Barnes—Matt's brother-in-law
John and Rebecca—Matt's nephew and niece
Captain Phil—Captain of the Excalibur
John & Aaron—Deckhands for the Excalibur
Jonas Andros—Director of Vatican Security
Noah Webster—Matt's coworker at Delta Defense
Pope Simplicius II—Current Pope
Suzie—Assistant for the Disciples
Red Taylor—Owner of Taxicab Company
Scratches—Matt's cat

Points to Ponder from Book One of The 12th Disciple Series...

- The 12th Disciple is found in the City of Angels.
- Samil represents the Angel of Death and everything evil in the world.
- Matt's visions take the Disciples to the Western Wall in Jerusalem.
- Matt finds the mysterious woman from his dreams at the Western Wall. Samil executes terror attack at the Western Wall.
- Mary, Matt's sister, is kidnapped by Samil and held in Gaza.
- Jonas Andros locates the Disciples in Tel Aviv and invites them to visit the Vatican and meet with Pope Simplicius II.
- World War III begins.
- Pope Simplicius speaks with Matt and Elisabeth about their calling and blessings from God.
- Dirty bombs are detonated in four major cities of the United States. President Palmer was in Concord, New Hampshire when two bombs are detonated.

****

"Vice President Crevan, Secretary of State Watt is here for his appointment." The Oval Office Secretary remained on the line for confirmation.

She hung up, "He is ready to see you."

"Thank you." Secretary of State Watt passed through an Oval Office door; the Oval Office hadn't changed for decades. The United States' seal on the floor, several pictures of past Presidents on the walls, plants, and a view of the Presidential garden directly behind Palmer's high back leather chair.

Mickey Watt and Alexander Crevan served together under President Palmer. They had also orchestrated one of the most significant coup d'états in recent history. Alexander Crevan had served as a no nonsense Massachusetts Senator before being selected as a Vice Presidential candidate for Palmer's campaign. Crevan was an important choice to gain votes and electorate appeal in the northeast. Senator Crevan had served in Desert Storm and Operation Iraqi Freedom. Crevan's position and leverage in the military afforded him the opportunity to foster adversarial relationships throughout the Middle East. Those relationships paid dividends in the successful assassination of President Palmer.

Mickey Watt served with Crevan in the Middle East on multiple tours. They would set up security forces and meet with tribes in Iraq and Afghanistan to maintain superficial peace. Watt and Crevan knew peace came at a price and they funneled billions of American dollars to warlords and tribal leaders to maintain a cease-fire in the territory. They paid off anybody and everybody to ensure the peace process looked successful to the public at home and abroad. By doing so, they were able to buy relationships that would bring them to eventual power and control of the United States.

"Have a seat." Crevan and Watt maintained militaristic professionalism and respect. He took a seat in front of Crevan's oversized oak desk, an oak desk that belonged to President Palmer a few days prior.

Watt opened up a folder with briefing documents he'd collected from an international team. He pulled his reading glasses up to his eyes, "The Excalibur left the Port at Flumicino 10 minutes ago."

"What direction?"

"Heading northwest."

"Is our target on the ship?" Crevan leaned back in his chair and crossed his fingers while tapping his thumbs together.

"She is, along with nine or ten Israeli Defense Sailors, the Captain and his crew, and an international security force protecting her."

"What is the connection with the Americans involved with her security force?" Crevan was testing Watt's ability to gather intelligence.

"We don't know yet."

"Why not?" Crevan wasn't impressed by the lack of intel.

"We were very close to the self-proclaimed Disciples in Los Angeles when they contacted Matthew Hiatt. Matt is a very well trained and decorated Marine serving in Special Operations. Even though he's young, he has served in some of the toughest missions around the world. Looks like Matt's sister and brother-in-law met up with them at some point between Los Angeles and Ashdod."

"What's the story with his sister?" Crevan didn't see the connection and why they would join the Disciples.

Watt shuffled some papers, "Stay at home mom raising two children. Graduated from the University of Colorado with honors. She was involved in the tragic shootings of Columbine High School. Even though she was in the library, she survived somehow and administered aid to those wounded or deceased. Pretty boring, no record, criminal or otherwise."

Crevan continued to tap his thumbs together and moved forward in his chair, "What about her husband?"

"Michael Barnes. He served in multiple tours for the Marines and Special Operations in Afghanistan and Iraq. Highly trained in weaponry and hand-to-hand combat. Many Medals of Valor for disabling or killing the enemy with his bare hands. Looks like Mike is very well known and respected in the Marines and Special Forces. Retired early to start his own business and become a family man."

"Touching." Crevan turned to look out the windows behind him.

"How soon can we have birds in the area?" Oddly enough, Crevan noticed Canadian geese flying south in formation for the winter.

Watt went to a map on a nearby wall; "We have birds in the area right now over France and Bosnia. We can have a couple Stealth fighters with payload there inside of 45 minutes."

"I'd prefer a visual with guided missiles to guarantee that we eliminate the target. Unleash the Stealth fighters and," Crevan paused, "no survivors." He turned the chair back around and smiled at Watt.

"These people and this boat are the only things standing in our way. I'll set up a news conference with the White House Press to update the world with our succession plan and groups responsible for the terrorist attacks on our soil." Crevan's smile grew wider.

"I will phone Secretary of Defense Drake and have him order the strike. Let's meet in the Situation Room in thirty minutes for a satellite feed of the attack." Watt gathered his papers from a nearby chair and exited the Oval Office. Crevan rotated his chair back around and peered out the windows. Some black birds were calling from a nearby oak tree on the South Lawn of the White House. A government that created a level of dependency like never seen before in the United States was about to take everything back.

****

Matt was on the stern of the Excalibur absorbing an Italian coastline. Compared to the Port of Ashdod in Israel, Flumicino was peaceful with lights flickering up and down the coast. He looked overhead and two anti-aircraft gun barrels reminded Matt of a transformation the Excalibur was undergoing to be wartime ready, much like the Disciples and sailors on the ship.

Matt thought about what Pope Simplicius II said with regard to Elisabeth and their calling. As he played back the conversation in his mind, Matt was a little embarrassed by the details of his predetermined relationship with Elisabeth. Matt knew that prearranged marriages happened all over the world, but not in the United States. There was something odd being told about a significant other and future child, especially from a Pope. Matt's mind was swirling and he was having a difficult time wrapping his thoughts around the details.

"Get a good look at it." Ethan walked up and stood at the right hand of Matt.

"Hey Ethan. Beautiful isn't it?"

"Yes, and amazingly calm right now."

Ethan continued, "I know that I was skeptical and difficult when we first met, I want to apologize for my behavior."

Matt turned to Ethan, "I understand. Probably feeling a little better since putting Seth in his place, six feet under."

"Much better." Ethan's grin cut through the darkness. "Seth had it coming, although I would have preferred to kill him with Trevor's 1911 .45 caliber."

"Why didn't you?" Matt was drawn into the conversation.

"Much braver and better to end a life with your own hands than a powerful weapon. I wanted to give him every chance to defend himself." Ethan went to the rail and looked out over the water.

"As opposed to western civilizations, building trust and developing relationships in my culture takes a little more time."

Matt recalled some of his own training in the Middle East. "When I was starting off with Special Operations, different branches of the military would be assigned to the same mission. There was one in particular that taught me about trust and confidence." Matt joined Ethan on the rail.

With an eyebrow raised, Ethan asked, "Which one?"

"A group of us were performing recon missions between the Pakistan and Afghanistan borders. At night, transport planes would drop us over the Pakistani side of the border. We knew the enemy was supplying pro Taliban forces with heavy artillery through Pakistan. The mission was simple."

"What was it?

"After the drop, we would move through the mountain trails and kill everyone we encountered, disable the weapons, and continue to the Afghanistan border." Matt paused for a moment as he looked out over the majestic Mediterranean. "We had seven hours to cover twelve miles of rough terrain on the good nights. The trails were numerous and our packs were heavy."

Matt thought about how many rounds he fired on those recon missions. "The enemy began to anticipate some of our drops and set up Improvised Explosive Devices and trip wires. Because the terrain was so rough, cell phones weren't practical for calling in trigger mechanisms. As the enemy would advance, they would deploy explosives along the trails. One evening, I was leading our unit when I came across an enemy stringing a series of IEDs. As he was dropping wire to the ordnance, my helmet flashlight exposed him as he fumbled to trigger the explosions. I raised my M249 and depressed the trigger…nothing. Behind me I heard, 'Down.'"

"I went down to a knee and an Army Ranger put a bullet through the enemy's forehead. I kept my light focused on the enemy and he failed to depress the trigger in the instant he was killed. A couple of our engineers hung back and found six IEDs in that area. Many of us would have died that night if the Army Ranger hadn't been prepared to act so swiftly."

"Wasn't that his job?" Ethan wanted to know Matt's perspective on the story.

"Yes. But different branches of the military are always touting how they are more superior to the others. I'd always believed that Marines were the toughest soldiers in the military. I came to find out that an Army Ranger would save many lives in my unit that night because he had my back. I was the one on point to protect our unit from enemy attack. I never thought my training was superior to anyone after that incident. We still stay in touch today, at least until you guys came along," Matt smiled at Ethan.

Ethan could relate, "You would have liked Trevor. A very humble man who had a keen sense about other people. He was a good friend, much like the Army Ranger you describe. In many ways, Trevor saved our lives when he exposed Seth for who he was."

The two men looked out over the peaceful waters, unaware of imminent danger. Lights were barely visible on the coastline and the Excalibur was propelling her way to the next destination. Captain Phil and the crew didn't know that Stealth fighters were barreling down on their location and would be there inside of twenty-four minutes.

****

President Crevan, Secretary of State Watt, and Secretary of Defense Drake were in the Situation Room with a live feed from the B-2s that were speeding toward the Excalibur. They could hear audio from both cockpits and easily identified their location over the Mediterranean via global positioning systems. The Situation Room had a digital global map that showed the planes, the signal from Excalibur, and the location of several ships and planes in the area. Since the attack on 9/11, the White House had fortified bunkers to be used for control rooms and living quarters, which could sustain life for months in the event of a nuclear attack on Washington.

"Raven 6, this is Raven 3, you have the lead and lock assignment on the vessel." A United States Air Force Captain came over the radio to assign orders.

"Raven 6 has lead and lock responsibility on vessel located at 33.137 and 34.497 heading northwest, over." The pilot paused for a moment as he checked his gauges. "Signal coming from the vessel Excalibur is strong and moving at an estimated 20 knots. Arming bombs and missiles."

The phone rang on the bridge of the Excalibur, "Captain, sorties in the area. Can't get a read on their location, but one of them just armed missiles."

Phil was on the bridge with Sesom, "Aircraft has a lock on Excalibur."

"How long until deployment?" Sesom rubbed his beard and maintained his cool.

Phil regurgitated the question to an Israeli Defense Sailor below deck monitoring all activity on the Mediterranean within a 500-mile radius.

"Missiles within distance right now; sorties will likely conduct visual surveillance before deploying. Please advise."

Phil was an effective messenger, "Missiles locked and within range of the Excalibur right now." Sesom kept on rubbing his beard, almost as if it was a rabbit's foot. "Sesom, mission control," Phil chuckled at the statement, "would like to be advised of our orders."

Sesom kept rubbing his beard and looked at Phil out of the corner of his eyes. "There are no orders, continue on our current course. These sorties are not the enemy."

Phil rolled his eyes, "Stand down and continue to monitor. Share information with Sde Dov in Tel Aviv. Let them know hostiles are entering Italian air space."

"Ay Captain." The sailor went to work communicating information with the Air Force Base in Tel Aviv. Stealth fighters were hard to track and even tougher to predict. However, the Israeli Defense Force (IDF) was certain of whom the Stealths were targeting.

Phil hung the phone up, "I sure hope your plan works!"

"Our plan my friend." Sesom gave Phil a wink. "There is no your in team." Sesom was still mixing up idioms of the English language.

"What?" Phil didn't understand Sesom.

"There is no YOUR in TEAM." Sesom emphasized a couple words.

"You mean I in TEAM." Phil began laughing at his friend.

"Exactly." Sesom seemed satisfied with Phil's translation. John and Aaron entered the door to the bridge.

"Everything looks good below Captain." John always felt compelled to update his captain on the status of Excalibur.

"Very well. Let's go dark." Phil motioned for Aaron to shut down all lights on the Excalibur, including the Captain's bridge. Aaron began to flip switches on a section of the control panel. Phil went over the intercom and made an announcement.

"Excalibur is going dark on the decks. Lower sections will remain lit. Should last about 20 minutes."

Ethan and Matt remained on deck. The flicker from the coastline seemed to grow brighter as the Excalibur extinguished her lights.

"Planes are coming in." Ethan looked out over the water.

"If they have a lock on our position, the lights won't matter." Matt knew that technology and infrared would easily give their position away.

"You're right." Ethan continued to look straight ahead.

****

"T minus 60 seconds until target is reached. Decelerating to deploy ordnance." The co-pilot of the Raven 6, B-2 was zooming in on the Excalibur to gain a visual before firing.

"T minus 40 seconds. Waiting for visual identification of target." The pilot of Raven 6 had his finger on the trigger ready to fire missiles and drop bombs.

"Raven 6, this is Raven 3, you are clear to engage when ready." Raven 3 was acting as wingman and cover for the mission of Raven 6.

The co-pilot of Raven 6 got a good look at the Excalibur and exclaimed over the radio, "Abort, abort…target is not the Excalibur."

"Raven 6, please advise." Raven 3 was confused.

"T minus 25 seconds until target is reached." The pilot of Raven 6 was still counting down the sequence.

The co-pilot of Raven 6 reiterated, "Target is civilian, and I repeat, is not Excalibur."

In the Situation Room of the White House, Vice President Crevan gave Secretary of State Watt a look. Watt responded with a shrug of his shoulders, as if he had no idea of what was happening.

Right after the co-pilot finished his sentence, both Stealth radars began to pick up multiple locations of the Excalibur on the Mediterranean Sea off the Italian coast.

"Raven 6. Are you seeing what we're seeing?"

"Copy. We have 12 Excaliburs from the coast of Sicily to the south of France." The co-pilot of Raven 6 couldn't believe what he was seeing.

"T minus 10 seconds and counting." Raven 6's pilot didn't know why he was still counting down the sequence. The pilot and co-pilot had a good view over the plane's dashboard of a well-lit fishing boat on the Mediterranean. Seven crewmembers appeared to be on deck and waving to the B-2 as it flew over.

"Raven 3, do you have a visual?"

"We do." As the pilot responded a warning light began to flash and an alarm went off.

"Raven 6, we have an enemy lock on our aircraft. Deploying countermeasures and taking evasive action. Evasive action didn't mean much for a B-2, as the plane was subsonic in speed.

A couple of Italy's F-15 Silent Eagles had taken positions behind the United States' B-2s. The F-15s had locked on both B-2s and were following their every move.

"This is IAF 127. Please identify aircraft and country."

The pilot for Raven 6 hesitated and responded slowly, "IAF 127, aircrafts are Raven 6 and Raven 3 from the United States of America. B-2 bombers."

"Copy Raven 6 and Raven 3 from the United States. You guys lost or something?"

"Negative 127, we are on a mission for the United States Air Force to seek and destroy ship in the Mediterranean. Over." Raven 6's pilot knew the explanation wouldn't appease an aggressive Italian Air Force that maintained superiority in the Mediterranean. The American pilot noticed that the warning light and alarm ceased.

"Raven 6 and Raven 3, we will escort you to Aviano. Be advised that you are to land at Aviano Air Force Base for debrief with Italian intelligence. You have entered Italian air space without permission or filing a flight plan with the IAF." The Italian pilot smiled and spoke with a heavy dialect.

"IAF 127, Raven 6 and Raven 3 appreciate the escort and will land at Aviano." The Raven 6 pilot slammed down the transmitter after he replied to the Italian aircraft. The Italian F-15SE pilots began laughing it up on their own secure channel. With the help of the IAF, the Excalibur was safe heading southwest to their next rendezvous points, Spain and Morocco.

Vice President Crevan turned his attention to Secretary of State Watt and Secretary of Defense Drake.

"It appears that our self-proclaimed Disciples are a little smarter than we anticipated." Crevan smiled at his colleagues.

"It appears so." Watt was still amazed that 12 ships were emitting a signal for the Excalibur.

"Excuse me Vice President Crevan, I need to make some phone calls to Aviano and the Italian Ambassador to the United States." Drake hesitated, "I'm sure they will understand our mistake in a time of war with hostile nations. I will let the Italians know that we are looking out for their interests as much as we are ours."

"Sounds like a good idea. Other nations will understand that we're a little on edge after dirty bomb attacks in Concord, New York, Los Angeles, and Miami. If President Lombardi requires a phone call from me, I'd be happy to pull some wool." Crevan displayed an eerie aura of confidence, almost as if he'd lived his life to take over the United States and bring in a new world order.

****

The lights came back up on the deck of the Excalibur and Captain Phil came over the intercom. "All clear. We will maintain our course to The Strait of Gibraltar, a day and a half to make the trip." Phil hung up the intercom.

"Your plan worked." Phil pulled a cigar out of his pocket and clipped the tip.

"The United States has always been overanxious to engage and destroy an enemy. Their predictability will play to our advantage down the road."

"I would have liked to see the look on those pilots faces when they realized they were targeting a tuna boat." Phil began to laugh.

"Those pilots can deal with the Italian Air Force now." Sesom came over and poured himself a cup of coffee. "John and Aaron, you want a cup?" Both the men gave nods as they continued to check gauges and turn lights back on. Sesom had spent enough time on the bridge to know how the deckhands enjoyed their java.

"I'm going to head below and check on the sailors; give them a pat on the back. John, you've got the com." Phil disappeared through the bridge door.

Sesom brought John and Aaron a cup of coffee. John was in the Captain's chair and Aaron was nearby.

"Sesom," Aaron wanted to vet some issues with Sesom.

"Yes Aaron."

"Now that the United States is hunting us, will we be able to achieve our goals?" Aaron knew the stakes were high.

Sesom knew the young men were concerned about the mission, the way their country would view them, and a very uncertain future. Talk of Revelation, the assassination of their President, and a coup d'état had them worried. Sesom would need to choose his words carefully.

"Aaron, we will achieve our goals regardless of what country takes exception with our mission. The United States has seen tough times for the past three decades. Now that bad members of their own country have successfully taken over the government, the United States is in great danger and in need of outside influence." Suddenly, the bridge door swung open and interrupted Sesom.

Jonas wanted to check on the crew and let them know that the Italian military was in full support of their mission. The Italians had embarrassed themselves during World War I and disgusted the world with their participation in World War II. The Vatican had taken a neutral position during WWII, which would haunt them in every political discussion since. The Pope's indifference to Jews during WWII was disgraceful, and the deportation of Jews from all over Europe to death camps was met with very little resistance from the Vatican. Much like the story of Revelation in the Bible, the Italians had been seeking redemption and a chance to prove their faith to the world through action. Jonas, a member of the Swiss Army, was just the person to bring atonement to The Vatican and Italy.

"You couldn't have shown up at a better time." Sesom gave Jonas a smile. Jonas had elected to become a Disciple, even though he hadn't been called to Sesom or identified through Matt's ethereal experience. A baker's dozen of sorts, Jonas knew that the Disciples would need help since the deaths of Liam and Trevor. Jonas understood how to navigate through diplomatic relations and call upon the Swiss Army to back his moves. The President of Italy and Pope Simplicius II had given Jonas latitude to make decisions on behalf of the Italian government and The Vatican.

"And why is that?" Jonas went to the coffeemaker to pour himself a cup. Cering had purchased a very expensive Kona for the wheelhouse and lower deck. She knew that Captain Phil and his crew would be working extended hours to keep their passengers safe.

"Aaron, John, and I are in a discussion about what's happening in the United States and the worldwide implications of their coup."

Jonas was meticulous about choosing his words and preparing a good cup of coffee. Jonas stirred some half-and-half into his cup. After tasting the coffee, he put another spoonful of sugar in the mug. He tasted the creation once again.

"Once worldwide economies and social media became global, what happened in the United States had an impact on other countries around the world." Jonas paused for a moment, "However, as much as countries became interdependent, emerging markets were able to establish an independence like never seen before."

"For example..." John posed the question to Jonas from the Captain's chair.

"Take an economy like Greece. The country is part of the eurozone and affects the overall economic health of other European countries. Because of their inability to manage debt and grow their economy, the Germans had to become very involved in government affairs and the financial future of Greece. The dependence of the US on Chinese money has similar implications." Jonas took another sip of coffee. "In essence, if the interdependence becomes unbalanced through trade, the borrower becomes slave to the lender." Jonas pulled a well-known passage from Proverbs.

"China is largely independent. They play by a different set of rules and manipulate currency to bolster their economy. The trade imbalances with China are overwhelming to other developed countries and they have been left unchecked by the worldwide community. In essence, they write their own set of rules and do so successfully." Jonas wanted to shore up his point, "All of the rhetoric with regard to human rights and fair trade pale in comparison to worldwide greed. People would prefer to have inexpensive Chinese goods than worry about what's happening to the people in China. This dichotomy has brought us to the place we are in the world today. A similar greed has successfully overthrown the US government in recent days. The bigger problem is the people who have overthrown the US government are part of a larger conspiracy, one that has religious implications."

Aaron was engaged, "I understand the economic implications, what are your thoughts about the religious implications?"

"Worldwide, we are seeing a crescendo of sorts with regard to good versus evil. The divide between good versus evil has more distance between it than any time in recent history. In some respects, radical Muslims are correct when they refer to their struggle as a jihad, a holy war. But the context within they are fighting a holy war misses its mark. If the fight were truly about good versus evil, religions worldwide would find themselves on the same side of the conflict, fighting the same holy war. But organized religions have made this more about the differences between them instead of what evil is doing to this planet." Jonas had thought much about the topic. He had visited with religious leaders from several different churches and ideologies; they were all in agreement, but they didn't know how to bring the masses to the same table to break bread.

Sesom was glad to see that Aaron and John took interest in the wisdom of Jonas. Jonas continued, "The Vatican has been guilty of being an unwilling spectator in some of the worst atrocities mankind has ever witnessed. That won't be the case this time around." Jonas had a sense of confidence and certainty with regard to the advent of Revelation. The Vatican knew the time was right, and they were committed to ushering in a period of redemption.

"How can you be so sure of yourself, or the Vatican?" Aaron wanted confirmation.

"I will be meeting with the Vice President of the United States in three days. The President of Italy and Simplicius have arranged my meeting with Crevan. The US is very interested in the Vatican's dealings with two highly decorated Marines, and an international force to protect a young woman." Jonas couldn't hold a smile back.

"You're kidding? You're meeting with VP Crevan?" John shook his head, as if to show he wasn't a big fan of the Vice President.

"I am. By that time he will be sworn in as President of the United States."

A silence fell over the wheelhouse. Crevan becoming the President of the United States had implications beyond what anyone could imagine. At one time, Crevan was an honest man with good intentions. The beginning of Crevan's career with the military was very successful and decorated. He became an important member to envoys that traveled through Iraq, Afghanistan, and Pakistan. After witnessing how politicians conducted business, Crevan became very cynical and began to leverage Middle Eastern relationships for his own benefit.

Crevan set up offshore accounts and funneled money from rebels, warlords, and governments to ensure that the people in power got paid, with blood money from the United States. The United States couldn't account for billions of dollars in government spending and there was a reason why. People in charge of the money could easily funnel millions of dollars through puppet security companies that had been set up to assist the United States. Crevan and his cronies even figured out that they could funnel monies earmarked for civilian reparations to their own bank accounts. They would make up names of civilians that were wounded or killed in the conflict and have the United States pay reparations to them. Many people were on the take, and that's how Crevan befriended Samil. Samil was recruiting heavily in the Middle East to disrupt any planned peace process for the territory.

Samil was very interested in partnering with a high profile up-and-coming military hero that was interested in seeking political office. Once Crevan finished his military tours in the Middle East, he still traveled to the territory as a civilian to broker the peace process. On the surface, he appeared to develop strong relationships with important leaders in the Middle East. Below the surface, monies were changing hands between key members of the peace process. Jonas knew the details of Crevan's background and his involvement with the mysterious death of the Turkish Ambassador to the Vatican. While Jonas didn't share the same intensity for revenge as Ethan, Jonas had plans for Crevan.

****

In the last days, God says, I will pour out my Spirit upon all people. Your sons and daughters will prophesy. Your young men will see visions, and your old men will dream dreams.

Acts 2:17

Matt and Dorje were still rooming together on the Excalibur. Dorje was one of the most interesting Disciples because of his Buddhist beliefs and broken English. The Dali Lama was involved with Dorje's decision to find Sesom in West Africa. Dorje came to enlightenment through his own dreams and visions while protecting his Holiness in Northern India. Dorje had dreams that his life was a continuation of the 12th Dali Lama, Trinley Gyatso. Gyatso had died of a mysterious illness at the age of 18 in 1875. Dorje's dream was that Gyatso experienced an untimely death to be reincarnated 115 years later. In essence, Gyatso had been reincarnated as Dorje and called to the Dali Lama to protect his Holiness and understand the impetus of Buddhism, to end the suffering in life.

The 15th Dali Lama and Dorje were both aware of a strong West African, with ties to Abraham, who would usher in a world with no suffering and the abolishment of evil. Dorje had been meditating in a Buddhist temple for several months when a name came to mind, Sesom. He began to chant the name and the Dali Lama took notice.

After Dorje finished chanting "Sesom", the Dali Lama came to his side and whispered, "You will find him in Morocco, in Marakesh. You must go to him and follow his words." Dorje packed a bag and left for Marakesh. He found Sesom, Cering, Amen, and Ethan at the Jemaa el-Fna plaza by accident. Dorje had arrived in Marakesh

knowing nothing about the city or how to find Sesom.
When Dorje came across the Jemaa el-Fna plaza, some
street boxing matches were taking place between young
adults. Dorje stopped to watch the action and recognized
Sesom on the other side of the makeshift boxing arena.
The African leader and the Disciples embraced Dorje
from the beginning, almost a foreshadowing of how
easily Seth would manipulate the Disciples in the future.

For the two nights Matt and Dorje would spend on
Excalibur to reach the southern tip of Spain, Dorje
volunteered to sleep in the bunk and let Matt take the
hammock. The hammock was very comfortable and
forgiving of the side-to-side and up-and-down
movements of the ship. Matt was sound asleep in the
hammock. Plenty of images and ideas were swirling in
Matt's head, one of which was Elisabeth. Matt found
himself back in Elisabeth's hotel suite at The Grand
Beach Hotel, with the smells of Jerusalem mint tea and
rugelach cookies wafting through the air. He also saw
himself in St. Peter's Square in an embrace with
Elisabeth, followed by an impassioned kiss that took
them both by surprise. Matt let off a grin as he slept in
the hammock; he tucked his hands behind his head. His
dream took him back to the Western Wall. This time the
plaza was filled with children running and playing on the
polished stone surface. There was no blood oozing from
the pores of sandstone, or black birds perched atop the
Wall.

Matt heard a whisper in his ears; "This Wall represents
everything that's right with the world, while at the same
time reminding us of what's wrong with it." Matt turned
to see the origins of the whisper and found nobody.

Children were still running in the plaza chasing each
other and playing tag. Matt was reminded of his
childhood and the innocence of being young. While
watching the plaza, Matt realized why Jesus had so

much trust and confidence in children. For the most part, children weren't born with aggression or hate; they learned those behaviors from adults. All children wanted to do was play, enjoy life, and enjoy each other. They weren't hung up on color, religion, status, or power; they merely wanted to play. Matt's thoughts were interrupted by six intercontinental ballistic missiles roaring overhead. The children didn't even notice the massive rockets streaming thousands of feet above them. The ICBMs were heading west.

"Not quite the rocket's red glare we sing about." Dorothy Hiatt was standing next to her son.

"Mom?" Matt was surprised to see his mother, even though her whisper sounded familiar.

"I miss you Matt." Dorothy hugged her son. Although Matt was dreaming, he felt like she was physically present. When the physical intersects the ethereal in dreams, separating what's real from what's imagined becomes indistinguishable. Matt had experienced dreams in the past that seemed real. When he was playing football or wresting for Columbine, the dreams took on a physical element he couldn't explain. Matt would wake up and have the feeling as if he'd been playing sports, or studying for an upcoming test. He'd also had night terrors about his parents' plane crash into the Pentagon on 9/11. Those dreams were unforgettable and terrifyingly real.

"Your father and I are happy the Disciples found you." Dorothy spoke matter-of-factly, almost as if she knew the Disciples were looking for him well in advance of recent events.

"They seem like a good bunch of people." Matt and his mother were still in the plaza watching children near the

Western Wall, another set of six ICBMs flew overhead heading west.

"I see that you've found Elisabeth too."

"More like we found each other." Matt turned to his mother.

"Elisabeth is a good name. She was the mother of John the Baptist and cousin to Mary, mother of Jesus. The angel Gabriel appeared to Elisabeth's husband and told them they would be blessed with a child, even though they were both advanced in age. Elisabeth's husband didn't believe a child was possible at their later stage in life."

"I think I remember the story. I've had my fair share of Sunday School lessons over the past month." Matt smiled at his mother.

"I know you have. One of these children was supposed to be Elisabeth's child, before her abortion." Dorothy became serious as she shared the news with Matt. They were interrupted by one more set of 6 ICBMs heading in the same direction as the others.

"Which one?" Matt was surprised by what he heard.

Without hesitation, Dorothy pointed to a beautiful young girl that appeared to be around the age of seven. She was playing with a group of girls. They were setting up hopscotch with chalk on the plaza floor of the Western Wall. The young girl had physical characteristics resembling Elisabeth. Matt couldn't believe what he was seeing and left speechless.

"There are other plans for all of us, including you." Dorothy spoke in a more serious tone.

"And what are my plans?" Matt remembered the visit from his father. He was curious to see what advice his mother would share.

"One of them happens to be in the plaza. She will be very important to the 2nd Coming of the Messiah. Your daughter."

Matt asked, "Really?"

His mother answered, "Really."

"Which one is she?" Matt's curiosity was peaked.

"What?" The response from his mother seemed confused.

"Which one is she?" Matt repeated the question, a little louder.

"What are you talking about?" Matt became frustrated by the response.

"Which one is she?" Matt was yelling at this point.

"Matt, wake up. Which one is who?" Elisabeth was seated at the right hand of Matt, pushing his shoulder. Dorje knew Elisabeth had entered the room. He smelled her hand lotion as she came down the hallway and through the door. Matt woke up suddenly and went for his 1911 .45 caliber. Before Elisabeth knew what happened, Matt had the end of the barrel positioned below Elisabeth's chin. Matt was breathing heavy.

"Please don't shoot me." Elisabeth didn't move and was in shock.

"I'm so sorry. I had no idea that was you." Matt pulled the .45 away from Elisabeth's chin.

"I was who?" Elisabeth had heard Matt asking about which one.

"Never mind. I'm just glad that I didn't shoot you. What time is it?"

"1:40 in the morning." Elisabeth was gaining her own composure.

"That's weird." Matt remembered something from a few weeks back.

"What's weird?" Elisabeth was finding Matt to be more and more mysterious.

"That's the time I made my last journal entry, after having visions of you at the Western Wall." Matt remembered he was happy to have a few more hours of sleep, 3 hours and 20 minutes to be exact until 0500. Everything in the military was about time. Everything in the Bible was about time, a time for everyplace and everything.

"Can we get some coffee?" Elisabeth seemed to be asking Matt on a date, at an odd hour of the morning.

"Sure." Matt looked over at Dorje. He knew that Dorje was awake while keeping his eyes closed, if not peeking on occasion. Scratches was at the foot of the bed with Dorje, curled up and comfortable. Dorje and Scratches had become companions on the Excalibur.

****

"You want coffee at this hour of the morning?" Matt was shocked about Elisabeth's choice to consume caffeine.

"Yes, please." Elisabeth sat down in the dining room of the Excalibur adjacent to the kitchen. Matt went to work on the coffeemaker.

"How do you like it?" Matt went to the fridge for some milk.

"Tan, with a lot of sugar." Elisabeth didn't appear to need caffeine. Matt was still waking up from a deep sleep, thinking about the conversation with his mother.

"What is it Matt?" Elisabeth saw that he was lost in thought.

"Strange dreams, like nothing I've experienced before." Matt was mixing parts of coffee, milk, and sugar like a chemist.

"Anything you'd like to share?" Elisabeth's connection had grown with Matt since their first kiss in St. Peter's Square.

"When you had dreams that angels, or whatever, were visiting you, did you think they were real?" Matt's skepticism shined through as he stirred the coffee.

"Initially, I was very suspicious, but when I became pregnant, I didn't know what was happening. I was in shock. I was still a virgin, yet with child. I didn't know if I'd been drugged and raped when I first found out the news. I had a strong connection with the baby and wanted to keep the unborn child." Matt brought the coffee with him to the table.

"Why didn't you run?"

"Run where? I had just found out I was pregnant when my father made arrangements with a family doctor. I didn't know the doctor was going to perform an abortion until after the surgery was complete. They put an I.V. in my arm, put me to sleep, and performed the abortion; it was as simple as that." Elisabeth took a sip of coffee and thanked Matt for the drink.

"It wasn't until after surgery the doctor reported to my parents that my hymen was still in place." Elisabeth seemed a little embarrassed.

"Your hymen?" Matt repeated the awkward word.

"My hymen." Elisabeth said the word again for Matt, hoping he would understand its significance.

"Remind me why the hymen is important?" Matt was drinking bottled water instead of coffee.

"The hymen usually remains in place until a woman's virginity is taken." Elisabeth smiled at Matt, almost as if they were finally having the private conversation they needed to have at the hotel in Tel Aviv.

"Oh." Matt didn't know what to say. Flashbacks of high school biology ran though his mind. How did he miss that?

"Oh?" Elisabeth began to laugh and grabbed Matt's left hand without thinking. Matt looked down at his hand.

"I'm sorry." Elisabeth retreated from Matt; she had invaded his space.

"No, I'm sorry…it's okay. I have a question to ask you anyway." Matt fetched Elisabeth's retreated right hand. She was happy he did.

"Do you…" Matt didn't know how to find the right words.

"Do I?" Elisabeth was trying to help him.

"Okay. Do you still have", Cering walked into the dining room, "your hymen?" Cering heard the tail end of the sentence and turned around to walk back out. Matt put his head down in embarrassment. Once again, Cering had accidentally interrupted a very important moment for an extremely important couple.

"Cering, come back, it's okay." Elisabeth and Cering were friends on their way to becoming sisters. Cering already knew the answer to Matt's question.

"According to Pope Simplicius, you're going to have to find out for yourself." Elisabeth whispered the comment and smiled before Cering reentered the dining room. She also leaned over and gave Matt a quick kiss on the lips. He was hoping for more, as his eyes were still closed and lips puckered as she pulled away.

"I'm sorry…again." Cering went to the cupboards and retrieved some tea. Cering didn't look at the couple as if to play like nothing happened. An awkward silence fell over the dining room.

"What are you doing up at this hour?" Cering came over and joined Matt and Elisabeth at the table.

"Discussing the Pope, dreams, and hymens among other things." Matt took an opportunity to lighten the mood. Elisabeth and Cering began laughing together. Matt turned red as he finished the sentence. He was waiting for the right woman to share his marriage vows and virginity with.

"My kind of conversation." Matt met Cering under very odd circumstances at Carlita's Café. Now that he'd shared meals, sparred, and saved lives with her, Matt had developed a deep admiration for the Egyptian woman.

Cering continued, "What's your plan when we reach the Strait of Gibraltar?"

Matt answered, "Sesom said, I mean demanded, that Elisabeth and I continue on to the Falkland Islands with Ethan, Li, my sis and kiddos, and the Excalibur. I have no idea what's up with the others, including Mike. Sesom isn't telling me much because he doesn't want me to leave the ship."

"I'll be leaving the ship with Mike, Amen, and Lucas. We will set out to meet with General Gilmore in Virginia. Sesom, Dorje, Kimi, and Talan will do what they can to disrupt Crevan's plans. News reports are stating that Crevan will be inaugurated tomorrow morning." Cering had been making travel arrangements through Suzie for the Disciples.

"What about Jonas?" Matt knew that his involvement would be crucial to the success of the Disciples.

"He has a meeting with Crevan in three days. US intelligence knows that some of their decorated servicemen have been converted to Disciples." Cering smiled and winked at Matt.

"Wow. Will he need help?" Matt was still looking for an opportunity to join the missions.

"Jonas? No. Those familiar with Jonas know that he doesn't need an escort."

****

Vice President Crevan looked straight ahead, almost as if he was looking through the camera in front of him. His national address was coming from the Oval Office.

"My fellow Americans. We have experienced more attacks on the homeland at the hands of terrorists. Tonight, our prayers are with the people of Concord, New York, Los Angeles, and Miami. Due to the nature of these dirty bombs, specialized teams are still working very hard to recover bodies in those areas. Dirty bombs pose a risk for citizens, first responders, and emergency workers in the targeted areas. I have spoken with state leadership and mayors of these cities to ensure that they have the full support of the Federal Emergency Management Administration and Homeland Security.

President Palmer was assassinated in the attacks a few days ago and will be laid to rest in a state funeral when it is safe. As the Vice President of the United States, I am committed to the domestic and foreign policies of our former President. President Palmer was an outstanding leader and worked hard to bring the country back from economic hardship and fractured relationships between political parties." Vice President Crevan's delivery was very believable and convincing, like any other career politician.

"I will be sworn in tomorrow morning, October 6th, as President of the United States. With multiple countries at war and our unwavering support of allies across the globe, I will continue what President Palmer started 5 years ago in this administration. Our pursuit of the terrorists that orchestrated these attacks will be unrelenting. God bless us all and God bless the United States of America." Crevan smiled at the camera before major networks returned to their regular programming.

The nation had heard canned speeches like these countless times before. Hope and change, a better tomorrow, we'll get the bad guys, had all been heralded before by decades of bad leadership in Washington, DC. Constituents were largely numb to the circumstances surrounding Washington and the dirty bomb attacks in several cities across the nation. The United States had experienced school shootings, 9/11, embassy bombings, and war for extended periods of time. Death and destruction had become a way of life for Americans, even though most Americans had been killed on foreign soil. Ever since the Cold War, the United States didn't seem to have a period of peace. Politicians evoked fear regularly to keep constituents dependent on bad leadership and bad government. Washington constantly reminded people the government was saving them from themselves. Hope and change had been replaced by fear and status quo.

The Colonists protested Vice President Crevan's decision to carry on with the Inauguration. They believed there was no better time than the present to restructure the Federal government and bring control back to the States. Even though the United States was involved in simultaneous battles around the globe, people were fed up with wars and spending billions of dollars overseas, while American people went hungry and homeless in hundreds of cities. The Federal government developed policies of dependence to split the country in two and influence voting patterns of the wealthy and the poor. Crevan was hoping to exploit the division of the country even further after the Inauguration.

After the camera crew packed their gear and left, Secretary Watt took a seat in front of the large oak desk across from Crevan.

"Quite convincing." Watt was impressed by Crevan's manipulation of words.

"I threw up in my mouth a little when I referred to Palmer's leadership and success with the country. If anything, he made our job a little more difficult." Watt nodded his head in affirmation.

"We received a call from the Vatican confirming your meeting with Jonas Andros on Friday. As you recall, he oversees the Swiss Army and is a security advisor to Pope Simplicius II. You have lunch scheduled with him in the Oval Office at noon." Watt was thumbing through papers.

"Should we arrest him once he arrives?" Crevan and Watt had discussed the Vatican visitor in a previous meeting.

"No. Let's see what he has to say first. Then we will arrest him as a war criminal. The White House press is working on the story to link Jonas to the terrorists on Excalibur. We can successfully link the Disciples to the bombings in Israel and the recent attacks in the United States. We will release the story after you meet with Mr. Andros. He will then be sent to Guantanamo Bay and rot with the rest of our war criminals. We'll try him at some point in the future, only after we manufacture enough evidence to put him to death." Watt had worked long enough with Crevan to cover all the bases and contingencies.

"And many citizens complain that we don't manufacture enough in this country." Crevan was amused by his own comment.

"What about the Colonists? There are thousands on Pennsylvania Avenue and tens of thousands spread across the mall and Lafayette Park." Watt looked over the rim of his reading glasses.

"The weather will help our cause. Many of them are likely Occupiers that have nothing better to do." Crevan continued, "Call up the National Guard and have them beef up security for the Inauguration tomorrow. Have them begin making arrests tonight to show them that we're serious. How are our brothers Samil doing?"

"After their underwhelming hostage negotiations in Gaza, they seemed to have pulled off the dirty bombs without error. If Samil could get organized, they may have a chance at ruling the world." Watt said.

"That's where we come in." Crevan knew that a US backed Samil organization would be unstoppable around the world.

"What is Samil's next target?" Watt knew that Crevan had a direct line to Samil leadership.

"The Holy Land. Religious hysteria creates a great diversion for world leaders. I'll let Mr. Andros know that we have every intention of marching on St. Peter's Square."

"How about some dinner?" Watt just remembered he hadn't eaten all day.

"Sounds good, I'm sure my wife has already dined. I'll meet you in the kitchen in about 30 minutes, I have a few phone calls that I still need to make." Crevan was all business. He had been preparing for this day since becoming a Senator of Massachusetts. A successful military career afforded him the opportunity to align himself with insurgents and sect leadership in the Middle East. Crevan knew that most everyone was on the take in Washington with lobbyists, foreign leaders, and big corporations. The only difference between Crevan and the politicians was that he wanted to change the world by leveraging his Middle Eastern relationships.

****

Sesom called a Disciple meeting at 10:00 am in the belly of Excalibur. Logistics were important, as the Disciples would split up at the Straight of Gibraltar. Sesom, Dorje, Kimi, and Talan would disembark and head for the Mohammed V International Airport in Morocco. Cering, Mike, Amen, Lucas, and Jonas would disembark and head for the Murcia-San Javier Airport. Captain Phil attended the meeting with John and Aaron. Even though the crew of the Excalibur would continue on with Matt, Elisabeth, Ethan, Li, Mary, and the kids, Sesom wanted the crew to attend. The Israeli Defense Sailors were in full control of the Excalibur as the Disciples met in the large gym a few levels below. Talan set up a projector and video presentations for the meeting. Suzie continued to conduct research and make travel arrangements for the team. The Disciples needed new passports and identification cards to get through customs and security checkpoints. Dorje and Kimi would travel as husband and wife, while Sesom and Talan would travel as computer software engineers. Cering and Amen would travel as a couple, while Mike and Lucas would travel as business partners brokering petroleum products. Jonas didn't need an alias as the Vice President was expecting a meeting with him on Friday, two days from today. Intelligence updates were important to those traveling on the Excalibur. The IDF gathered information from around the world and shared it with sailors on the ship. The sailors were constantly monitoring and updating Captain Phil and Sesom with information from Israel.

"The United States and China are now at war over a small island to the southeast of China. China is working on a ground invasion. The US has moved two aircraft carriers into the Taiwan Strait; tensions are high in the area. The Taiwanese are encouraging the Chinese to invade with ground forces, the Taiwanese want their independence." Sesom showed satellite images of the territory.

Sesom moved to the next image, "Indonesia has experienced a Muslim uprising calling for an end to Israel and Jewish rule. Indonesia is lending full support to Iran and the Palestinians. Australia and the Philippines are responding to the uprising and allowing the Japanese and India to use their military bases for air support. Indonesia doesn't have the resources to make a global difference in the war."

The next slide showed Russia from a satellite image. Sesom focused on Eastern Russia first. "Russia is moving hundreds of thousands of troops to North Korea. They have pledged aid and support to the North Koreans."

Sesom moved the satellite image to Western Russia. "Russia is also moving hundreds of thousands of troops to the border of Georgia. They are threatening to move across Georgia, down through Turkey, and into Syria. They aren't pleased about Israel's involvement with Iran. Iraq, Saudi Arabia, and Afghanistan are on high alert. Syria is so unstable that Russia could march through the country with hardly anyone noticing."

Sesom moved through the other slides more quickly, "Venezuela has threatened to use nukes against the United States, which seems odd because the US has been rocked to its core with dirty bombs in major cities. Venezuela may have a maximum of two nuclear weapons. They seem to want attention. They may get it; Crevan won't tolerate threats from dictators."

"Lastly, Iran is being struck with tactical nukes to destroy infrastructure and minimize their ability to launch a nuclear warhead. The US and Israel have pounded Tehran, Mashhad, Esfahan, Tabriz, and

Shiraz." Sesom went from city to city showing major destruction and smoldering rubble.

"The US and Israeli forces are concentrating on areas with over one million people in population. Unfortunately, Iranian leadership strategically placed their nuclear warheads in densely populated areas; hoping civilians would serve as human shields from a foreign attack. Tens of thousands of civilians and military personnel have been killed in the attacks so far. There will be no ground troops involved with these operations." Sesom knew that Mesopotamia would never be the same.

"What are your plans after you leave the ship with Dorje, Kimi, and Talan?" Matt spoke first.

"After Jonas meets with Crevan, we will have a clear idea of his intentions and what the administration plans to do." Sesom stopped at that.

"How does Samil play into all of this?" Ethan wanted clarification.

"They are responsible for the attacks on Israel, the kidnapping of Mary, and recent dirty bombs being deployed in the US. They are very much involved with several of the countries mentioned in the presentation supporting uprisings across the globe." Sesom paused, "After Crevan's Inauguration, they will become better managed and more organized. Many agents of the US intelligence community will become double agents. They won't have the slightest idea that they're supporting missions for Samil. Very similar to what Crevan and Secretary of State Watt did while serving in the Middle East. They are masters of illusion and execution."

"How can Crevan be stopped?" Amen knew the US President was more protected than anyone else in the world. The Pope came in a close second with protection from the Swiss Guard.

"Once he assumes office, he will broaden the Secret Service and call on branches of the military to beef up security wherever he travels. Our best time to strike will be right after the Inauguration. The government will work slowly to enhance the Secret Service and call on military branches to provide additional support. The US government is more hare than tortoise."

"You mean tortoise than hare." Kimi and Phil began giggling.

"That's what I said; regardless, they are slow to accomplish anything." Sesom was proud of his English. "Talan, please share with us the intelligence you've gathered from the Israeli Defense Force and Suzie."

Talan left his chair and took Sesom's place at the front of the gym. He began a presentation that would leave the Disciples speechless.

"With the help of our Israeli Defense Sailors and Suzie in the United States, we are certain that Crevan will begin a smear campaign of our group shortly after the Inauguration. The Disciples will be put on an international most wanted list with the Federal Bureau of Investigation and Central Intelligence Agency, if we aren't already. According to Suzie and insiders at the White House, we will be framed for the attacks in Israel, the United States, and several disruptions in the Middle East."

Talan showed a slide of the air base at Aviano, "The US B-2 bombers from last night were forced to land and given a debriefing by the Italian Air Force and State

Department of the US. Needless to say, the US was embarrassed by the events and were asked not to involve themselves in matters of Italian airspace without prior approval."

Talan moved to the next slide of Los Angeles and Matt interjected, "I recognize that place."

Talan continued, "Vice President Crevan will be visiting Los Angeles next week and pass over areas hit hard by the dirty bombs. As you can see, radiation damage is far more extensive than the destruction caused by the detonations. The United States' government has quarantined areas in Los Angeles, New York, Miami, and Concord to contain the radiation. Many people still lay dead and are unrecoverable at this time, including President Palmer."

Another slide showed the Beverly Wilshire in Los Angeles. "We have received a tip from the Secret Service and FBI that Crevan will be staying here for his upcoming visit to LA. Once Amen and Cering reach New York with me and Sesom, they will travel to Los Angeles and meet with Red's Cab Company."

Mike looked at Cering, "Change in plans?"

"We know some people in Los Angeles that may be interested in supporting our mission." Cering and Mike knew that plans could change at a moment's notice.

"A cab company?" Matt was confused.

Amen explained, "I met some people in Compton that may be able to help us. The US government would never think to look in Compton, or investigate the people I met. We may find connections to the Wilshire through this group of people. When people in the United States betray us, sometimes the only people we can trust are strangers. I believe we can trust this group of people."

"How can you be so sure?" Mike continued prodding and remembered an earlier conversation he had with Amen at Disneyland about the disappearance of Matt's Mustang.

"Let's just say one of them owes me a favor." Amen smiled

"Good enough." Mike was ready to move on.

"Because we will know Crevan's motorcade route prior to his visit, Sesom and I will work to cause distractions and disruptions along the way. The city of Los Angeles will be on edge since the attacks; this will play to our advantage."

Talan continued, "At the same time Jonas is meeting with Crevan at the White House on Friday, Mike and Lucas will meet with General Gilmore in Virginia near the United States' Marine Headquarters. General Gilmore has agreed to speak with Mike and Lucas over lunch. He is aware of the circumstances surrounding Mike and Matt and is willing to listen."

"Dorje and Kimi will travel to Los Angeles and support Sesom and me with preparations for Crevan's arrival. They can lend a hand to Amen and Cering in Compton if necessary. Suzie has made arrangements with private contractors from Rabat in Morocco to pick up our teams on the Excalibur and transport us by way of helicopters to the Mohammed V International and Murcia-San Javier airports tomorrow morning. Envelopes with further instructions will be provided for our trips to the United States. Take only what you need and don't check weapons. Even though Suzie has chartered flights for us, security and customs will be on high alert."

Talan finished up his presentation, "Wear hats, sunglasses, change the way you wear your hair, and provide good cover with clothing. Long sleeves and business attire works well; act like tourists." Talan revealed a slight smile to the group.

"Kind of like at the Western Wall." Matt winked at Sesom as he returned to the front of the room.

"Any questions?" Sesom always left the door open for his friends. The Disciples, Mike, and Jonas knew exactly what to do. They had served on many missions, assumed identities, and traveled abroad under dangerous circumstances. The Disciples were the best of the best and needed to be in order to survive what was becoming a largely secular, selfish world. No questions were asked.

****

The west steps of the US Capitol were packed with photographers, congressmen and women, justices, constituents, and heavily armed Secret Service and National Guard troops. Riot police were holding protesters back at Constitution and Independence Avenues. The Inauguration of Vice President Crevan was contentious for many Americans, regardless of their political affiliation. President Palmer had become a very likeable President at a time when politics weren't so popular. Constituents weren't very excited about a mysterious Vice President assuming the highest office in the United States by default. Politicians made decisions to carry votes in all parts of the country, and Vice President Crevan was selected more for his constituents in the Northeast than his character or political record. Many times, state politicians didn't transfer well to the Federal level and Crevan struggled to win people over in the White House and Congress.

But all of that didn't matter today, on a day that was dreary and unusually cool for a Fall in Washington, DC. The nation was still numb and didn't understand what was happening to their homeland, a situation eerily similar to the post Kennedy assassination period. To make matters worse, President Palmer's body couldn't be recovered because of its location and proximity to an intense radiation field. The military had set up perimeters in Los Angeles, New York, Concord, and Miami. No-fly zones had been established over the cities to prevent the media and curiosity seekers from taking photographs and publishing them within the pages of newspapers and tabloids, or ubiquitous social media and other Internet outlets. Anyone that violated the no-fly zone would be shot down and prosecuted, if they survived.

Several of the protestors were Colonists that didn't want to see the Federal Government move forward without substantial changes; the abolishment of the House of Representatives, the dismantling of the Federal Reserve and Departments of Education, Transportation, Interior, Housing and Urban Development, and Commerce. The Colonists wanted states to manage programs with their own tax dollars and resources. Federal highways would be managed by the states and maintained through tolls. States would work with corporations on tax rates and regulations to keep the free market competitive. Many states would need to look at legislation and regulation to keep companies from migrating to other states. In essence, manufacturing would return to the United States, and states would have an opportunity to compete for businesses. Many domestic and international corporations were very interested and supportive of the business models touted by the Colonist party. The differences between Occupiers and the Colonist Party were substantial. One of the biggest differences was the Colonists had a platform that outlined change in government while the Occupiers just wanted retribution or more government services. One movement fueled anarchy while the other fueled a Revolution. Either way, both movements were strong and gaining thousands of supporters every day. President Palmer was popular because of his emphasis on a balanced budget amendment for the Federal government and focus on cutting programs that were ineffective and costly; the government had several.

But all of Palmer's aspirations and hard work didn't matter because Crevan would take the Presidential Oath on the steps of Capitol Hill like many Presidents before him. Supreme Court Justice Stalin led Alexander and Caprice Crevan from the Inaugural Parade up the west steps of the Capitol. They looked the part. Big smiles, conservative dress, waving to crowds on all sides of them as they followed Justice Stalin up the carpeted steps to a platform and lectern. Cameras were flashing and the crowd roared with insecurity, a mix of heckling and anxious applause. Hecklers were escorted to the outer boundaries of the National Mall on Constitution and Independence Avenues. Government crackdowns on protesters and demonstrators had become commonplace across the nation. A country that was founded on principles of free speech and demonstration had evolved into an oligarchy of political power and corporate influence. The government had no tolerance for people who wanted to speak out or change the status quo; there was too much wealth at stake for the elite. Unbeknownst to United States' citizens, the CIA had trained and targeted political activists under the power of the Patriot Act. Many activists would disappear and turn up murdered. They were thrown off bridges, set in concrete, compacted in cars, or cremated and their ashes dumped in rivers. President Palmer worked slowly to return the United States to a more Constitutionally friendly country. Palmer was trying to abolish the Patriot Act and end Federal programs that weren't provided for in the Constitution or that infringed upon individual rights. Even though the Colonists agreed with what Palmer was doing, they didn't believe he was moving fast enough with a favored states' agenda.

Justice Stalin stepped up to the lectern and began to speak.

"Vice President Crevan, please raise your right hand and repeat after me." Crevan followed the order and raised his right hand.

"I do solemnly swear," Justice Stalin began.

"I do solemnly swear," Crevan repeated.

"That I will faithfully execute the office of President of the United States."

"That I will faithfully execute the office of President of the United States."

"And will to the best of my ability."

"And will to the best of my ability."

"Preserve."

"Preserve."

"Protect."

"Protect."

"And defend the Constitution of the United States."

"And defend the Constitution of the United States."

In 35 words, Crevan assumed the highest office in the free world. In less than a minute, power had transferred from a popular deceased President to an ally of Samil. The United States' Constitution had become nothing but a footnote in recent history. The United States' tax code had grown to four times the length of a Bible and contained 2,500,000 pages of regulation. By comparison, the Constitution contained 4,543 words while The Declaration of Independence contained a paltry 1,458 words. Lyndon Baines Johnson had taken the same oath on Air Force One at Love Field following the assassination of John F. Kennedy. LBJ's rush to the highest office in the United States provided fodder for skeptics. President Crevan knew that an Inauguration couldn't be rushed after the death of President Palmer. Crevan wanted people to understand the magnitude of what happened in four major cities of the United States. People would mourn and look to the government for their next leader; they needed time to absorb the circumstances of the past several days.

Crevan would prey on the vulnerability of a dependent populace. Most people love heroes and despise villains. The United States' government had succeeded in developing villains over the past several decades: North Korea, Russia, Vietnam, Iraq, Afghanistan, China, and Iran. Crevan knew that a hero was just as dependent on a villain as US citizens had become on their own government. Helpless people provided a ripe environment for Crevan to take over the highest office in the free world. The founding fathers established the Constitution to protect the people from someone like Crevan. The Federal government had done everything in its power to unravel the Constitution over the past 60 years. A perfect storm of sorts, Crevan would work with Samil to spread evil and establish dictatorships for unstable countries all over the world. The rewards were money and power. Crevan would address the nation ten minutes after his Inauguration. He needed to quickly define the villains for US citizens to hate, so Crevan could become their new hero.

****

TV coverage continued as Crevan returned to the White House and greeted dignitaries and ambassadors from the State Department and several countries. The media predicted that President Crevan's upcoming address might be the most viewed televised broadcast in recent history.

"Well that was depressing." Matt didn't take his eyes off the television. The time was 7:12 pm on the Mediterranean.

"More disappointing than depressing." Mike looked at his younger brother-in-law and folded his arms in front of his chest.

"Wait until Crevan addresses the world." Amen spoke from behind Matt and Mike.

"More good news?" Matt put his left hand on Mike's right shoulder.

"He will paint us as terrorists, murderers, and an enemy of the United States and Israel. They will make us responsible for what Samil has done." Cering was sitting down next to Elisabeth and watching the same television.

"Hold on, here he is again, speaking from the Rose Garden." Matt was still standing in front of the television mounted to a wall.

"My fellow Americans. I appreciate your patience and support during this difficult transition." Grey clouds and a light drizzle continued to blanket the city.

"Now that formalities have been executed, my staff and I will work tirelessly to protect the homeland against further attacks by terrorists. Our intelligence community, working at home and abroad, has identified those responsible for the recent attacks in the United States and Israel. I would like to share our intelligence with you, so people worldwide can be vigilant and help us capture these criminals."

Mike turned to Sesom, "You never told me we'd become criminals in this group of Disciples."

Sesom shrugged his shoulders; "I believe you would call this an oversight in your country."

Crevan continued, "Two of the terrorists are former Special Operations' Marines that served the United States in Iraq, Afghanistan, and other territories around the world." A split screen showed pictures of Matt and Mike in full uniform.

"The enemy on the left is Matthew Hiatt from Los Angeles. While serving in the Marines and Special Forces, Mr. Hiatt also worked for a government contractor on defense and advanced weaponry systems. We believe he has classified documents and property belonging to the United States' government."

"The enemy on the right is Michael Barnes, a brother-in-law to the terrorist on the left. They left the country several weeks ago before the attacks in Israel and the United States. While Michael Barnes is a decorated veteran of the Marines and Special Forces, he has chosen family and terror over his oath to defend the United States of America."

Mike turned to Matt, "Family and terror every time." They began to laugh together.

"We believe the Americans were recruited by Sesom Ishmael to carry out the attacks on the homeland and abroad. He is a self-proclaimed Messiah and leader of a dangerous group of terrorists." A photo of Sesom was displayed on the television.

"You're the Messiah? I thought Elisabeth was responsible for that dynamic of our group? We need to get our own story straight." Sesom didn't say a word and stuck out a fist. Matt gave it a friendly bump.

"The group is traveling with and funded by Cering Kadesh. Her Egyptian family has ties to major corporations around the world. They have indirectly funded terrorist organizations associated with the Arab Spring and rebels in the Sudan." Sesom's photo was replaced by Cering's.

"He could at least pronounce my family's name right. This won't sit well with my family or the Egyptian people." Cering said with defiance.

"Another Egyptian in the group, Ethan Mubarak, grew up in similar cities as Ms. Kadesh. They may be in a relationship and share similar terrorist connections." A photo of Ethan flashed on the screen. The photo was taken at the Western Wall in Jerusalem. Ethan looked at Cering and moved his eyebrows up and down. Cering began laughing at the romantic inference.

Crevan brought up a photo of Talan. "Talan Sarin joined up with this group of terrorists in France. He is highly trained in computer engineering and intelligence gathering. Many cyber attacks on the United States were devised by Mr. Sarin over the past five years."

Everyone in the room turned to look at Talan. He smiled and shrugged his shoulders. Sesom roared with laughter.

"Dorje is one of the most dangerous terrorists in this group of evil mercenaries. Dorje is from Tibet and banned from ever stepping foot in China again." Crevan was pitching political half-truths to his audience. Dorje wasn't able to return to his homeland because of his security work with the Dali Lama. China chose to occupy Tibet during the late 1940's and relationships between the two countries crumbled. The Dali Lama had lived in exile since 1959 and Dorje began providing security for him in 2009 in Northern India. Dorje's family had lived in the Tibetan mountains for thousands of years. Some of his family were persecuted and killed in wars with the Chinese since the 1950's. Dorje's grandparents were instrumental in helping the Dali Lama flee from the Potala Palace to India in 1959.

Crevan continued by showing another photo, "Kimika Kei joined up with Sesom and the other terrorists in Morocco. She is from Japan and very skilled in martial arts. The people she's traveling with refer to her as Kimi."

"Interesting how Crevan keeps referring to us as terrorists." Mike and the others noticed how many times Crevan used the word terrorists. Word association was very important in Presidential addresses. Crevan's repetition of the word terrorists helped frame the Disciples and Mike as enemies of the homeland.

"That's not a flattering picture of me." Kimi joked about her photo at the Western Wall in Jerusalem. The picture was taken as she began to pursue Samil with Ethan after the deadly explosions.

"Li Che is a Chinese dissident who is no longer welcome in his own country. Much like Dorje, Mr. Che is an enemy of China and responsible for unnecessary uprisings and terrorists attacks within several Chinese cities. Che is trained in martial arts and advanced weaponry."

Crevan continued, "Lucas Tavares is from Brazil and traveled to Europe to meet up with Sesom and this group of terrorists. Before that, he was a common criminal roaming the streets on the outskirts of Sao Paulo. As you can see by the photo, Lucas is a man of big stature and trained in martial arts. He is also very proficient with weapons." Lucas looked straight ahead at the television. Being a fan of The Old Testament, Lucas knew that Crevan had it coming. An eye for an eye and a tooth for tooth; Lucas was confident that Crevan's days were numbered, he would make sure of that if he had the chance.

"Lastly, Amen Jordan is from Israel and likely devised the plan at the Western Wall in Jerusalem. The State Department has not verified if Mr. Jordan is a wanted terrorist within Israel. We know that he is well trained and served with Special Operations in the Israeli Defense Force. Mr. Jordan may have recruited Israeli Sailors to assist with operations. We believe the terrorists are traveling by ship. The Excalibur is the name of their vessel and is heavily armed. Several weeks ago, the Excalibur encountered two Russian fishing vessels on the Pacific. The crews were found dead after their boats were disabled and destroyed by the Excalibur." Crevan advanced to a photo of the Excalibur and Captain Phil.

"Captain Phil Alland of the Excalibur is transporting the terrorists and dangerous cargo. Mr. Alland has modified the Excalibur to carry artillery and weapons of mass destruction. Anyone who encounters the ship should notify authorities immediately. These terrorists should not be approached because of their destructive capability. We ask that you call the number at the bottom of the television screen for tips and information regarding these terrorists." Crevan put down his papers and looked into the camera.

"All of this information is posted at World Wide Web dot Whitehouse dot usa. We appreciate your advance support in helping us catch those responsible for the attacks on our homeland and Israel."

Crevan shifted directions, "The top priorities for the United States are protecting our homeland, catching those responsible for these recent acts of terror, and continuing to legislate strong fiscal responsibility for our nation's future. I will continue to work with Congress, representatives of the Colonist party, Tea Party activists, and Federal Agencies to find ways to continue the great work of President Palmer."

Crevan read the teleprompter for his closing statements. "Our nation has been through these types of attacks in the past. Our people have rallied before and we will rally again. I ask for your prayers and blessings as we move forward together as a nation and meet these challenges without hesitation. God Bless and God Bless the United States of America." President Crevan collected his papers and walked away from the lectern and Rose Garden of the White House. His first address focused on doing what politicians do best, defining the villain. Once the villain was defined, the American people would do the rest.

****

The time was 9:12 am on the West Coast at Delta Defense.

Dan showed up at the doorway of Noah's office.

"Noah."

Noah turned from his computer in his wheelchair to face his supervisor.

"Yes Dan." When Noah answered, two men in suits and a decorated Marine fell in behind Dan.

"These gentlemen are here to see you." Dan had a nervous crack in his voice.

"Are they the interns you've been talking about?" Noah was always up for a good joke.

One of the men in a suit stepped forward, "Noah Webster?"

Noah started looking around, "He's stepped out for a moment, would you like to make an appointment?"

The FBI agent wasn't amused, "Mr. Webster, I'm agent Davis with the Federal Bureau of Investigation, we need to take you in for questioning."

"You pick the guy who's elderly and in a wheelchair? Aren't there laws against profiling in the FBI?" Noah took it in stride. Dan was still in shock that one of his most talented employees and friends was being arrested. Noah wheeled from behind the desk to the door.

"I'll call the attorneys for Delta." Dan wanted to help.

"No need sir. The Patriot Act allows for terrorists to be captured and detained without due process. He will be held indefinitely."

Dan spoke, "Where are you taking him?"

"To a place he won't be a danger to the United States." Noah was searched and given a pat down. The other FBI agent began to wheel Noah away. Delta Defense employees took notice and began to clap for him. Everyone who worked with Noah knew that he was an upstanding guy. The office at Delta also knew that Matt was involved with covert operations and Noah was probably assisting him. Ever since the controversy surrounding 9/11 and the Guantanamo Bay Detention Camp in Cuba, many Americans had become suspicious of the United States' government and their interrogation practices. The Patiot Act had provisions allowing the US government to spy on their own citizens without checks and balances or recourse. Civil liberties were a thing of the past.

The Marine turned to Dan, "We have some unfinished business as well."

"With regards to?" Dan knew whom the Colonel was talking about.

"Hiatt and his brother-in-law. Let's step into your office." Colonel Lash followed Dan into his office.

The Colonel spoke first after the men took seats, "I'm not quite as gung ho as the FBI agents who took your employee away. I trained Matthew Hiatt and served with his brother-in-law, Michael Barnes, in Special Operations. Both men are very important to the United States' Marines and me. Hiatt was selected by the Commandant to serve in Special Operations."

"He has been a great asset to our team at Delta Defense; he left abruptly." Dan was still shifting and nervous from the morning's activities.

"I want to bring Hiatt and Barnes home safely. I'm afraid the situation with them has spun out of control. Have you communicated with Hiatt recently?" Colonel Lash didn't waste time.

Dan was still unsure of the Colonel's intentions. "And why should I trust you? Looks like you and the FBI guys are playing a little good cop, bad cop."

"I convinced the FBI not to take you in. They know Hiatt called you shortly after he left the United States."

Dan interrupted the Colonel, "Wasn't much of a conversation. He said that he needed to tend to some personal matters and would phone me back later. I never heard from him after that."

"Do you know who he was traveling with?"

"No. The conversation was brief. I said if he didn't return the following day he would be excused from the shoulder harness project." Dan began to relax a little.

"The same harness he used in Gaza?"

"Exactly."

"Any idea of where he is now?"

"None. The last record we have of his whereabouts is Gaza."

Colonel Lash pulled a business card out of his jacket, "Please don't hesitate to let me know if Hiatt contacts you. Hiatt and Barnes have been outstanding Marines since joining the service. While the Federal government may rush to judgment with regard to these situations, I'm interested in the rest of the story. Thank you for your time."

Dan took the card and nodded at the Colonel. He picked up the phone and called an attorney with Delta Defense as Lash left the office.

****

"There they are," Captain Phil pointed to the left side of the bow. The Excalibur was waiting for helicopters in the Strait of Gibraltar. The groups were on deck preparing gear and travel bags, the time was 1:12 am. The Disciples had to travel lightly as a cargo ladder was the only means to board the choppers. A harvest moon glistened on the Mediterranean. Weather was clear and winds were calm, perfect for disembarking the Excalibur and traveling by helicopter to Spain and Morocco.

John opened up the bridge door and whistled to the group. He waved his right arm and moved it in a circular motion over his head like a propeller. He pointed with his left arm in the direction of the helicopters. Sesom gave John a thumb's up.

Sesom began a cadence of orders, "Dorje, Kimi, Talan, and I will board the first chopper. Cering, Mike, Amen, Lucas, and Jonas will catch the next chopper for Spain. Remember, the helicopters will have envelopes with further instructions and travel arrangements. Do not, and I repeat, do not travel with any weapons. We don't need to draw any unwanted attention from airport security or customs." The first chopper was overhead and dropped a cargo ladder.

"Ladies first." Sesom held the ladder for Kimi as she scaled up the rungs of a flimsy ladder. The climb was about 40 feet to the door of the chopper. One-by-one, Kimi, Dorje, and Talan climbed the cargo ladder and entered the helicopter with their travel bags. Before Sesom made the climb, he went around and hugged each of the Disciples, Mike, Mary, and Elisabeth while Aaron held the ladder. Sesom smiled at Aaron and gave him a pat on the head.

Sesom called out as he began the climb, "We'll catch up after we finish this journey." He winked at Matt and turned toward the sky. Matt barely heard Sesom as the helicopter blades drowned out much of what was said. Once Sesom entered the chopper, the ladder was retracted and the chopper peeled off to the south. The other helicopter positioned itself over the bow of the Excalibur. Aaron caught the ladder and held it for the second group.

Matt winked at Cering, "Ladies first." Cering went up the ladder like a cat. Lucas was ready to climb when Matt interrupted him.

"Hey big man," Matt had to yell over the whirring sound. Lucas turned toward him. Matt had the Cristo de Redentor necklace in his hand. He let the crucifix fall while he held the chain. Lucas looked at the necklace.

"Take this with you. I insist." Matt handed over the necklace. Lucas gave Matt a smile and began the climb.

Jonas began the climb as Mike hugged Mary and kissed her neck.

"I love you."

"I love you too."

"A few weeks and I'll see you in the Falkland Islands."

"No more than two weeks though." Mary followed the statement with a nervous laugh. Her eyes were tearing up. Mike knew that he couldn't hang around as the departure would become much more difficult. He had to do what he had to do.

"Take care of my wife."

"She was my sister before she was your wife." Matt smiled at Mike and gave him a hug.

"Good luck with Gilmore." Matt gripped Mike's shoulders.

"No luck, we're Marines." Mike smiled and began the climb. He'd left his wife and family many times before. Leaving his family didn't get any easier, he just got better at it; one of the traits acquired over time for US military personnel. Amen was the last one to leave the ship. He spoke to Matt and Mary.

"I will look after him much like I looked out for you," Amen paused for a moment, "and that cat of yours." Amen smiled.

"I'm worried more about the big guy." Matt got serious.

"Lucas?" Amen was surprised that Matt was worried.

"No," Matt shook his head, "Sesom."

Amen got serious with Matt, "The big man will take care of himself, he always has." And with that, Amen climbed quickly into the helicopter. The cargo ladder disappeared and the chopper peeled off to the north. In a few seconds, the Mediterranean became peaceful again. The engines hummed as the Excalibur cut through the Strait of Gibraltar. Mary and Elisabeth remained on deck with Matt while Li and Ethan went below.

"Part of me wanted to jump on the ladder and board a chopper." Matt knew his sister would understand.

"You and Mike are just like dad. Always wanting to serve and take risks." Mary had a blanket around her; she offered part of it to Elisabeth.

Matt's cell phone vibrated. He thought Mike would be giving him a hard time about hanging back with the ladies. There was a new email from Dan at Delta Defense.

To: Matt Hiatt

From: Dan Richards

RE: Noah

Matt,

I hope this email finds you. Noah was taken away by two FBI agents this morning and charged with terrorism against the United States. I have no idea where they've taken him. I called attorneys from Delta and they said there's nothing they can do to help. Ever since the Patriot Act, the government has unchecked powers against people they claim to be terrorists at home and abroad.

I also spoke with Colonel Lash from Pendleton. He was curious to know if I had spoken with you or knew your whereabouts. He showed interest in your brother-in-law as well. He wants to speak with you and listen to your side of the story.

I'm worried about Noah. Let me know if there's anyone I can contact through the military to find out where they've taken him. I need to do whatever I can to support him and lobby for his release from the FBI.

Thanks,

Dan Richards
Project Manager-Delta Defense

Even though the military and government would be monitoring emails from Dan and Matt, Dan had to send a message to see if he could help his colleague.

"What is it?" Elisabeth saw that Matt was concerned.

"Bad news." Matt looked at the ladies.

"What happened?" Elisabeth continued with the query.

"The FBI picked up Noah from Delta Defense. Probably because of his involvement with me and the shoulder harness in Gaza." Elisabeth had a look of confusion.

"The weapon that I was using in Gaza came from Delta Defense, the place I used to work. Noah was responsible for project development and deployment. They know he's involved with the weapon used in Gaza that's traced back to me."

"Oh no." Mary knew that a person detained by the US government connected to acts of terrorism would be held without due process or legal representation.

"Oh yes, and this one is my fault. I requested the weapon from him when I left from Los Angeles." Matt felt responsible.

"What are you planning to do for Noah?" Elisabeth knew that Matt wouldn't leave his colleague and friend behind. Mary and Elisabeth looked like a couple of college students wrapped up in a blanket at a football game.

"I don't know yet." Matt knew that Sesom wanted him to remain on the Excalibur and make safe passage to the Falkland Islands with Elisabeth, Mary, and the children. Sesom wouldn't approve of Matt leaving the ship for any reason.

****

Matt was in a deep sleep having a dream about his friend Noah. He was alone in a cell, awaiting transfer to Gitmo. The FBI had taken his wheelchair away. Noah's face had been bloodied and his hair was disheveled.

Matt turned from the cell and saw his father, Robert Hiatt. His dad spoke first.

"I know you understand what's happening to your friend. I also know that your first impulse is to save him from the interrogation process. Noah sacrificed himself for the Disciples. He knew that helping you meant certain capture and interrogation. He was prepared for this."

"I wasn't." Matt was firm as he made eye contact with his father.

"Matt, we all make sacrifices. Noah made his. You must not get involved with Noah's affairs. He will find his own way." Robert knew that Noah was critical to the success of Mary's release from Samil. The shoulder harness was a modern marvel that had performed as expected and successful in the field. Even in earlier conversations, Noah had joked with Matt about his capture by the government once the shoulder harness was deployed in Gaza.

"I believe Semper Fidelis applies as much to Noah as it does to those in uniform. If it wasn't for him, Mary, Elisabeth, and I may have been killed in Gaza." Matt turned to find himself at Omaha Beach in the harbor. He was in the ocean and small waves splashed against his shins. His father knew all about the tradition of Semper Fidelis.

"When the Americans invaded this beach, they did so with eleven other allies. Not much is written about the involvement of those eleven countries during the invasion, but they were here. Twelve countries came together to invade this beach and push back an evil empire. Sometimes we can't see beyond our own experience to gain a broader perspective of what's happening in the world." Robert began to walk from the water to the Les Braves Memorial on the sand. Matt continued to look out over the harbor and imagined how D-Day must have unfolded on June 6th, 1944.

"Initial estimates were incorrect for those allies who perished on D-Day. The loss of life was immeasurable for those storming the beach and risking their lives. The sand and water were soaked with blood that day." Robert watched as his son looked out over the water.

Matt was vacillating between scenes of the D-Day invasion and the absolute serenity of Omaha Beach with his father. Troops were humping gear up the beach after being delivered by amphibious transport units. Matt couldn't believe how many men were rising from the water and getting mowed down by thousands of bullets. Artillery shells were exploding all along the beach as planes flew overhead. Complete chaos is what Matt witnessed. He turned to his father. Once again the setting was peaceful as his father sat next to the Les Braves Memorial.

"Why are you showing me Omaha?"

"Everybody makes sacrifices Matt, some more courageous than others."

Matt turned around and saw a prison camp with barbed wire and smoke stacks in the distance. A white ash was falling from the sky. Matt heard his father's voice behind him.

"The people on the beach were sacrificing their lives so these people could reclaim theirs." Robert and Matt had traveled to a death camp at Auschwitz. Robert's eyes began to mist and spill over his lower eyelids. Matt had never seen his father cry while he was alive.

"I never get used to that smell." Robert looked in the distance as he watched Jewish prisoners line up for roll call and a lice inspection. They were filthy, emaciated, and stoic as German guards began their cadence for prisoners. Matt couldn't take his eyes off the stacks in the distance. He knew what was burning in the chimneys. He knew why ash was falling from the sky. The Jewish prisoners would be gassed and burned, thousands a day, like clockwork. As the war intensified and the Germans gave up ground to the Allies, the Germans stepped up their efforts to kill as many Jews as possible. All told, estimates of 6,000,000 Jewish people were killed in death camps or directly from the effects of World War II.

"Matt, World War II wasn't random." Robert wiped away the moisture below his eyes as he looked straight ahead. "World War I prepared the Germans for an evil empire of unimaginable proportions. The people of Germany had been through tough times and economic hardship. Many welcomed a war effort and the jobs available to prepare the country for conflict." Matt interrupted his father.

"Much like what the United States has done for the past 30 years to stimulate the economy?"

"In some respects. But the US lost their purpose fighting wars over the past 60 years. Instead of fighting against evil empires or ruthless dictators, they chose to fight for political agendas or vendettas. In some respects, the United States became a new promised land for those looking to escape persecution and begin a new life. In less than three centuries, the promise has become elusive and largely unattainable for the masses."

"All the more reason to protect those who serve others." Matt referenced the capture of Noah.

"Like I said Matt, Noah has served a purpose and understood the consequences of his actions." Robert was still trying to convince his son to dismiss Noah's capture as collateral damage. Robert knew that Matt would expose himself to great danger if he went after Noah. In many respects, Samil wanted to draw Matt in by detaining Noah.

"I understand the purpose of an Allied invasion to eliminate an enemy from friendly soil, but what purpose does that serve in any part of the world?" Matt pointed to the smokestack as he reached out his right hand. He turned his palm over and caught a big piece of ash. Matt understood the dynamics of military affairs and operations. In many cases, unless a financial benefit could be defined through the use of military force, the United States' government wouldn't get involved. The Sudan and Syria were perfect examples of countries in decline that didn't matter to the rest of the world. Because the affairs in the Sudan and Syria didn't represent an economic benefit to the free world, the countries stood by as hostile governments slaughtered their own people.

"The purpose is pure evil. Samil got it wrong during World War II. Hitler underestimated the strength and response of Allied Forces across the globe. Samil won't make the same mistake twice." Ash fell from the sky into Matt's eyes. He rubbed them to regain his sight. In front of him was Hiroshima. A shadow was cast on the building in front of him.

"That serves as a reminder for this city and its people."

"A reminder for what?" Matt had no idea where he was. His eyes were still watering and itchy.

"Buildings and infrastructure can be rebuilt, but people can't be replaced. The person in front of you vaporized when the atom bomb hit. All that's left of her is a shadow."

"Her?"

"Her."

"She was carrying a newborn in her arms and turned to shield them from the blast. Hundreds of thousands of innocent Japanese lives were sacrificed in an instant to end World War II. She was about the same age as Elisabeth." Matt gave his father a strange look.

"Why is that important?"

"Why is what important?" Robert began to fade from Matt's vision.

"The Elisabeth angle. That this woman was the same age and carrying a newborn." Matt was raising his voice and pointed as his father's image began to disappear.

"Remember what I said about gaining a broader perspective of the world." Matt's father vanished.

"Wait." Matt was tossing and turning in bed.

"Matt."

"What do you mean?" Matt was still asking questions in his dream.

"Matt, wake up."

Matt opened his eyes and saw Elisabeth. He sat up and asked, "What is it?"

"Scratches came down the hall to my room." Elisabeth was sitting on the side of the bed cradling scratches. Scratches was purring as Elisabeth stroked her head.

"Well at least the cat approves." Matt sat up.

"Approves of what?" Elisabeth looked confused.

"Never mind. We've got to quit meeting like this." Matt's 6'3 frame was chiseled. He was shirtless with flannel pants. Elisabeth let Scratches down on the bed. Elisabeth noticed scars on Matt's chest and shoulders.

"What are those from?" She pointed to the flesh wounds.

"Barbed wire, a few knives, and a small piece of shrapnel." Matt looked over his body as he sat up and pointed to a few locations. "These scars are pretty typical for a Marine in Special Operations." Elisabeth touched one of the scars on Matt's back.

"This one is pretty big." Elisabeth traced the scar with her finger.

"That one was stitched by one of my buddies in the field. When we were covering parts of Tora Bora in Afghanistan, we couldn't call in medical support unless injuries were life threatening. I lost my footing, tumbled down a hill, and landed on a sharp rock. My buddy stitched the wound up with no anesthetic. That's why it looks pretty ratty."

"That must have hurt." Elisabeth showed genuine sympathy.

"Pain is something we learn to live with in Special Operations. Shrapnel, knives, boils, and blisters; they all feel the same over time." Scratches came over to Matt and began to rub her side against his left arm.

"Why did you wait?" Elisabeth was curious.

"Wait to dress our wounds?" Matt was still looking over his arms and chest.

"No. Wait to share your virginity with a woman?" Elisabeth felt more confident discussing private matters with Matt after their conversation with the Pope.

"I had chances. But the chances didn't feel or seem right at the time. After I lost my parents, my sister became a sense of strength for me. I always treated women like they were somebody's daughter or sister, not objects of my own sexual desires. Even though I had the same desires and feelings as my buddies, I always respected women as if they were sisters. I made a few mad by denying them my sensual side." Matt blushed at the thought of his past relationships.

Matt continued, "As I look at the bigger picture, maybe I was waiting for some other reason, or someone like you." Matt developed a serious tone as he finished the sentence.

"Really?" Elisabeth sounded insecure.

"Really." Matt reaffirmed what he said.

Elisabeth leaned over and began to kiss Matt. They tasted each other as their lips came together. Matt noticed that Elisabeth tasted sweet; a combination of peppermint flavored toothpaste mixed with her own saliva. Her tongue was soft and inviting while her lips were moist and supple. Elisabeth wasn't forceful at all; she was more receptive to Matt's kiss and his taking the initiative. He laid Elisabeth down and continued to kiss her lips and neck. Nothing was said between them.

Elisabeth continued to rub Matt's back and arms. She was amazed how hard and defined his body was. As Matt supported his weight with his arms, his triceps flared and biceps were tight. She brought her hands up to his face and continued to kiss his lips. Elisabeth could feel herself becoming aroused. She could feel Matt becoming aroused. She knew they were heading to a point of no return.

"We shouldn't," Elisabeth didn't want to stop, but knew she should.

"You're right. We shouldn't do this here. We should go down below." Matt didn't realize that Elisabeth wanted to stop altogether.

"No. We should wait." Elisabeth was ruining the moment.

"Isn't a blessing from Pope Simplicius enough?" Matt was trying to be funny as he continued to kiss Elisabeth's neck. He was working his way down to her breasts. Elisabeth was in a black camisole and a matching pair of panties. Her long black hair was down and she looked beautiful as a light shone through the porthole in Matt's room.

"The Pope's blessing was reassuring, but I need to know that you love me and will stand by me through all of this. Don't forget that I'm a virgin too. I have saved myself as well."

Matt rolled over to Elisabeth's left side and began to trace the outline of her face. "You're right. This needs to be special for both of us." Matt leaned in and kissed Elisabeth one more time. He hopped out of bed and went to the dresser for a t-shirt. Elisabeth was disappointed they wouldn't consummate their relationship on this morning. Matt whispered in her ear.

"C'mon, let me take you back to your room." Matt offered up his right hand to escort Elisabeth. She stood up and they exited the cabin. Ethan was standing outside the door.

"What are you doing up so early?" Matt gave Ethan a strange look.

"I couldn't sleep. Trying to get used to the sea again." Ethan wasn't convincing.

Matt looked back at the cabin, pointed and said, "You were spying on us, weren't you?"

"Oh no Matt, why would you think that?" Ethan was even less convincing.

"It's a little early in the morning to be on a stroll, isn't it?" Matt gave Ethan some sarcasm. Ethan looked at his watch and agreed with a nod.

"Yes it is. But this is merely a coincidence." Ethan had given up on convincing.

"A coincidence? Sesom put you up to this didn't he?" Matt knew what was going on with Ethan. "Didn't he?" Matt repeated the question for Ethan.

Ethan lowered his head, "Yes, he did."

"But why?" Matt was confused.

"He wants updates on your progress." Ethan looked sheepishly at Matt and Elisabeth.

"Our progress?" Matt was still confused.

"Your progress with…" Ethan turned sideways and made a semicircle motion over his midsection. As he made the motion, Ethan said, "Your progress with this."

Matt and Elisabeth began laughing. Elisabeth offered insight, "Really? He wants to know about this?" Elisabeth imitated the motion made by Ethan.

Matt began to laugh even harder as Ethan's face turned red. "Are you sure he doesn't want to know about this too?" Matt began to perform pelvic thrusts as he brought his fists to his hips. Ethan became more embarrassed with Matt's theatrics.

"I'm sorry. I will not intrude on your privacy again." Ethan was genuine with his embarrassment. Elisabeth heard a baby cry in the distance.

Elisabeth excused herself, "I'm going to help with Rebecca." She made a rocking motion with her arms for Ethan.

"Wait up, I'll get John." They both walked past Ethan as he stood against the wall.

Elisabeth knocked on the door as she entered Mary's room; Matt was right behind her. Mary was breastfeeding Rebecca. They were staying in the largest suite near Captain Phil's quarters. Having young children stay next door didn't bother Captain Phil; he could sleep through just about any disturbance. When ship captains worked, they worked hard; when they slept, they slept even harder.

"Hey guys. What are you doing up so early?" Mary had the look of a perfect mother. She wore an oversized white pajama set with lambs printed in a pattern across her shirt and pants. As she rocked back and forth in a chair, she grabbed a pair of glasses to focus her eyes on Matt and Elisabeth.

"We came to get a dose of birth control from you?" Matt's humor didn't come off so well at such an early hour. Mary looked confused. Matt clarified.

"The kids. We're going to give you a break." Matt smiled at his sister.

"Oh...okay. Let her finish feeding and I'll share my *birth control* with you." Mary emphasized the last part of the sentence and began to chuckle. Matt went over to John. He was sleeping in the lower part of a bunk bed.

"I'll take him to my room." Matt loaded John onto his right shoulder and disappeared into the hallway. Elisabeth sat next to Mary in another rocking chair.

"Such a beautiful child," Elisabeth admired the serenity of Rebecca.

"Thank you. She's been a blessing and sleeps through the night." Mary began to lightly burp Rebecca; she had fallen back to sleep.

"Are you having more children?"

"No. We were lucky to have a boy and girl. Two are enough for me and Mike." Mary wiped Rebecca's mouth and handed her to Elisabeth. Elisabeth lit up with a smile as she moved her hair away from Rebecca's face and began to rock.

Mary gathered some items for Elisabeth, "Here is a pack that has the essentials, including some formula."

"I will take good care of her."

"I know you will. She'll do fine in a bunk, just put some pillows near the edge."

Elisabeth got up and put the baby pack over her shoulder while holding Rebecca tight to her breast, "Okay." Elisabeth was careful with every step as she took Rebecca back to her room. She prepared the lower bunk with small pillows and retrieved a tiny stuffed animal from the baby pack. Rebecca was peaceful. She had no idea the world was at war. She had no idea that Samil assumed power in the United States of America. She had no idea her father was on his way to Virginia to meet with a powerful General in the Marines. Rebecca was peaceful, an innocent kind of peaceful that is lost during the adult years of life. Elisabeth thought for a minute about how the world could learn a lot from children and how they see life.

****

"Red." A uniquely familiar voice was on the phone.

"I need a ride." Amen smiled wondering if Red would recognize his voice.

"Where you at?"

"The intersection of South Compton and East Butler."

"You lost or something?" Red knew the area was rough.

"No. Just looking for a ride." Amen's grin got wider.

"How you payin'?"

"Cash."

Red remembered a very similar conversation a few weeks back. "You're not that fella in the blue blazer and jeans are you?"

"I am."

"Be there in 10 minutes."

Cering and Amen had taken a cab from LAX to the intersection in Compton. The couple stood out against a backdrop of closed buildings and overgrown vegetation. The time was 9:12 am. A black Escalade with custom rims rolled by. The driver and passengers took note of a very beautiful woman from the Middle East dressed in jeans, a black tank top, and sandals. Cering had her hair in a ponytail and black shades concealed her eyes. Neither Amen nor Cering noticed the predatory vehicle in front of them.

Amen turned to Cering, "About 10 minutes."

"That might be the average life span at this intersection." Cering gave Amen a nod. They'd both been in much rougher cities in worse situations. The Escalade came rolling by again. One of the tinted windows rolled down as the vehicle slowed and a man with sunglasses admired Cering.

"Hey baby. You need a ride? We got room for one more. We'll have to leave the John behind." The stranger smiled as he finished the proposition. Cering just smiled back and shook her head no. The SUV continued on. Other men in the vehicle began to give the front passenger a hard time over his failure to entice the woman.

"They'll be back." Amen understood the nature of men and their agony over rejection, especially by women.

"I know." Cering knew the predictability of men even better. She had been on the receiving end of catcalls and predator advances by the opposite sex for years.

"You want me to handle it?" Amen knew the answer before he asked.

"No. I got it." Cering enjoyed putting men in their place.

The Escalade rolled through the intersection again. This time the front passenger was more determined.

"C'mon sugar, we don't want to beat up your boyfriend." The passenger flashed some brass knuckles to Amen. Amen pointed at himself and mouthed, "Me?" The couple looked at each other and shrugged their shoulders. The vehicle kept moving by them at a slow rate of speed.

Cering reached behind the small of her back and pulled a 9 mm with a silencer. She shot out the right side tires and went down to her right knee, rolled, and shot out the left side tires. The Escalade rolled forward with the thumping sound of deflated rubber until the brake lights illuminated.

"Oh no you didn't!" The driver came out and went for his weapon.

Amen hit the driver in his right shoulder with two Chinese stars. They were sharp and penetrated the driver's shoulder about half way. Li taught Amen how to construct, sharpen, and throw the deadly weapons. Amen put a star near the second perpetrator's head in the frame of the passenger's side door. He threw one more and it traveled from horizontal to vertical as it stuck in the center of the dashboard.

"You just sit there. I wouldn't want to be responsible for beating you or your girlfriend up. We'll be leaving in a few minutes. Don't do anything more stupid than you already have." The driver returned to his seat holding his shoulder.

"Those are flesh wounds and you'll be fine. However, pulling those things out will be painful." Amen put the remaining stars back in a small case and returned them to his pocket. A red cab pulled up and rolled down the passenger side window.

"You lookin' for the ride?" Red smiled as he leaned across the seat.

"Yes sir," Amen and Cering grabbed their backpacks as Red got out of the vehicle. The passenger in the front of the Escalade got out of the car.

"What happened to the Caddy Santana?" Red popped the trunk.

"They happened?" Santana pointed at Amen and Cering as they put their bags in the back.

"These are good folks Santana. Not a bright idea to mess with them though. They've been trained to handle difficult situations. Is that why the Caddy has four flats?"

"Yeah," Santana was surprised Red knew the couple.

"You provoked them didn't you?" Red shut the trunk and went around to open the doors for Cering and Amen.

"Yeah," Santana had known Red for years.

Red opened the driver's door, "I'll do you boys a favor and call Checker's Wrecker to come get you. You don't want to ride on those rims. Is Kevin alright?" Kevin stuck his left hand out the window and waved.

Santana pointed at Amen as he got into the front seat. "That homey put two pieces of metal in Kevin's shoulder. He's bleeding some. He'll be okay."

"What did you do to him?" Red reached over and pulled down the meter.

"He went for a weapon and I hit him with a couple Chinese stars. Those have a tendency to tug on the skin as they get yanked out. He'll probably need a few stitches too." Amen looked at the Caddy in front of them.

"It's good for those kids to meet their match every once in a while. They may be more inclined to treat others with some respect in the future."

"We usually kill anybody that pulls a weapon on us. Because of your previous hospitality, they lived."

"I'll take the matter up with their parents. Where to?" Red pulled around the disabled Escalade.

"Do you have a place we can sit down and have an early lunch? We'd like to meet up with you and Robert to discuss some more business."

Red laughed, "There were some suits from the FBI that came looking around after your last trip to Compton. I guess they had some tips on that Mustang you drove the last time you were here. The military was looking for the owner of that vehicle; said that he was involved in some home invasions and explosions near UCLA."

"How did you leave it with them?" Amen looked at Red.

"Like we do with other authority figures that come snooping around Compton, we left them with nothing. We learned a long time ago you couldn't trust the government or police. They're always planting evidence and making up their own rules. Their rules don't apply here anymore. Nobody will talk to them."

****

*I appeal to you therefore, brothers, by the mercies of
God, to present your bodies as a living sacrifice, holy
and acceptable to God, which is your spiritual worship.
Do not be conformed to this world, but be transformed
by the renewal of your mind, that by testing you may
discern what is the will of God, what is good and
acceptable and perfect*

Romans 12:1-2

Jonas arrived at the White House and was being
screened by the Secret Service. Shoes, belts, rings, and
necklaces had to be removed to enter 1600 Pennsylvania
Avenue. With heightened security, Secret Service was
running visitors through two screenings.

"No cell phones sir." An agent was holding Jonas's
phone.

Jonas retorted, "I'll need to communicate with the Holy
Father from the Oval Office. Can we ask President
Crevan for an exception?"

The agent took the cell phone to a nearby White House
phone. After speaking with the Secret Service
Commander, the agent came back to Jonas. He
disassembled the phone, removed the battery from the
back, and then put the phone back together. Once the
phone had powered up, the agent dialed a number and
made a call. His own cell phone rang and he ignored the
call.

"Mr. Andros, you have been cleared with the use of your
phone. Only use the phone in the Oval Office." The
agent maintained the same level of dryness and
professionalism as when Jonas arrived.

"I will." Jonas followed a Secret Service agent down the hall; another agent was shadowing him.

The Oval Office Secretary welcomed Jonas, "Mr. Andros, President Crevan is ready to see you." She stood up, shook his hand, and escorted him into the Oval Office. President Crevan came over and shook Jonas's hand.

"Your reputation precedes you," Crevan squeezed Jonas's hand.

"And you too President Crevan." Both men knew that Jonas was verbally jabbing the new President.

"Please, come sit down. Can I get you something to drink?" Crevan took a seat in the high-back leather chair.

"No thank you, I'm good." Jonas meant business.

"How is the Holy Father?"

"He's well, albeit very concerned about what's happening in the United States and the Middle East." Jonas wasn't interested in small talk.

"The United States is concerned as well. As we've seen in the past with Libya and Syria, we don't want dictatorships to have unchecked power over their people and the territory. Al Qaeda is still determined and organized, as we witnessed recently in the attacks on the United States." Crevan linked terror back to an easy target.

"The Holy Father received intelligence from the Middle East with regard to the dirty bomb attacks in the United States." Jonas pulled out his phone.

"Really?"

"Really."

"And what was said?" Crevan played the part.

"Let me pull up the information." Jonas began to navigate through his smart phone. He put on some reading glasses.

Jonas continued, "The information we received implicated the United States in covert operations to attack Los Angeles, Miami, New York, and Concord."

"And who supplied this information?" Crevan already knew the answer.

"You should know," Jonas implicated Crevan.

"You believe this administration had something to do with attacks on our own homeland?" Crevan played stupid.

"President Crevan, the facts are indisputable…we know." Jonas looked over the top of his reading glasses at the deceptive leader.

"Really?"

"Really." Both men experienced a bit of déjà vu.

"Jonas, the allegations are absurd. However, we have our own intelligence pointing to the Vatican's involvement with these self-proclaimed," Crevan raised his fingers and made quotation marks, "Disciples. In fact, we know that you traveled with Hiatt, Barnes, and the rest of the terrorists."

Jonas smiled and began to tap a series of numbers on his smart phone, 231611. The bottom of the phone opened up and exposed a dart, a syringe, and a small tube with a thicker gauge needle attached. Crevan failed to notice what Jonas was doing with his smart phone.

Jonas made eye contact with Crevan once again. "Alexander. Secretary of State Watt and you are responsible for the mysterious death surrounding the Turkish Ambassador to Italy. You also rallied Samil to carry out dirty bomb attacks on the United States, conveniently placing blame on Al Qaeda and their terrorist networks. Your plot failed at the Western Wall, failed in Gaza, and ultimately failed to sink the Excalibur off the coast of Italy. Your record of failing is quite remarkable."

Jonas raised his phone, pressed the call button, and shot a dart above Crevan's collar into his neck. Crevan didn't even know what hit him. He passed out on the desk before Jonas left his seat. Jonas went to work and retrieved the small tube with the thick needle from his phone. He grabbed a tuft of Crevan's hair and pulled his head back against the leather chair.

"This won't hurt at all." Jonas injected the needle below Crevan's left jaw. He moved the needle around a little before he was satisfied with a location to administer a small tracking device. The tracking device was covered with materials to mimic bone should an x-ray of Crevan's jaw be taken. The Disciples and Israeli Defense Force could now track Crevan's position and listen to his conversations.

Jonas took the syringe from the smart phone and lifted Crevan to his feet in front of the chair. While holding Crevan with his left arm, Jonas injected a counteractive serum to the Versed like sedative he'd administered with the dart. Crevan would come to in a matter of seconds. Once Jonas finished the injection, he put the items back in his smart phone and closed the compartment. He pushed the numbers 231611 and the compartment closed and sealed completely. The secret compartment would never open again. Jonas placed the phone in his right pant pocket.

"You may feel this a little." Jonas took Crevan and threw him into a table that was behind the Presidential desk. A lamp and a couple pictures came crashing to the floor as Crevan broke his fall with an oak table that matched the oversized desk. Jonas went over to Crevan and showed concern. The Secret Service came barging through the door.

"What happened?" An agent had pulled a gun. Three more agents followed him into the room.

"He got up from the desk and collapsed onto the table?" Jonas took Crevan's pulse. "His pulse is normal."

An agent radioed for the medical staff to come to the Oval Office. President Crevan began to regain consciousness. He rubbed the back of his head.

"What happened?"

"Stay down Mr. President, you had a nasty fall."

Crevan sat up and looked at the attending agent, "I don't remember getting up from my desk."

"We have medical on the way."

Secretary of State Watt came rushing into the room.

"Arrest this man." Watt pointed in Jonas's direction. "We have intelligence showing his recent work with terrorists in the United States and abroad."

"Watt, you know those allegations are false." Jonas had prepared to be framed for his work with the Disciples. Two Secret Service agents forced Jonas's hands behind his back. One of the agents began to read Jonas his Miranda rights. Jonas depressed a button on his watch that sent a message to the Vatican and Talan through his cell phone.

Watt walked up to Jonas and said, "You won't have the right to remain silent, you will not be provided an attorney, and you will most certainly rot in prison at Guantanamo Bay. We don't care what country you're from."

"I'm sure you had a similar conversation with our Turkish Ambassador, before you killed him." Jonas wasn't intimidated.

"Get him out of here! Turn him over to the Navy and have them hold him at Gitmo." Two Secret Service agents escorted Jonas from the Oval Office while the other two helped Crevan to his feet. White House Medical staff rushed into the room to check on their President. Crevan returned to the leather chair.

"Thank you." Crevan was still shaken up and bleeding from the back of his head. A doctor put a blood pressure cuff on him while a nurse began to clean a sizeable laceration.

"What happened?" Watt was concerned about how his leader fell over.

"I'm not sure. I remember asking Mr. Andros if he wanted something to drink. Everything went blurry after that." The doctor finished taking Crevan's blood pressure.

"BP is fine. We need to snap some pictures of your head to ensure there isn't internal bleeding." The doctor was insistent.

"I'll be fine." Crevan wanted to brush off the embarrassing encounter.

"No Mr. President. Protocol is that we take you in and run some tests to be safe." The doctor was insistent as the Speaker of the House entered the Oval Office.

The Speaker had become Vice President through a natural progression and Crevan's encouragement. Even though Lance Morgan wasn't fond of Crevan and his style of dirty politics, he agreed to help the President in a transitional government. Morgan was one of the good guys, a moderate who believed in less government and more liberties for the American people. He was popular with congressional leaders and constituents in Texas. Coming from the south, he held strong Christian convictions. Morgan was shocked to see the President bleeding from the back of his head.

"Is he okay?"

Crevan wanted to speak for himself. "I'm fine, just a misstep."

"We're going to take him to emergency for some scans and blood work." The doctor wasn't backing down. Jonas utilized sedative agents that metabolized quickly, there would be no trace of the drugs in Crevan's system found in a blood test.

"Sounds like a good idea." Morgan assessed the damage.

"You've got a pretty nasty cut on the back of your head."

"I think the plant got the worst of it," Crevan made light of his head wound.

The nurse disagreed, "The plant will be fine, your head needs to be stitched."

"Great." Crevan didn't want to leave the White House.

"Who was the person being escorted by Secret Service?" Morgan saw two agents taking a man away in a black sedan. He looked at Watt.

"One of the Pope's men. It appears the Vatican has been working with a terrorist organization that loosely defines itself as Disciples. We have very good intelligence to hold him indefinitely."

"The Vatican?" Morgan was in disbelief.

"Yes. The Vatican." Watt gave the impression he wasn't kidding.

"Wow. Has anybody notified Simplicius of this?" Morgan knew the fallout between Rome and the United States would create a public relation's nightmare.

"No. I think it would be a good idea if you made the call seeing as the President will be requiring medical attention." Watt presumed Morgan was volunteering.

"I know nothing of the circumstances," Morgan objected.

"Just let Simplicius know the President will be following up with him shortly, after he visits the hospital." Watt pushed even harder.

A few more Secret Service agents entered the Oval Office. "Mr. President, we're ready to roll."

Watt volunteered, "I'll come with you and the doctor. You'll need to stand in as President for a few hours," Watt pointed at Morgan.

****

Lucas and Mike pulled up to the Lettuce Head restaurant. The time was 12:40 pm.

"What is this Lettuce Head?" Lucas spoke in a deep baritone.

"A small deli near Marine Headquarters." Mike pulled into a parking space. The lunch crowd was beginning to thin. "General Gilmore has agreed to meet us here."

Both men got out of a rental car and entered the restaurant. The Lettuce Head served some of the best sandwiches and soups in town. Locally owned and operated, the deli had become a popular diner for tourists and repeat customers. General Gilmore greeted him at the door.

"Mookie."

"Gil."

The men gave each other a long hug. Mike saved the General's life while they served together in the Middle East. The men earned each other's trust and respect in Special Operations. Mike didn't want to make a career out of the military. General Gilmore dressed down for the meeting.

"Are you gentlemen ready to be seated?" A hostess interrupted the men.

Gilmore asked, "Anymore coming?"

"No." Mike grabbed Gil's shoulders. He was happy to see his friend.

The hostess led the men to a booth. Lucas couldn't fit between the bench and table. "I think a table might be better." Mike led the hostess to a more comfortable table. Before the men sat down, Mike did the honors. "General Gilmore, this is Lucas, a good friend of mine."

"It's a pleasure to meet you Lucas." Gilmore extended his hand to the supersized Brazilian.

Lucas's hand engulfed the General's as he smiled and said, "It's a pleasure to meet a friend of Mike." The men took their seats and menus were distributed. Drink orders were taken before the men got down to business.

Gilmore took the lead, "The United States' government is looking for you and Matt. Something about you guys being involved in a terror plot in Jerusalem and Gaza. They've distributed pictures, intelligence data, and even linked you guys to the recent dirty bombs in New York, Los Angeles, Miami, and Concord. I believe I saw a photo of your Brazilian friend in Jerusalem. The FBI has put out a million dollar reward for your capture. In fact, each of you is worth a million dollars. I never knew what two million dollars looked like," Gilmore gave a grin. Lucas took off his sunglasses.

"I may turn you in myself," Lucas looked at Mike. "The shelters of Sao Paulo could use that kind of money for orphans."

"A million apiece? Don't let Mary know." Mike began laughing and continued, "Vice President, I mean, President Crevan has a very deceptive agenda set up for the United States and other countries abroad. He lost his way while serving in the Middle East envoys and became corrupt. The relationships he built and connections he formed are solid in Iran, Syria, Yemen, Lebanon, Egypt, and Libya. He wants to leverage those relationships quickly."

Gilmore began a series of questions. "How can you be so sure?"

Mike shared details, "A Turkish Ambassador to Italy had very credible intelligence that the State Department was involved with Syrian operatives recruiting Turkish paramilitary to carry out the bomb attacks in the United States months before they happened."

"Where is the Ambassador to Italy? Why hasn't he come forward?"

"He met with the Swiss Guard and Vatican months ago to reveal the incriminating intelligence. The Ambassador was concerned about numerous sources in Turkey sharing similar stories about how the US wanted to recruit trained personnel to carry out dirty bomb attacks. The US government wanted to stage the attacks to look like Al Qaeda or some other terror network. Soon after the Ambassador shared the information, he mysteriously died."

"Who shared this information with you?"

"His Holiness shared the information with our group at the Vatican. Jonas, the leader of the Swiss Guard, witnessed the conversation between the Pope and the Ambassador as well. Jonas is in Washington meeting with Crevan as we speak. Not sure how that meeting will go."

"What's the nature of their meeting?"

"The Pope isn't pleased with the war in the Middle East, tensions in the Orient, offensive moves by Russia, and the death of a friendly Ambassador. Jonas went to vet President Crevan to understand his intentions."

The General sipped some coffee. He thought hard about what he wanted to say and chose his words carefully.

"Alexander and I served together in the Middle East on several occasions. While my roles were geared more toward troop exercises and deployment, Crevan was always negotiating with tribal leaders and recruiting rebels to join the fight. The envoy handed out tens of millions of dollars and caches of advanced weaponry. In many cases, our Marines would be called upon to train rebels how to use the weapons. We did and they would return to their villages or go fight the war on their own fronts."

Mike and Lucas listened carefully as Gilmore continued, "In many reports, several Marines documented that they were fighting the same rebels we were arming and training. I took the matter up with Crevan and he stood by the rebels and their commitment to the US. At the time, Mickey Watt seemed to carry out Crevan's wishes; they were thicker than thieves. We quit trusting the Middle East envoys and their support of puppets in the territory."

"Did you and Crevan work out your differences?" Mike wasn't surprised by Crevan and Watt's reputation in the Middle East.

"No. We agreed to disagree. I was surprised that Palmer selected him as a running mate during the campaign. While Crevan helped carry votes for Palmer in the northeast, he also carried plenty of baggage."

Mike had Gil's attention, "Crevan was paying Syrian operatives to recruit Turkish paramilitary. He is responsible for the attacks on the United States and assassinating Palmer in New Hampshire."

"Are you ready to order?" The waitress caught both men off guard.

"You guys want shrimp po boys?" Gilmore didn't need a menu.

"I'll take two." Lucas had an appetite.

"Sure." Mike closed his menu.

"Four po boys with fries and hush puppies."

"I'll have those right out." The waitress gathered up the menus and went to the kitchen.

Gilmore got back to business, "Those are pretty serious allegations."

Mike reiterated, "We're in some serious conflicts across the globe right now. Crevan and Watt coordinated the attacks on US soil to retaliate against countries of their choosing. They want to establish their own leadership throughout the Middle East, Africa, parts of Europe, and Indonesia. Eventually they will turn on Israel and establish a new world order. The Muslim world will follow Crevan's lead if he destroys Israel." Lucas nodded his head in affirmation.

"The American people won't go for it," Gilmore thought about the constituency.

"They will when government programs dry up and affect our national economy. Crevan and Watt have a plan for the United States as well. They will create class warfare to keep focus away from foreign policy. In some respects, seems like we're at the beginning of the end." Mike had said enough.

"Is there anything I can do to help? I've never been a fan of Crevan and his cronies." General Gilmore shared his support as food was being delivered to the table.

"Well, we could use some help getting onto Guantanamo Bay. There is a person of special interest we need to release from the detention camp." Mike took a bite of his po boy. Lucas quietly blessed the meal and began eating. Gilmore nodded his head and thought for a moment.

"I have some friends in the Navy who owe me a favor. They can be trusted. Once you're on Gitmo, you're on your own." General Gilmore knew how far he could go without jeopardizing Mike's mission.

"Good enough. What do you think Lucas?" Mike took another bite of his flavorful po boy.

Lucas shoveled half a sandwich in his mouth while speaking, "We can handle the rest. We will do our best not to kill anybody on the Base. We will evacuate the prisoner from Santiago de Cuba. We have some connections on that part of island." Lucas seemed more preoccupied with his sandwich than a reconnaissance mission.

General Gilmore quipped, "Lucas, if you were coming at me with a weapon, I might be more inclined to drop mine and run." All the men had a good laugh.

****

"It's never too early for soul food." Red parked the cab in front of Soul-to-Seoul, a popular mix of fried foods with a Korean flair. The restaurant was still located in a tough section of Compton.

Cering said, "I'm not sure if I've ever had soul food."

"If you're going to miss church on Sunday, don't forget some food for the soul during the week." Red began laughing as he held the door for Amen and Cering. He was wearing a Cincinnati Reds' jersey with a Boston Red Sox hat. Red was in his early sixties and in good shape. After years of lugging bags and working multiple jobs at once, he'd made it as a taxi driver for his own company. With a white beard and a short white Afro, some people referred to him as Santa Compton. Red even volunteered at the Boys and Girls' Clubs in Compton during Christmastime and other holidays.

Time stopped momentarily when Cering and Amen entered the establishment. Except for a Korean cook in the kitchen, Cering and Amen were the only non-African American patrons in the diner. Robert was the first to greet them.

"Our table is over here." Robert, Sneakers, Michael, and two of their friends had saved a table for eight. Red followed them to the table.

Michael stood up, "Good to see you man. Looks like the kitty is all grown up." He admired Cering as he shook hands with Amen. Cering gave Amen a funny look.

"I'll explain later. Gentlemen, this is Cering, a dear friend of mine from Egypt." Cering shook hands with the men as Amen pulled out a chair for her.

"Hey Red," Sneakers welcomed his old friend and a familiar face from the neighborhood.

"Hey fellas," Red tipped his hat to the young men and took a seat.

A very large African American woman came over to check on the table.

"Relatives of yours?" Alabama Evans pulled a pen out of her hair.

"C'mon Bama, of course they are. I'm royalty in Saudi Arabia. Can't you tell? These folks are here to share details about my kingdom and throne." Michael was having fun with one of his favorite waitresses.

"You just sat on your throne a few minutes ago before these fine folks arrived. Don't know if you want to share those details?" Bama was a veteran of quid pro quo banter.

All of the men began to slap each other and giggle into their fists. Red gave Bama a fist bump to welcome her to the table.

"Can I get you fine folks something to drink?" Bama began with Cering and Amen. They both ordered coffee with cream. She took drink orders and gave instructions, "Menus are on the table and specials on the board. We're out of the blackened catfish omelet and I'd avoid the shrimp soufflé. Even though the chefs like to mix it up, we don't do French well; unless it's from the bayou in Louisiana."

The diner was very clean and packed with a late morning crowd. Cering noticed how clean the black and white checkered floor was. The tables were made of stainless steel and lined with red, white, and blue chairs. She also noticed two police officers were enjoying an early lunch and taking a break during a shift.

Robert spoke up, "What brings you to Compton? Not necessarily a destination spot for travelers."

"We have more business for you, if you're interested?"

"We're always open for business." Michael was mature beyond his years. Growing up in Compton with one parent taught him more about survival than anything else.

"We can trust these two gentlemen?" Amen motioned in the direction of Michael's friends, two men he didn't recognize from an earlier encounter.

"Sporty and Tiny have been running with me since kindergarten. They wouldn't be here if we couldn't trust them." Michael's confidence was convincing.

Sporty spoke up, "Any chance you ran across some MF812s this morning? Word on the street is you put some metal in the driver's shoulder after blowing out four tires. The driver is a younger brother of the gang leader. Those guys are looking for you."

Red interjected, "The driver's name is Kevin, he'll be fine. They were disrespecting the lady. He had it coming to him."

Amen interrupted, "Sporty, we're not worried about minor distractions or mixing it up with LA gangs. We have no interest in turf, territory, or colors. We're here on business. People who interfere with our business will be dealt with accordingly. We have no business with the 812s."

"Fair enough." Tiny, whose body frame was everything but, wanted to move the conversation forward.

"What's your business with us?" Sporty was beginning to understand how Amen operated.

Cering took over, "In three days President Crevan will tour LA and focus on the areas hit by the recent dirty bombs. We have credible sources indicating that he will stay at the Beverly Wilshire Hotel. Any of you know someone working at the hotel?"

The drink orders arrived and Bama noticed the menus went untouched, "Don't tell me you haven't looked at the menus yet? You guys going to need to sign a lease or somethin'? Let's pick up those menus and order up. Anything dead and fried is a safe bet." Bama pulled the pen back out of her hair.

"Please begin with them," Amen shared a menu with Cering. They were both more interested in what the group was ordering. Most of the men ordered a mix of Korean and soul food. Red ordered a fried chicken sandwich with collard greens and red beans and rice; Amen and Cering ordered the same dish.

Bama smiled at the guests, "Great choice. I'll have your food right out."

Sneakers picked up the previous conversation, "I know one of their line chefs and someone on the hospitality crew."

"I know a couple people as well." Tiny came from a large family and had several relatives in the area.

"Did you say President Crevan? What are your plans?" Michael was out of his comfort zone. "Isn't the President protected by a thousand people?"

"He is," Cering agreed with Michael.

"Don't they put people away for life that mess with the Prez?" Robert was curious.

"They do. Unless they put them to death first." Amen was matter-of-fact.

"That's some heavy stuff." Michael sat back in his chair. "What do you want us to do?"

"We need you to create distractions for the Secret Service. We need you to slow down the motorcade so we can remove the President from office." Cering knew honesty was the best policy. The Disciples were already wanted by the FBI, CIA and anyone else looking to cash in on a million dollar bounty per Disciple.

"How are you proposing we do that?" Tiny realized the absurdity of the request.

Cering smiled, "We have credible sources in the Secret Service, CIA, and FBI. We will know the motorcade route for President Crevan. You have strength in numbers. The distraction will come from a bridge above the route. We will provide all necessary supplies for the diversion. You will be paid handsomely for your efforts."

"How much?" Michael enjoyed the business aspect of a transaction. He wasn't concerned about the amount of risk involved with an operation.

"Twenty million." Cering said.

"What? What did you say?" Michael couldn't believe his ears. Red and all of the young men moved to the edge of their seats.

"Twenty million of your US dollars." Cering repeated the number.

Robert spit up his soda; some of which came pouring out of his nose. Red handed Robert a napkin.

Michael said, "Down payment?"

"Two million dollars will be transferred into an offshore account belonging to Mr. Taylor; I believe you refer to him as Red. He will be responsible for disbursements and tracking monies. We believe that several of you and Red can successfully handle the operation. Once the operation is complete, the account will grow by an additional eighteen million dollars."

"Where will the diversion take place?" Robert regained his composure as food was delivered to the table. Amen and Cering were amazed at the size of their chicken fried sandwiches.

Bama exclaimed, "Good for the soul. What else can I deep fry for ya?"

Amen smiled and winked at the waitress, "I think this will feed us for a few days."

"Bamalicious as usual." Sneakers grabbed a fork and began to tear into his lunch.

Bama turned to notice a commotion at the front of the diner. Three men had entered the building and were looking around the establishment. They were wearing trench coats and sunglasses.

"Friends of yours?" Bama spoke to Michael.

Michael looked at Amen and Cering, "Friends of theirs. They're 812s looking to repay a debt from this morning."

By the time Michael finished his sentence, the men noticed a table of eight in the corner. Two of the patrons matched the description of a man and woman at the corner of Compton and Butler this morning. One of the men motioned for the others to follow.

Bama headed off the men halfway to the table, "No trouble fellas. Soul-to-Seoul is a safe zone. You got trouble, take it elsewhere." The men blew off Bama and marched to the table.

"We've got some unfinished business with you," One of the men addressed Amen.

Michael spoke up, "C'mon Spyder, your boys were disrespecting the lady this morning. They got what was coming to them."

A voice came from behind Spyder, "Is there a problem gentlemen?" Both police officers had made their way over to the table. The officers knew exactly what was happening in the corner.

Amen stood up, "No problem here officer. These men were just joining us." Cering retrieved a few more chairs.

"What?" Spyder was still defiant.

"Have a seat Spyder, we'll talk it out." Amen was insistent that his enemies join him at the table. The officers left and returned to their meal. The diner was still bustling and preparing for a busy lunch crowd.

Amen looked at Michael, "You know each other."

"Yeah. We went to school together. We played ball together. Spyder was an All-District running back a couple years back." Michael looked at Spyder and his friends.

"Can we get you something to eat?" Cering waved Bama over to the table.

"We didn't come here to eat," Spyder was still upset.

"We didn't come here to fight either," Amen looked at Spyder.

Bama had her pad ready to go, "Nice to see you decided to stay Reggie. Can I get you and your friends the usual?" Spyder looked at his buddies and gave them a nod.

"Yeah Bama, three chicken sandwiches and chocolate malts." Reggie, known as Spyder to the MF812s, took a seat and removed his knit beanie. The other men took a seat next to Tiny and Red.

"What's up Red? What are you doing here?" Spyder was surprised to see Red at the table.

"Just having an early lunch with some friends. What are you up to Reggie? You didn't come here looking for trouble? Did you?"

Spyder said, "Maybe. I received word that these two perps mixed it up with some of my boys this morning."

Robert shared the truth, "Santana was disrespecting Cering. Cering disabled the vehicle and Kevin drew a weapon. Amen would have killed them, but out of respect to Red, he let them live."

Amen took a bite of his sandwich and nodded his head, "Robert speaks the truth. Most people who disrespect my friends or me don't live to tell about the experience. I made an exception because your friends didn't have any idea of who we are or what our business is in Compton." All of the men and Cering looked at Spyder.

Spyder said, "So, what's your business?"

Amen smiled, "I'm just getting my wallet." Once Amen retrieved his wallet, he pulled out $2,000 and placed it in front of Spyder.

"We probably don't want the police to see that. That should cover the four tires this morning." Amen pulled out another $1,000.

"That should cover the flesh wounds and any psychological damage your friends suffered this morning." Amen smiled at Spyder. Spyder moved the cash off the table and into his pocket.

Amen wasn't done yet, "Our business is confidential and we only operate with those whom can be trusted. We trust Red, Robert, Michael, Sneakers, and their friends. The question is, can you be trusted?"

Michael looked across the table at Reggie. They were old friends caught up in rival gangs. There was a time when they used to hang out, go on double dates, and play sports together. There was a time when they had each other's backs. Things changed when they had to start making money and figure out how to survive on the streets. Michael gave Reggie a nod of affirmation, letting him know that Amen and Cering could be trusted.

****

Ethan, Phil, and Aaron were enjoying an early morning cup of coffee when Matt entered the dining room with his nephew.

"Sorry about last night," Ethan was sincere, and somewhat embarrassed.

Matt began laughing as John took a seat at the table with the guys. "No big deal. Based on the past several weeks, we're all a little jumpy and curious as to what's happening. To put your mind at ease, *THAT* hasn't happened yet. Johnny, you want some cereal?"

"Yeah. I want some of that Captain Phil stuff."

Matt looked at Phil, "You're famous. Not only are you wanted by every branch of the government and military, but you're also being confused with a popular cereal character."

"If I had a choice, I'd prefer the cereal box right now." Captain Phil took everything in stride. He knew that he was with the right people, on the right side of good versus evil.

Matt poured cereal and sat down at the table. John had become used to the rocking, heaving, and pitching of the ship. He had begun to enjoy riding on the high seas and the company of interesting people.

"Pretty rough this morning." Matt sipped some coffee. The coffee on the Excalibur was the best he'd ever tasted. He looked forward to a good cup before working out, training, and helping out as a deckhand on the ship. Matt was training for the eventual, the inevitable, and a future meeting with Samil.

"We'll have rough seas across the Atlantic. Cold fronts are lined up one after the other. Won't really let up until we're well south of the equator." Phil dipped a donut in his coffee.

"Where's Elisabeth?" Ethan asked.

"She's sleeping with Rebecca, giving mom a break. Seems like it would just be easier to have Rebecca as the anointed one." Matt grabbed a donut, even though he was training hard during the day.

Mary entered the kitchen in her pajamas, "Didn't mom used to tell us that the easy road wasn't a path to righteousness."

"Yeah, especially when I'd tell a lie or embellish my grades before report cards came out," Matt looked at Ethan.

"I wasn't always the chosen one." Matt dipped the donut and followed Phil's lead. "How long until we reach the Falkland Islands?"

"About ten days until we reach the narrows of Port William. We will lay low in Gypsy Cove until everyone finds their way to the Falklands."

Elisabeth entered the kitchen with Rebecca. Rebecca was hanging onto Elisabeth and playing with her long dark hair.

"Looks like you need a cup of coffee. Can I pour you one?" Mary was doctoring a cup of her own.

"Yes please." Elisabeth placed Rebecca in a high chair that Phil had fastened to the kitchen floor. Ethan grabbed a box of Cheerios from the table and put a few in front of the one year old. Li made his way to the kitchen as well.

"You getting used to this yet?" Captain Phil knew Li wasn't fond of water or boats.

"No. But the medicines and ginger drops help." Li sat down on the other side of Rebecca.

"Coffee Li?" Mary had finished prepping Elisabeth's cup.

"Please."

"Milk and sugar?"

"Two and two. Thank you." Li pulled a sweet roll from a plate on the table. Mary was the obvious mother figure on the ship. She was patient, kind, and great with her children. She was always looking to make people feel welcome and comfortable. Elisabeth admired Mary's maturity and demeanor. Even though Mary abruptly left her home in New Jersey, was on a boat in the middle of the Atlantic, and her husband was somewhere in the United States, her resolve and character were unwavering with the other travelers. During the tragedies of Columbine and 9/11, Mary learned to control her emotions and work through difficult circumstances.

"Here you go," Elisabeth brought coffee to Li.

"Warm ups?" Mary brought the pot around and poured a caramel colored coffee into oversized ceramic cups.

"What's the word from Sesom?" Li knew Ethan had been speaking with their leader.

Ethan pulled up his phone and went through a laundry list of updates.

"We all know about Noah. He's on his way to be detained with other enemies of the United States' government at Guantanamo Bay. Amen and Cering met with the owner of the cab company in Compton and are developing plans for Crevan's arrival in a couple days. Los Angeles is already crawling with additional security and reservists. Jonas was taken into custody by the Secret Service yesterday and will be interrogated and shipped off to Guantanamo. Looks like Jonas and Noah will be neighbors in the very near future. Talan, Dorje, and Kimi are hacking their way into the infrastructure of Los Angeles. They will have control of street signals, emergency response, and air space in Los Angeles before the President arrives."

Mary spoke up, "They detained Jonas? For what?"

Ethan explained, "They are holding him because of his connections with us. They are fabricating stories about his involvement with supposed terrorists, the Western Wall bombing, and dirty bombs in the United States. The US government is sharing a story with Turkish officials that the Swiss Army poisoned the Ambassador to Italy after he revealed his knowledge of covert operations in Turkey."

"Jonas is a good man. That's terrible." Mary made her way to the table. Everyone was drinking coffee and sharing sweet rolls and donuts.

Matt said, "Mike has been communicating with General Gilmore and learned some interesting news. Militias are vowing to support the Colonist party if any more attacks are carried out on US soil. They will target the White House and Congress first. Washington has always been concerned about militias taking to the streets."

"Some of this may be playing into Crevan's plan. He doesn't care about the future of the United States or its citizens. The more chaos he creates, the better off he'll be. If he is who you think he is, the American people fighting each other will create a distraction from what's happening worldwide." Captain Phil sat back while considering the magnitude of what was happening in the US.

Elisabeth and Mary sat together at the table. Since finding Elisabeth and understanding her importance to the Disciples' mission, there was an air of awkwardness with regard to what her role with Matt would be in the future. Mary's story was a little different. Looking back at what she'd done for Matt since Columbine and the death of their parents, her role was significant in guiding him through some formative years.

John came into the kitchen with a message for the captain. He handed off the message, filled up a cup of coffee, and went back to the wheelhouse.

Captain Phil put on his reading glasses, "Looks like the seas will get a little rougher. Tropical storm Peter has become a hurricane and is headed for the east coast of Central America. Seems to be sweeping northwest through the middle of the Atlantic."

Li put his head down on the table, "I must speak with Sesom about the travel arrangements."

Everyone at the table had a laugh at Li's expense.

****

"My fellow Americans, I bring this message to you from one of the most symbolic monuments in our country." President Crevan was walking around inside the Lincoln Memorial.

"President Lincoln said 'America will never be destroyed from the outside. If we falter and lose our freedoms, it will be because we destroyed ourselves.' The United States has experienced some difficult challenges over the past several weeks. From war beginning in the Middle East to dirty bombs being detonated on our own soil, we have experienced the challenges of living in a free and democratic society. We must not let the recent challenges break our resolve."

Crevan stood in front of Lincoln as he continued the address. "The man behind me also said, 'Don't interfere with anything in the Constitution. That must be maintained, for it is the only safeguard of our liberties. And not to Democrats alone do I make this appeal, but to all who love these great and true principles.' These words are just as meaningful today as they were one hundred fifty years ago. I come to you tonight with the same appeal as Abraham Lincoln."

"Unfortunately, for decades our government has been unsuccessful balancing a budget. Deficit spending and entitlements have drained our country to the point of bankruptcy. With wars taking place overseas, and the fact that several foreign countries own large portions of our debt, we must take drastic action to reduce our liabilities as a country. Beginning tomorrow, I will begin signing a series of executive orders that cut entitlements in half, while eliminating some programs completely. Most of the remaining budget will focus on military payments and healthcare for retirees. Food stamps, welfare, and disability payments will be hard hit by dramatic cuts to the Federal budget. I have met with the Council of Economic Advisers and we are in agreement that swift action must be taken to preserve the value of our currency. Because Congress has not been able to agree on anything to do with the fiscal policy of our country for years, I'm taking a unilateral approach to fix our financial problems to protect the union. While I understand that decreasing the size of our government may not be popular for some of you, I'm sure the private sector will do its best to fill the void. The private sector and non-profits have done a more than adequate job of serving the needs of those who have fallen on hard times for centuries."

Crevan continued, "On a brighter note, the FBI has successfully captured two individuals involved with the recent terrorist attacks at home and abroad. One of them worked for a defense contractor in the United States, the other is from foreign soil and helped mastermind the dirty bomb detonations in the United States. For security reasons, we cannot release any further information with regard to the detainees."

"As we find ways to reduce our debt and bring the country back to days of stronger fiscal policy, we must work together. I'm calling on the private sector to do what it's always done, create jobs and provide for American families. For years the government has become too involved in the everyday life of Americans. As we decrease the size of government, we look to restore the very liberties this country enjoyed after the Revolution. God bless and God bless the United States of America."

Clapping echoed in the Lincoln Memorial. Secretary of State Watt stepped out of the darkness with a smirk on his face. Secret Service surrounded the perimeter as the camera crew broke down equipment.

"Bravo. You almost had me believing in the future of the United States." Watt shook Crevan's hand.

"Over half of the people in this country have become dependent on the United States' government to take care of their needs. The government was never designed to take care of one hundred fifty million people. Wealthy Americans will embrace this speech as an equalizer. Those who rely on the government to survive will be lost and begin to panic. They have become so reliant on entitlements; they won't know what to do or how to take care of themselves. While our financial woes have been years in the making, we will take full advantage of the situation by starting class warfare." Crevan was quite pleased with himself.

Watt smiled and complimented his boss, "Brilliant. What will Morgan think of the executive orders?"

"He'll think I'm nuts," Crevan began laughing.

"He was going to find out sooner or later." The men started laughing as they walked down the steps of the Lincoln Memorial in front of the Reflecting Pool. Secret Service had the grounds covered well. Two helicopters landed to the south near the Ash Woods. Crevan and Watt boarded Marine One and left the area. The second helicopter served as a decoy for Marine One. Blackhawk helicopters were in the area to provide additional security for the President.

Talan leaned back in a leather chair with headphones on. He had been watching the Presidential address from a desk in a hotel room.

"Did you get that?" The question was directed at Sesom, Kimi, and Dorje. They were also wearing headsets to pick up audio from the speech. President Crevan didn't realize the Disciples had been listening in since Jonas was captured at the White House.

Sesom removed his headphones. "Interesting. Crevan is smarter than I realized. He will utilize the general population's dependence on government to create chaos and class warfare. The strategy will keep US citizens distracted from what's happening internationally. Crevan will also have to call up reservists and bring back military troops to keep the peace at home."

Kimi continued his sentence, "To allow Crevan and Watt an opportunity to prop up some of these Samil friendly puppets across the globe."

Talan concurred, "Exactly. By creating a civil war within his own country, he can support evil dictators in strategic countries."

Dorje offered insight with his thick accent; "Tibet has seen many war for hundreds of years. When communist China invaded my country in early nineteen fifties, they wanted to wipe out our people and culture forever. The Chinese knew that Tibet was a strategic land, one of rich soil and resource. After the invasion, neighboring countries turned their backs on us. The United Nations condemned the actions of China on paper, but did nothing through sanctions or penalties. Once the Chinese realized they could do whatever they pleased in Tibet, they massacred our people and ruined our land. They dumped nuclear waste in many parts of Tibet, causing sickness and death."

"What did you learn about the Chinese?" Sesom wanted to understand the lessons from Dorje's perspective.

Dorje thought for a few seconds before answering the question, "What happened in Tibet can happen anywhere, like what happened in the Sudan and Syria. Many generations take time to put a great society together. All of that can be destroyed in the blink of an eye. People you count on to help you never do when things get violent. Most people don't understand that doing right takes a strong mind and hard work. The path of evil is easy and appealing, but comes at a greater cost to an individual. Eventually, evil people turn on each other because they can't trust one another. That's why I like being with Disciples." He smiled as he finished the sentence.

Dorje was a simple and quiet man. He had lost several family members through previous wars with the Chinese and subsequent Chinese occupation of Tibet. By losing everything, Dorje understood the value of family and friendship. Even though he missed serving the Dali Lama in northern India, Dorje understood the importance of being a Disciple and following Sesom.

****

Talan adjusted a camera in an empty warehouse while standing on a chair.

"We're ready when you are." He stepped down from the makeshift ladder and joined Sesom, Amen, Cering, Kimi, and Dorje at a table. Sesom punched keys on the laptop in front of him. He had established a videoconference with Mike and Lucas. The teams were on opposite coasts of the United States. Once Sesom signed in, he could see Mike and Lucas on the computer screen. Talan set up additional monitors with cameras and microphones so everyone could communicate with ease.

"God Bless you Mike and Lucas," Sesom had a familiar grin.

"And you too Sesom," Lucas's booming voice was easily heard through the computer speakers.

"How are things in Virginia?" Sesom knew the men had already met with General Gilmore.

Mike shared details, "Good. General Gilmore was interested in our story. He shared many of the same concerns we had with regard to the new administration. Gilmore and Crevan have a bit of history with each other. The good news is that Gilmore has a good relationship with Vice President Morgan. Morgan served as Speaker of the House before Palmer's assassination. Palmer and Morgan worked together passing critical legislation to scale down the spending of the Federal government without crippling the US military. General Gilmore was very much involved in the budgetary process with the Department of Defense and Ways and Means Committee. The General said he wanted to stay in touch with us and close to the situation. He said that he may involve VP Morgan when the time is right too."

Lucas was curious, "How are preparations going on the west coast?"

Sesom was pleased with the progress, "Quite well. Talan, Kimi, and I have made our way past the Firewall for the city's mainframes and infrastructure. We will have complete control of streetlights, cameras, emergency response, and air control when Crevan arrives." Sesom turned his attention to Amen.

"Would you like to update us with details about our new friends?"

Amen nodded, "Sure. We met up with Red's Cab Company and some other people in Compton at a diner. Without going into much detail, there were some surprises at lunch that will help us capitalize on creating distractions for President Crevan's motorcade. I believe we can trust this group of people. They don't have a real high regard for authority figures."

Cering continued, "The President will be staying at the Beverly Wilshire in Los Angeles. Based on communication with the people we met at our lunch meeting, we will have access to the Wilshire and be able to monitor the President's movements."

Mike dug a little deeper, "Speaking of movements, what about Jonas and Noah?"

Sesom answered, "Jonas's capture was expected. Noah's circumstance was unforeseen and unfortunate as well. They will soon be together at Guantanamo Bay and we will deal with their situation down the road. We must stay focused on President Crevan's visit and the execution of our plan in Los Angeles. We could use help if you're done in Virginia."

Lucas evoked a serious tone, "I don't think our mission is complete yet."

Sesom queried as he was a little confused, "What else can we help you with?"

Mike spoke up again, "Matt had every intention of rescuing Noah from Gitmo. He was planning on leaving the Excalibur for Cuba without anybody knowing."

"What stopped him?" Sesom knew that Matt wouldn't leave anybody behind. Matt felt responsible for Noah's capture and transfer to Guantanamo Bay. He wouldn't let him rot in a prison for long.

"I did. He shared some thoughts with me after Jonas was taken prisoner at the White House and subsequently turned over to the CIA. He was running the idea by me because of my experience with Gitmo and intricate security systems on that portion of the island." Mike paused for a moment, "I told him to wait until I met with Gilmore."

"And he waited?" Sesom seemed surprised.

"Absolutely. Matt and I have an understanding. If he gets out of line or upsets his sister, I'll work him over. Part of the growing process as a family," Mike laughed as he finished the sentence.

"What is your play then Mike?" Sesom knew that he had already thought the problem through.

"This will be Lucas's play too. General Gilmore can get us over Cuba on a high altitude drop. We'll pack lightly with ammunitions, taser guns, and small explosives. Once boots are on the ground, I anticipate we'll have Noah and Jonas released inside of 10 minutes. From there, we'll hump to the coastline and catch an evac chopper with them."

"Isn't Noah disabled?" Sesom was concerned.

Mike put his arm on Lucas's shoulder and professed, "A few hundred yards is a warm up for this Brazilian. I don't think Lucas will have any problems getting Noah to the beach. Jonas and I will provide cover as they lead the way."

"Then it is settled, do you need anything from Cering or Suzie for the mission?"

"I think we're good. We'll use the Egyptian accounts if we need further supplies." Mike seemed relieved that Sesom agreed with the plan.

"When do you plan on making the trip to Cuba?"

Mike hesitated, "When is your rain on Crevan's parade in Los Angeles?"

****

"What's it like?" Matt and Elisabeth were in the belly of the Excalibur as it was being tossed around on the Atlantic. Vehicles, weapons, wires, and pipes surrounded them. The cargo ship creaked and moaned with each wave.

"What's what like?" Matt couldn't read Elisabeth's mind.

"To kill a person. To take a life." Elisabeth had seen Matt in action; she'd also seen his scars.

"When I graduated from Columbine, the United States was in a post 9/11 world. I could have gone to college, but I wanted to serve my country. Looking back, I really wanted revenge. I wanted to locate terrorists in the crosshairs of my sniper rifle and wipe them out. I wanted to kill terrorists with my own hands, and I did. I wanted revenge for the death of my parents."

"Did you get your revenge?"

Matt thought for a second. He was surprised how Elisabeth asked the question. "Not really. No."

"Why not?" Even though Elisabeth was from the West Bank and seen the atrocities of war and suicide bombers, she didn't understand the purpose behind much of the killing.

"No matter how many people I killed, the killing never brought my parents back. At first, I thought I might feel better if I killed the people responsible for my pain. The killing just numbed the pain, buried it."

Elisabeth could tell that Matt loved his parents and missed them. Her situation was different. She had been disowned by her family and banned from her own home. Anything that brought disgrace to a Palestinian family was dealt with severely. Even though Elisabeth understood why her parents reacted the way they did, she missed and loved them. Elisabeth sat down on the hood of an SUV.

"So what does it feel like?" She continued to prod Matt for an answer.

"You don't want to know." Matt turned away from Elisabeth and looked at the hull of the ship.

"I wouldn't ask if I didn't want to know." Elisabeth had a serious tone. She wanted to know how this handsome man could become a killer in a matter of seconds. If she was going to carry his child, she wanted to know how he felt about ending a life.

"When I pulled a trigger, collapsed a trachea, broke a neck, or caused shock to someone's chest cavity, I could feel life leave the body. The feeling is unexplainable. Like something is being sucked out of the area. Then there is complete silence. Unless of course, I'm firing rockets and heavy artillery from the top of an SUV at an enemy." Matt gave Elisabeth a smile as he worked his body between her legs dangling from the SUV.

Elisabeth put her arms around his oversized shoulders. She gave him a kiss as she worked her hands through his soft hair. Matt was equally interested in Elisabeth's tight body and luscious lips. She put her legs around his waist and drew him near.

Matt pulled back and looked into Elisabeth's eyes, "We need to quit meeting like this."

"You're right." Elisabeth nibbled Matt's lower lip and continued to kiss him with her tongue. The embrace grew tighter as they explored one another's bodies. The Excalibur continued to rock back and forth as the ship plowed through rough seas created by Hurricane Peter.

"Do you think you can fall in love with me?" Elisabeth pulled back and wanted confirmation from Matt.

Matt smiled, "You're the only girl I've ever dreamed of."

Elisabeth pressed, "Can you?" She kicked Matt in the backside to show she was serious.

"Absolutely. I'm beginning to enjoy the time we're spending together." Matt had never fallen in love. He'd never allowed himself to. He was busy with the military, special ops, and exacting revenge for his parents' deaths. In a strange way, Matt was beginning to understand how he could avenge his parents' deaths by falling for the beautiful woman in front of him. A woman that had been chosen for him, a woman that would carry his seed.

Scratches jumped up on the hood of the SUV next to Elisabeth. The cat began to rub the sides of her body against Elisabeth.

"You see. The cat approves," she smiled.

Matt began to rub scratches. "This cat showed up on my doorstep at the same time I started dreaming about you. She's been great company."

Matt prompted Elisabeth's next question, "Do you still dream about me?"

"No. I've been dreaming about my parents. The dreams are so real, it's almost like they're not dreams at all. In some respects, my father and mother are guiding me through the dreams. They provide me direction and inspiration. My parents seem to know you as well; at least they do in my dreams."

"Really?" Elisabeth was stunned.

"Really." Matt paused for a second, "What about you? Are you experiencing any *unusual* dreams?"

"I talk to her," Elisabeth looked forward.

"To whom."

"To Mary." Creases formed on the side of Elisabeth's mouth. She was grinning.

"My sister? What kind of dreams are you having about her?" Matt began laughing. Elisabeth gave him a look.

Elisabeth continued, "Not that Mary. The *other* Mary."

Matt shook his head, "I'm not following you. What *other* Mary."

"The mother of Jesus. My name is taken from John the Baptist's mother, she was a cousin to Mary." Elisabeth never knew the biblical connections would have so much significance in her own life.

"What does she say?" Matt was curious to see if there were any similarities between his dreams and hers.

"She reassures me. She gives me comfort." Elisabeth grinned again.

"And what does she think about you traveling on a boat in the middle of the Atlantic?" Matt continued to feel the ship listing.

"Nothing specific to the journey, but very important

details with regard to the destination."

"Am I at the destination with you?" Matt was hoping that he didn't get killed off along the journey.

"Yes, with our child."

Matt's phone buzzed in his pocket. He was so focused on what Elisabeth was saying the vibration startled him. The Israeli Defense sailors had high-powered receivers and transmitters on the ship that allowed cell coverage in the middle of nowhere. They scrambled phone calls and texts coming to and from the ship. In a unique move, they could generate signals from anywhere in the world and send them encrypted. The sailors worked closely with the Israeli Defense Force to travel with stealth operations. Matt pulled up the text.

To: Little Hiatt

From: Mookie

RE: Ark Engineer

M,

Met with Gil. Lucas and I will handle the 2x2 with Ark Engineer. Please remain in place and stand by for further instruction. Hello to M, J, and R. Get busy with E…lol.

Over

"Who is it?"

"Mike. He's having some success on the mainland."
Matt put up his phone, "Let's go up top."

Matt and Elisabeth returned to the deck level. Ethan and Li were helping John and Aaron on the stern of the ship. They were securing tarps over lifeboats and gear. As they emerged from a steel door, Ethan looked up at the couple. Elisabeth came out of the doorway first and moved her right hand up and down over her belly in a semicircle motion. Matt was right behind her doing a hip thrust with fists at his side. All of the men began laughing as rain dumped on the open deck of the Excalibur. The men were in need of a good laugh.

"Let's go hang with Phil in the wheelhouse." Matt grabbed Elisabeth's hand and held it tightly as they moved their way to the bow of the ship.

****

Crevan and Watt were pleased with the results of the previous night's address. Many Americans had taken to the streets to occupy parks, buildings, churches, and picket government offices over the President's plan to unilaterally cut the deficit. Thousands of people were protesting in California, a state already bankrupt from overreaching entitlement programs and declining sales tax revenues. The Secret Service was worried about the local government's ability to handle security in a hostile environment. The National Guard had already been called up by the state government to protect the neighborhoods affected by the LA dirty bombs. People in Los Angeles were angry, and a small group of Disciples and gang members looked to capitalize on heightened emotions.

The Disciples were still hanging out in an empty warehouse. Matt's Mustang was being equipped with electrical harnesses and computer chips. Talan and Dorje were testing receivers, transmitters, and cameras installed in the Mustang and syncing them with software in Talan's computer. Other than a nervous tension in the air, Los Angeles was enjoying a beautiful Fall morning.

Michael, Reggie, and Red were there for a meeting with Sesom, Cering, and Kimi. Robert had arrived early to assist Talan and Dorje with modification of his Mustang. The Mustang had already been through a chop shop to assume a new identity. Cering had even acquired a replacement ride for Robert, and this time his Mustang was legal. Amen was scouting rooftops on each side of Highway 405 at the Palms Bridge. He was also mapping out the storm sewer system for an evacuation of the area.

"The President will arrive at 1:00 pm this afternoon." Cering was looking up information she'd acquired from inside sources. "Have you shared the secure transmitters with your sources at the Wilshire?"

Michael nodded his head, "We have two on the inside. They will be wearing the transmitters after 1:00 pm."

"How many people have you recruited?" Cering made eye contact with Michael and Reggie.

"I have fifteen plus me." Michael handpicked his close friends for the operation.

"I have seventeen plus me." Reggie was meticulous as well in picking his close friends.

Sesom said, "Do they understand the danger? Do they understand they may not live through this evening?"

Reggie's words rolled off his tongue. "These people have known danger their whole lives. They look at this as an opportunity to escape the life, to end their time in the gang. There's no guarantee they'll live through this evening anyway, regardless of your operation."

Kimi retrieved a couple of large bags and tossed them in front of the men.

"Your team will wear the past Presidents," she turned to Reggie, "your team will wear Halloween masks. I have included pairs of leather gloves in your bags. Everyone must wear gloves and masks, no exceptions."

Kimi turned to Red, "You know that car dealership you shared with us?"

"Yes." Red knew everyone in Compton.

"Here are keys for 4 SUVs sitting on the lot. The key tag number corresponds to the number hanging above the dash. The vehicles have been paid for and scrubbed.

They have no vehicle identification numbers, they have clean license plates, and they've been washed and filled with gas. All you need to do is pick them up. Use these vehicles to pick up your teams. Remember, don't stop at convenience stores, banks, or any other places with security cameras. Don't worry about cameras at intersections or the highways; we have complete control of those."

Red took the keys from Kimi as she continued.

"In order to give the government a taste of its own medicine, the weapons in the corner have been bought on the black market in Juarez, Mexico. They can all be traced back to the Fast and Furious program of the US government conducted several years ago. Each weapon has three clips with twenty-seven to thirty rounds. I doubt anybody will get through his or her second clip. Use lethal force only if necessary. The Secret Service will use lethal force against you given the opportunity. Remember, they are not the enemy, but will be protecting the President with their lives. Please take the weapons with you as you leave."

Michael and Reggie looked at each other. The Disciples meant business. They were glad the Disciples were concerned about the wellbeing of their teams.

Sesom emphasized, "After you engage the motorcade, leave all of the weapons behind. Red will be waiting for you at the auto yard a few blocks away to dispose of the vehicles and any evidence."

Cering reminded the men of additional supplies. "Three duffel bags with ballistic vests are sitting by the weapons. Ensure that your teams are wearing the vests, gloves, and masks. Your survival on this mission is just as important as the objective."

Michael asked again, "And what's the objective?"

Sesom smiled, "To remove the current President from office."

Michael and Reggie shook their heads. Reggie weighed in on the objective, "That's some heavy stuff."

Kimi wanted the men to understand the gravity of the situation, "Very heavy. You don't want to be exposed or caught in this operation. Based on the way Crevan's government operates, you will be tried for treason and executed. No man or woman left behind on this operation."

Sesom had a map on an easel, "Once we compromise the bridge at 405 and Palms Boulevard, you'll close in behind the motorcade by coming over the wall on both sides of the freeway. We want the motorcade to continue south under the bridge where we'll engage them. There will be very little time to execute the operation, as F-15s will be in the area. Please set your watches for 30 seconds. Beyond that, we will be facing major firepower from the air. They will be able to lock on vehicles and global positions. Do not let them get a lock on your position."

Kimi continued, "Here are the sections where you will come over the walls. There is a side street to park the SUVs on the east side. Get there early, as traffic will be backed up due to Highway 405 closing for the motorcade. The President will be meeting the mayor and governor of California at the Wilshire for a late lunch. After that, he will be briefed on the status of the war and make phone calls to Generals engaged in the conflict. Once he finishes those calls, Crevan will head back to the airport to catch Marine One for a tour of the area affected by the dirty bombs. We expect that to happen at 4:15 pm. Because people won't know the route of the motorcade, you shouldn't have any issue getting hung up in traffic on the side streets. Give yourselves an escape route and designate a driver. Remember, masks, gloves, and vests; don't let anyone know your identity. There will be plenty of cameras out taking pictures. If need be, abandon the road, cross these fields and get on side streets. Everything will happen quickly."

"What about eyes in the sky?" Michael knew that helicopters would be canvassing the area prior to the motorcade arriving.

"Dorje will handle any birds in the area. We will have control of air space by that time. Your biggest threat will come from Air Force jets. Dorje can't do anything about those, they are too quick." Cering continued to hack away on the computer as she spoke.

"How are you doing over there?" Cering enjoyed Red's personality. He didn't say much and knew what to do. Red served in the Army after graduating from high school and retired after Desert Storm.

"You get these boys to me, I'll get them home." Red smiled at Cering as he removed his Red Sox cap and rubbed his white hair.

****

Lucas and Mike walked along the tarmac at Langley Air Force Base. They were staring at a B-2 Stealth directly in front of them.

"A Stealth, we're riding on a Stealth?" Lucas was giddy as a schoolboy.

"Not riding, flying. We're flying on the Stealth in front of us." Mike smiled as he corrected the towering Brazilian. The men carried bags with gear for a HALO (High Altitude Low Opening) drop and weapons to extract Noah and Jonas. The CIA had transported Jonas to Guantanamo Bay to begin his interrogation. Mike briefed Lucas on the landing and extraction points; both the men were expert paratroopers. General Gilmore made arrangements with the Air Force to transport Mike and Lucas to a drop spot over Cuba at 37,000 feet. Mike contacted a local Cuban contractor to pick them up at Windward Point and fly them to Communist Manzanillo after the mission. All of the files were classified. No identities, no names, and no record of the B-2 flight.

A pilot and copilot were waiting at the plane for Mike and Lucas.

The pilot said, "Good afternoon sir. Code name of the operation?"

"Cuba Libre." Mike shook the pilot and copilot's hands.

"Affirmative. We leave in five minutes to rendezvous at the drop zone. Drop is scheduled for 1900 hours."

Because the mission was classified, very little was said between the men. The B-2 would take about three hours to reach Cuban airspace. Mike and Lucas would gear up with thermal clothing and ballistic armor. They would need oxygen until 15,000 feet of elevation. Once they descended into an oxygen-enriched altitude, the men would peel their tanks and ready themselves for hostile territory. In order to be successful during the recon operation, they would need to land on top of a building at Camp Delta. If they missed their mark, they would jeopardize the mission. Mike and Lucas carried some of the highest tech weaponry available to the United States' military. Years ago, Mike shared his philosophy with Matt about preparing for Special Forces, "Training gets you in the game, tools make sure you win it."

****

Matt looked up at a sun surrounded by a deep blue sea of
sky. He could feel the warmth on his face. The sun
didn't burn his eyes and he was able to keep them open
as he looked about. Matt lowered his head and realized
he was back at the Western Wall. The plaza was
completely empty and peaceful. There was no blood
oozing from the pores of sandstone or large black birds
perched atop the wall. Complete serenity. Matt noticed
three crosses in the distance. He was reminded of a time
when a great speaker, leader, and healer had given his
life for the sake of others.

"You're known by the company you keep." A young
girl's voice emanated from behind Matt. She was the
same girl he'd seen setting up a game of hopscotch in a
previous dream. She sat down on some steps next to
Matt leading into the plaza. Matt took a seat next to her.

"I might be in trouble then." Matt started laughing.
"You're the same girl I saw before in the plaza playing
with friends."

She pointed in the distance, "He was hung on a cross
between two convicted thieves. The crowd before
Pontius Pilate chose a known criminal over the Prince of
Peace. In some ways, the world is doing the same thing
today."

Matt looked out over the wall at the crosses. The young
girl was right. The world hadn't changed much from two
thousand years ago.

"What does that say about the company he kept?"

"The thief comes only to steal, kill, and destroy. He
came that they may have life and have it abundantly. He
came for them as much as he came for you and me." The

young girl who resembled Elisabeth smiled at Matt.

Matt said, "What's your name?"

"Lisa. My mom's name is Elisabeth."

Matt was stunned. This young girl had been aborted just after the first trimester of development. She was sitting next to Matt carrying on a conversation as if she'd known him for a lifetime.

"I like the name Lisa."

Lisa said, "What's your name?"

"Matthew Hiatt."

"I like the name Matthew."

"You can call me Matt."

"I'm glad you found my mom Matt," Lisa traced her shadow on the stone floor of the plaza.

"Me too. She helped save my sister in Gaza. Do you know where that is?"

"That way." Lisa pointed to the southwest.

She continued, "I was playing with a girl named Hiatt the last time you visited."

"Really?"

"Yes. She is a nice girl. She's my sister." Lisa smiled at Matt.

"What's your sister's name?" Matt was curious to see if his daughter had a name.

"Ariel."

"Ariel's a pretty name." Matt was given the name for his daughter.

"She is a pretty girl too. You know she's waiting for you?" Lisa spoke matter-of-factly.

"Where is she waiting?"

"Down the hall." Lisa got up and pointed to the plaza. There were children of all ages playing hopscotch, jump rope, jacks, tic-tac-toe, football, tag, and catch. "This place is why the man on the cross loved children. He knew each and every one of us before our journey."

Lisa continued in a more serious tone, "Go to my mother. Make this dream your own. Ariel is ready for her destiny." Lisa turned and ran back to the plaza. As she reached the other children, they faded into the rays of sunshine. The plaza was peaceful again. Matt slowly began to open his eyes as the plaza in his dream was replaced with an open door and hallway of the Excalibur. The boat was still being tossed around from the affects of Hurricane Peter. Matt's bedroom and hallway were dark and the boat continued to moan with stress as she plowed through the Atlantic.

Sitting up in bed, Matt reached for a t-shirt he'd tossed on the floor before laying down. He rolled his wrist over and looked at the time, 11:00 pm. He'd gone to bed less than 30 minutes ago. Placing his feet on the ground, he noticed the cold nature of the steel ship. As the earth rotated and cold fronts began to push their way south from the northern hemisphere, he could feel the temperature change in the body of Excalibur. In a bit of role reversals, Matt would go to Elisabeth and check on her. He noticed down the hall that her door was shut.

As Matt walked along the hallway, the ship pitched from left to right. On a few occasions, Matt had to use the walls to keep from losing his balance in the hallway. Elisabeth's door was not locked. As quietly as he could, Matt turned the knob on the door and looked into her room.

"Can't sleep?" A voice came from behind Matt and shocked him. Elisabeth was returning from the common bathrooms down the hall.

"You startled me." Not many people were successful sneaking up on a Marine.

"You're peeping in my room and I startled you?" Elisabeth began to giggle. She was wearing black shorts and a black tank top. A band held her long black hair that draped along the left side of her chest.

Elisabeth motioned to him, "You first, Scratches in on the bed anyway. What's one more?"

Scratches was at the foot of the bed and Matt sat down next to her. She was purring and happy to see him.

"The storm wake you up?" Elisabeth plopped down at the head of the bed and put a pillow over her crossed legs.

"No. I was sleeping and woke up after a dream." Scratches stretched out as Matt rubbed her belly.

"You want to talk about it?" Elisabeth assumed that's why Matt made the trip.

"Did you have a name for your child?"

"No. Everything happened so fast. I was thinking of

giving her a family name, something a little more modern, a little more western. Why?"

"I just had a dream about your daughter, your aborted daughter." Matt didn't know how else to describe the dream. Elisabeth's eyes began to tear up.

"Really?" She put her hand over her mouth.

"Yes. When I saw her, she was about seven years old. She was in the plaza of the Western Wall. Her name is Lisa."

Elisabeth was sobbing by the time Matt finished the sentence. Scratches moved from the foot of the bed to the head. She could sense that Elisabeth needed a companion and some comfort. Matt also moved closer to Elisabeth and put an arm around her. Elisabeth tucked herself under Matt's right shoulder; she wanted to make herself as small as possible. Matt let Elisabeth cry. He didn't interrupt her or tell her everything was going to be fine. He just let her cry. Matt was reminded of times when Mary needed a shoulder to cry on. When he held his sister after their parents' deaths as emotions flowed from her body. As Matt grew closer to Elisabeth, he realized how much she resembled the personality and character of his mother and sister.

"Lisa is a good name," She continued to sob.

"Another name was revealed to me." Matt wanted to share a surprise with Elisabeth and lift her spirits. She became quiet and looked at Matt.

"What are you talking about?"

"Lisa let me know that she met a girl named Hiatt and played with her in the plaza. Said she is a nice girl too." Matt couldn't believe what he was saying. He couldn't believe the nature of his dream. The consummate skeptic was describing dreams that were amazing, almost incomprehensible.

He continued, "Lisa said she is waiting for us. Waiting for us to bring her into this unforgiving world."

Elisabeth shook her head. She couldn't believe what Matt was sharing with her. They had experienced several dreams about being blessed with a baby. A very important baby that would help usher in Revelation and change the world as they knew it.

"She also mentioned our daughter's name."

"What is it?"

"Ariel."

Elisabeth said, "Ariel is a beautiful name. Ariel Hiatt." She wiped the tears away from her eyes and looked at Matt.

"Lisa mentioned that I should come down the hall and make our dreams a reality." Matt was embarrassed by what he just revealed. He was embarrassed that a seven-year-old girl from a dream had to encourage him to seek out his destiny.

"In what way?" Elisabeth grabbed a tissue nearby and blew her nose.

Matt paused for a moment. "In *that* way. The way we connected in the belly of the ship and my room."

"What about waiting for marriage?" Elisabeth wanted to remain pure for her husband.

Matt laughed, "Based on my recurring dreams and the

condition of the world, I'm not sure if we can wait."

Elisabeth was matter-of-fact, "It is that time of the month."

"Maybe waiting is a good idea then."

"Not *that* time of the month, the good time of the month. I'm between cycles and ovulating." Elisabeth began laughing. Her eyes were still puffy and her nose was running.

"Oh…well if that's the case, what do you think?" Matt moved his eyebrows up and down. He really had no idea what he was doing.

"I'm sure that I look wonderful right now. This isn't necessarily the love boat either. But I do love you and want to carry your child." Elisabeth even looked beautiful after a good cry.

"I love you too and I promise we'll marry when the Disciples make it back from the States." With that, Matt began to kiss Elisabeth. He embraced her and moved her long dark hair from her eyes. She reached up and pulled the band from her hair, hair that fell softly to her waist.

Elisabeth stood up and disrobed her. Matt began to tremble a little. He was nervous and inexperienced; even though he was obviously aroused by her physical appearance.

Matt pulled her body close to his. He kissed her belly and moved his way up to her breasts. Elisabeth threw her head back, as she knew this was the moment something sacred would be shared between them. Even though Matt had killed people with his bare hands and feared nobody, he trembled at the thought of making love to this woman. His heart pounded as nature took over and

Matt's body was saturated with hormones to encourage procreation.

He pulled her down onto the bed and began to kiss her lips and neck. Matt was in love with Elisabeth and attracted to her gentle spirit. Even though her outside beauty was stunning, Matt connected on a deeper level with Elisabeth's character and ideals. When she stood her ground in front of the Pope, he knew that her resolve was unmatched with any woman he'd ever met before. Elisabeth had been brave at the Western Wall and Gaza in the face of great danger. Matt was attracted to her determination and will to live. He knew that she would make a great mother to any child, especially a child from God. She was chosen for good reason and a specific purpose.

They continued to kiss each other's bodies until Elisabeth removed Matt's clothing. Matt was still trembling as Elisabeth held him. Elisabeth took the lead, partially because of her nurturing ways, and partially because she was genetically engineered to be a mother. She wanted Matt to see and feel her beauty, and understand how beautiful the moment was they would share together.

****

After President Crevan landed, he traveled with close to 25 vehicles in the motorcade north on 405. Two presidential limos, a host of SUVs that served multiple purposes, press vehicles, and local police were part of a caravan wreaking havoc with the Los Angeles traffic. Several angry citizens hung signs indicating their displeasure with the new President and his decision to cut funding for thousands of government programs. Many people had taken to the street to toss trash and rocks along the motorcade route. The city of Los Angeles had called up several independent security services to help with protests and crowd control. Crevan was pleased with the distractions.

The gang members had dropped off Dorje near the Palms Bridge at a storage facility. Dorje removed a lock from the storage building and entered a unit that had supplies acquired by Suzie. Talan and Cering were monitoring the movements of everyone, including President Crevan. The motorcade had arrived on time to the Beverly Wilshire. After a late lunch, power nap, and a few phone calls, the President was preparing to travel south again to the airport for a tour of the dirty bomb zones. Kimi was on top of an apartment building on the west side of the freeway just south of the bridge. She was covered in clothing and body paints to blend into the rooftop. Kimi carried automatic weapons and a few surface-to-air heat-seeking missiles. Once again, several of the automatic weapons had been purchased south of the border in Mexico or acquired from terrorist organizations in the Middle East. Sesom wanted to give Crevan a taste of his own medicine.

Sesom was at the John Wayne airport. Suzie had made arrangements through the Israeli Defense Force to transport a Blackhawk helicopter to a private hanger. Transporting a Blackhawk helicopter to the United

States through a port was not an easy assignment. The helicopter was only partially assembled and shipped in a container to the airport. From there, Suzie had to find an independent contractor that could reassemble the parts in the airport hanger and test the aircraft without being discovered in a day's work. She had to find someone that was previous military and wouldn't discuss the job. Money has a tendency to maintain confidentially, and the thought of working with good paying customers in the future has a certain appeal with small independent contractors. The IDF had removed all serial numbers from engines, transmissions, the chassis, propellers, and anything else with traceable numbers on the aircraft. If the Blackhawk should go down, the CIA wouldn't be able to determine the country of origin. The Blackhawk was armed with Hellfire missiles and an M60 machine gun.

Talan ran through a system's check with the Disciples and gang members. They could communicate openly with a scrambled signal that was embedded in layers of encryption. Cering had provided two earpiece devices to the gang members working at the Wilshire Hotel. The earpieces were similar to ear buds, but they were flesh colored and equipped with microphones to detect the smallest vibrations from a jawbone. They fit inside the ear and couldn't be detected unless someone was looking for them. The time was 4:12 pm.

Cering spoke into a headset, "Wilshire, update on POTUS."

A man spoke, "CIC is still in suite. Motorcade assembling outside the hotel. Media and protesters making a mess of Rodeo and Wilshire. Riot police have been called in."

Cering said, "Sesom, standby. Once POTUS has left the building, you will ready the bird."

Talan came over the radio, "We have control of cameras, traffic signals, and air space. Be advised that the 405s and 812s are in position on east and west Rose. Wait for my signal."

Cering smiled at Talan, "Dorje, are you out there?"

"Yes. Ready for POTUS." Dorje's voice echoed in the storage unit that was comprised mostly of corrugated steel.

Cering said, "Kimi, are you in place?"

"10-4," Kimi was sighting an assault rifle on the southwest side of the bridge.

Cering said, "We will go silent until we hear from the Wilshire. Wilshire, let us know when POTUS is rolling."

The same voice came over the radio from the hotel, "10-4."

****

The B-2 Stealth pilot came over the radio. "T minus 45 seconds until drop zone. Please put on your oxygen masks as we will be losing cabin pressure. Stay clear of the bay doors until we reach the zone." The pilot turned to give the men a thumb's up.

"Remember, you pull at 2000 feet. I'll be right behind you at 1800. Follow me to Camp Delta. We will land on the largest building at the site. Make sure you switch your shield to night vision after we jump. It's going to be dark down there." Mike had a specialized rifle with a long barrel.

"What's that?" Lucas saw the odd looking weapon.

"You'll see." Mike winked at Lucas and put the jump helmet over his head. The helmets were equipped with audio so Mike and Lucas could communicate during the high altitude drop.

"T minus 25 seconds until drop zone. Bay doors opening." The large belly of the B-2 opened up and pressure dropped in the plane. The plane immediately dropped in temperature. Mike and Lucas watched the indicator lights on the side of the plane to show them when to jump.

"T minus 10 seconds and counting." The indicator light went from red to yellow. Mike gave Lucas a thumb's up.

"T minus 5 seconds and counting." Mike readied his weapon and waited for the green light.

The light turned green and Lucas went first. Mike saluted the pilot and went feet first through the bay doors. They were in a free fall at 35,000 feet. For the most part, Cuba wasn't lit up like most cities in North

America. Havana and a couple other major cities were sparkling with lights, but the island was dark for the most part. Mike and Lucas had GPS devices that kept them in line with Camp Delta on Guantanamo Bay. The drop would take a few minutes to execute.

****

"POTUS is on the move at Wilshire." A familiar voice came over the radio.

Another voice came over the radio inside the hotel. "10-4, waiting for visual in the lobby."

Cering said, "Sesom, roll the bird and fire it up."

"10-4." Sesom had some contractors help transfer the helicopter from the hanger to a helipad out front.

Cering adjusted her headset, typed some commands on the keyboard, and spoke to the flight control at John Wayne airport. She had already logged the flight plan and manifest with the airport in their database. According to what flight control could see, the helicopter belonged to the National Guard and was supporting the security detail for the President.

The tower cleared Sesom for takeoff, "Guard Rider One, visual flight rule departure to the northwest at or below 1500 feet."

"Copy tower one," Sesom answered through the helmet.

Sesom had flown Blackhawks in Egypt during the Arab Spring and revolution of 2011. Even though he had been hired by the Egyptian military, he was specifically instructed to keep peace between both sides. After the military and protestors began clashing in Tahrir Square, Sesom flew missions on a regular basis as a peacekeeper. He had become very familiar with the controls and handling of a Blackhawk.

Talan spoke into his headset, "Dorje and Kimi, provide air support from your positions."

"Roger," Dorje opened the storage door and quickly scaled a wall to the roof. He was in camouflage to prevent detection from the air. Kimi was prostrate on the roof with weapons lined up to her right and left. Automatic weapons were on her right, surface to air missiles on the left. They were covered with tan netting to blend into the shingles.

Cering called out, "405s and 812s, be ready to roll on our signal. Target should be acquired in less than five minutes."

She turned to Amen, "Let the horse run wild."

He gave her a smile. Talan, Cering, and Amen had computers and monitors set up on an oversized metal table. Directly in front of them was a large projector screen showing the locations of Crevan, the gangsters, Dorje, Kimi, and Sesom. Crevan and Sesom were on the move. Both gangs had taken up locations on each side of the highway north of the bridge at Palms and Highway 405. Everybody was in place to ambush the motorcade.

Amen rolled to his left in an office chair and positioned himself in front of a steering wheel, pedals, and a monitor. He depressed a button on the wheel and Robert's Mustang started up on Tabor Street. The Mustang was transmitting video from the dash, both side mirrors, and the rear of the vehicle. Amen had a split screen showing all cameras, the most prominent view coming from the dash.

"Here we go." Amen mashed the accelerator to the floor and moved onto Tabor Street heading west. In front of him, he could see the traffic was heavy on Inglewood. The Mustang had been modified with tires that were heavily reinforced with steel radial belts, perfect for driving on lawns, sidewalks, and over mailboxes. Amen elected to drive the Mustang on the sidewalk to navigate through traffic that was gridlocked due to rush hour and the Presidential motorcade. In Los Angeles, people driving on the sidewalks when traffic bottlenecked didn't surprise motorists. They had seen everything from people escaping riots to OJ Simpson's infamous trip down Highway 405.

Amen elected to stay on the sidewalk once he reached Inglewood. Other than clipping a couple mailboxes and a fencepost or two, the path along the sidewalk was largely unimpeded as he headed east toward the bridge. He noticed a black and white to his left sitting in traffic. As he blew by the officer, the car lit up and began pursuit.

"2 minutes until lead car reaches Palms and 405." Talan kept Amen updated.

"Got one in pursuit, others likely en route," Amen was busy steering the wheel and controlling the pedals.

A satellite image showed real-time traffic conditions at the bridge. A few police cars and one motorcycle were stopping or directing traffic away from the overpass.

"You have two cars and one motorcycle at the west entrance of the bridge. It appears that your friend has radioed for backup. A couple of the officers are retrieving shotguns from their vehicles."

Amen turned the wheel hard to the left to miss a homeowner checking her mailbox. He sideswiped a vehicle waiting in traffic. The camera on the left rearview mirror lost its signal. The police officer had to make the same maneuver; he hit another vehicle waiting in traffic.

"One minute thirty seconds until lead car of the motorcade reaches the underpass." Talan was calm as he counted down the pace of the motorcade.

"No problem. I'm going to get there early." Amen mashed the accelerator as he saw an opening at an intersection in front of him. The Mustang jumped back up on the sidewalk and smashed into some newspaper dispensers. Papers flew everywhere. One of them stuck to the Mustang's windshield before Amen turned on the wipers to remove the obstruction.

"Two more patrol cars coming to assist the roadblock at the bridge. Looks like they are pulling out stop strips too." Talan adjusted the microphone in front of his face.

"Stop strips? You mean spike strips?" Amen winked at Talan.

"You have one minute until the motorcade reaches the bridge.

"This is exciting. At one point I promised Matt that I would take care of his Mustang. I just ran over some person's fountain in a front yard. Probably not his idea of respecting the Mustang." Amen kind of felt bad, but was enjoying himself way too much for it to matter.

Cering, Talan, and Amen could see the Mustang's location on the large projector. Amen was almost there.

"Talan."

"Yes Amen."

"Blow the windshield."

"Yes Amen." Talan pulled up a program tied to the performance enhancers of the Mustang. He brought up a diagram with the front of the car and expanded the windshield and dash. He clicked on the lower portion of

the windshield. The computer program asked him if he
wanted to execute the command.

"Blowing windshield." Talan left-clicked the mouse and
a small explosion occurred at the bottom of the
windshield. The camera shook and the windshield was
blown from the car.

"That's better." Amen could see clearly. No papers,
debris, water droplets, bugs, or anything else to impede
his vision. He didn't have to worry about bullet holes
shattering the windshield either. Amen was somewhat
impressed with the driving skills of the police officer
behind him.

"Thirty seconds until lead car passes underneath the
bridge." Cering was watching the screen in front of her.

"Just arrived at Sawtelle." Amen saw the spike strips in
front of him. The officers began to fire at the Mustang.
Pedestrians and vehicles stuck in traffic began to panic
and flee the area. Bullets and shotgun pellets penetrated
the Mustang and began to ricochet from the body. Amen
ran over the spike strips and his tires re-inflated, just
before the Mustang smashed into the front of two police
cars forming a barrier. Robert had installed a heavy-duty
grill guard while assisting the Disciples with
enhancements to the Mustang. The grill guard easily
moved the patrol cars out of the way.

"I'm here." Amen performed a 180° maneuver and
depressed a blue button on the steering wheel. Seven
smoke grenades skipped across the ground, which
frightened the officers and created a diversion.

"Lead car is under the bridge. Fire in the hole." Talan
left-clicked his mouse again. A portion of the northwest
concrete wall collapsed from the bridge on top of
Highway 405 heading south. The hazardous materials

SUV and a squad car slammed on their brakes in front of the falling debris. The Stagecoach (vehicle carrying Crevan) and Spare (decoy vehicle) limousines were a half-mile from the bridge when the Secret Service began to radio other vehicles in the motorcade.

"Ready for take off." Amen performed a donut as police cars approached the Mustang from the east. They were firing on the vehicle. Amen drove through an opening in the concrete wall created by the explosion. Before the vehicle fell to the highway below, Amen depressed a red button on the steering wheel. The Mustang blew up, sending shrapnel everywhere.

While the security vehicles of the motorcade sped up to engage the hostiles, both limousines began to slow down.

An order came over the Secret Service radio, "Abort, abort. Run November Echo escape route. Hawkeye and Bravo, engage enemy at the bridge. Control and Counter, stay with the Stagecoach. Air support, engage any hostiles at the Palms Bridge and 405." A couple F-15 Eagles and three Lockheed Martin VH-71 Kestrel helicopters were in the area, so was Sesom and his Blackhawk helicopter.

A command was given by the Control car of the motorcade, "Federal Aviation Administration, ground and divert all flights to and from Los Angeles airports. Only authorized military aircraft in LA airspace."

Flight Control at LAX and the John Wayne airport had Sesom's Blackhawk identified as air support for President Crevan, they began to ground all flights ready for take off at both airports. Incoming flights were diverted away from all airports in Los Angeles. The Decoy limousine continued its course toward the bridge.

"We have an ID on the Stagecoach." Cering came over the radio. "812s and 405s, time to rumble." Both gangs came over the highway walls on each side of the interstate. They weren't interested in the Presidential motorcade; they were interested in fighting each other. In their respective colors, the gangs met at the highway median and began pounding each other. Michael and Reggie were out front throwing punches keeping an eye on the motorcade and their respective gangs.

"Stagecoach, we have hostiles to the north. They seem to be attacking each other. Control and Counter, take the lead and engage the hostiles to clear a path for the Stagecoach." The Control and Counter vehicles passed President Crevan's limousine with a few police cars and came to a stop about 40 yards from the gang fight. A voice came over a loudspeaker.

"Disperse or you will be fired upon with lethal force." Because the gangs weren't threatening the motorcade, protocol required a verbal warning to be executed before lethal force was deployed. The gangs paid no attention to the warning and kept fighting each other.

"Guard Rider One, do you have a visual?" Cering spoke to Sesom.

"I do, beginning decent." Sesom was racing toward the bridge, so were two F-15s and three helicopters.

"Sesom, the F-15s are 40 seconds away and the helicopters will be there in 15 seconds. Be advised."

"10-4. Let's see if they modify the escape route. Dorje, stand ready."

"10-4." Dorje activated a specialized weapon that sent high-powered magnetic impulses through the air. When fired at most aircrafts, the magnetic pulses would fry all electronic controls. The F-15s traveled too fast for the magnetron weapon to be effective.

One of the Secret Service officers gave the order, "Fire at will." Military operatives and local police exited their vehicles with automatic weapons, high-powered rifles, tear gas, M202A and AT-4 rocket launchers.

Michael yelled to the gang members, "Take positions." Half the gang members on the most northern section of the fight moved to the front with ballistic shields. The other half pulled out handguns and assault weapons. The gang members were more than 30 strong in number. Some of them had even been trained by the US military and deployed in the Middle East to fight wars against terror. Many of them utilized the military training to teach each other about hand-to-hand combat and the use of advanced weaponry. They opened fire at the motorcade and local police. They were instructed not to aim at the security detail protecting the President. They were instructed to shoot up the vehicles to send Crevan's limousine to the south.

"Get POTUS out of here. Head south." The commander from the Counter vehicle gave the order. The Stagecoach turned south and headed for the underpass. Vehicles from the motorcade returned fire from the gangsters. Reggie called out to the men, "Rocket launchers. Get down on my order."

One of the Kestrel helicopters made it to the scene. Sesom was in position to the south of the bridge with the Blackhawk. The pilot radioed the communication's vehicle known as Roadrunner to alert them of the danger.

"Roadrunner, Blackhawk helicopter not part of security detail. I repeat, Blackhawk helicopter not part of security detail. Jam radio frequencies. Engaging the aircraft."

Security associated with the motorcade didn't even notice the Blackhawk's position south of the underpass. By the time the Kestrel helicopter noticed the anomaly, President Crevan's limousine was under the bridge. From the top of the storage building, Dorje fired the magnetron weapon at the Marine helicopter. The pilot noticed the helicopter's controls began to malfunction.

"Get down," Reggie yelled at the top of his lungs to alert the gang members of incoming rockets. At once, the men up front with the ballistic shields dropped to their knees and rolled to their right. They turned the shields on their sides and butted them together. The men behind them ceased fire and lay on their backs. Each of them pulled two smoke grenades and tossed them to the south in the direction of the motorcade. Two rockets from an AT-4 flew over the gang members and detonated farther north up the highway. One rocket from an M202A flew over the gang members and detonated 40 yards away. Another rocket fell short and the last rocket was a direct hit on the east side of their barrier line. Robert was holding a ballistic shield that was hit by debris from the rocket. He was knocked unconscious and shrapnel penetrated his clothing. The smoke grenades prevented any further rockets from being deployed.

Sesom saw the Stagecoach rush under the Palms Bridge. His heart began to pound, as this was an opportunity to eliminate one of the most evil men on the planet. Sesom steadied the stick, locked on the Stagecoach, and fired a Hellfire missile. The Hellfire traveled a few hundred yards before hitting the ground on the driver's side of the Stagecoach. The Secret Service driver swerved to avoid a direct hit from the missile. Impact from the blast caused the limousine to roll a few times before resting on its top.

Cering gave the order, "812s and 405s, evacuate now."

Another Kestrel helicopter reached the hot zone. Dorje aimed the magnetron and brought the helicopter down to the south of Sesom's position.

"Time for an evac Sesom. F-15s are 10 seconds away." Talan spoke with urgency. The Disciples didn't know if Crevan was dead.

Sesom set the Blackhawk down beside the Stagecoach. He grabbed the M60E3 affixed to the helicopter and a 7.62 mm belt of bullets and ran to the limousine. The limousine had survived the blast, even though a few windows were blown out and the driver's side had noticeable depressions in the steel reinforced doors. Sesom made his way around to the back passenger door. Crevan was crawling out of a blown out window.

"You have the entire motorcade bearing down on you." Cering gave an imminent danger warning. Sesom threw some smoke grenades in response to the north.

Crevan landed on the pavement and rolled, his left leg was broken from the crash. President Crevan was in great physical shape from his days in the military and continued dedication to personal training while serving as a Senator in Massachusetts.

"You must be Sesom." Crevan looked up at the large African man standing over him. The sun was behind Sesom setting to the west. Sesom stood in the sun's path and cast a shadow over Crevan. Talan, Cering, and Amen watched the projector in front of them; the gang members were scaling the east highway wall. Michael and Reggie would ensure that Robert made it over the wall, even though he was still unconscious from the M202A missile blast.

Sesom lowered the M60E3 machine gun and a shot rung out. He lowered the weapon further and fell to his knees.

Another shot hit Sesom in his ballistics' vest and penetrated the armor. He slumped backward as blood began to spill from his mouth. The first downed helicopter Marine had taken position next to his aircraft and successfully killed Sesom with amour piercing bullets.

Another shot rang out. Kimi dropped the helicopter pilot, as Sesom's body lay lifeless on Highway 405. Kimi had watched the first Kestrel helicopter fall from the sky after Dorje disabled the aircraft with magnetron bursts. She thought the pilot would have been injured badly or killed from the crash.

"Sesom, come in." Kimi began calling to her fallen leader in a worried voice, "Sesom, please come in."

She called out to the others, "I'm going after him."

Amen came over the radio, "Stand down Kimi, there will be no rescue operation." Cering had her mouth covered with her right hand; she couldn't believe Sesom was down. Talan watched the screen in front of him with amazement.

The third Marine helicopter arrived on scene and fired two Hellfire missiles at the Blackhawk and destroyed the aircraft before landing to evacuate the President to safety.

Amen continued, "Let them be, we can't risk further loss of life. Kimi and Dorje, evac the area now." Kimi was disappointed that the Disciples would let Sesom stay as he lay.

Reggie and Michael affixed a rope around Robert's shoulders and waist.

"Make the climb." Reggie wanted Michael to scale the

wall first.

"We'll go together, after they pull Robert up." Michael
pulled the rope tight around Robert's waist. He had a
few shrapnel wounds that were bleeding but not life
threatening. Robert was semi-conscious from the blast.

Michael yelled, "Pull him up Tiny." Tiny gave a hand
signal and Robert was being pulled to safety. Both gangs
were pulling together from the other side to raise Robert
to the top of the wall. Tiny was waiting for Robert to
make his ascent. Once Robert reached the top of the
wall, Tiny grabbed the rope and began to lower him.
Even though Tiny was wearing gloves, the rope began to
cut into his hands and burn his palms. He didn't even
notice the pain. The group immediately whisked Robert
off to the vehicles waiting on Sepulveda. Michael and
Reggie scaled the wall quickly and Tiny joined them in
their descent to the other side. Smoke grenades were
being tossed everywhere as a diversion and to provide
cover for the gangs. Two F-15s roared overhead to show
air support for the motorcade.

Amen took over, "The 15's will fly over again and try to
gain your position. Wait to enter the SUVs until I say so.
We can't let them lock on your vehicles."

Dorje came flying down the roof of the storage building
and ran 20 yards to a manhole cover. The cover was
made out of plastic instead of steel. He removed the
cover, went down a few rungs on a ladder, and replaced
it. Dorje would hump two miles through storm sewers to
a rendezvous point on the east side of Highway 405.
Kimi was on the third floor of an apartment building
roof. She scaled down the roof and jumped to a concrete
landing near some stairs. In a matter of seconds, she was
on the main level and sprinted west about 75 yards to
another manhole cover. The cover was plastic and she
dropped into the storm sewer system. Kimi returned the

cover to its original position and turned on a flashlight. She couldn't believe that Sesom lay lifeless on the highway a few hundred yards away.

****

Lucas pulled his parachute at 2000 feet. He was carefully watching the GPS guidance system to ensure a successful landing. Mike flew past Lucas and pulled his cord at 1800 feet. Both men had stripped their oxygen tanks and tossed them during the descent. Mike immediately armed the specialized weapon with rounds that resembled darts. To be safe, he loaded seven in the magazine and one in the chamber. A high-powered scope allowed Mike to see the guard stations of Camp Delta. He depressed a few buttons on the weapon and pumped it like a shotgun. Without thinking about direct hits, Mike sited in the guard stations and began to fire the darts. The darts were heat seeking and would target the warmest parts of the body near the cardiovascular system or genital area. They were filled with sedatives that would disable the guards for at least an hour. Four guard stations lined Camp Delta at the corners and one was in the middle with a 360-degree view. Once the darts hit their targets, the guards would drop within a few seconds, leaving them no time to make radio calls.

Mike used five darts and kept three in reserve. He focused on guiding his parachute to the main building of Camp Delta. Mike and Lucas could see each other's positions with the GPS system.

"That's the building Lucas." Mike was at 800 feet.

"I see it. I'll follow your lead." Lucas was directly above Mike.

"Time for the Cubans to spice it up a little." Mike pulled out a two-way radio and gave a command.

"Es el momento para Cuba Libre." Mike was calling to some of his friends on the east side of Gitmo, just beyond the American fence.

"Estamos Listos!" A Cuban voice came over the radio. A dozen Cubans began to launch mortars, send up flares, fire machine guns into the air, and set off fireworks. They weren't aiming at anything in particular; they just wanted to make a big impression. Mike and Lucas could see the fireworks display off to the east. An alarm sounded throughout the naval base and soldiers began taking positions and planning a counter attack in the direction of the disturbance. Most of the Cuban attacks were nothing more than irritants to the Navy and provided them a chance to play war games with some of America's elite servicemen and women.

Mike and Lucas landed on the largest building of Camp Delta 1. During the fireworks, nobody noticed a couple of paratroopers landing on the roof of a building. Nobody noticed the guard stations were unmanned either. When alarms sounded on Gitmo, the prisoners would rake items against the steel mesh walls of their cells and yell at the guards. Mike knew the Cuban distraction would keep the prison guards busy for several minutes. Many of the guards would move from buildings to the perimeter to protect the compound. Lucas armed four tasers and chambered a round in a Glock 23. He also had several small C4 explosives.

Mike threw five smoke grenades in the direction of Camp's 2 and 3. Jonas and Noah were being held captive in the Charlie Building of Camp 1. Mike had a ballistics' weapon very similar to the one Amen used to disable the SUV in front of Matt's townhome. He set three charges for 10 seconds and loaded them into the weapon. The first and second charges were directed at a side door of Charlie Building. The third charge was shot through the fence and struck a door on the Oscar Building of Camp 2.

"Let's go." Mike jumped from the main building roof.

Lucas followed closely behind. They took positions on each side of the door at Charlie Building, Camp 1.

"Detonation." Mike called to Lucas and shielded his face from the explosion; Lucas did the same. The steel door was blown off its hinges and tumbled down a corridor with cellblocks on each side. An explosion in Camp 2 did similar damage to the Oscar Building. Mike leaned over with a launcher that shot concussion grenades; he knew where the guards would be stationed in Charlie Building. After unloading five rounds he shouted to Lucas again.

"Fire in the hole." The concussion grenades detonated in succession.

"Let's go. Jonas should be on the right a few cells down and Noah will be on the left all the way down this hall." Lucas entered the building first. Prisoners were going crazy thinking they would be released in a rescue attempt. Mike followed closely behind with a taser gun in his right hand and a Glock 19 in his left. Smoke was everywhere in Charlie Building.

Lucas called out, "Jonas, where are you?"

"I'm here." Jonas reached out his hand and stopped the Brazilian in his tracks. Mike blew past Lucas to release Noah.

"Stand back. Hopefully this will be a smaller explosion." Lucas put a small amount of C4 on the hinges of Jonas's cell door. He inserted two small metal prods into the plastic explosives and flipped a switch to activate the detonators. Lucas moved out of the way and depressed a red button on a remote detonator. The steel hinges were blown off and the cell door fell to the floor. Jonas immediately exited his cell.

"Take these," Lucas handed a taser, fully loaded Glock 23, and some smoke grenades to Jonas. "If you can, try to taser the guards. If that doesn't work, the Glock is your best defense," Lucas smiled at Jonas. Jonas looked like a prisoner of Guantanamo. He was wearing a white jump suit and his hair was disheveled. Over the past day, Jonas had received a black eye and bloodied lip courtesy of the CIA. Both men took off down the hall.

"Fire in the hole." Mike set off two explosions at Noah's cell. As Mike rushed in the cell, Lucas fired a taser at a guard that was beginning to gain his composure. The taser automatically discharged thousands of volts for five seconds into the guard's body, rendering him unconscious. Lucas left the gun with the guard and grabbed another one from his belt.

Lucas was laughing as he yelled out to Jonas, "Like that!"

Noah was happy to see someone took interest in him, "Any chance you brought a wheelchair? These facilities aren't necessarily ADA compliant."

"I think we can do better than a wheelchair. Lucas, time to carry your weight on this mission." Mike smiled as Lucas came from behind him and shook Noah's hand. Lucas handed a Glock 19 to Noah.

"You will be the eyes in the back of my head. Please don't shoot me, Mike, or Jonas." Lucas chambered a round and handed the weapon to Noah. Before Noah could respond, his belly rested on Lucas's right shoulder.

"Let's get out of here." Mike gave the order and the men headed for a different side exit of Charlie Building.

"Mookie wait." Mike recognized the voice, but he knew the accent didn't belong to Jonas, Lucas, or Noah. He turned to see an Arab man in a white jumpsuit and turban standing behind a cell door.

Mike replied, "Sallah. Is that you?"

"It is. Take me with you." Sallah smiled at his old friend.

Mike took C4 and blew open the prison cell. Sallah came out and gave Mike a hug.

"No time to catch up." Mike pulled a Beretta from an ankle holster and tossed the gun to Sallah. Sallah pulled the clip to see that it was full and chambered a round.

"I have the front. Jonas and Sallah, cover the back. Guard stations have been neutralized. Let's roll." Mike kicked a panic bar on a nearby steel door and the men exited the building. He immediately threw three smoke grenades into the wind in the direction they were going. The Cubans were still firing off mortars, fireworks, and shooting machine guns into the air. Most of the Navy's security detail were responding to the east and oblivious to the rescue operation. Prisoners at the camp continued to yell and rattle their cages.

"We need to make the beach." Mike motioned to the men to head southeast. Sallah shot a guard responding to the situation. He hit the man in his left hip.

Lucas instructed Sallah, "Try not to kill them, they are not the enemy."

Sallah replied, "Maybe not to you, but you haven't lived here for the past two years." Sallah kept moving swiftly behind Lucas. Jonas shot a guard in the thigh to his left. Mike tossed a few more smoke grenades and pulled out a battery operated grinding wheel to cut the fence. The wheel cut through the chain link fence like butter. The group began to take on small arms fire. Lucas set Noah down and went for his backpack. He began to toss smoke grenades in all directions, to confuse the advancing security detail of Gitmo.

"We're through." Mike pulled back the chain link fabric and the men ducked as they went through the opening. Lucas grabbed Noah's arms and pulled him through. They were on the other side. Guards had begun checking towers to see what happened to their counterparts. As they reached the birds' nests, the guards fired up spotlights to see what was happening at the perimeter. There was so much smoke in the yard, the guards had a difficult time determining who was attacking Delta Camp 1 and from where. They could hear some of their fallen brothers calling out for help.

Lucas picked up Noah and threw him over his shoulder like a sack of potatoes. The men had successfully breached the perimeter and needed to cover 440 yards of sandy beach before catching a rendezvous Mi-24 helicopter at the shoreline. Mike knew that Gitmo helicopters would be in the air in a matter of seconds to gain control of the situation. The group could see and hear the commotion to the east. Even with the extra weight of Noah, Lucas was bearing down on Mike as they humped to the coastline.

As they reached the 200-yard mark, Mike could see the Mi-24 helicopter land on the beach. In Mike's mind, the longest part of any mission was the evacuation, especially by helicopter. Mike hadn't even met Noah, yet they were all risking their lives together for his freedom. The more they ran, the helicopter looked farther away, even smaller. Mike knew this was part of the experience. As the human body responded to dangerous situations and adrenaline began flowing, senses became more acute and time slowed down. He was disciplined enough to use the biological response as an advantage. Small arms fire whizzed by them and impacted the sand nearby.

Noah could see flashes coming from the base of a guard tower closest to their position. He decided to return fire with the Glock 19. His first shot hit the sand about 15 feet behind them. The next shot hit a water tower to the left of the guard's position.

"Quit bouncing me so much." Noah yelled at Lucas.

"No time for a trot." Lucas laughed and yelled back.

Noah closed his left eye and tried to line up the rear and front sites. Guards were climbing the tower ladder and he hit a rung above their position with a bullet. The guards stopped climbing for a brief moment and Noah fired another round. He hit the water tower again. Once the guards reached the tower, they began to fire automatic weapons at the men. The Mi-24 on the beach returned fire with a Shturm V missile that took out the tower. Helicopters from Gitmo were taking off by the time Mike, Jonas, Lucas, Sallah, and Noah reached their chopper.

A Cuban MIG-23 flew overhead and launched missiles in the direction of two US MH-60M helicopters. The missiles struck a position near the birds as a warning to the pilots to remain grounded. The MIG tailed off to the south and headed for Cuban airspace. The US helicopters landed safely as the pilots knew they were outmatched against a MIG fighter. A different alarm sounded as the Gitmo Naval leaders realized they were experiencing a full-scale attack. The Cuban Mi-24 helicopter took off safely from the beach and headed southwest; the men were in route to Santiago de Cuba. From there, the group would catch a private plane to Caracas, Venezuela and fly south to Buenos Aires, Argentina. Their next stop after Buenos Aires would be the Falkland Islands, to regroup with the Excalibur.

Mike peeled off his helmet and checked on Noah. Noah looked worn out and beat up. He had a few cuts on his face and his left eye was bruised.

"Noah, I've heard great things about you from my brother-in-law." Mike stretched out his right hand.

"And who may that be?" Noah still didn't know who was responsible for his rescue.

"Matthew Hiatt. He wanted to make the trip himself, but we couldn't let him." Mike smiled as he shook hands with Noah to celebrate their successful mission.

"We'll get you a warm meal, hot shower, and a good night's sleep before we head out tomorrow." Mike pulled a water bottle from his belt and handed it to Noah. Noah didn't reply as he looked out of the open door of the Mi-24 helicopter into the darkness. He had a look of relief, relief that he'd been evacuated from Camp Delta. Noah contemplated the irony associated with his transfer from Delta Defense to Camp Delta in a matter of days. He didn't know what the future would hold, but anything was better than Gitmo and the hell he'd experienced at the hands of his own countrymen.

****

The F-15s came roaring overhead again.

Amen said, "Make your move. Choppers are seconds away."

"10-4." Michael tucked the 2-way into a belt and called for the gangs to move out together. "Leave all of the weapons behind, let's go."

They were only a few yards from the SUVs. Michael and Reggie continued to carry Robert. He was moaning and wincing in some pain, still unconscious. The 812s and 405s were on their way. Robert was the only injury during the campaign and the gangs had served their purpose. They heard the news about Sesom over the radio during the exchange between Amen and Kimi. Most of the young men were surprised they'd made it out alive. They entered the getaway vehicles and rushed to the wrecking yard.

"How's he doing?" Michael asked from the backseat.

"He's coming to!" Tiny was pulling Robert's vest from his body. He was bleeding from areas around his arms and legs. The shrapnel had ripped off parts of his skin.

"C'mon man, wake up. Let me know you're good." Tiny was talking to Robert while patting his cheeks.

Reggie called out to Red, "A few blocks away, we're coming in hot."

"Copy." Red was in the middle of the wrecking yard and gave a hand signal to the crane operator. The crane operator gave him a thumb's up and was ready to dispose of the SUVs. A lookout employee was posted at the large, corrugated steel doors at the entrance to the yard. Red flashed a hand signal to the lookout and closed his hand to make a fist. The lookout was ready to shut the doors once the SUVs safely entered the yard.

Robert opened his eyes for the first time. He saw Tiny hovering above him. Tiny smiled and moved his lips; Robert still couldn't hear anything. He looked to his left and saw Michael stretching out an arm from the backseat. He grabbed Robert's right hand and smiled. Robert began to hear sounds, almost as if someone was speeding up a song on the radio. Then came clarity; Robert could understand what Tiny was saying.

"You made it man, you did it. Stay put, you got some nasty cuts."

Robert looked at Tiny and smiled. He squeezed Michael's hand to let him know that he was there and back with the group. The SUV was speeding to its final destination. As the four vehicles entered the yard, Red motioned for them to line up in front of the crane.

Robert emerged from the third SUV. Reggie put his arm around Robert and helped him away from the vehicle. He was limping and bleeding from several cuts on his arms and legs.

Red was concerned, "Robert, you going to be alright?"

Robert responded with a thumb's up, "I'm going to make it. Wish my ears would quit ringing." Robert was a young gang member who did well in school and avoided violence or fighting within the group. Most of his friends were in gangs, and his membership was a natural progression from the streets. He had learned too much from his father to get involved with the criminal elements of a gang. The other members respected Robert for his decisions to do well in school and avoid jail time. Red was quick to bark orders.

"There are first aid supplies in the break room. Reggie, make sure Robert gets some butterflies on those cuts."

Red instructed them, "Strip down gentlemen. Leave all gloves, vests, shields, weapons, shirts, pants, and anything else with DNA in the vehicles. Keys remain with the vehicles too. Let's move."

The men did as instructed and left everything with the SUVs, including their shoes and socks. The gang members were stripped down to their underwear.

"Head into the break room. There are clothes waiting for you. Don't worry about colors." Red pointed to a door that served as a common area for employees. The crane began to pick up the SUVs and set them into a crusher. From there, the vehicles would be chewed up into small pieces of steel and sent to a recycler. Typically, vehicles would be stripped of rubbers and plastics before being shredded into pieces. The SUVs would be chewed up whole, with everything remaining inside. The wrecker yard would burn off the remaining materials.

Red saw the F-15s fly over the highway again. Helicopters began to converge on the President's position. Crevan was immediately evacuated from the area and taken to a nearby hospital. Aside from a broken left leg, the President's injuries were superficial. Sesom's body was recovered by a group of Navy Seals and flown out to sea in a Blackhawk Stealth helicopter. Without wrapping the body, Sesom was tossed into the Pacific Ocean with chains and weights to keep him from resurfacing. Sesom's final resting place would be twenty-five miles from the coast of Los Angeles near a depth of 700 feet.

News channels were reporting everything from the President had been in an accident to his assassination.

The truth lay somewhere in between. Panic and rioting took to the streets of Los Angeles. The people didn't feel safe and didn't know who was attacking their city. The Colonists had warned the President that future terrorist attacks on the homeland would compel them to take back their government. They would look to make good on their promise. Since the Civil War, the United States had not experienced people taking up arms against their government in protest or to protect liberties. The Colonist party leader, Thomas Sawyer, had garnered noticeable support and donations from thousands of Americans to reclaim the United States from its runaway government. Sawdog, as he was nicknamed in Washington, was no nonsense and tired of the endless red tape and indecision from Congressional bureaucrats and lame duck Presidents.

The gangsters emerged from the break room, all of them wearing black pants and white button-down shirts.

Red smiled, "You gentlemen look nice."

He continued, "Two million dollars has already been deposited into our offshore account. Amen and Cering will make good on the rest. We need to meet up with them at The Third Baptist Church in Compton."

One of the gang members said, "There's a third?"

Red nodded, "Yes Ace, there are several churches in Compton. Now that you have an opportunity to leave the life, you may want to explore the mysteries of Rome."

Ace responded, "Why Rome?"

Tiny cut in, "Man, shut up. Red, what's with the costumes?"

"Those aren't costumes. They're appropriate clothes,

especially if you're on mission work from Utah."

"Mission. What mission? I thought we just carried out our mission?"

Red laughed, "You did, and you did well. The clothes and mission are cover in case the authorities stop us. You see those three vans over there?"

The men looked in the direction Red was pointing.

"The backs of those vans are filled with Bibles. Grab one and keep it close to your chest. Let's all pray that we make the journey safely out of this wrecker yard. Let's go." Red tossed Michael, Reggie, and Tiny keys to the vans.

"Single file and follow me. We don't want to break the law and bring unnecessary attention to ourselves." Red was already wearing black dress pants and a white button-down shirt. He continued to wear his lucky Boston Red Sox cap. The group of gangsters would meet up with Amen and Cering at The Third Baptist Church in Compton. Talan controlled traffic signals to make the trip less congestive for his Disciples and the gang members.

****

"Vice President Morgan, you have a call on the red phone." An administrative assistant paged him over an intercom system at the residence of 1 Observatory Circle. Morgan had been in constant contact with President Crevan's Communication team since the assassination attempt.

"This is Morgan."

"Seems like matters are getting worse." Thomas Sawyer and Lance Morgan had served together in Congress for close to a decade. During Sawyer's tenure, he had denounced both major political parties several years prior and left Congress to support the Libertarians. Tea Party members supported Sawyer's ideas to strip down the powers of Federal government. He believed that a strong military was necessary in a hostile world, but he didn't support the government's overreaching policies and burdensome regulation. Bureaucracy had infiltrated the military and reduced the efficiencies of the armed forces while increasing costs. Sawdog looked to change the direction of the country, by way of negotiation or revolution.

"If our second President would have been assassinated within a few weeks of President Palmer, matters would be worse." Morgan stated the obvious and avoided a debate with Sawyer.

"You know that recent developments will create a strain between the current administration and my party."

Morgan knew this conversation was coming, "What kind of strains?"

"The Colonist party and millions of Americans are tired of a two party system that does nothing but bicker and spend copious amounts of money on failing programs. As the mouthpiece of the Colonist party, I warned that future terrorist attacks on our homeland would be met with consequences from people supporting our party. The Colonist party will not allow our do-nothing Federal government to continue spending money on pork while domestic and foreign terrorists attack the people of the United States. In our opinion, the government has lost control and become what the Anti-Federalists feared during construction of the Constitution. Even though we don't call the President a king, he has become one through the abuse of executive orders and Presidential privilege. We won't be ruled by a king."

Morgan was firm, "You know the problem runs deeper than one person."

Sawyer concurred, "I agree, the legislative branch of our government will be restructured as well."

"You know that military action against the US government will be met with retribution and charges of treason. Is there a possibility we can meet to open up some dialog?" Morgan desired a more peaceful resolution to the matter.

Sawyer respected Morgan and knew that he was a moderate with solid roots. He had also served on several committees to try and scale back government programs and push for a balanced budget amendment. The government had become so weighed down in partisan politics and serving lobbyists, most of Morgan's work had been passed over or fallen on deaf ears. Sawyer knew that Morgan wouldn't waste his time, so he gave him a little breathing room.

"You have thirty days until we organize and call for the resignation of the executive branch and House of Representatives. The Colonists are ready to take action now, and we have members of the military that will join our ranks. Because you and I have worked together in the past, I trust that you understand the urgency of this matter."

Morgan retorted, "And because we've worked together in the past, I trust that you know I'll do everything I can to compromise with the Colonist party to keep our government in tact and working for the people of the United States."

Sawyer said, "Fair enough. I'll phone you next week for lunch. I can call the dogs off for thirty days; after that, you're either with us or against us."

Sawdog took a page out of George W. Bush's playbook with his last statement. He wanted Morgan to understand that there was no room for neutrality. Many cities of the United States were boiling over anyway. Social unrest had already claimed dozens of lives and caused hundreds of injuries. The rest of the world wasn't fairing much better. Israel wiped out key nuclear facilities in Iran and hostile cities in Syria and Lebanon. In a surprise move, Jordan and Saudi Arabia sided with Israel and shuttered their borders to prevent extremists from moving through their countries. Egypt vowed to support Israel's extermination and tensions flared up on the border between the two nations. Saudi Arabia moved air support and ground troops to the southern border of Israel. Jordan moved troops to the north to keep Syria from entering the Holy Land. The entire region was a mess and thousands of casualties were reported daily.

India and Pakistan had begun a war of their own, each of them threatening the use of nuclear weapons. China had successfully invaded Taiwan and taken over the government; the US didn't have enough resources in the Taiwan Strait and South China Sea to hold the Chinese military back during the invasion. Any resistance from the Taiwanese people was met with immediate execution of entire families. Australia was bombing Indonesia to protect the interests of the Philippines and Vietnam. Jakarta had fallen to hardline Islamic leadership and they controlled the military. Even though the Indonesian Navy had sent ships in the direction of the Philippines, they were warned by US submarines to return to Manado Naval Base. At one point, Indonesia had been considered a moderate Democratic government. With the Arab Springs and recent success of radical Islamic governments, the islands of Indonesia didn't stand a chance against an Islamic uprising.

****

Ethan opened up the door to Elisabeth's cabin. The time was a little after midnight.

"Get dressed and come quickly to the dining room." He shut the door and disappeared down a stairwell.

Neither Matt nor Elisabeth was sleeping. They were still contemplating the physical connection they'd just shared together. Emotions of joy and excitement were coupled with insecurities that came from sharing a sacred part of one's being. They had consummated their relationship, elevated their bond to a higher level, and connected in ways they hadn't experienced with anyone before them. In a growing secular world that put emphasis on sexuality and conquests, Matt and Elisabeth knew their connection would last a lifetime. Even though they hadn't shared the sacrament of marriage yet, the connection was decided and part of a greater experience.

"I wonder if there are more pirates?" Matt slipped on his clothes. He still carried around his modified .45 on the ship and chambered a round.

"There are pirates out here?" Elisabeth didn't understand the reference. She didn't know the Excalibur was boarded on their trip across the Pacific. Matt leaned over and kissed her on the lips.

"They were Russian. I doubt there are Russian pirates off the coast of South Africa." Matt didn't mention the Excalibur had a bounty placed on the ship after the Russian encounter. Pirates across the globe were interested in capturing the Excalibur and her crew to cash in on a large reward.

Elisabeth put on a pajama top and bottom. A hair band was applied to hold her long hair together. Before they left the cabin, Matt gave her one more kiss. The engines had stopped, which seemed strange to Matt. He hadn't noticed before leaving Elisabeth's cabin. The Excalibur took on the nature of her surroundings. The steel was getting colder and the cabins were less humid as the earth rotated the northern hemisphere away from the sun. The couple made it to the dining room. Captain Phil, John, Aaron, Ethan, and Li were waiting for them.

"Where's my sister?" Matt looked around; she was conspicuous by her absence.

Ethan replied, "We didn't wake her." Matt headed for the coffee. After the past hour, he knew sleep wouldn't be an option.

"Anybody else?" Matt held up the pot and offered some to the group.

"Please, a little cream and sugar." Elisabeth smiled as she brought her index finger and thumb within an inch of each other to indicate her idea of a little. Captain Phil held up his cup. Nobody was saying anything. Obviously, the group was waiting for Matt to get his coffee. Matt brought over Elisabeth's coffee and filled up Phil's cup. He took a seat at the table with the others, next to Elisabeth. The couple appeared very happy, almost giddy.

Ethan was cupping his coffee with both hands. He looked up, "Sesom is dead."

"What?" Matt's mood changed.

Li followed up, "Sesom is dead, he was killed in the mission to wipe out Crevan."

"Yeah sure, you guys are always kidding around and playing pranks." Matt didn't want to believe what he heard. He wanted to return to Elisabeth's warm bed and feel her body close to his. Matt looked around the table and nobody gestured, all of them were serious.

Matt looked at Ethan, "Sesom can't be dead. He's the one who set all this up, brought us together, put this in motion. He's responsible for finding me and taking us to the Western Wall. If it weren't for Sesom, we would have never found Elisabeth. That's impossible."

Ethan replied, "Things happen Matt."

Matt became angry, "Things just don't happen to this group, we make them happen." He jumped out of his chair in disbelief. Matt had lost important family members during his life. He was tired of losing people close to him, who meant something to him. Over the past several weeks, Matt and Sesom had formed a tight relationship. Even though Sesom was like many of his military leaders, the relationship transcended rank; Sesom taught Matt about life and how to become a better person. They had sparred, shared mutual feelings over a cup of coffee, and seen each other in action. Sesom was a rock and represented the foundation of their group. Matt was talking to himself and dropped his head. Elisabeth held her hand over her mouth as tears spilled over her fingers. She remembered Sesom's nature, and how nonjudgmental he was when they first met.

Matt was still facing the wall; he didn't want the others to see him upset. "What about Crevan?"

"Injured with a broken leg and some cuts. Sesom had the drop on him when he was shot to death." Ethan's eyes were watering.

"I should have been there," Matt immediately felt guilty. He knew that, given the chance, he would have done everything in his power to save Sesom, even lay down his own life.

"How?" Matt came back to the table, even though he had tears rolling down his cheeks. He wiped away the tears and put a hand on Elisabeth's right leg.

"The mission was going as planned. Crevan's limousine was disabled and rolled a couple of times. Sesom put his chopper down and left the bird. Cering called for Sesom to get out of there because security forces were bearing down on him from the air and ground. He continued to the limousine anyway. As he came up on Crevan, he readied his machine gun to take him out. Sesom was unaware that a helicopter pilot providing cover for the President had survived a crash and escaped the wreckage. The pilot put two bullets in Sesom's armor. The bullets were piercing and Sesom died instantly. He didn't suffer."

"What happened to his cover?" Matt knew that Disciples had to be in the area providing protection.

"Dorje was north of the bridge and couldn't see the pilot. Kimi was focused on the entire motorcade bearing down on Sesom from the north. She heard shots coming from the east side of the median. By the time she heard the shots, Sesom was dead."

Matt took his first sip of coffee; this would be a long morning.

Li said, "She feels terrible. Kimi wanted to go in and retrieve Sesom's body. Amen had her stand down and evacuate the area with Dorje."

"Where is his body?"

Li continued, "A group of Marines picked up Sesom in a Blackhawk Stealth helicopter and flew him out to sea.

His body was dumped about 25 miles west of Los Angeles; very close to the debris field of Flight 261 that crashed several years ago."

Matt said, "Should we attempt to recover his body?"

Ethan replied, "No, too predictable. His body is probably deeper than 500 feet in that part of the Pacific. According to Islamic tradition, he must be buried within 24 hours of his death. If the US government believes that a land burial isn't appropriate, the sea becomes the next best option."

Matt sipped his coffee, "Oddly enough, I probably know half the Marines that were sent to dump Sesom's body. What about the rest of the team?"

"Amen and Cering are meeting with some people in Compton. Talan is picking up Kimi and Dorje at locations east and west of Interstate 405 along the storm sewer systems. Mike and Lucas have successfully rescued Noah and Jonas from Gitmo without incident. They should be safe in Santiago de Cuba by now."

Matt broke a little smile, "They got Noah."

"They did." Ethan smiled back.

"That's got to be a sight to see." Matt rotated his cup on the dining table. He was looking down into the cup wondering when he'd see Noah again, knowing that he would never see Sesom again.

Matt wiped his nose and continued, "Cap, what do you think?"

Phil paused and let out a sigh, "Two Disciples passed on before Sesom. Trevor and Liam are probably hanging with him right now lighting up some good Cuban cigars.

Sesom had an idea that he might die before seeing this mission to completion. That's why he was always questioning us, challenging our critical thinking, and forcing us to become better leaders, better people. He also knew that the reigns would be passed on to one of you should he be killed. We've been through a lot together, that won't stop because we lost another Disciple. I'm in for the long haul. Sesom would want us to carry on."

John and Aaron shook their heads in agreement with Captain Phil. The world was spinning out of control and one of the safest places to be was on the Excalibur with the Disciples and Captain Phil. The Israeli Defense Sailors were settling in and keeping to themselves for the most part. They would always share meals with other shipmates during the evening, allowing them an opportunity to catch up on news or play a game of cards. Matt felt great admiration for the IDF and an appreciation for the Israeli Special Forces. In recent years, Israeli Special Forces had assisted the United States with missions in the Middle East. Whether they were focusing on rogue nuclear scientists, or striking terrorist camps, Israel was very much in the game, even though they didn't publicize their involvement.

Since World War II, the nation of Israel vowed to never let any country or leader prey upon Jewish people again. To make matters worse, several neighboring countries denied the holocaust ever happened. Even though Israel had been baited for several decades, they had remained on the sidelines while missile after missile was launched against their country day after day. Israel had been preparing for a war with the Muslim world since reoccupying the country after World War II. The territory had known war for way too long, since the days before Roman occupation. This time, there would be peace in the Middle East, regardless of who was left to enjoy it.

****

The Third Baptist Church of Compton was quiet. No evening services were planned for this day and Red was an Elder for the church. The vans made the trip to the church without incident. The gangsters were still dressed in black pants and button downs. Red opened a side door to the church and the men entered the chapel.

"Might be a good idea if we took some time to reflect before Amen and Cering arrive." Red dimmed the lights and lit some candles. The gang members were sitting together on the right side of the church. There was a large crucifix in front of them, to remind them of who made the ultimate sacrifice for their existence. Many of the young men stared at the wood carving of Jesus on the cross. His head hung to the side as a crown of thorns dug deep into his skull. Romans and Jews alike scorned a man whom represented everything pure in a hostile world. Jesus had cried out to his Father to forgive the people, for they knew not what they did. The same held true in today's world, for many people, including these gangsters who had committed unspeakable sins in the past.

After Red lit candles, he sat in the front pew. He bowed his head and prayed for Sesom. He knew that Sesom didn't return from the mission. Red had also known several people that didn't return home from school, church, or a night out with their friends in the past. Red knew the Disciples were doing their best to prevent an evil dictator from assuming the highest office in the so-called free world. He also knew the United States had been on a steady decline for decades. From greed to secularism, the United States had lost its collective consciousness. People of the country used to be proud, work hard, and focus on the family. By losing its collective consciousness, many people had given up, taken to the streets, and abandoned the American Dream.

Amen and Cering entered the chapel through the same side door. Red stood up and greeted them. They gave each other hugs and Amen stepped forward.

"You guys did great out there today. How are you doing Robert?"

Robert smiled, "I'm okay. My head hurts a little and I got a couple scrapes. That shield saved my life. What about that Sesom guy? He okay?"

"No. He didn't make the trip back." Amen pressed his lips together.

"I'm sorry to hear that. Anything else we can do to help?" Robert had a servant's heart.

"No. You guys did everything we asked. Cering has some good news for you."

Cering stepped forward, "I've initiated a transfer of $18 million dollars to pay off the balance. You earned the $20 million. The money is sitting in Mr. Taylor's account and will be split up between all of you equally. You performed courageously today, be proud of yourselves."

Cering stepped back and Red spoke, "I know that you guys run with different friends and protect your turf. I ask that you leave the life. You no longer need to hustle, run drugs, or collect rent. You have enough money to take your family out of this place."

Red pointed at the crucifix. "This man had much less than we do. He never asked anything of anybody, other than for some people to follow him. He knew that he was going to die for your sins. He knew that those who loved him would betray him. He knew that he would rise again and come in glory to judge you and me. I ask that you leave the life. You can only stay in Compton if you choose to change your ways and become a role model for the young kids, all of them. Denounce the gang life and leave your past right here, right now."

Red paused, "As you walk out of the chapel, understand that the life you once lived is gone, and the life you will live is just beyond that door. The money will help, but you have to make a decision to leave the life. You acted as one out there today, and you shall walk as one tomorrow. If anybody should ask you about the event, you don't know anything. If anybody should ask you where you were, you were at the church with me, planning a surprise party for Pastor Paul. Nobody talks and that's the way it stays. When we leave this chapel, you know nothing. The reason you're wearing those clothes? Because I made you, for the church meeting. I don't ever want to see you wearing colors again. It's over."

All of the gang members respected Red. He knew all of their parents. They looked at him as a father figure, someone they could trust and turn to in a bind. The chapel was completely quiet; the men knew that Red meant business.

"Now for the fun part. I will set up individual accounts for each of you tomorrow. They will be offshore and tax-free. If we learned anything from fat cats and politicians, it's how to hide money and prevent the government from taxing it to death. You will be the only one with access to the account. If you're a minor," Red looked at Robert, "I will serve as your custodian. I plan on speaking with your parents or guardians so they understand the money is legit. I'll tell them that you earned the money without gangbanging, and someone hired you to do some heavy lifting on the streets. I won't tell them what, where, when, how, or why. I'll tell them the money is as good as gold and you own it without strings. What's my one condition?"

Half of the church replied, "Leave the life."

Red brought his right hand up to his ear and motioned with his left hand for more participation.

The entire church answered, "Leave the life." Red stepped back to let Amen wrap up the meeting.

"Once again, thank you for helping us. You have earned every penny of that money. Red is right. Don't speak about the events of today. If anybody strays from the path Red described, we'll find you. I don't anticipate any of you would be foolish enough to challenge our authority. Please don't forget that we have the resources to take on the President of the United States. Even though we didn't end his life today, we will continue to hunt him down and hold him accountable for what he's done and plans to do. There is no doubt he will be hunting us as well. Don't make yourself part of his agenda."

Amen looked at the pews, "Any questions?"

One of the gang members raised his hand slowly, "Will we see you again?"

Cering smiled, "We will see each other again, in this life or the next."

Amen nodded his head in affirmation. "Any other questions?" The church was still. The men looked around to see if anyone else had a question for the Disciples. Amen and Cering began to shake hands with the gang members and thank them for their involvement with the operation.

"You going to be okay?" Amen checked on Robert.

"Yeah, I'll make it. I can't wait to share the money with Pops and help him with our family. Since mom died, he's done his best. This will lighten the load for him."

Amen smiled and knew that he'd changed several lives. He hoped they continued to seek challenges with purpose that came with a payday. When considering groups of people, gang members had undying loyalty and kept their mouths shut. Many workers in corporate America lacked the aforementioned skills. As Sesom planned for the event in Los Angeles, Amen knew where to find assistance and diversion in the City of Angels. The gangs had done their job, now they would move forward as leaders in a different capacity.

****

Samil had legitimate concerns. President Crevan and Secretary of State Watt benefited greatly from Samil's brazenness to dirty bomb the United States. Crevan and Watt had successfully recruited and paid Samil to carry out multiple operations worldwide. In light of Samil's success, a rogue group of Crusaders seemed intent on preventing Samil from taking over the world country by country. Crevan's assassination attempt preceded by the Disciples successful reconnaissance mission at the Western Wall had him worried about Crevan's security detail. The Disciples and Samil had encountered each other at several crossroads over the past couple of years. Samil knew the dangers that came with a group of Disciples focused on an operation. Even though they had lost a leader, they would come back harder and stronger.

A Secret Service agent entered Crevan's hospital room.

"Mr. President, you have a visitor from the Republic of Yemen. We've run him through security screens. He's insisting that he see you."

Crevan was sitting in a leather chair near the window of his hospital room. He knew that Samil would be concerned and want to meet with him.

"Send him in." Crevan preferred sweats and a t-shirt to a hospital gown. His broken leg had already been set and casted. He was waiting for a few more tests to come back before he could be discharged.

"Yes sir." Secret Service had canvassed the hospital. The department knew that a coordinated assassination attempt required multiple groups of people working in concert together. Those same people were likely still at large in Los Angeles. The threat level was still very high and real. Ahriman entered the hospital room.

"Ahri, how are you?" Crevan motioned for Yemen's Ambassador to join him at a table nearby.

"Better than you it appears." Crevan had a few cuts and bruises on his face. Ahri took a seat at the table near Crevan's leather chair.

"Could have been worse. The one they call Sesom had a drop on me. If it wasn't for a Marine helicopter pilot, you'd be dealing with Vice President Morgan."

Ahri rubbed his beard and explained, "That's what we're afraid of. If they get to you, Morgan would disrupt our plans. Are you safe within your own administration?"

"Yes. Taking out Sesom will damage the leadership of these self-proclaimed Disciples. However, after they work through the loss, they will come back with resilience. We must continue with our plan. How is Samil doing in Indonesia?"

"Jakarta is ours and the other islands are submitting, including nearby Malaysia. We control the military in the area."

Crevan asked, "What about Russia?"

"They are holding lines to the east and west. Based on conversations we've had with their interior ministry, they will surprise China with a preemptive strike in the next few days. Russia is aware at some point in the future the Chinese will invade them for strategic land resources. China doesn't have enough resources to sustain itself for the long term. The Mongolian people are ready to go. They look forward to an opportunity to become a great empire again and will show allegiance to Samil."

Crevan smiled, "War brings out the best in people."

Ahri countered, "Not all people. These Disciples are very determined to disrupt our plans. What about the girl?"

"The Samil clairvoyants seem to believe that the woman rescued at the Western Wall will begin John's Revelation from the Bible. They predict that she will give birth to a child that will pave the way for the 2nd Coming of a Messiah. The man she is with, Matt Hiatt, has been called to protect her from us."

Ahri thought back to a time before World War II and looked out the window into darkness. "Germany was very much like your modern day United States before World War II. The country was disillusioned, politically divided, and in financial trouble before Hitler's rise. The country was ripe for a Samil takeover and we almost succeeded. Samil was very much entrenched in the Axis Powers of Germany, Italy, and Japan. Hitler should have chosen religion instead of race as his primary motivator to divide the country and world. The secular society of the United States will yield more followers to your message. The Axis Powers would have succeeded if their reasons for dominating the world were more singular in focus. The conflict of nations and differences between Christianity, Islam, and Judaism will work in our favor during these world wars. God has worked through chosen individuals to bring salvation to his people in the past."

Crevan said, "And we must prevent God from working through this group of Disciples to usher in John's Revelation. If we can stop the 2nd Coming, we will rule the earth and everyone on it. One of the flaws with free will is that people can make decisions to affect outcomes, yielding different results."

A Secret Service agent entered the room. "Mr. President, Secretary of State Watt is on the phone. The call is waiting for you on our secure line."

Crevan looked at his guest, "You may want to stick around for this."

****

Mike, Lucas, Jonas, Sallah, and Noah were on a plane to Caracas when Lucas received the news from Cering that Sesom was dead. Sesom had been a father figure to Lucas since meeting up with him in Brazil at a futbol game. Oddly enough, Lucas didn't weep at hearing the news. He celebrated Sesom's life and what he'd accomplished before passing on from this physical world. Jonas understood the jubilation felt by Lucas, but Mike and Noah were surprised by his reaction.

"Aren't you upset in the least bit?" Mike shared his bewilderment.

Lucas smiled and leaned back in his seat, "Me? No, not at all."

"I guess I'm having a difficult time understanding Disciples. You're not upset that the leader of this group, the man you believe lived his life based on a higher calling, has just been killed and dumped in the ocean."

Lucas continued to smile and spoke in his recognizable deep voice, "Mike. You must understand that you're looking at Sesom's death in a very physical manner. A manner that suggests his life has ended and all is lost. What I believe to be true is much different."

Mike smirked and pressed for information, "And just what is it that you believe to be true?"

Lucas had thought of resurrection in great detail. "Jesus, Mohammed, Buddha, and many other great prophets had to die in order to see their teachings come to fruition. Other people, or Disciples as you've mentioned, needed to pass on the parables and teachings of their spiritual leaders. No one person, in the flesh, can change the world by himself. I believe Jesus Christ is the Messiah, and he rose from death to show us there is life beyond this physical world. The idea of a resurrection is shared by other orthodox faiths, but Christians share a message that those who believe in Jesus will find their path to God. Sesom chose such a path as well, even though he was Muslim by birthright."

Mike began to interrupt Lucas and was immediately silenced. "But before you form your own opinion, your own path so-to-speak, just because I believe Jesus Christ is the Messiah doesn't mean I diminish the importance and influence of any other religion. I have learned a lot from studying other religions and their teachings, including what Sesom taught me. He believed that Christianity and Islam were closer together than most people recognized. Sesom also believed that man focused more on the differences between religions than their inherent similarities, to create great division between the people of God."

Mike was surprised. Not so much by what Lucas was saying, but by how much he was speaking. Mike had never heard Lucas put such a string of words together in the past. Mike thought about what Lucas said.

"The mystery of faith."

Lucas became more serious, "Exactly. If followers of any religion applied their principles to real life without prejudice, we wouldn't be having this conversation. We probably wouldn't have to do what we're doing."

Jonas entered the conversation, "Lucas is right. All religions have failed to uphold the basic principles of their teachings at some point in history. The Catholic faith was humiliated by the actions of the Vatican during World War II. The Church's strict neutrality during the war can be better described as all that is necessary for evil to triumph is for good men to do nothing."

Mike looked at Jonas, "That's Edmund Burke. Most people mistake the quote as something from the Bible. He was supportive of the American Revolutionaries when the thirteen colonies elected to break from British rule."

Jonas smiled, "You know your history."

"In the hopes of not repeating it. Which is easier said than done."

Jonas continued, "Humans are disappointingly predictable and fail to internalize life's lessons. When Simplicius II was elected, he committed himself to understanding and sharing truths. He didn't want to be perceived as inaccessible or political. Simplicius has recognized that the Church did not serve some people and groups well in the past. By revealing such truth in history, he looks to change how the Church will approach geopolitical issues that affect the Catholic faith and world going forward."

Mike said, "There shouldn't be a shortage of issues for the Church to embrace."

Jonas replied, "I agree. I'm excited that Simplicius was elected to the Papal Office. He will serve the Vatican well as the world enters a dark period of war and decadence. Simplicius also knows that Matt and Elisabeth will bear a child of great significance to this dying planet; nothing like the world has seen since the coming of Jesus Christ."

Noah didn't engage in the conversation, he just listened. His world had changed in a matter of days. Everything he'd learned and understood about the United States was tarnished. No due process, no attorneys, and no trials. The CIA had tortured Noah to coerce a confession in a terrorist plot at the Western Wall in Jerusalem and a recovery mission in Gaza. They even took his wheelchair. He didn't tell them anything and denied any involvement by Matt with a terrorist organization. Noah believed that his partner at Delta Defense was on a mission to rescue a family member. Even though he'd heard news reports pegging his friend as a terrorist, Noah didn't believe any of the details. Noah knew Matt loved his country and would sacrifice his life to protect the United States. He had no idea that Matt would send people to rescue him from Gitmo. Sallah was sleeping next to Noah in a window seat on the plane.

Lucas wanted clarification, "What can be bigger than the coming of Jesus Christ?"

Jonas knew he had an audience for the answer and took some time. "As you've witnessed at the Vatican, there are many reasons for us to believe that God will hold humanity accountable for its actions. Free will is a gift, and has resulted in unintended consequences for mankind. God has worked through people in the past and will continue to do so in the future. That's why we're on an early morning flight headed to Buenos Aires. I'm hoping we'll catch up with the others at the Falklands soon."

Mike asked, "And what about our competition, the people we're up against?"

Jonas replied, "As the world becomes more secular and divided, Samil becomes very attractive to several unstable governments across the globe. They seem to have unlimited funds and an endless stream of people interested in their cause and subsequent rise to power. High unemployment rates and young people angry with their leadership provide Samil unlimited resources. On the inside, the group has always struggled with deception and organization. Members of Samil will crawl all over each other to gain favor within the group. They do not serve a higher purpose, they serve themselves."

****

After Crevan was discharged from the hospital, he toured the sections of Los Angeles hard hit by the dirty bombs. Emergency response teams issued full body suits and oxygen for people entering the areas. The military had armored vehicles equipped with ovens that could cremate the dead on site and preserve their ashes for family members. A special hospital was set up at a nearby school for those that survived the blast but were sickened from the radioactive fallout. The casualties ranged from flu like symptoms to those killed by the blast. Every age group was affected by the blasts and fallout. Unfortunately, many of the people exposed to radiation would eventually die from cancer. From the air, Crevan could see cleanup operations taking place in the City of Angels. The immediate areas affected by the detonation would take several months to clean up before residents could return to their homes. Plants, pets, and water supplies would be disposed of immediately. Much of the debris would be buried or flown out to sea and dumped. Areas would need to be washed with solutions and sand blasted in some cases. Response teams in Los Angeles, New York, Miami, and Concord were well trained to handle the situation. Homeland Security and the State Department anticipated something like this would happen on American soil, and were well prepared.

After touring Los Angeles, Crevan boarded Air Force One and returned to Washington. Even though his lower left leg was broken, he insisted that doctors set and plate the bone so he could use a walking cast and cane. He didn't want to be seen on crutches or a wheelchair while recovering. Many people would be watching the President to gauge his resolve and leadership during a time of terror and war. Even though US citizens had no clue of the details surrounding the assassination attempt, most believed that Al Qaeda, Hezbollah, militias, or some other unidentified terrorist organization planned the attack. Even after 2000 years and the crucifixion of Jesus Christ, people still had a tendency to rush to judgment and let their emotions get the best of them. A handful of people on the planet knew what the truth really was regarding the assassination attempt and how a group of Disciples were trying to prevent Crevan from setting up puppet governments across the globe.

Once again, protestors lined the street of 1600 Pennsylvania Avenue. The National Guard was providing full time security for the White House and adjacent national monuments. Washington, DC had increased security detail at airports, bus, and train stations due to the heightened threat levels issued by the Department of Homeland Security. Washington, DC couldn't have been safer, mainly because the person responsible for orchestrating the US terror attacks lived in the White House and held the highest office in the US government.

Vice President Morgan had requested an audience with Crevan upon his return. Even though the President had arrived later than scheduled, Morgan wanted to discuss the Colonist party and overtures made by Thomas "Sawdog" Sawyer. Sawdog knew that he would need the military to overthrow Crevan's administration. Crevan's secretary escorted Morgan into the Oval Office. The President looked like he'd been on the wrong end of a fistfight.

"Good evening Lance," Crevan was annoyed with Morgan's persistence to conduct a meeting so late in the evening.

"Good evening Mr. President. How is the leg?"

Crevan said, "Better than my face. What can I help you with?"

"Thomas Sawyer phoned me after the attempt in Los Angeles. He's given us a deadline."

"What kind of deadline?"

Morgan looked at his watch, "29 days and 3 ½ hours."

"Until what?"

"Until he demands that the current administration stand down and resign their positions."

Crevan wasn't even seated. He was looking out the window in the direction of the South Lawn Fountain. Crevan was surprised the fountain was still operational based on the recent cold temperatures.

"Are you suggesting that he may attempt a coup?"

Morgan was careful with his words, "I'm not suggesting anything. I'm merely stating that he's given us a deadline."

Crevan thought for a few seconds, "Well, he's assured us that any more terror attacks on US soil would be met with outrage and resistance by the Colonist party. How many members make up the Colonist party?"

Morgan said without delay, "7 million plus are registered with the party's website and social pages. Close to 300,000 people in the DC area support the Colonist party. Their base is energized and made up of several demographics. Regardless of income, race, religion or whatever, they seem to share the same disdain for the Federal government's two party system."

Crevan moved over to his high back leather chair and elevated his broken leg on a footstool. "Do they have any support within the legislature or military?"

"Fragmented support within the legislature. Sawyer and General Gilmore have shared a friendship over the years. I wouldn't be surprised if the dealings of the Federal government and current administration came up in their conversations."

Crevan tapped an index finger on his desk. "General Gilmore and I have chewed some of the same dirt. We had some disagreements in the Middle East about how to fund and arm the freedom fighters. Can't say that we had a positive relationship during the surges of Iraq and Afghanistan. Do you think I need to speak with him?"

"With whom?"

"General Gilmore."

Morgan didn't follow the President, "About what?"

"About his loyalty to the military and current administration."

Morgan became more confused, "Based on what? The idea that you didn't see eye-to-eye on policies in the Middle East? If that's the case, you may want to round up more than half the legislature and several leaders of the US military." Morgan began chuckling.

Crevan thought for a minute, "Yeah, several of us have shared many disagreements over how to handle the Middle East and leadership. Speaking of which, what's the latest in the territory?"

Even though Crevan changed the subject, he archived the comment about General Gilmore. Crevan would follow up with Watt regarding General Gilmore and anyone else sympathetic to the Colonist party in the military.

"Israel has taken back the West Bank and Gaza. Refugees from Gaza moved into Egypt and the refugees from the West Bank have been encouraged to travel north to Turkey for safety. Israel has forced the Lebanese north to Turkey and plan to invade Syria in the next few days. Our coalition of US, British, Australian, Italian, and French troops are in a fierce battle to the east of Turkey. The Iranians have sent hundreds of thousands of troops to their western border to invade Turkey. They are calling on jihadists worldwide to support them in their march to the Holy Land."

Lance left his chair and went to a map on the wall. "Unfortunately, thousands of Pakistanis have made the pilgrimage over Hindu Kush into Afghanistan. We've had to pull back our troops from Kabul, Khost, and Kandahar to the Iranian border and we'll likely have to evacuate Afghanistan over the next several weeks. Iran has sent thousands of troops to their eastern border to ensure that we don't enter the country. We don't want to be caught in a crossfire. Many of the former Soviet countries like Turkmenistan, Tajikistan, and Uzbekistan have large percentages of Muslim populations interested in a jihad against the great Satan. We aren't getting much help from diplomatic relations with those western Asian countries."

Crevan appeared almost bored with the briefing. "Interesting. I'll take up the matter with the Joint Chiefs and have them make recommendations to keep our troops safe."

"There's one other thing." Morgan pointed to Russia.

Crevan yawned, "What's that?"

"We are receiving some interesting intelligence about Russia."

"And?"

Morgan stepped away from the map and looked at the territory. "Sources, albeit not very reliable, are claiming that Russia is considering an invasion of northern China."

"That's silly. What do they have to gain from invading China?"

Morgan looked at Crevan, "They don't have much to gain, but they do have a lot to protect. China is outgrowing their resources. Instead of depending on trade and imports, they would be much better served invading Russia for land at some point in the future."

Crevan knew Russia's plan. The Russians were on board with Samil leadership and knew that the Muslim world would be critical to destroying western civilization. Russia was very familiar with former Union of Soviet Socialist Republic (USSR) countries that were predominately Muslim. They had even invaded Afghanistan and learned about the resolve and ruthlessness of a people that had been at war for thousands of years to protect their culture and tribes. In order for the country to survive a world at war, Russia knew that they had to partner with Muslim leadership and overthrow the Chinese. What the Muslim world didn't know was that the training grounds for Islamic extremists provided a haven for leaders of Samil. Their shared hatred for western civilization created a great environment for developing jihadists and military leaders. People from the Middle East flocked to training camps to fight a war against the west and Israel. What they didn't understand was that Samil managed the camps and daily operations to recruit soldiers. Under the marquee of radical Islam, Samil could energize an entire region of the world. Samil didn't care if people wanted to practice Judaism, Islam, Christianity, Buddhism, Hinduism, or cultism. Samil wanted to rule the world and prevent John's Revelation from occurring. They wanted to control the currency and culture of the world.

"Mongolia appears to be on board with the Russian plan." Morgan studied the map again as he moved his finger down from Russia, through Mongolia, and into China.

Crevan said, "China has moved several resources to the south and southeast as they struggle with the Taiwanese. An invasion from the north would be a surprise and leave Beijing exposed."

****

The Falkland Islands were beautiful. Gypsy Cove was located a few miles from the capital city of Stanley. Lined with white beaches and thousands of Magellanic penguins, Captain Phil and the others were happy to anchor in the cove. Surprisingly, foothills and small mountains surrounded several of the coves and harbors around the Falkland Islands. Mike, Lucas, Jonas, Noah, and Sallah made the trip safely from Cuba. Amen, Cering, Dorje, Kimi, and Talan were expected to land at the Mount Pleasant International Airport during the afternoon. Even though the mood was somber because of Sesom's death, the group was excited to reunite and discuss a plan for the future.

Mike and Mary were taking a stroll on the beach in the bay. John and Rebecca were fishing from a lifeboat with Matt and Elisabeth near the shore. The weather was warming up in the southern part of the hemisphere and producing some nice days for South American countries.

Mary was happy to have her husband back. "How was your little excursion to the States and Cuba?"

"Good. General Gilmore seems interested in what's happening in Washington right now. He was able to assist us with a plane to Gitmo for the recon mission. Noah was in pretty bad shape when we found him. I don't think he was prepared for how harshly his captors would treat him."

"What about Sallah?"

"Sallah is a good man and will be able to help us with the Middle East. He knows the territory, the tribes, the languages, and details of several past operations of the United States. He's been trained by the Central Intelligence Agency."

"What was he doing at Gitmo?"

"He sniffed out some of the questionable operations taking place in Syria and Afghanistan. Sallah had an idea the US was recruiting terror cells to carry out a mission in major cities on the homeland. He began asking questions, was detained, and left to rot in Gitmo. The CIA turned on him and made him an enemy of the US."

"We can trust him?"

Mike replied, "With our children."

"How can you be so sure?"

"I've seen him in action. He's saved Americans from ambushes and suicide bombers. We spent some time on missions together. Even though he's a bit of a goofball, you'll end up liking him."

Mike continued, "How is Matt?"

"He was upset when he heard the news about Sesom. Matt seems to be embracing his involvement with the Disciples more and more. I'm not sure if Sesom's death will shake his resolve. I believe that Elisabeth may be helping him work through some of the emotions."

Mike smiled, "Really?"

Mary replied, "Really. They've been spending more time together on the ship, some of it alone time. They would like to get married and say their vows with all of us as witnesses."

"Marriage?"

Mary put her arm around Mike's waist. "Yes, marriage.

Have you forgotten how quickly we fell in love with each other and wanted to tie the knot? Matt and Elisabeth are no different than we were back then. I see it in their eyes. They are embracing the importance of their callings."

Mike placed his arm around Mary's shoulders. "Your little brother?"

"My little brother."

Mike said, "The thought of that makes me feel older."

"You are older," Mary giggled at the reference.

"Not too old to pull some people out of Gitmo without incident." Mike regained his confidence.

Mary retorted, "I thought Lucas did most of the heavy lifting on that operation."

"Lucas is a monster. He's one of the strongest people I've ever met. Noah was shooting behind Lucas as they were both heading to the helicopter on Gitmo. He yelled at Noah and told him to move the gun away from his right ear. His ear is still ringing from the blasts." Mike began laughing.

"I'm glad you made it back to us safely, our children depend on it."

Mike became serious, "I know. Leaving becomes harder and harder. I'm glad I retired from the Marines and Special Operations. You know that Matt will want revenge for Sesom's death."

"I know. He will need everyone of us involved to pull that mission off."

Mary asked, "Can this be your last mission?"

"Let's hope. If we are successful, it will be the last mission for a while. We won't be able to return to our lives back in Jersey though. Even though I don't understand the particulars of what's unfolding, Samil appears to be capitalizing on instability around the world. Stabilizing the United States will be a priority of the Disciples moving forward. The way the US goes so does the rest of the world. Matt will need to step up as the leader of the Disciples. The Colonist party will get involved in the next couple of weeks. They've already provided Crevan an ultimatum to restructure the government or step down. Matters will get very messy in the near term. Matt is the perfect leader based on his service and involvement with special operations. The only way to overthrow the government is through military leadership."

"How can you coordinate a coup?"

"We'll need General Gilmore. I also understand that Colonel Lash is looking for Matt. We will need to start with people we've served with in the armed forces that will listen. President Crevan doesn't hold up well in a popularity contest. His ruthless style of military leadership and politics is well known throughout Washington. I don't believe President Palmer was a big fan of Crevan before the election. He needed Crevan on the ticket to carry the northeast. Who would have known that Crevan would turn on his own administration?"

The couple continued to walk along the beach. At several points along their walk, they noticed sections of the beach were closed due to minefields. When Argentina elected to invade the Falkland Islands in 1982, they set up minefields along the beaches in anticipation of an amphibious landing by the United Kingdom. The conflict lasted a little over 70 days and was won by the

British army. Mike and Mary also noticed artifacts from World War II. They were both surprised that such a small island with limited resources could be involved in the major conflicts of World War's I and II.

****

The Israeli Defense sailors were enjoying an afternoon lunch together. Phil came into the kitchen and poured himself a cup of coffee.

"Gentlemen, I have some papers for you."

The group of sailors became quiet for the announcement. Papers in the military could mean several different things. The papers could signify the end of an assignment, the beginning of another, discharge, promotion, and a whole host of other possibilities. The IDF sailors enjoyed sailing on the Excalibur and the relaxed style of Captain Phil.

"Pack your bags for a couple of weeks and return to your families. We've made arrangements for you guys to return home by way of the Royal Air Force this afternoon. You'll catch a commercial flight in London to Tel Aviv."

The men smiled and began to high five each other. Even though they hadn't been gone long, any chance to return home was met with anticipation and delight.

One of the men spoke up, "Thank you Captain, when would you like us to return?"

"Amen will handle details of your return. In fact, he'll meet up with you at the airport. We're putting a boat in the water so you can travel to the dock in Gypsy Cove. Tie off the boat once you're there so Amen, Cering, Kimi, Talan, and Dorje can return to the ship. From there, a couple of vans will transport you to the airport. The Excalibur will remain in the cove until we can determine a course of action."

Another sailor spoke up, "Hey Cap, sorry to hear about

your friend in Los Angeles."

"Thanks Gabe," Phil paused for a moment as he thought about the years he spent with Sesom.

****

The sailors made their way off the island and the group of Disciples returned to the Excalibur. Amen called a meeting with everyone on the ship before dinner. They needed to regroup; they needed to recharge their batteries.

Matt was walking the bow of the ship with Mike and Mary. The kids were a few decks below in the pool with Kimi and Cering. Kimi needed to take her mind off what happened in Los Angeles. Even though Sesom's death wasn't her fault, she was having a hard time separating herself from what happened.

Matt stopped, "So let me get this straight. We lose a Sesom and pick up a Sallah?"

Mary interjected, "The Lord works in mysterious ways."

Mike said, "I'm surprised you never worked with him in the past. He has great knowledge of the Middle East and CIA operations. Sallah was very embedded in what was happening in Pakistan during Operation Neptune Spear to kill Osama Bin Laden. Sallah exposed several terror plots coming out of the region over the past several years. I'm surprised he didn't get ripped apart at Gitmo, the CIA was probably counting on the prisoners wiping him out."

Matt looked at the landscape surrounding the ship, "After speaking with him, he's a pretty likeable guy. Kinda goofy though."

Mike began laughing, "He always reminded me of that Russian astronaut in the movie Armageddon."

Matt did his best impersonation of the Russian, "Components. American components, Russian components, all made in Taiwan!"

Mary smiled, "Oh brother. Must you guys rely on movie quotes and relate them to your testosterone overloaded lives?"

"Was that a question?"

Matt replied, "I think so, I don't believe that was a statement."

"Could have been a statement."

"Yeah, I guess it could have. Regardless, the answer is always."

Both Mike and Mary smiled at Matt. They were happy to spend time with him, regardless of circumstances. The discussion became more serious.

Mike took a seat near the rail, "Mary said that you and Elisabeth want to get married on the island."

Matt would have rather stuck with movie quotes, "Tying the knot is important to Elisabeth."

"What about you?"

Mary and Matt sat down next to Mike. Mary held her brother's hand as he asked, "What do you think of Elisabeth?"

Mary responded, "I really like her. Your experiences are somewhat similar, even though your heritage is completely different. She has a great foundation as a person, there is a reason she was chosen by the angels."

Mike added, "She's kinda hot too."

Mary hit her husband in the arm and said, "Looks will get you so far, just take your brother-in-law for instance," Mary winked at her husband, "I knew Mike was the perfect father for our children after a few dates with him. Regardless of his looks, I knew that he was a great person for me and our future family."

Matt replied, "That's pretty heavy."

His sister explained, "What you're involved in right now is pretty heavy Matt. We've left our homes, I've been kidnapped, we met with Pope Simplicius, and you found out that Elisabeth would offer something to this world we can't comprehend. Doesn't get more heavy than that."

"Your sister is right. Elisabeth is estranged from her family based on unfortunate assumptions her parents made. Even though I'm not a biblical scholar, sounds similar to what Joseph and Mary must have experienced when they brought Jesus into this hostile world, in a barn nonetheless. None of the inns would take them in. You and Elisabeth have had to endure some tough family circumstances to prepare you for this calling. The Disciples have committed to seeing your visions through, even if the mission means giving up their own lives. I can't put all of the pieces together, but the calling is reminiscent of several stories told in the Bible."

Matt looked at his sister, "I've been having dreams about mom and dad."

Mary looked surprised, "Really?"

"Yes. They are so vivid and connected. Almost like I'm stepping into another world and meeting with them."

Mary said, "After their deaths, I began to pray every day for strength, understanding, and forgiveness. After a few months, mom began appearing to me when issues got complicated and difficult. I didn't know where else to turn or whom to trust, so I began praying. When dad appeared, he was so real and practical in the conversations I almost believed he was alive again. In many respects, they guided me through that tough period at the University of Colorado. I worked hard to keep us together in the house."

Matt asked, "Do they still appear in your dreams?"

Mary replied, "Not since Mike and I had Rebecca. For whatever reason, mom appeared to me and was insistent on the name. The entire dream was bizarre. I was very pregnant running the incline in Colorado Springs. Mom and I were running together discussing my pregnancy. Out of the blue mom told me to name our daughter Rebecca. At the time, Mike and I didn't know the sex of our child. He was spending a lot of time at the pizzeria and we hadn't scheduled an appointment for an ultrasound. When we finally did, the technician asked us if we wanted to know the sex. Of course we did and she said the baby was a very healthy girl. I have no idea why, but I said 'Rebecca' after the tech mentioned we were having a girl. Mike looked at me and said, 'What a beautiful name,' and the rest is history."

Mike agreed, "I remember that. I miss Maria's too."

Matt asked, "How is the pizzeria doing?"

"I don't know. I cut off all communication with Pat for their safety. I told him to move into the house, manage the pizzeria, and not contact me. That was several weeks ago. I'm sure he's doing fine. He can have the house and the restaurant. I doubt we'll be returning anyway."

Mary was curious, "What about your dreams Matt?"

"I've had several. Mom and dad ask how you and the kids are doing. When dad appeared, he apologized for being away so much when we were younger. He said that they didn't suffer in the crash at the Pentagon. They seem to know about Elisabeth and our destiny with the Disciples. I tried to pry more information from dad, but he just smiled and said that I needed to figure things out on my own."

Mary laughed, "Boy, that sounds familiar."

"Doesn't it. I still feel like a little boy when I think of dad or he appears in one of my dreams. Wish we could have shared some time together as grown ups. I've had some bizarre dreams as well. I really need to begin documenting them again. I haven't chronicled anything since I left Los Angeles. I almost forgot that Samil has my journal."

Mike interjected, "They've obviously poured over your thoughts. The details from your journal led them to the Western Wall, unless somebody tipped them off."

"You know how the intelligence world works. Most of the time it lacks meaningful intelligence."

Mary had to keep the men on point, "What bizarre dreams have you experienced?"

"One involved Elisabeth's aborted daughter. She was playing with a bunch of children in the plaza of the Western Wall. Mom pointed her out to me. She was around the age of 7 and I later found out her name is Lisa."

Mike couldn't help himself, "That's weird."

"You're telling me." Matt considered what he just recounted to his brother and sister.

Matt continued, "Lisa appeared to me in another dream. We had a conversation much like we're sharing right now. She sat down next to me on some steps and began to tell me about how she had played with a girl named Hiatt. I was a little stunned that she knew my last name and that she'd played with a girl that shared my name. Lisa went on to say that the girl named Hiatt is my daughter and she's waiting for me."

Mary said, "Where is she waiting?"

"According to Lisa, in the place that children stay before they are born, or where they go when their lives have ended prematurely. I guess? My unborn daughter also has a name."

Mary got excited, "And what's her name?"

"Ariel."

Mary smiled, "Ariel is a beautiful name."

Matt had done his homework, "I did some research on the name. The literal meaning is lion of God and often referred to when speaking of Jerusalem. Mike will find this funny, but it is also the twelfth and brightest moon of the planet Uranus."

Mike looked confused, "Myanus?"

"No. Uranus."

Mike was unrelenting, "Mary's anus?"

"Why did I bother telling you that? That's gross and you're referring to my sister. Do we need to go down below so I can teach you some manners?" Matt backed up and did some Wushu moves before reaching out his right hand to invite Mike to a fight.

"Yes, you are the one little brother," Mike did his best character impersonation, "*Mr. Anderson.*"

"You guys and your movies." Mary was amused and embarrassed by the sophomoric behavior of the two grown men.

Mary asked, "Have you shared this with Elisabeth?"

"Yes. Obviously, discussing anything with regard to her aborted child evokes several different emotions."

Mary clarified, "I was referring more to the name of the child she will carry for you?"

Matt said, "Yes, we've discussed Ariel as well."

Before Matt finished his sentence, Sallah came busting out of a nearby door.

"Mookie, is this your family? I can't believe it. You must be Mrs. Barnes?"

Mary offered up her hand, "And you must be Sallah?"

Sallah looked at her funny while kissing her right hand, "You know who I am? Mike has shared information about me with you? I am honored."

Mary began giggling, "Me too."

"And you must be Matthew," Sallah hugged him and put his head on Matt's left shoulder. Matt didn't know how to handle the hug and let Sallah relish in the moment. Sallah rose up his head and squeezed Matt's shoulders.

"Your brother saved me from that awful island. I had no

business there. I began asking questions about American intelligence in Turkey and the CIA arrested me and labeled me a 'terrorist'. I was sent off to Cuba and detained with the very people I'd helped your government capture. I'm lucky to be alive!"

Matt said, "We're lucky to have you. Mike tells me you're familiar with Middle Eastern tribes and policy makers."

Sallah looked at Matt and waved his finger at himself, "You tell me what you need and I'll get it. If you need to meet someone in the region, I can arrange that. I'm familiar with most of the tribal leaders and how they function. My family has traded with major cities in the region for hundreds of years. We broker sugar cane sales in the territory, which provides a great cover for CIA work."

Matt was confused, "If you were a successful salesman with a family owned business in the Middle East, why would you want to bother with the CIA."

Sallah tilted his head and smiled as he continued to squeeze Matt's shoulders for emotional emphasis. "I wanted a life of action and adventure, much like your movie stars Dirty Harry and Indiana Jones. I don't like sales anyway. My family has plenty of money; I just wanted to become a spy and work for the United States' government. More for the thrill than anything else."

Matt asked, "And your family was okay with that decision?"

Sallah put his hands together, "They don't know. I was using the sugar sales position as cover for covert operations. My family was disappointed when I was transferred to Gitmo, but they don't know the circumstances surrounding my transfer and involvement with the CIA."

Matt laughed and put his right hand on Sallah's left shoulder, "Well played."

Mike interrupted, "Sallah was an important operative for several of our missions in Afghanistan, Pakistan, Iran, Syria, and Libya."

Sallah got excited, "I signed up to ride motorcycles and set bombs on vehicles transporting Iranian nuclear scientists. I was also involved with a major viral attack on Iranian computer mainframes at nuclear facilities. That mission was impossible, much like your movies with Ethan Hunt. I had to infect a laptop for a scientist working for all of the underground nuclear facilities, that don't exist of course. When he updated the software for mainframes at the reactors, they all shut down simultaneously. The program was brilliant and developed by software engineers with the Israeli Defense Force. I'm not surprised the countries originally went to war. Very nasty over there right now; many people dying."

Matt looked out over the rail, "Some of ours have died as well. Aren't you concerned about retaliation against you and your family?"

"A little, but that's the life we live in some countries of the Middle East. My family is well known in the sugar business and they will publicly disown me, much like Osama Bin Laden's family did to him. We will still see each other and stay in touch. That's the way the game works. America and other western countries focus on the financial gain from their influence in the region long term, even though most of the countries are broke when considering their governments. Western Asia and the Middle East fight more about land and religious disciplines. The struggle is more religious than financial, and people will fight harder for their religion than money in our territory. That's why attempts to westernize Saudi Arabia and the United Arab Emirates have been met with harsh criticism from traditional Muslim counties. Very complicated."

Mary agreed, "Sounds like it. Do you have a wife or children?"

"No. If I was exposed during an operation, that would put a wife and children at great risk. They would most certainly be killed. I couldn't allow that to happen." Sallah shook his head.

Sallah said, "I heard about Sesom. He was well known in northwest Africa and Morocco. Islamic ministers in the region were recruiting him to become an Imam after his involvement with the South African National Defense Force. Sesom led several missions to return territories to the government that had been overrun by coups guided by religious leaders."

Matt asked, "So why didn't Sesom become an Imam?"

"He was too moderate. Sesom was a friend to Christians and Jews as well. He didn't believe that any one religion was superior to the ideas of another. Eventually, a few people were called to Sesom and began to follow him. That's about the time I was detained by the CIA and shipped off to Gitmo. You were called to follow Sesom as well?"

Matt replied, "No. Sesom found me."

Sallah got excited, "That's a great honor. Many people believed that Sesom was involved with some significant religious event. A few thought he might be involved with the return of our God in the very near future."

Mike, Mary, and Matt looked at each other. Each of them had come to know Sesom personally and what he represented to the group. The Disciples knew that Sesom wouldn't lead them forever, but they had no idea he would be killed at such a crucial point in their journey together. President Crevan had survived the ambush, albeit injured and shaken by a highly tactical strike against his motorcade. The Colonist party had warned Crevan and his leadership about future terrorist attacks on the homeland. The clock was ticking down to a possible confrontation between Americans with different ideologies. The talking points had gone nowhere and several citizens of the United States were ready to take action, violent action to protect a few pages that outlined life, liberty, and the pursuit of happiness developed in 1787.

Matt was done with the heavy conversation and stretched out his right hand to Sallah, "We're glad to have you, you may want to join us for a meeting before dinner. You'll have an opportunity to meet everyone and understand what we're trying to accomplish."

Sallah was serious, "I would be honored. Is that okay with you Mookie?"

"Absolutely. We need all the help we can get at this point."

Sallah went to the rail and exclaimed in Arabic, "Allahu Akbar." Sallah yelled so loud that several seabirds on the ship took flight. He was happy to be part of such a diverse group of highly trained operatives. In Sallah's mind, he was living the life of John McClane or Dirty Harry. Like many Arabic people the west had counted on in the past, Sallah was trustworthy and loyal to a fault.

****

Phil, John, Aaron, *Matt*, Elisabeth, Mike, Mary and the kids, Sallah, Jonas, Noah, *Amen*, *Cering*, *Kimi*, *Dorje*, *Li*, *Lucas*, *Ethan*, and *Talan* convened below deck in the gym of the Excalibur. There was no presentation or props for the meeting as Amen called for everyone's attention. Amen wanted an open forum so the group could discuss how they wanted to proceed. Introductions were first.

Amen gave instructions, "Mike, please tell us about your friend."

Mike stood up, "Sallah and I worked together on several missions in the Middle East. He is well connected and his family owns a company that focuses on sugar distribution. Oddly enough, Cering has worked with Sallah's parents and traded with them throughout the region. Sallah used his cover as a sales agent for the family owned business to work with the CIA. The business, his parents, and friends had no idea that he was participating with CIA operatives. Crevan and Watt shipped Sallah off to Gitmo when he began to question the motives of CIA operatives in Turkey. Based on information we learned at the Vatican, the CIA operatives were recruiting terrorists to carry out the dirty bomb attacks in Miami, New York, Los Angeles, and Concord. Those attacks killed POTUS, have shaken financial markets, and started another world war. Sallah is a good man with good intentions. He is also very well trained by the CIA."

Amen welcomed Sallah, "Any friend of Mike is a friend of ours. You are welcome to stay as long as you wish. We will take all the help we can get."

Sallah could hardly contain his excitement, "My lifelong dream has been to work with intelligence agencies and save the world. I couldn't be in a better place right now. I will help you until I breathe my last breath."

"Thank you Sallah. We look forward to working with you. Matt, would you mind introducing your friend to us?"

Noah was still pretty shaken from the Gitmo experience. Cering had acquired one of the finest wheelchairs she could find for the former Senior Programmer at Delta Defense. Noah had access to every level of the ship with the assistance of a couple of freight elevators. Because Noah and Captain Phil shared similar interests, they had started a friendship on the ship by discussing maritime law while sharing coffee together. The men were "Deadheads" and enjoyed discussing the albums and live shows of Jerry Garcia. Day-by-day Noah was becoming more comfortable with the passengers and crew of the Excalibur.

Matt stood up and walked over to Noah, "This is my good friend Noah. He has saved my life on more than one occasion. I owe a debt of gratitude to Mike, Lucas, and Jonas for helping him escape the confines of Gitmo. Once we are successful with our mission of removing POTUS from the White House, I will pay a personal visit to the men who tortured my friend. Noah and I worked together at Delta Defense for a couple years. He also sent the shoulder harness weapon to Cering's warehouse in Jerusalem. The weapon helped save Mary from Samil and return us safely to the Israeli border." People familiar with the story began laughing and Matt corrected himself. "Okay, I see. The weapon definitely helped Elisabeth and Mary return safely."

Mike began laughing and interrupted his brother, "Elisabeth, his hard head may be the most redeeming quality." The group began laughing as Matt pointed to the boxing ring set up nearby. He placed two fingers up to his eyes and pointed at Mike. A sense of humor was paramount to dealing with tragedy.

Matt continued, "Noah may have been the most intelligent programmer working for the military. I'm not sure how Delta Defense will survive without his technical ability. Noah served in the United States' Navy during his younger years and became a disabled veteran while serving on a Los Angeles class nuclear submarine. After he was discharged from the Navy, he was hired by Delta Defense to develop and test high tech weaponry. I was able to test much of the weaponry while deployed on worldwide Special Op's missions. Much like Sallah, Noah is a good man and I'm happy he's with us. Talan will really benefit from Noah's computer knowledge and experience."

Matt sat down and Mike gave him the thumb's up. Sallah brought a notepad to the meeting and was ready to take instructions from Amen. Most of the Disciples were worn out and ready for rest, Sallah was keyed up and ready to start the next mission.

Amen became serious, "The mission in Los Angeles came close to succeeding. We proved that the President of the United States is vulnerable and that we can infiltrate his security detail. Sesom took a risk and paid with his life."

Amen paused and began walking around the gym. "After the deaths of Liam and Trevor, Sesom knew that his days might be numbered with us. That's why he spent time training us, teaching us, coaching us, and developing us. Not only would Sesom have wanted us to move on, he would have wanted us to move on as a stronger unit. With that said, we need someone to lead this group."

Dorje looked confused, "I thought you were leading us?"

Amen continued, "We will not make assumptions in the absence of Sesom. We must work this out as a unit. The remaining Disciples will make a decision on who leads us."

Kimi was still angry with herself, "If I would have noticed the helicopter pilot to the east, Sesom would still be here with us."

Talan defended Kimi, "Sesom knew the risks. We warned him to evacuate the area. Like Amen said, he made the decision to go face-to-face with Crevan."

Li asked, "What would Sesom have wanted?"

Lucas answered, "He would have wanted what's best for us. What's best for this group."

Ethan retorted, "So what's best for the group?"

Amen responded, "Ethan, you know that answers weren't quite that simple with Sesom."

Matt didn't say a word. He was the newest member of the Disciples and had the least amount of experience with the group. In Matt's mind, he believed Amen would be a great leader for the Disciples. He had successfully recovered his cat, guaranteed safe passage of his family to Japan, and was tough as nails. When Matt first encountered Amen at Carlita's Cafe, he was impressed with his quick reflexes and resolve. Matt baited Amen when he threw a punch at his face, but Amen caught his fist and returned it with a smile.

Ethan was also quite capable of leading the group. Even though Matt didn't like him at first, he had shown great leadership at the Western Wall and killed Seth with his bare hands. Matt and Ethan trained together on the voyage from Rome to the Falkland Islands. Ethan was a skeptic by nature and challenged popular beliefs, but once he trusted another person, his loyalty was unwavering. Ethan and Trevor had become close Disciples in the beginning. When Seth approached the Disciples, Trevor didn't trust him and shared his concerns with Ethan and Sesom. After Seth betrayed the group and killed Trevor, Ethan became angry with Sesom and challenged his judgment. Sesom embraced the challenge and worked through the issues with Ethan.

Cering and Kimi had leadership qualities as well. They knew how to fight, use weapons, take charge, and more importantly, show compassion. Cering and Kimi had been wonderful travelers on the Excalibur and taken care of John and Rebecca on several occasions. On one hand, they could fight Samil hand-to-hand; and on the other, they could be playful and gentle with young children. By all appearances, nobody could tell that Cering and Kimi were mercenaries that would stop at nothing. Having a woman lead the group might be a good idea.

In Matt's mind, Lucas, Talan, Li, and Dorje were better followers. They took pride in executing plans and following orders. After years in the military, Matt knew that well-trained followers were just as important as great leaders. Leaders only became great when they had disciplined followers. Jesus Christ was able to change every corner of the earth through his twelve followers, even with one betraying him. After Jesus' death, most of his Disciples were martyred because of their faith and teachings. Even though Matt lacked knowledge of the Bible, he respected the leadership of Jesus and how he changed the world for the better.

Dorje looked at Matt, "What you think?"

"I think that several of you are capable of leading this group."

Dorje pointed at Matt, "What about you?"

Matt replied, "I'm honored Dorje, but I've only been with the Disciples for a few months; a few unforgettable months. I doubt Sesom ever saw me leading this group."

Amen responded, "How can you be so sure Matt?"

Matt was confused, "What do you mean?"

"Ten of us found Sesom. You were the only Disciple Sesom set out to find. He knew that you were military and from the City of Angels. Sesom's visions became more lucid as we approached Los Angeles. He knew that your name was a combination of the 8th Disciple of Jesus and heaven. Sesom also figured out that the combination of your first and last names closely resembled Matthias, the 12th Disciple of Jesus who replaced Judas Iscariot. Your name became more significant after Seth betrayed us. You are the Omega Matt. Sesom was the Alpha of this group and you are the Omega."

Matt countered, "Doesn't that mean I'm the last in line, the end of the alphabet?"

Talan stood up and took over for Amen, "Omega means much more Matt. From the Christian Bible and Revelation, there is a passage that states that God is the first and the last, the beginning and the end. The Alpha period of our group has ended and Sesom took us so far. Maybe this group and the world are entering our period of Omega."

Mike added, "I was very suspicious when I received the phone call from Matt a few months back. I'm not a religious guy and I'm always a little suspicious of people who claim they know God and his wishes. My wife is one of the most spiritual people I know." Mary held

Rebecca as she placed her left hand on Mike's thigh. Little John had become bored with the meeting and was punching a heavy bag in the corner.

He continued, "The events at the Western Wall were a turning point for me. Samil's decision to bomb innocent civilians in the plaza during Rosh Hashanah was gutless and provocative. Lucas and I wish we could have traveled to Los Angeles to assist with the POTUS mission, but we're pleased to have Jonas, Noah, and Sallah with our group. While we may have lost Sesom, through no fault of yours Kimi, we've added three more to our group. We also have the attention of General Gilmore and Colonel Lash. Thomas Sawyer is ready to restructure Washington through diplomacy or force; he has significant numbers supporting him through militias and Tea Party followers. For the most part, the Colonist party believes that Washington will only be changed by force."

Amen agreed, "Not much different than what we believe."

Mike concluded, "Matt, as Amen said, this may be your time to lead. You have the skills, the determination, and support to make your visions a reality. Obviously, through divine intervention or strange inexplicable coincidences, you're being called to usher in a period of Biblical proportions. I have no idea if we'll survive the events, or if they will even come to pass, but you have my support." Mike could feel a punch on his thigh, "And your sister's."

****

Morgan and Sawyer elected to meet at a waterfront restaurant and crab house in Annapolis. Home to the Naval Academy and some of the best blue crab on the east coast, the men were happy to meet up in Maryland to escape the confines of Washington. When considering politics, most everything and everyone had become phony in Washington. Between relentless lobbyists and unending scandals, the city was bought and paid for a hundred times over. In most cases, the constituency was the farthest thing from a legislator's mind, when he showed evidence of one. Morgan was a moderate and believed in the power and simplicity of the US Constitution. In years past, much debate and blood had been spilled over the Bill of Rights and subsequent Amendments to the Constitution. Rethinking the political wheel wasn't an option for Morgan; the foundation had been laid by the founding fathers and should be followed with less restriction.

In many respects, Sawyer felt the same way. The Constitution had become convoluted and diluted with way too many laws and government regulations. Sawdog also believed that Washington politics had very little to do with the masses, and more to do with individual greed and back scratching. The Colonist party had reached the breaking point. They felt as if their Congressional leaders were doing nothing to move the country forward and improve the American condition. Endless wars, unemployment, wasteful spending, and poor leadership had left the country in shambles. Many families had moved to the streets because they couldn't find work or afford shelter. The private sector was doing its best to feed and clothe children, but the numbers were too staggering to overcome for the children in poverty. The United States had learned an important lesson, which was that entitlement monies would eventually dry up over time with less and less people paying into an inefficient system. President Palmer had begun to work on raising tax revenues through more corporate revenues in America. He had also cut funding for several entitlement programs, which wasn't popular but necessary. Much like Abraham Lincoln, Palmer was opposed to corporations rewriting laws through lobbyists to protect their own interests. Palmer knew the American worker was the key to a successful Republic. Sawyer and Morgan shared more in common than not.

Morgan brought up the topic, "Is there any way that the Colonist party will consider a peaceful option?"

Sawyer responded, "Is there any way that everyone in the House will resign along with your President?"

Morgan took a bite of crab, "He is still our President, is he not?"

Sawyer rolled up his sleeves and dug into the plate of crab, "Whether we want to split hairs about this three weeks from today or right now, I don't consider Crevan to be the President of these divided states. His actions have always been suspicious, especially during his envoys to the Middle East."

"I can't say that I disagree with your assessment. As Speaker of the House, he asked me to sign on as Vice President during his interim government. I would say that Secretary of State Watt has a better relationship and audience with President Crevan than I do. We haven't necessarily agreed on much policy over the years."

Sawyer was curious about the assassination attempt. "The rumors coming out of the State Department are interesting right now. Two of our own have joined a group of international 'Disciples' to take out the President?"

"We are still gathering intelligence from what happened in Los Angeles; looks like a joint operation of some sort. Regardless, the group was very well trained and fortified. We have very few traces of who was involved."

Sawyer pressed, "What about the two Marines from Special Operations?"

"Matt Hiatt and Michael Barnes left the country a few months ago. We have surveillance of their involvement at the Western Wall and intelligence indicating they may have crossed into Gaza around the same time."

"Gaza? Why Gaza?"

"We don't know. The CIA detained one of Hiatt's coworkers from Delta Defense in Los Angeles shortly after the Western Wall explosions. The coworker provided a specialized weapon to Major Hiatt that was utilized in a recon mission south of the Israeli border."

"And what became of this coworker?"

Morgan paused for a moment, "He was transferred to Gitmo and interrogated."

Sawyer shook his head, "Oh, this just keeps getting better. Anything else you want to share with me about our own citizens being detained as war criminals without due process?"

Morgan picked up his cup of coffee and paused again, "You and I share a level of confidence and trust with each other. I don't anticipate that you will share details of our conversation with anyone."

"Oh spare me Morgan, you and I go way back. We could have buried each other long along, but we chose the high road. That is my only path with our conversations."

"Gitmo was breached a few days back. We believe Lieutenant Colonel Michael Barnes may have been involved with the release of three prisoners from the camp. During the operation, Noah Webster, Jonas Andros, and Sallah Salaam escaped from the facility. They were able to work in connection with the Cuban Air Force and Revolutionary Armed Forces to pull off the mission. Obviously, on Crevan's orders, the entire breach will remain classified."

Sawyer asked, "Why does the name Jonas Andros sound familiar?"

Morgan clarified, "Andros is in charge of security detail for the Pope. He's served with the Swiss Army for years."

"Why would Jonas Andros be detained at Gitmo? Why would Lieutenant Colonel Michael Barnes be rescuing the Commander of the Swiss Army from Gitmo? Why is the Executive Branch making unilateral decisions in private?"

Morgan said, "Jonas was detained after his visit to Washington to meet with Crevan on the Pope's behalf. Crevan and Watt had intelligence showing that Jonas traveled to Tel Aviv and met with the Disciples after the attack at the Western Wall. The Disciples then traveled to the Vatican after the war started and met with Pope Simplicius II. Because of the circumstances and subsequent implications surrounding Andros, Crevan believed that he was justified in sending him to Gitmo for war crimes against the United States."

"I'm sure the Pope is quite pleased that we sent his Commander to Gitmo based on limited intelligence. The whole thing reeks Morgan."

Morgan was quick to respond, "You know how I feel about Executive Powers and Orders. We are certain that Jonas met with the Disciples, but we have little knowledge of what his involvement is with the group."

Sawyer pressed, "And the body dumped in the Pacific Ocean?"

"The man buried at sea was Sesom Ishmael. As far as we know, he was leading this group of self-proclaimed Disciples. Several of them traveled to Morocco and other parts of the world to follow his leadership."

Sawyer was confused, "For what? To assassinate the President of the United States?"

"We don't believe so, but we're not sure either. This group seems more complicated than that. As far as we know, they have no connections with any terrorist organizations in the world. Based on the reports of people we've interviewed in Morocco, Israel, and Brazil, the group's calling transcends geopolitical power or financial gain. We don't have a clear idea of what they intend to do, or why."

"Any ideas on where the Disciples are right now?"

Morgan shook his head, "No. They have plenty of financial support and resources at their fingertips too. We have reason to believe the Israeli Defense Force is supporting their efforts."

Sawyer looked perplexed, "The IDF. Why would they be involved with this group?"

Morgan smiled, "As I said earlier, their motivation transcends geopolitical power or financial gain. You've been to Jerusalem. Many people worldwide believe that the end times are upon us. The Disciples have recently been to the Western Wall and Vatican. Feel free to draw your own conclusions."

Sawyer was incredulous, "What you're suggesting is nothing more than fairy dust and tall tales for many others. The people of God and atheists have rivaled the legislature in their division and gobbledygook for the past several decades. I shall reserve my conclusions for a future date, when we both have better intelligence."

Morgan had become more confident that Sawyer would open up about details within the Colonist party. "In three weeks, what does the Colonist party intend to do?"

"Demand the resignation of the President and the House of Representatives. The Colonist party would also like to see one union of our states, dissolution of Cabinets, and more states' rights. You've read our plan and understand its details. The Federal government will become much smaller in size and scope."

Morgan asked, "And the timeframe?"

"Two weeks. After two weeks, we will call up militias and move to forcefully extract the President and House of Representatives in a coup."

Morgan stated the obvious, "And what about me, Sawdog?"

"The Colonist party has no qualms with you and your interpretation of the Constitution. We would ask that you continue to serve as Vice President for the interim government. After the coup, the people of the United States would need to pick a President and Vice President from the Colonist party. There would be no more two party systems for the Senate in their next election cycle. Anyone wanting to run for the legislature would do so in the Colonist party. In the words of John Adams, 'There is nothing which I dread so much as a division of the republic into two great parties, each arranged under its leader, and concerting measures in opposition to each other. This, in my humble apprehension, is to be dreaded as the greatest political evil under our Constitution.'"

"And the states?"

"We don't care what the states do. If they wish to remain divided under a failed two-party system, they may. However, if the representatives wish to run for the US Senate or Presidency, they will do so in the Colonist party. The Colonist party will hold the President accountable to uphold the Constitution of the United States, and party affiliation will become a moot point. Our goal is to unify the country under one banner that is neither red nor blue, but red, white, and blue."

****

Give thanks to the LORD, for he is good; his love endures forever.

1 Chronicles 16:34

Elisabeth was looking out over Gypsy Cove. Mary, Cering, and Kimi were standing beside her dressed in silver gowns and holding bouquets of white lilies. Elisabeth was wearing a gold gown and tiara formed from olive branches.

Cering smiled, "You look so beautiful, just like a princess."

Kimi agreed, "The gown is perfect and your hair is flowing. Matt is a lucky man."

Mary added, "I'm blessed to call you my sister. You and my brother are perfect for each other. I'm relieved to have someone else help me tone down the testosterone in the family."

Elisabeth moved a curl away from her left eye, "I am a lucky woman as well, lucky to be with a great group of people. Thank you for everything you've done for me."

The women hugged each other and Elisabeth asked, "How can I ever repay you for the sacrifices you've made?"

Kimi patted Elisabeth on her lower stomach, "What you intend to do will be more than sufficient. By the way, Aunt Mary, Aunt Cering, and Auntie Kimi have a nice ring to them."

The women laughed as the men readied themselves for the ceremony. Jonas had spoken with Pope Simplicius and asked for the Holy Father's permission and blessings to perform a wedding for Matt and Elisabeth. The Pope was excited about their union and accommodated Jonas's request. Pope Simplicius texted a prayer that he wanted Jonas to say during the ceremony.

All of the men were wearing blue. Aside from being Sesom's favorite color, he believed the Disciples were called to unify heaven and earth. Aaron, Captain Phil's deckhand, finger picked Canon D and other wedding songs on a guitar. Instead of standing on Matt or Elisabeth's sides, the men formed a partial circle that would be filled when Jonas, Elisabeth, Mary, Cering, and Kimi joined them. Jonas approached the group of women.

"The men are waiting, just over the knoll. May I escort you?"

"You may," Elisabeth could feel the butterflies taking flight in her stomach.

"Remember, we will complete the circle once we arrive. Matt will be on my right and you will be on my left. Mike and Mary have wedding rings for the ceremony."

Elisabeth smiled and hugged Cering, "Thank you so much."

"Even though we've been a bit distracted, the rings are too important to overlook for your wedding. All of us pitched in when we visited the Vatican. The rings were blessed by Simplicius and have special meanings. Jonas will share the story of the rings during your ceremony."

Elisabeth began to tear up, "When did you have time for the rings?"

Kimi smiled and provided the answer, "When you, Matt,

and Sesom met with Pope Simplicius in his quarters for coffee."

Elisabeth said, "So you knew all along?"

Mary countered, "We had an idea. Once we found you at the Western Wall, Matt's dreams became a little more than a fairy tale for me."

Elisabeth shared a long embrace with Mary. She considered the miracle of Matt finding her based on visions he'd chronicled in a journal for almost a year. Many people in the world had given up on the idea of dreams and miracles. They failed to see the beauty of a flower, the engineering of an ant farm, and the transformation of a caterpillar to a beautiful butterfly. The secular world had dismissed such miracles as a byproduct of chance and evolution. Samil had capitalized on declining interest in a higher power and religion worldwide. The United States had tossed God and prayer out of schools and public places, and most young people had never stepped foot in Sunday School or seen the inside of a chapel. Evil had been organizing for years through social media and secret societies. Through recruiting efforts and endless financing, Samil created a worldwide power that infiltrated just about every aspect of humanity. There was nothing more damaging to a society than a majority of people that believed in hope and change, and had little idea of how to produce either one.

Jonas took Elisabeth's hand and walked with her along the path. Mary, Kimi, and Cering followed behind them single file. Celebrating a wedding was something new for the Disciples. Kimi and Cering had been busy with their careers in Japan and Egypt before being called to Sesom. Even though the women attended a few weddings as young ladies, they'd never participated as bridesmaids or given much attention to what was said by a pastor. The women were trained killers and mercenaries, but they enjoyed any opportunity to spend time with children and people they loved.

As Jonas and the women came over a small ridge, the men took notice. Elisabeth, Mary, Cering, and Kimi looked beautiful. The sun reflected off the gold and silver dresses and the women appeared radiant. There was a light breeze that flirted with the women's hair. Matt couldn't believe his eyes. Elisabeth was biting her lower left lip and looked nervous. She exuded an innocence that Matt had never witnessed before. Elisabeth's appearance reminded him of the dream he had when she was standing in a rivulet near a stream, which reinforced his feelings for her and their destiny together. Mike held Rebecca as John stood on his right side. Little John was dressed up for his uncle's ceremony.

Jonas walked up to Matt and took his left hand. He welcomed the Disciples, Mike, John, Sallah, Phil and his shipmates. Matt and Elisabeth wanted a late afternoon ceremony so they could see the sun dip into the South Atlantic Ocean. The sunsets were beautiful as the Atlantic swallowed up the sun until the earth rotated enough for her to rise again on the other side of the coast. Jonas called upon the Lord Jesus Christ to be with the group as they held hands in prayer. Jonas talked about the book of Revelation and how John experienced several visions about the 2nd Coming of the Messiah. How the world would lose its way and turn away from God over a period of years. Then Jonas shared an interesting Native American prayer that Pope Simplicius sent for the ceremony:

O Great Spirit, whose breath gives life to the world,
and whose voice is heard in the soft breeze.
We need your strength and wisdom.
Cause us to walk in beauty.

Give us eyes ever to behold the red and purple sunset.
Make us wise so that we may understand what you have
taught us.
Help us learn the lessons you have hidden in every leaf
and rock.
Make us always ready to come to you with clean hands
and steady eyes, so when life fades, like the fading
sunset, our spirits may come to you without shame.

Jonas then spoke of Sesom, "A man of great knowledge
and spirit has gone before us. From what I knew of
Sesom through his actions and stories recalled by
friends, he was a man of God. He died committed to
what he believed in, and what he shared as the truth of
his faith. He brought this couple and our group together
by following his dreams and visions, and for that, we
owe him a debt of gratitude. We will carry on and
support the union of this beautiful couple. A couple
called together with higher purpose. The rings," Jonas
motioned to Mike and Mary, "represent the importance
of your union. They have been held at the Vatican for a
thousand years and were discovered in Wales during the
Crusades. They are made from platinum and rose gold.
The outer platinum frames Celtic knots that are woven
with rose gold and go on forever. They represent the
eternity of your vows and commitment to your eternal
relationship with God." Mike handed Elisabeth's ring to
Matt and Mary handed Matt's ring to Elisabeth.

Jonas continued, "Mike and Mary serve as great role
models for marriage. Look to them and counsel with
them for the challenges that befall any union between a
man and a woman. Observe how they love each other,
love their children, and love their friends and family.
Take note of how they respond to trials, and understand
their relationship becomes most important when faced
with life's challenges. You have a group of people
before us committed to the success of your union and
family."

Jonas read the Gospel and said a few prayers. He blessed the couple and began saying vows for the couple to repeat. When he asked the couple to exchange the rings, Jonas explained their importance.

"These thousand year old rings remind us of a time when Christians fought to take back territories in Europe and Israel that were of great importance to their faith. We are reminded that billions of people have fought for the opportunity to wear a crucifix and worship freely in the Holy Land and beyond. As you place the rings on each other's fingers, understand that the struggle of good and evil continues to play out in our world. Faith has brought you together and will live well beyond the days of humanity."

The couple exchanged rings, finished their vows, and sealed their covenant with a kiss. Cering had rented a hall in Stanley and the wedding party utilized the secure SUVs for transport to the reception. The reception had a few toasts, fine dining, and dancing. Because Mary, Elisabeth, Cering, and Kimi were outnumbered, they danced with everyone well into the evening. As the evening began to wind down, Amen approached Matt and Mike.

Amen was relaxed but focused. Matt kicked off the conversation, "No time for a honeymoon?"

"Not unless you want to honeymoon in Compton."

Matt was curious, "By the way, what happened to my Mustang?"

Mike began laughing, "This should be good."

Amen said, "I ask for your forgiveness in advance."

"Forgiveness for what?"

Amen felt bad, "Forgiveness for what I'm about to tell you."

Matt remembered what his father used to say, "That asking for forgiveness is easier than asking for permission?"

"Something like that."

Matt pressed, "Well…you're forgiven."

Amen began to tell the story. "I had to make your car disappear. After I killed the five Samil in your neighborhood, I knew the authorities would be looking for you and the vehicle. Your Mustang was bugged too. Samil was tracking your movements; for how long I don't know. I met up with some people in Compton that knew what to do with your vehicle. In fact, these are the same people that helped us with the attempt on Crevan's life."

Even though Matt had lost interest in the Mustang since his abrupt departure from Los Angeles, he wanted Amen to feel some pain for the welsh on his commitment.

Matt played the part, "You're kidding? Tell me that you put the Mustang in storage and pulled the plates. You know how long I worked and saved to buy that car? I couldn't even afford a new one coming off the line. Based on what I wanted, I had to wait a few years and purchase a Mustang that was slightly broken in."

Amen looked disappointed, "I know Matt. I made a commitment to you and I feel terrible. After what happened at the townhome, I had to dispose of your vehicle. I made sure that your Mustang was left in good hands." Mike began laughing harder.

"Whose hands?"

"A young teenager that I met in Compton. He knew exactly what to do with the car."

"Oh brother. You didn't at least leave the vehicle at a car lot or with a wholesaler."

Amen continued, "I couldn't. The vehicle needed to disappear. In fact, we used it in Los Angeles as a diversion on the Palms Bridge over Interstate 405."

Matt continued with his award winning acting performance. "I can't believe this? Didn't I tell you how much the Mustang meant to me? I should have known when you peeled out in front of Carlita's Café that the car was doomed." As Mike continued to howl with laughter Matt gave him a wink.

"Look Matt, I will make it up to you. I would like to buy you another vehicle when things settle down. A wedding present of sorts," Amen was grasping for ways to appease the newest, yet most important, Disciple.

Matt laughed, "When things settle down? More than half the world is at war right now and our leader was just killed in Los Angeles. Just when do you anticipate things will settle down?" Matt couldn't contain himself and began to chuckle a little.

Mike gave Matt a high five as Amen realized he was on the other side of a prank. Amen looked at the men and shook his head. He was relieved that Matt wasn't upset about the Mustang. The group began to discuss what happened in Los Angeles and how the Mustang detonated with C4 before hitting the interstate to distract President Crevan's motorcade. Matt and Mike were fascinated by the story and how close the Disciples had come to succeeding in the City of Angels. Mike also shared details about the reconnaissance mission in Cuba and how the locals did a great job of creating a diversion for their mission. As Mike told the story, the men noticed Sallah on the dance floor performing a Russian Cossak dance.

Matt looked at Mike, "You sure about this guy?"

Mike and Amen were laughing, "Absolutely. If anything else, he'll provide some great entertainment for everyone." The remaining group on the dance floor began to clap as Sallah squatted down and kicked his legs out in front of him. Noah was on the dance floor laughing and clapping. He was slowly regaining his confidence and identity back. Little John mimicked Sallah's dance and they began competing with each other for attention.

"Looks like Sallah has some competition." Amen began clapping to the beat as well.

Matt whistled, "C'mon Johnny, show him how it's done." Matt noticed Elisabeth on the dance floor with the other women. His bride was stunning and smiling from ear to ear. She looked at Matt and waved with the innocence of a schoolgirl. They were in love.

Ethan walked up to the men, "Congratulations Matt." He offered his hand to the Marine.

Matt gave a hug in return. Ethan and Matt were becoming close, almost as close as Ethan and Trevor were before his untimely passing.

Amen addressed the three men, "We will vote on a leader for the Disciples tomorrow."

"There goes the honeymoon," Matt took a sip of club

soda.

Amen continued, "As Sesom alluded to before his death, we must keep the pressure up and strike while Crevan's government is still forming. They will continue to beef up Secret Service and security for the President."

Matt was aware of the resources available to the President. "Getting close to him will be a challenge."

Amen responded, "Not really."

Mike and Matt looked puzzled. Amen explained, "When Jonas went to visit President Crevan before his capture, he lodged a small microphone in a lower portion of his jaw. We have twenty-four hour audio surveillance and can track Crevan's position anywhere."

Mike was amazed, "How did he pull that off?"

"Between the Swiss Army and Talan, we have access to some useful gadgets. He carried a phone that was equipped with a dart and syringe. Once Crevan was incapacitated, Jonas injected the tracking device into his jaw line."

Matt knew the power of technology and tracking devices. "Any chance they'll find it?"

"Not likely. The microphone mimics bone and transmits low power frequencies only when we're monitoring. To add injury to insult, Jonas tossed Crevan into a table before he regained consciousness."

The men had a good laugh and continued to watch Sallah capture the attention of an audience gathering on the dance floor. Even though Sesom's absence was conspicuous, Matt felt that the group was finally together. Noah, Jonas, and Sallah were natural additions

to the group of Disciples and crew of the Excalibur. The
men quit discussing business and rejoined the
celebration.

****

"What do you mean we have no traces or leads on the Disciples?" Crevan was conducting a weekly Cabinet meeting.

Secretary of Defense Drake responded, "Our last known position of the Disciples was west of Italy. We all know how that turned out."

Crevan turned his attention to the Director of Homeland Security Mitch Reed. "They were obviously involved with the assassination attempt in Los Angeles. For crying out loud, one of our Marines killed their leader and we dumped his body into the sea. We have no trace of the remaining Disciples?"

Reed answered, "None. We know the group utilized storm water systems for cover and movements. After that, they disappeared. This group is highly trained with expert knowledge of covert operations and technology. There wasn't even a driver for the Mustang that crashed through the highway partition and exploded before impact. When we went to retrieve video from local surveillance cameras on Palms Boulevard, they were disabled. Whoever made the attempt on your life also controlled the streetlights and flight control at the nearby John Wayne Airport. Because many citizens are suspicious of our government, we can't get anybody to talk. Many of our leads are coming up empty because people won't assist us with the investigations."

Crevan wasn't surprised, "Wonderful. I will work with the White House Press Secretary to increase the reward on each of these Disciples to five million dollars. People can be bought and we will continue to utilize the public to assist us with a capture or kill campaign for these terrorists. Once again, I will interrupt prime time television to remind the world we are committed to bringing these terrorists to justice."

Crevan turned his attention back to Drake, "Update us on the wars happening around the globe."

Drake pulled out his reading glasses and retrieved a report from the Joint Chiefs of Staff. "Indonesia has fallen into the hands of radical Islam. Israel has wiped out sections of several cities in Iran. Unfortunately, Iran was using heavily populated areas to cache weapons of mass destruction. Iran has been utilizing Syria and Lebanon to fire short range missiles into Jerusalem, Tel Aviv, and Haifan. Both sides have inflicted many casualties. Israel has deployed strategic nukes in Iran to take out their hot zones. Taiwan has been outmatched by the Chinese military; rebels have vowed to fight China until their deaths. We are supporting the Taiwanese with drops of aid and munitions. China has threatened to engage our military planes and helicopters, but they don't have the firepower from the air to be effective. We have warned the Chinese that we will go to war if they interrupt our humanitarian efforts in the region."

Drake took a sip of coffee, "We have pulled back in Afghanistan and retreated to the Turkmenistan border. From there we will conduct an evacuation from Towraghondi. There are too many refugees fleeing over the Hindu Kush mountain range from Pakistan, creating instability in the territory. India continues to drive Pakistan from the border cities of Kasur, Sialkot, and Lahore. Many Pakistani citizens are concerned that the Indian Army will march to Islamabad. Pakistan deployed two short-range tactical nukes, but they were intercepted by India's Advanced Air Defense missile system. In a surprise move, the Indian government declared they would not retaliate with nukes, but would invade territories of Pakistan to remove any future threats of nuclear or chemical weapons. They want the war with Pakistan to end peacefully with a surrender and subsequent peace treaty to work with the Indian government in the future. Looks like India is more interested in the geography than a war with the Pakistanis."

The Cabinet remained focused as Drake continued with his briefing. "As usual, Russia remains silent and suspicious. They are well armed to the east and west within their country. Russia has denounced Israel's use of force. In an interesting move, and we don't understand if it's offensive or defensive, they have opened the hatches on the silos of their medium and long-range nuclear warheads. Several of our adversaries in the region are Russian allies."

Secretary of State Watt said, "I'll check with Russia's Minister of Defense and see what prompted them to open the hatches on their silos. I'm sure it's nothing more than a show of force."

Crevan asked, "What DEFCON are we at right now?"

Drake said, "We're yellow, DEFCON 3."

Crevan responded, "Are we still receiving threats from Venezuela?"

"Yes Mr. President."

"Let's remove the threat. Send bombers and fighters to take out the positions we've identified. I'll make an announcement to the world that the United States takes any threat of nuclear attack seriously and will respond accordingly, either through diplomatic channels or force or both. I don't want other countries to believe they can make such threats against us without consequence."

Vice President Morgan interjected, "We've never taken threats from Venezuela seriously. There are a handful of dictators in Venezuela, North Korea, Egypt, and other places around the world that want attention through saber rattling and fist pumping."

Crevan reminded Morgan of some different world history, "Let's not forget Germany, Iraq, Libya, Syria, and many other countries that went unchecked when they began to rattle sabers and pump fists. Now that the world is at war, we will take every threat against our country seriously. We will send fighters and bombers to the territory and park one of our aircraft carriers nearby in the Caribbean Sea."

Morgan knew that an argument with Crevan wouldn't change his mind. In some respects, Morgan understood both positions. Syria had murdered thousands of their civilians. North Korea hadn't been deterred from pursuing enriched uranium and a long-range ballistics' program. Hitler created one of the most despicable and evil empires in modern history. Morgan knew that dictators in several parts of the world wreaked havoc on their civilians and surrounding countries. While Morgan had grown frustrated with dictators during his political career, he didn't know if Venezuela was worth considering or even bombing. In his mind, there were several other countries with greater instability and posed greater risks to the United States. Then again, Morgan didn't know if he was sitting before one of the world's most powerful dictators.

****

Amen, Dorje, Li, Cering, Lucas, Kimi, Ethan, Talan, and **Matt** remained in the dining area after a late breakfast; the Disciples had work on the mind. Gypsy Cove isolated the Excalibur from rough seas and high winds.

Amen addressed the group, "While we mourn the passing of our leader and friend, we must move forward as a group. In order to move ahead, we must elect a new leader to guide us in the days to come. Our group has known only one leader, and his style was unique and empowering. By electing a new leader, we are not looking to replace anything we've known, learned, and experienced so far. We will continue to collaborate, we will continue to disagree, and we will continue to come together and serve each other as one. With that said, we must have someone guide us, weigh our opinions, and make decisions based on facts and faith. Questions?"

Li asked, "How are we voting?"

"Cering has pieces of paper and pens. Because there are nine of us, we won't need a tiebreaker; therefore, all of us will cast one vote. On the pieces of paper, you will write the first name of the person you believe should lead our group."

Cering began to distribute the pens and papers. Amen continued, "The floor is open to discussion before we take a vote."

Dorje enjoyed any opportunity to practice his English, "I believe anybody in this room can lead. We have men and women that make good leaders. I still trust that Sesom made right decision by taking us to Matt in City of Angels. I like Matt. If this is our destiny, maybe Matt should lead?"

Li asked Matt a question, "Now that we have found Elisabeth and you've made her your wife, do you want to put yourself in harm's way?"

Matt thought the question was fair. "For the past several years, my life has always been in harm's way. Even after finding Elisabeth in Jerusalem, rescuing Mary in Gaza was a huge risk for the entire group. In some respects, I've never changed my mind based on the level of risk. Elisabeth and I have taken vows, but that doesn't change who I am and what this group needs to do. While I appreciate Dorje's kind words, I'm still the newest member of our group and surrounded by very capable people."

Lucas whispered in a baritone, "I was thinking the same thing Li. I'm excited about our future, but I worry about Matt and Elisabeth taking unnecessary risks. Sesom took a risk by leaving the helicopter to execute Crevan face-to-face. He wanted to kill him while staring into the dark abyss of his eyes. That decision ended Sesom's life. I'd hate to see the same thing happen to Matt."

Matt retorted, "Whether I'm leading or following, I will stand by your side in our struggle to defeat this evil enemy. Much like Jonas said during the ceremony, the conflict between good and evil dates back thousands of years." Matt held up his ring finger and displayed the newly acquired hardware. "There were millions of people that went before us, to bring us to this place, so I could put this ring on my finger and a matching one on my wife's. We shouldn't consider their risk to be in vain, should we?"

Nobody answered Matt's question. He was right. In the struggle of good versus evil, nobody could measure the contribution of one person's sacrifice. They were all equally important, regardless of time period or circumstance. Unfortunately, the world had become a place of less faith and sacrifice. People had become more self-indulgent and preoccupied with material possessions. Sacrifice was something other people did, and less people were willing to make them. Secularism didn't have a means to hold people accountable. People were free to believe and do what they wanted without consequence. Sin was something of the past and was merely written off as an inconsequential mistake made by fallible human beings. Sins were not only excused, but also expected in a secular society.

Matt continued, "Regardless of how you vote, I will stay with this group until my death or we succeed, whichever comes first. I have nothing to go back to in the United States."

Cering was curious, "What about you Matt, who's earned your vote?"

Matt had already given the leadership role some thought. "I'm pretty traditional when considering leadership qualities. I know that Amen was the first to find Sesom in Morocco, and has spent more time with him than anyone else in our group. He also retrieved Scratches and safely traveled with my family from Washington, DC to Tokyo. I haven't been able to repay him yet; I will with my vote for his leadership."

Amen smiled, "Thank you Matt. Please don't forget that you are the Omega of our group. Sesom was the first and you are the last. While everyone serves a purpose between the Alpha and Omega, finding you was what our group set out to do a few years ago. Trevor and Liam gave the ultimate sacrifice to find an obscure man in Los Angeles. When you and I first met at the café, you tested my skills to see if I was worthy of protecting everything important to you. I knew that you weren't interested in a scuffle, but finding out if I could be trusted. I felt your strength and determination; it was at that point I knew you would make a great leader. I will return the favor with a vote for Omega."

Amen continued, "Are we ready for a vote or would someone else like to have the floor?"

The Disciples closest to Sesom knew this day would come. Sesom had predicted he would lay down his life for the Disciples in an effort to protect the world from evil. Once Matthew Hiatt was found in Los Angeles, Sesom knew the Disciples would have strong leadership moving forward. On the outside, Mike Barnes was a very capable brother-in-law with connections in the military and Middle East. After a few seconds of silence, Amen called for a vote.

"You have a single sheet of paper and pen in front of you. Take your time and call upon the wisdom of God to guide you in this important vote. Selecting a leader is not the be-all, end-all of our group. All nine of us have a voice and responsibility for the execution of our decisions. Our leader will weigh options and give us the best chance for success in our mission. While the mission has evolved over the past several months, we have been sent to protect Elisabeth and her blessing of a child." Amen stopped for a moment and eyed Matt. Matt shrugged his shoulders and gave a bewildered look. "Our mission also includes removing Samil leadership from the United States' government before they set up puppet governments at key locations around the world. Samil will continue to hunt us down until they kill Elisabeth. We will not let that happen. Please take your time and vote."

Amen took a seat and voted. He had already revealed his vote by sharing his admiration for Matt. Amen had come to know Matt's family and respected their values. Mike and Mary were strong people with wonderful children;

Amen knew the family dynamic would be important to Matt over time. The other Disciples took their time voting. Many of them had not even considered a vote or who would replace Sesom. The group of Disciples transcended politics and posturing, they were confident they would make the right decision to elect a new leader. Regardless, they were all committed to Elisabeth's safety and wiping out Samil. Captain Phil had an empty tin coffee can in the kitchen. Amen went to retrieve the can and waited for everyone to vote and fold over their papers. Once the voting was finished, Amen passed the can around the table.

Amen reached into the can and pulled out the first piece of paper.

"Most High." The first vote was for Matt.

Then came the second, "Omega."

And the third, "AJ." The initials for Amen Jordan.

Amen read the fourth, "The 8th Disciple of Jesus." Matthew Hiatt had received another vote.

Amen read "Omega" for the next five votes. Other than Matt voting for Amen, everyone else voted for the newest Disciple. Matt was shocked. He didn't know the group felt so strongly about his ability to lead.

Amen smiled again, "You have the floor Mr. Hiatt."

Matt shook his head, "Sesom used to call me that and it drove me nuts."

Amen shook Matt's hand and gave him a hug.

Matt started, "Let's bring in the others and discuss our next steps together."

Captain Phil, John, Aaron, Jonas, Sallah, Noah, Elisabeth, Mike, Mary, and the kids were on the forecastle of the Excalibur. They were enjoying coffee and watching fishing vessels in the cove.

Cering opened a door to the deck and said, "Matt would like you to join us." Instantly, the group knew the result of the vote.

Aaron spoke to Mary, "John and I will stay up here with the kids. Take your time."

"Are you sure?"

"Absolutely. This is an important day for the Hiatt family."

Mary was humble, "Thank you Aaron and John."

The Disciples pulled up extra chairs as the rest of the group joined them in the dining room. Matt was all business.

"Let's call the Israeli sailors back to the ship." Amen gave a nod and answered, "They'll be here in 48 hours."

Matt turned to Talan, "Please provide us with an intel update."

Talan pulled a docking station and recording device from a nearby backpack. He began to play a conversation that was recorded in Los Angeles during President Crevan's hospital stay. The group listened to about five minutes of recording before Talan stopped the playback.

"As many of you know, when Jonas visited the White House he implanted a microphone in Crevan's jaw. We are able to track his position and listen to his conversations. Because of the microphone's position, we can't hear what the other person is saying, but we can clearly hear Crevan through the device. We now know that he was speaking with the Yemeni Ambassador to the United States in the hospital, Ahriman Abraxas. He may be the highest-ranking official of Samil. As you can hear, he seems to have the undivided attention of Crevan."

Mike asked, "What do you make of the references to Russia and China?"

"Russia holds their cards close to the vest. They have obviously fortified the areas around Turkey and North Korea. Even though we don't have credible information, there is chatter about Russia invading the northern part of China. The Mongolians have interest in partnering with the Russians to engage the Chinese and take some of their resources. The Russians know that the Chinese would look north once they begin depleting their natural resources; a preemptive strike on the part of the Russians and Mongolians."

Jonas commented, "That would be a fight to see."

Talan agreed, "Yes it would, but most of the battle will be fought with ground forces and air support. Neither country is interested in nuclear war because of their proximity. With winds constantly changing, and resources scarce in some parts of the region, they will not deploy either tactical or strategic nuclear weapons. China seems oblivious to an attack from the north, and they've allocated a number of assets to the southeast."

Lucas interjected, "Where can we find this Ahriman?"

Talan answered, "The country of Yemen has an Ambassador's office in Washington, DC. He is known as Ahri in political circles and spends most of his time in the Middle East. Well connected and very wealthy, similar to a man who came out of Saudi Arabia during the Soviet-Afghan War. Any more questions for me?"

The room was silent as Talan packed away the docking station and recording device. As Matt returned to the front of the room, Talan shook his hand and congratulated him on the recent promotion. Matt was humble and more concerned about the next steps for the Disciples.

Matt said, "Noah, work with Talan and see what you can find out about Ahriman and his present location. We need to get close to him. While you guys are conducting surveillance, let's see if we can find out about Crevan's movements over the next couple of weeks."

Noah was excited about the opportunity to work again, "I'd be honored to work with Talan."

"Thanksgiving is right around the corner. The President will have plenty of photo ops planned for the holiday. With the war in full force and soldiers deployed overseas, I'm guessing the President will make a surprise visit to the Middle East, maybe Israel. Because I'm guessing that both of our targets will be in the Middle East, we will set sail for Ashdod the minute our IDF sailors return to the ship."

"We're going back?" Captain Phil was curious as to the intent.

"We have to," Matt was matter of fact.

Captain Phil commented, "I thought we came here to lay low and protect Elisabeth from Samil?"

Matt responded, "We did, and a few of you will remain

with the Excalibur at all times, including Elisabeth, for her protection. When we reach Israel, Amen will ask for added security from the Israeli Navy and Air Force. We will not be docking at Ashdod, in case the threat of nuclear war becomes a reality. The Excalibur will need to be far enough from the coast of Israel to remain safe."

So far, Matt's briefing impressed the group. "We will send two teams into the Middle East to pursue Crevan and Ahriman once we arrive. I'll have Cering make arrangements with the Israeli Defense Force to transport us by Sikorsky CH-53K Super Stallion helicopters. Cering, Ethan, Li, Lucas, Jonas, and I will be Team 1 and pursue Crevan. Amen, Mike, Kimi, and Sallah will be Team 2 and pursue Ahriman. Talan, Dorje, and Noah will remain on the ship with Captain Phil, the crew, Mary, the kids, and Elisabeth.

Sallah sheepishly raised his hand. He didn't know if he was able to participate in a briefing for the Disciples.

Matt chuckled, "Yes Sallah?"

Sallah looked around the room. He couldn't believe that he was on a mission with some of the most technically trained people in the world.

"I know of this Ahriman from Yemen. The Yemeni people have tried hard to establish a new government of good leaders, law, and order for the past several years. The problem is that the country remains very poor and people can be bought to serve radical leadership. Ahriman is one of the radical leaders who keeps recruiting and paying young men to train at terror camps in the territory. In fact, he is funneling hundreds of millions in US aid to terror camps in Yemen, Somalia, and the Sudan. Based on what I've heard about Samil's growth and leadership, I wouldn't be surprised if Samil is running most of the camps. Depending on when Samil began their campaign in the Middle East, they may be responsible for all of the hate speech surrounding the Muslim world and radical Islamists. The Islamic faith is often the most slandered religion in the world. Many people of the world don't understand Islam because there are thousands of radicals that commit heinous crimes in the name of Islam. These people continue to call on other Muslims to join a jihad against the enemies of Islam, and there are many. If Samil is using terror camps as a means to fulfill their destiny, they have found thousands of people committed to their spiritual struggle against western civilization and the nation of Israel."

Matt said, "Thank you Sallah. We have placed you on a team with Amen, Mike, and Kimi to track Ahri and inflict some street justice on him."

Sallah was confused, "What is this street justice?"

Mike answered, "We won't turn him over to the authorities once we capture him. We'll be responsible for bringing him to justice and disposing of his body."

"Oh." Sallah was beginning to understand the stealth nature of their mission.

Matt wanted to wrap up the meeting, "Mike and I will travel to Toronto and meet up with General Gilmore and Colonel Lash. Regardless of our plans, we will need the support of the US military to be successful with a coup."

Matt turned to Cering, "Can you have Suzie set us up with two plane tickets early tomorrow morning? I will contact Colonel Lash and Mike will contact General Gilmore to meet us for dinner at the restaurant in the CN Tower. With a flight time of 12 hours, we'll need to leave early."

"Got it." Cering made a note of the request.

Matt asked, "Any more questions before we close?"

People around the room began to congratulate Matt on his new role for the Disciples. They were pleased to see that he was moving forward swiftly and not wasting time. When considering the Disciples' targets, minutes were important to executing a successful mission. No questions were asked.

****

As planned, Matt and Mike left early from the RAF
Mount Pleasant International Airport. General Gilmore
and Colonel Lash agreed to meet with the men in
Toronto near the top of the CN Tower at a restaurant.
Because military leaders were involved with classified
operations, Gilmore and Lash had no problem taking a
stealth trip to Toronto. The men elected to drive to
Toronto from Washington, DC; a trip that would take a
little over 9 hours in a car. They didn't want to risk
being followed, photographed, or part of a network of
elaborate surveillance cameras set up at airports, service
stations, and road intersections throughout the country.
Big brother was everywhere in the United States and the
government could access video cameras at any time.
Because the CIA wanted Mike and Matt dead or alive,
and the reward was a sizable sum of cash, the military
leaders didn't want to risk anything. They would even
pick up a rental car in Jamestown, New York before
crossing the Canadian border.

Amen called the IDF sailors back to the ship and they
would be transported by the Royal Air Force back to the
Falkland Islands. Upon the sailors return, the Excalibur
would leave immediately from Gypsy Cove. Once again,
the ship was looking at a long haul of 17 to 18 days
depending on weather. For the United States, the
Thanksgiving holiday was 20 days away. The Disciples,
Mike, and Noah believed President Crevan would travel
overseas during the Thanksgiving holiday. He could also
meet with Samil leadership while visiting US military
bases in the region. Talan and Noah had already
determined that Ambassador Abraxas traveled back to
the Middle East after speaking with Crevan in the Los
Angeles hospital. If nothing else, Ahriman Abraxas
would receive a surprise visit from the Disciples.

Mary and Elisabeth were sad to see their husbands leave

the Excalibur. Mary was ready for Mike to wrap up risky missions with the Disciples. Elisabeth had never experienced a husband leaving for a risky mission. While the uneasiness was similar for both women, Mary was experienced with the emotions and butterflies that came with a deployment. The women were comforted by the fact the men were together. They were some of the most highly trained and decorated members of Special Operations for the United States Marine Corp.

Even with heightened security, traveling was uneventful for both groups of men. Matt and Mike arrived at the Toronto Pearson International Airport at 6:30 pm. A dinner reservation was made at the CN Tower for 8:00 pm. The hotel was within walking distance of the tallest freestanding structure in the Western Hemisphere. The men would have just enough time to check into a hotel and head for the restaurant. After a quick elevator ride, Matt and Mike would be overlooking a beautiful Canadian skyline at 1150 feet of elevation.

Matt walked up to the reservation stand, "Four for dinner."

The host asked, "Under what name?"

"Charlie."

"Mr. Charlie, two other guests have already arrived, follow me this way." Matt and Mike followed the host through the dining room. Mike stopped for a second and realized the dining room was rotating 360 degrees.

"Hey Matty, the room is spinning."

Matt and the host stopped for a second. The host looked very unimpressed with Mike's discovery. Matt said, "You've never been here? We'll have to bring our ladies back when the time is right." The host looked even more unimpressed with the men.

"Right this way gentlemen," Matt and Mike continued to follow the host to the table. The table was located at the edge of the dining room in front of picturesque window.

Gilmore and Lash were sitting across from each other. Gilmore was drinking a Manhattan and Lash was savoring a whiskey sour. The men stood up as Matt and Mike approached the table. They shook hands, hugged, and returned to their seats. Mike took a seat next to Gilmore and Matt sat next to Lash. Matt hadn't seen Colonel Lash since he returned from his last deployment in Afghanistan; they had traded a few emails back and forth to check in on each other. The host handed Matt and Mike menus and outlined specials for the evening. Even in a time of war, the restaurant was still busy.

Gilmore started up the conversation, "How was the trip?"

"Good." Mike didn't provide any more details than that. Even though General Gilmore and Colonel Lash could be trusted, the people they worked for couldn't be. Mike didn't want to give any indication of how long the trip took them to arrive in Toronto.

Matt returned the courtesy, "And yours?"

"Lash and I drove up for obvious reasons. We ditched our car in the southwest corner of New York. Typical precautions in case we're being followed, I don't think we were."

Lash said, "I'm glad that you contacted me. I came up short when I visited your office in Los Angeles."

Matt summarized, "That's not what Noah Webster shared with me. Said he was detained without any charges or due process. According to what he told me, you were there when he was detained." Matt was more than a little upset with his former Colonel.

Lash responded, "There was nothing I could do. Once the FBI and Homeland Security became involved, they were looking to hang somebody. They wanted to arrest your boss, Mr. Richards, for aiding and abetting a known terrorist. I convinced them not to."

"How did you manage that?"

Lash picked up his whiskey and laughed, "I convinced them that you might be stupid enough to contact Mr. Richards or return to Delta Defense at some point in the near future. Looks like Dan sent you an email when Noah was detained, but there hasn't been any correspondence since. Because of the assassination attempt in Los Angeles, resources have been reallocated and Mr. Richards is no longer a high priority."

Gilmore continued, "You two are the priority for Federal, State, and local authorities in the United States. The Canadians could care less what the Disciples are doing or not doing, because they've experienced the ills of our mismanaged government over the past few decades. According to limited intelligence, I guess one of the Disciples served in Canada with the JTF2. When he returned home to visit an ailing relative, the hospital was ambushed and he, along with several family members, were killed."

A waitress stopped by the table, "Drinks gentlemen?"

Mike said, "I'll take a coffee with cream."

Matt nodded in affirmation, "I'll have the same, water as well please."

Lash noticed the ring on Matt's finger, "You got married?"

"I did. A friend of the family." Matt looked at Mike and smiled.

"Congratulations. I had no idea." Lash raised his glass and took a sip of his own drink.

Matt got down to business, "We called because we need your help."

Gilmore and Lash knew the men would need assistance. Much like Gilmore assisting Mike and Lucas with their reconnaissance mission in Cuba, connections to the US military would be an important element to the Disciples' success with their next mission. Drinks arrived at the table for Matt and Mike.

"Are you ready to order?" The waitress then realized the menus hadn't been touched.

"Give us a few if you don't mind," Gilmore excused the waitress from the table.

Gilmore looked at Matt, "How can Colonel Lash and I assist you?"

Matt said, "You know that we're involved with an international coalition. One that is determined to end the presidency of Alexander Crevan for a host of reasons."

Lash wanted clarification, "What are your reasons for removing President Crevan from office? Seeing as we're committing treason by sitting here, I think we should know."

Matt explained, "At some point during Operation Enduring Democracy, Crevan became twisted and delusional. The Middle East envoys he was overseeing began to funnel US dollars into the wrong hands. The people we met up with, otherwise known as Disciples, refer to the wrong hands as Samil. Samil is a Hebrew word meaning the angel of death. In short, they represent everything that is evil and wrong with the world today. Crevan is utilizing Samil to set up puppet governments worldwide. They now control Indonesia, Russia, the Sudan, Egypt, Libya, Yemen, Syria, and Afghanistan. By all appearances, several of these countries appear to be led by radical Islamists. In reality, billions of dollars have been funneled through Samil leadership to set up puppet governments and terror training camps in several countries."

Gilmore was interested as he'd heard conflicting stories about leadership in the Middle East, "For example?"

Matt opened up his menu, "Maybe we should decide on what we're eating first." The men opened their menus and made dinner selections. The waitress stopped by as Mike closed his menu and took their orders. As Matt sipped his coffee, he realized the Kona on the Excalibur was smoother and had more flavor. He thought for a moment before answering Gilmore's question.

"As we were traveling in Europe, I met up with Pope Simplicius II and some of his staff. As I say that, I realize how strange it must sound because I've never really been a religious person. Anyway, while sharing some coffee together, he told me about the Turkish Ambassador to Italy. The Ambassador made a special trip to the Vatican to meet with the Pope and Director of Security for the Swiss Army. He reported that Syrians were crossing over into Turkey and recruiting paramilitary to carry out a mission in the United States. The Syrians needed Turkish terrorists for their knowledge and work with explosives. Once the Syrians got their hands on some enriched uranium, they needed the Turk's experience with a trigger to detonate devices in Concord, New York, Miami, and Los Angeles."

Lash asked, "How does that involve Crevan?"

Matt answered, "All of the financial aid heading to the Middle East, including some of Pakistan's millions, were diverted to Samil leadership and terror camps. Crevan's envoys assembled an intricate system of funneling money to the very groups we are fighting in Afghanistan, Pakistan, and Iraq."

Gilmore was connecting the dots, "So that's why he was so interested in arming the rebels."

Matt added more sugar to his coffee, "Been going on for several years from what I know. Once he was selected as President Palmer's running mate, Crevan stepped up his efforts to arm Samil and support appointed leadership in the region. Many people in Washington, including Palmer, believed that Crevan was working with rebels to establish democracies in countries with unstable governments. Turns out that Crevan was working with people loyal to Samil and interested in setting up evil dictatorships."

Lash commented, "Some of the dictatorships were evil to begin with."

Matt continued, "Samil has been around for hundreds of years. They never had the backing or money to garner the support they needed. Once they found someone in the United States' government willing to listen and support their efforts, power and control began to shift immediately. Some of the current dictators in place may be supporting Samil; the ones that don't will be targeted for removal by any means necessary. Samil is propping up people to manage their puppet governments and run countries into the ground. Some of these countries have nuclear warheads too. I'm not sure if the intelligence community is picking up on Russia's intentions, but they plan to invade China with the Mongolians any day. China has been preoccupied with the messes in Tibet and Taiwan, leaving them exposed to the north. Russia looks to capitalize on their weaknesses."

Matt continued to share timelines and details of Samil's plans before food arrived at the table and the men began eating. All four of them were hungry from a long day of travel.

Gilmore paused for a moment and stated, "I still don't understand the Samil angle and their evil intentions. Why is Crevan interested in them?"

Matt took his cloth napkin and wiped his mouth. He took another sip of coffee before explaining the method to the madness, "You ever read the Bible?"

"Outside of Sunday School and an occasional visit to a Bible Study group? No."

Matt confessed, "I hadn't either, until I met the Disciples. Even though they come from different backgrounds and religions, they have a knack for reciting scripture. I've learned more about the Bible in the past two months than I ever wanted to, especially the book of Revelation."

Lash said, "Isn't that the end of the Bible and the end of the world?"

Matt replied, "Yes."

Lash asked, "You found a wife and religion during the past few months?"

Mike looked at Matt and answered the Colonel, "Look

gentlemen, I found the entire story unbelievable and farfetched when Matt told me a few months ago. Mary and I met up with him overseas because, at first, we thought he was in some real trouble. I've traveled with this group and I've come to know them as brothers and sisters, they are the real deal. The Disciples, which includes Matt, are well connected and highly trained. They look to balance the scales of good versus evil."

Gilmore asked, "Why aren't you part of the Disciples?"

Mike laughed, "Plain and simple, I wasn't called. But that doesn't mean that I won't stand side-by-side with them and fight an evil enemy. I've probably fought some of them already on tours in the Middle East. Samil has been successful utilizing radical Islamists as a cover to carry out their operations in the name of Islam or a jihad against western civilization. In reality, the goal of Samil is much bigger."

Matt piggybacked on what Mike said; "We need you guys to stand side-by-side with us to take back the White House. President Palmer was moving things in the right direction. A man ambushed him with selfish interests and evil ambitions. If we don't stop Crevan now, our world at war will spin out of control and we'll lose the United States forever."

Colonel Lash asked, "What about the Disciples and their link to what you've learned about Revelation?"

Matt didn't sugarcoat the answer, "They believe that we're at the end of times, at least the times familiar to us. With the decline in religion, economies, governments, morals, and values over the past several decades, the Disciples believe they have been called to help usher in a new period; a period that separates good from evil and holds humanity accountable. The world is filled with skeptics, and many people don't believe Jesus rose from the dead."

Gilmore was curious, "What do you believe Matt?"

"I've weighed my circumstances and decisions. Several nights I've laid awake and thought about the magnitude of what I'm involved with, what we're involved with right now. After the crucifixion of Jesus, the remaining Disciples must have felt abandoned and isolated against the world. The man they followed, the one who performed miracles, died and was buried. If I was a Disciple of Jesus, and I witnessed him die on the cross, I would have thought that the mission was over. I would have thought the Son of God couldn't even save himself from the Romans and Jews."

Matt took another sip of coffee and enjoyed a bite of his meal before continuing. "Then their leader rose from the dead and appeared before the Disciples on several different occasions. If it wasn't for the resurrection, the Disciples would have likely disbanded and gone their separate ways. Once Jesus appeared to them, and showed them that he was flesh and bones before his ascension, the Disciples had no more doubt. Many of them went to their graves spreading the word of God. They were beaten, crucified, speared, and John was exiled until he died of old age. After witnessing the resurrection, the Disciples didn't fear death. They knew salvation was waiting for them. That's what I believe."

The table was quiet for a moment. Gilmore spoke first, "What is the next play?"

Mike was proud of his brother-in-law, he was beginning to lead and not worry about what other's thought. Matt said, "We will succeed on the next mission to wipe out the President of the United States. Based on urgency and timelines, Mike and I believe that Crevan won't see a day in December.

Colonel Lash asked, "If you have this mission figured out, what do you need from us?" Lash was relieved that he wouldn't have to participate in a mission to assassinate the President.

Matt responded, "Taking out the President might prove to be difficult, but the mission won't be as complicated as establishing a new government for the United States of America." Lash lost the feeling of being relieved.

Gilmore looked at Matt, "We're not politicians, we're soldiers."

Mike said, "That's what makes your involvement so appealing to the Disciples."

"And just how can our involvement be appealing?"

Matt said, "Vice President Morgan is one of the good guys. He can lead the United States in a transitional government, one that will be by the people and for the people. Thomas Sawyer will be interested in setting up a government that favors Constitutional law and less government. In my opinion, the two party system has outlived its usefulness."

General Gilmore knew Lance Morgan fairly well. They had served together on budget committees and passed appropriation measures to cut spending without damaging the military strength of the United States. With technology improving and missile defense strategically placed at all borders of the country, the men knew that the trade off was to reduce the headcount of each branch of the military. Gilmore and Morgan developed a plan to cut military spending over a period of forty years with little impact to the safety or readiness of the armed forces. Troops would actually receive more training and Special Operations would increase their numbers to deploy at several locations around the world at any given time. From the study of biological agents to computer hacking, Special Operations would utilize several skills to protect freedom across the globe. Gilmore liked Morgan too.

"And what about the people we report to?" Gilmore knew that he answered to people, many people.

Matt was quick to respond, "Colonel Lash needs to be near the Pentagon and you will need to stay close to Capitol Hill when this goes down. They will follow your lead. Let them know that Mike and I will make a televised announcement when the mission is complete. In the meantime, contacting Morgan will be paramount to this mission's success. He'll go along with the coup, trust me."

Colonel Lash was finishing up his meal, "It appears you guys are pretty confident of the outcome."

Mike smiled, "We're not politicians either."

The men began to laugh and concluded the meal with coffee and dessert. Even though Mike and Matt weren't old in military years, and had no interest in a decorated career with the armed forces, the men reminisced about the good old days, when leaders led and troops followed. They talked about Stormin' Norman and the success of Operation Desert Storm in Iraq. The men shared their battle scars and discussed how wars were successful until politicians became involved with their own agendas and self-interests. War was war to these men and they shared a common bond of keeping each other alive during conflict. Even though General Gilmore and Colonel Lash didn't openly show their affection to Mike and Matt, they had great admiration for what they'd accomplished in a brief military career.

****

The Israeli Defense sailors returned without incident and the Excalibur departed for the coast of Israel. The Excalibur transmitted an encrypted signal that only allowed the Israeli Defense Force and Disciples to see the precise location of Captain Phil's massive cargo ship. The Israeli Defense Force retransmitted signals of the Excalibur's locations as decoys throughout the world. To date, the Excalibur had 2609 decoys sailing at sea and on lakes around the globe. The IDF knew that the United States and other nations wouldn't waste time trying to find the Excalibur with thousands of decoys. Some were even sailing on the Great Lakes according to reports from the United Nations. One of the decoys was apparently docked at the Hall's Crossing Marina on Lake Powell. Noah and Talan working hand-in-hand with the IDF provided the Disciples a great technological advantage.

Mike and Matt convinced General Gilmore to provide them one more trip to Gitmo. They wanted to pay a special visit to the Commanding Officer responsible for the treatment of Noah, Jonas, and Sallah. The CIA worked with the Commanding Officer on Gitmo to utilize several different torture techniques on Noah and Jonas to coerce a statement from them. While Jonas had the physical and mental training to endure such torture techniques, Noah didn't handle the stress very well. He became lethargic and socially withdrawn from other prisoners in the camp. Noah couldn't believe that his own country, the one he'd served inside and outside the military, would treat him so harshly.

Working with Talan provided Noah new hope to serve on a team to accomplish specific goals. Even though Noah didn't understand the particulars of why the Disciples would target President Crevan, he was happy to be working with Matt again in the field. Noah and

Captain Phil were always up early drinking Kona coffee and playing chess. They had become good friends. Everyone on the ship was happy to have Noah and Sallah join the group. While Noah was an encyclopedia of knowledge, Sallah provided comic relief for everyone on the ship by telling stories of his involvement with the CIA and his time at Gitmo. Sallah was a master at maneuvering through, in, and around conversations to persuade people to believe his ideas and opinions. In some respects, he was a master manipulator, which is one of the primary reasons he was able to stay alive at Gitmo after his arrival. Even though Sallah had assisted the CIA with capturing several of the detainees on the island, he was able to convince the prisoners that he was working with the Taliban to infiltrate the CIA, to throw them off course and lead them away from America's most wanted at large in Afghanistan, Pakistan, Iran, Iraq, and Syria. He made up elaborate stories about how the prisoners would have been captured sooner if it wasn't for his misleading stories and ideas about where the prisoners were located. In some respects, Sallah became a hero to the prisoners at Gitmo because of his efforts to keep them from being captured sooner.

When members of the military needed to hold one of their own accountable, like the Commanding Officer at Gitmo, they would take matters into their own hands. Matt and Mike didn't work well within the confines of government bureaucracy; they believed in the Golden Rule and applied the ideas regularly in their days of military leadership. After leaving Toronto, Matt and Mike jumped an Air Force plane to Langley Air Force Base in Virginia and made a connection with a familiar B-2 Stealth pilot.

"Good to see you again Captain," Mike smiled at the pilot.

"You too sir," The pilot returned a grin.

Matt looked confused, "You guys know each other?"

Mike put his index finger up to his mouth, "Classified information Major. Captain, we're looking for a ride. Call sign on this mission is Whiskey, Whiskey, Mike, Mike, Delta."

The pilot said, "WWMMD. You guys ready to leave?"

Mike replied, "Yes sir."

Matt knew not to ask questions. Everything was classified. No names, no flight log, everything had to remain stealth to protect the ground crew, pilots, passengers, and orders coming from General Gilmore. This flight experienced more turbulence than the first, reminding Matt and Mike that winter was coming fast. They were equipped with specialized backpacks, outfitted in wet suits, gear for an ocean drop, an assault rifle, two Glocks, and various types of grenades. Unlike before, this wasn't a rescue attempt, but a reconciliation mission. Both Matt and Mike were angered at how Commanding Officer Gerald Booth handled the interrogation techniques of Sallah, Jonas, and Noah at Gitmo. While they knew the CIA was involved, the Commanding Officer is still in charge of detainees and their humane treatment during imprisonment. The men were making a special trip to remind Booth of his duty to prisoners and the military. Mike made arrangements with some of his connections on Cuba to pick them up by boat once the mission was complete. No need for distractions, fighter jets, and helicopters to be involved with WWMMD. Matt and Mike would utilize several stealth techniques to convince Booth that he should be operating under a different set of procedures. They would surprise the Commander while he slept.

Matt and Mike wore helmets with microphones and ear

buds. They were dialed into the frequency of the B-2 Stealth so they could listen to the pilot and copilot. No reference was made to the last mission. The men discussed football and their favorite college teams. They also discussed fantasy football and players on hot streaks. The military loved their football and any sport that referred to the game as a battlefield. Because of the rough weather and turbulence, Matt and Mike would be dropped from an elevation of 39,000 feet. Another HALO drop meant oxygen and covering exposed parts of the body. The men were excited because this was the first military mission they would serve on together. Even though the FBI, CIA, Homeland Security, and the military were hunting Matt and Mike, they were determined to spend a little quality time with Commander Booth on the island of Cuba.

The pilot came over the radio, "We've got a small break in the weather in two minutes for a good drop zone. Green means go." Matt and Mike looked to the front of the plane as the Captain gave a thumb's up.

He continued, "You guys be safe out there."

Mike said, "Thanks Cap, you guys be safe to your next destination."

Mike turned to Matt, "Remember, you follow me."

Matt laughed as he put on gloves and snapped his oxygen mask on, "I'm more comfortable leading."

Mike did the same and said, "The Caribbean is rough right now. We'll go into the water 500 meters from shore. Unload your oxygen and detach from your chute before going into the water."

Matt gave a nod to Mike as the indicator light turned green. Once again, the B-2 bay doors opened and Mike went headfirst into the darkness. Matt was not far behind. Mike was utilizing global positioning systems to locate Matt and zero in on a position just south of Hidden Beach off the coast of Guantanamo Bay. Because of the cloud cover, the men couldn't see the island of Cuba; the ceiling of clouds rested at 7,000 feet. After emerging from the clouds, the men would pull the cords to their parachutes. A thunderstorm was raging on the southeast corner of the island.

"Quite the light show." Mike was impressed with the amount of lightning transferring between the clouds and to the ground.

Matt said, "Looks like we'll go right through it."

Mike laughed, "Hope your religious connections keep us protected."

Matt replied, "I'm not sure if the man upstairs intended for us to make an unplanned stop at Gitmo."

"Nothing we can do about that now." The men were plummeting to the earth at 120 mph. Passing through the clouds was even more ethereal. At terminal velocity, the men felt as if they were floating through the sky. When lightning lit up the clouds, white rolls of moisture surrounded them. The men had to remain focused on their instruments and not become disoriented with lighting traversing the clouds. Once they passed through the clouds they deployed the parachutes, dumped oxygen tanks, and peeled off clothing from their high altitude drop. They retrieved flip fins that were strapped to their packs. Even though the men were tossed around by gusts of up to 20 mph, they successfully dropped from their canopies at 35 feet. The current was strong and waves were 10-15 feet high. Matt and Mike began their swim of 1500 feet to the shore.

****

"You sleeping?" Morgan was mindful of the late hour at which he was making a call.

"Morgan?"

"Yeah Sawyer, it's me."

"Is everything alright?"

"Yes. Sorry about making a call this late. Hope I didn't wake you."

Sawyer was sarcastic, "No. I was just catching up on some late night news. I'm not sure at what point news agencies stopped reporting and just began making up their own stories."

Morgan laughed, "Right after Al Gore invented the internet."

Sawyer asked, "So, what can I help you with Vice President Morgan?"

"Do you have time to meet for a really late dinner or very early breakfast? Not something we should discuss over the phone."

Sawyer looked at his watch, the time was 12:40 am. "Yeah, what were you thinking?"

Morgan thought for a few seconds, "Chicken and waffles, maybe a beer. You know that dive on the west side of Rock Creek Park?"

"Yeah, best chicken and waffles in the DC area."

Morgan looked at his watch, "Let's meet up there at 1:15

am."

"Look forward to it." Sawdog knew that Morgan would want to discuss the Colonist party and the imminent deadline that was rapidly approaching.

****

And shall come forth; they that have done good, unto the resurrection of life; and they that have done evil, unto the resurrection of damnation.

John 5:29

Mike removed the burlap bag from Commander Booth's head. The bag was soaked from Mike's swim and a hard rain falling on the southeast coast of Cuba. The time was 1:00 am and the men were to the east of Hidden Beach on the island. The Commander was coming to, from the effects of the chloroform used to quietly capture him.

Matt was directly in front of him and wore a ski mask to hide his identity. Mike was directly behind the Commander with a ski mask on as well. They had both participated in approved torture techniques in the Middle East. They each wanted two minutes with the American soldiers exposed at Abu Ghraib in Iraq; they didn't believe in treating prisoners like animals. There were other ways to get people to talk and share important information. The men always believed that a soldier should kill somebody in the name of combat before treating them like animals; there was no honor in treating people subhuman. They followed the procedures and guidelines adopted by the Geneva Convention from 1864 to 2005. The only time Matt and Mike would stray from the Geneva Convention is when they found out about captors taking torture methods into their own hands. If captors showed no mercy, neither would they. Commander Booth had shown no mercy with Noah, Jonas, and Sallah.

Matt looked him in the eyes, "Good morning Commander Booth. Seems like you've had some unanticipated security breaches over the past few weeks." Rain fell hard as lightning lit up palm trees and bushes rocking back and forth near the beach.

"Who are you?"

"We are your conscience, the collective soul you've forgotten about. A few prisoners escape Delta camp recently?"

"How would you know about anybody escaping?"

Matt looked disappointed, "I'll ask the questions." Matt kicked the Commander in the chest. He fell backwards in a chair that Matt and Mike had strapped him to with duct tape and rope. Mike picked the chair up off the sand. Booth was trying to catch his breath.

Matt repeated the question, "Did a few prisoners escape the camp recently?"

Commander Booth insisted on playing difficult, "Go to hell."

"You first." Matt nodded at Mike and the men picked up the chair and placed it in seawater that was knee high.

Mike said, "The seas appear pretty rough, let's see what kind of balance he has." The Marines left the chair and returned to shore. Commander Booth could feel the chair losing stability as the undertow began to sweep sand away from the legs. Booth was able to escape the blow of a small wave, but a 7' wave wiped the chair off its legs and it went tumbling; the current pulled the chair out to sea as other waves crashed on top of the Commander.

Mike hit a button on his stopwatch and said, "We'll give him 30 seconds to start." At 25 seconds the men went to retrieve the chair and bring it to shore. Booth was coughing and had sand in his hair. Based on how he was tethered to the chair, Booth couldn't control his balance after toppling over in the ocean.

"Well done Commander, 30 seconds underwater. I doubt anyone will notice you missing until 0600 hours. Which gives my partner and me about 5 hours to see how well you perform with endurance exercises. The next time segment will be 45 seconds."

"Let me repeat the question. Did a few prisoners escape the camp recently?"

The Commander was stubborn, keeping his head down and not answering the question. Matt, once again, nodded at Mike and they placed the chair back in the ocean.

Mike showed the Commander his watch and said, "Forty-five seconds. Looks like you may be a little out of shape for this exercise. Big difference fifteen seconds makes while underwater, sometimes the difference between life and death."

Matt and Mike knew that torture techniques were more about head games than anything else. They wanted Commander Booth to think about what was happening to him. They also wanted him to understand the torture would progress until his cooperation. Booth needed to feel helpless and completely vulnerable. He needed to feel like other prisoners at the camp, like nobody was watching out for them.

The chair crashed around, went upside down, and the Commander swallowed salt water as he tried to catch a breath. At 40 seconds, Matt and Mike retrieved the chair and brought Booth to shore again.

Matt said, "Impressive Commander. Obviously you know the routine by now. Another 15 seconds added to your time. You either talk or drown, your choice. This is our version of extreme water boarding, almost as extreme as what you did to our friends inside those buildings. All three of them had no business being detained here."

Mike knelt down by the Commander, "We have no demands. We aren't interested in anything you possess or what you can do for us. We made a special trip to give you a dose of your own medicine."

Mike stood up, "Whether you live or die is of no consequence to us, but may be to your family and those whom depend on you. If you don't answer his questions, you will die."

Matt continued, "You tortured a man paralyzed from the waste down. We know the CIA was involved too. Who's authorizing such treatment of your prisoners?"

Commander Booth looked straight ahead. He refused to answer the question. Once again, Matt and Mike picked up the chair and set it in the ocean.

Mike said, "One minute Commander. As you're tossed about by the waves, think of those who would like to see you in the morning. If you don't survive the endurance exercises, nobody will ever know what happened to you, or your body." Matt and Mike returned to the shore.

Matt said, "You think he'll cooperate."

Mike thought for a moment, "Yeah. A minute is a long time to hold your breath. He probably realizes that he can't go for another 15 seconds."

The Commander was tossed around and flipped several times in the water. When the Marines went to retrieve him, he gagged and coughed to catch his breath.

Matt said, "I think you reached your limit Commander. We've reached ours as well. I'll give you one more chance to talk. Who's authorizing the torture techniques on your prisoners?"

As Matt finished the question, a lightning bolt struck a palm tree a few hundred yards from their location. The thunder was deafening and Matt didn't even flinch. Once again, the Commander was silent, until Matt and Mike went to pick him up.

"Okay, okay, I'll talk." Commander Booth was yielding to the realization that he wouldn't make the next trip back to the shore alive.

Mike began to cut the bindings from Booth's hands and body. Once the tape and rope were removed, Mike chambered a round in his Glock 23 and put the gun to the Commander's right temple.

"Nothing stupid, or you'll wish you were surfing again."

Matt said, "Who gave the orders?"

"The CIA came down with the first prisoner, the man from the Swiss Army. They were on strict orders from Secretary of State Watt to coerce a statement. We did everything from light control to hypothermia. Neither one of the men would crack, which made the CIA angry and more determined to inflict pain and harm to the men. The paralyzed man was in disbelief. In my opinion, he didn't know much about what we were asking him."

Matt looked disgusted, "You broke his left leg, right in front of his eyes." Matt pulled out a set of nunchucks that Kimi gave to him during their Kendo training. He slowly began to work them around his body.

Mike covered the Commander's eyes, "Be silent and take the pain."

Matt sped up the nunchucks and whizzed them over Booth's head and around his ears. Booth was quiet and knew what was coming.

Matt said, "An eye for an eye Commander Booth. Don't make us come back here again." Matt flung the nunchucks into the air and punched Booth on the chin. By the time he caught the weapon, Booth was knocked out and flat on his back from Matt's right cross. The men left him on his back and rendezvoused with a nearby motorboat.

****

As expected, albeit a big surprise to the Chinese, the Russians and Mongolians attacked China from the north and began their march to Beijing from Erenhot. Up until Russia's act of aggression, the Chinese believed their Slavic friends to the north were allies. The Mongolians wanted to avenge the demise of their empire during the 14th century. The Russians had positioned elaborate missile deployment and defense systems on the borders of Mongolia and southern portions of Russia; the Chinese had believed the Russians were running exercises to protect their borders from radical Islamists. As a war strategy, the Russians and Mongolians wanted to push the Chinese to the south and have them forced into further conflict with Taiwan, South Korea, Japan, and India. India had been at war with the Chinese before and they respected the Dali Lama and independence of Tibet. Once the Russians and Mongolians made their moves, countries to the east, southeast, south, and southwest of China began to attack. The goal was to break up China and strip them of their superpower status. The country was divided into several regions and the invading countries pledged to absorb the areas peacefully after China surrendered. The invading countries encouraged Chinese citizens to turn against their oppressive government. Even though the United Nations didn't approve of the surprise attack, President Crevan was vocal about the importance of returning economic balance to the territory while improving human rights for the Chinese people.

Realities were a sharp contrast to Crevan's public platitudes. Russia was a major supporter of Samil and didn't care much about Chinese land. As long as China was broken up and lost their superpower status, Russia didn't care what territories other countries absorbed through a Chinese surrender. They were more interested in supporting radical Islam and their efforts to decimate

the Holy Land. Once Samil used radical Islam to prop up
their leadership, they would abandon the nation of Islam
for a government of their own.

****

Amen met with the Disciples, Jonas, Sallah, Mary, and Elisabeth in the kitchen of the Excalibur. The ship was headed back to hostile territory. Israeli sailors and the IDF were working with Captain Phil to help guide the ship through stormy seas.

Amen said, "Russia and Mongolia have invaded China. Taiwan, South Korea, Japan, and India have offered their resources to help overthrow the country. Even though China attempted to launch short-range missiles, Russia intercepted them and threatened to use their nuclear arsenal against the Chinese if they persisted."

Sallah asked, "Why would the Russians want to invade China?"

Jonas replied, "As a diversion. Several countries of eastern Asia have been suspicious of Chinese leadership for years. The Russians made the move to amalgamate several border countries of China and the Chinese people. Amen and I don't believe the Russians have much interest in China at all. The move was more preemptive because Russia and the Chinese would eventually cross paths at some point in the future over natural resources in the region."

Lucas interrupted, "So why the diversion?"

Amen replied, "Samil is entrenched in Russian leadership. They have more interest in what happens to the west, specifically around the Holy Land. Russia has supported Iran, Syria, and other dictators in the Middle East for decades. Once Israel is removed from the equation, Russia will have great influence over the Middle East. With President Crevan holding the highest office in the United States, Samil hopes to control the east and west by dismantling religions and stripping people of their liberties. Much like Germany's Kristallnacht, Samil plans on burning the churches of all religions worldwide."

Ethan added, "Ahriman Abraxas is working with hundreds of leaders in the Middle East and Russia to coordinate rebels and military brass in a ground invasion from the north of Israel. Samil is using the Internet and social networks to plan highly structured attacks. The message boards are coded and provide specific instructions. They update their code every two weeks, so we can't follow their plans as they share information. On average, decoding their communication is taking 4-6 weeks. As far as I know, Russia and Iran will launch nuclear weapons against Israel if they don't leave the Holy Land."

Captain Phil walked into the kitchen, "That's why we'll remain in the Mediterranean far from the coast of Israel. I've been speaking with the Israeli sailors; they're very concerned about their country and families. This time around, they don't know if they'll ever see them again."

Amen spoke, "Sallah."

"Yes Amen," Sallah sat up in his seat.

"You will disembark with Cering when we pass the coast of Sierra Leon. Once again, a helicopter will rendezvous with the Excalibur and transport you to the airport in Gambia. From there, you will take a charter to Egypt and meet up with Matt and Mike in Dahab and determine your course of action. Matt and Mike want to find the location of Ahri before the President arrives. Even though Ahri won't be as difficult to find as Osama Bin Laden, he will be heavily guarded and on the move. Once the Excalibur arrives off the coast of Israel, Team 2 will take over the mission to extinguish Ahri."

Sallah was all smiles. Matt had requested that Sallah and Cering accompany the men through the Middle East as they searched for the location of Ahri. The Disciples knew that Ahri and President Crevan needed to be killed to stop a global epidemic of Samil leadership from continuing its course.

Amen continued, "The rest of us will remain on the ship to protect its crew and passengers. Once we arrive at our destination, we should have a better understanding of Ahri's location and when President Crevan plans to travel to bases in the Middle East for Thanksgiving. We still have a strong signal from the device Jonas implanted in Crevan's jaw. The White House has no idea we are tracking Crevan's position and listening in on several of his conversations. Depending on the intelligence we gather, we may be able to assist Matt and Mike with Ahri's location. Talan and Noah will maintain constant surveillance on Crevan and let us know if plans change. We must show some restraint and hit our targets simultaneously when the time is right."

Jonas said, "You have the full support of Pope Simplicius and the Swiss Army. Several countries of the European Union are not pleased with the aggressive actions of the United States and Russia. Many of our European allies believe that Russia will not stop at Israel and the Middle East, but they will continue to march to the west and invade more countries. Great Britain has been very vocal about keeping Russia's power in check. They have also been disappointed that the United States appears more interested in Middle Eastern affairs than what Russia intends to do. We have an idea that Samil leadership has resurfaced in Germany and may serve as a gateway for Russia to enter the EU."

Lucas spoke softly, "Interesting how the more things change, the more they remain the same."

Elisabeth got up and left the kitchen area. She went to a nearby bathroom and shut the door.

Dorje asked, "She okay?"

Kimi answered, "I think she's had some seasickness for the past several hours. I'll go check on her."

Kimi followed Elisabeth's steps to the nearby bathroom and knocked on the door.

"Is everything alright?" Kimi could hear Elisabeth getting sick in the bathroom.

Elisabeth tried to put Kimi at ease, "I'll be out in a minute."

"You want me to come in and pull your hair back?"

Elisabeth felt terrible and caved. She unlocked the door and Kimi went to work. Kimi retrieved a towel and wet it. She pulled back Elisabeth's hair as she threw up in the toilet. Once Elisabeth stopped, Kimi placed a cold cloth on her forehead.

"The seas are a little rougher." Kimi wiped away some sweat and smiled at Elisabeth.

"The seas aren't causing the sickness." Elisabeth sat up against the wall and pulled her knees in tight to her body.

"Do you have the flu?"

"I don't think so. I haven't run a fever or felt achy." Elisabeth wiped her forehead.

Kimi smiled even wider, "Are you pregnant?"

Elisabeth looked up at Kimi and nodded, "I think I might be."

Kimi clapped her hands softly and hugged Elisabeth. "Oh I hope so. Would you like me to see if Captain Phil or Mary have a pregnancy test?"

Elisabeth chuckled, "I'm not sure why they would, but feel free to ask."

Kimi said, "I'll be right back. Take it easy." She motioned for Elisabeth to stay still and closed the bathroom door behind her. She leaned up against the door, said a brief prayer while facing the ceiling, and then she headed to the kitchen. The group was still discussing the world war and imminent danger to the Holy Land.

Kimi went over to Captain Phil and whispered, "You don't have a pregnancy test in your medical kits, do you?"

Captain Phil smiled, "No, I've never needed one."

Kimi remained focused and went over to Mary, "You don't have a pregnancy test, do you?"

Mary was more shocked by the question and looked at Kimi with a quizzical stare. She then looked down the hallway to where the bathrooms were located.

Before Mary could answer, Amen interrupted the women. "What is it Kimi?"

She began to move to Amen's position at the front of the kitchen and he stopped her. "No Kimi. We won't keep secrets from this group. If you have something to say, share the message with everyone."

Kimi knew that she would not convince Amen that the message was more personal than secret. Amen crossed his arms and gave Kimi one of *those* looks.

Kimi took a seat beside Li and Dorje, "I'm looking for a pregnancy test."

Amen looked alarmed, "When would *that* have happened?"

Kimi gave Amen a nasty look, "Not me." Kimi pointed down the hall.

Amen figured it out and felt embarrassed, "Oh, okay, a pregnancy test."

Kimi asked, "Does anybody have a pregnancy test?"

Everyone looked around the room at each other. They were all excited at the possibility Elisabeth might be pregnant again. Nobody had a test.

Noah spoke up, "With the technology available in smart phones today, Talan and I can make up a test that will work with an application. I'll check with the Israeli soldiers and see what meters, probes, and wiring they have. We'll find a way to measure Elisabeth's human chorionic gonadotropin with a smart phone and give her the results."

Li looked at Noah funny, "Probes?"

Noah laughed, "Talan and I won't probe anything. However, a probe may be useful to measure the hCG in urine, much like over-the-counter pregnancy tests made available to the public. In essence, we'll measure Elisabeth's urine to detect a specific pregnancy hormone."

Amen said, "Very well Noah. Let's see if we can perform a test in the next 24 hours to put Elisabeth's mind at ease. If her test comes up positive, we have more reason to stay on the ship and guard her precious cargo."

Mary, Cering, and Kimi looked at each other. They had a feeling this may be the epiphany for the Disciples. Mary was proud of her little brother and amazed that he was part of a higher calling, a significant life experience for humanity. She knew that he was committed to helping others and protecting the liberties of civilians, but she had no idea that his stewardship would be called upon to usher in a period of biblical proportions. Matt was a genuine, caring person; but his spiritual self had been dormant since Columbine and his parents' murders. Mary was witnessing the reemergence of Matt's spirituality, and combined with his leadership skills, the Disciples were beginning to regain a confidence they hadn't felt since finding the 12th Disciple in Los Angeles.

****

Noah checked with the Israeli sailors and they had several meters and PH probes to measure the salinity of drinking water on the ship.

Noah dialed in Suzie on a secure line for a videoconference. Suzie was at the office of a reputable gynecologist to inquire about a pregnancy test at sea.

"Hello Noah," Suzie was receiving a strong signal through her tablet at the doctor's office.

"The pleasure is mine Suzie. I understand that you're responsible for most of the coordination and support for our group. Thank you for working with Cering to free me from the confines of Cuba. My leg is healing up quite well. Glad Mike and Lucas made it when they did or else gangrene would have set in."

"No problem Noah. Matt was adamant that we moved and moved quickly. Mike and Lucas were in a perfect position for the reconnaissance mission; think nothing of it. I'm here with Doctor Schwartz and we'll discuss some possibilities for a pregnancy test."

"Good afternoon Dr. Schwartz. Talan and I are grateful for your time."

"My pleasure Noah. What kinds of devices do you have?"

Noah held up some items, "We have a voltage meter, some PH probes, and we can pull gauges from the ship and vehicles we have on board if need be for a test."

The doctor said, "PH is good for alkalinity and possibly predicting the sex of a child. We may be able to recalibrate some of the probes to detect hCG in urine flow. Let me send you the markers for a woman that is not pregnant and one that is. There is also an application made for smart phones that will assist you in determining the presence of hCG. You shouldn't have too much trouble converting the physical properties of hCG to electrical signals for your smart phone. Seeing as you have a few women on the ship that aren't pregnant, they will serve as controls for your testing and two-point calibration. Make sure that the calibration is as accurate as possible before you test the pregnant woman. A couple wires, PH probe, and a good connection to a smart phone should help you appropriately administer and measure a good sample."

Suzie said, "I'll send the link for the application and the doctor's control readings for women that are pregnant and those whom aren't. Those will be coming to Talan's secure email."

Talan confirmed, "Thank you Suzie, we'll look for the email and we appreciate the good doctor's help."

Dr. Schwartz smiled, "No worries gentlemen. Because I'm a scientist at heart, please send me the results so I can analyze and see if your plan worked."

Noah responded, "You bet."

The groups signed off the call.

****

Noah and Talan went to work. They downloaded the application to measure hCG in a pregnancy test and set up the doctor's results as models. Mary, Cering, and Kimi were kind enough to provide samples to the men so they could work on calibrating the best PH probe they had. The trick was determining how the probe would measure specific elements of the samples and comparing them against the doctor's models.

Talan looked at his smart phone and a nearby computer, "I think we've got it."

Noah wheeled himself over to Talan's laptop and looked at the smart phone while studying the computer screen. He looked at Talan and nodded his head.

"I'll let Elisabeth know that we're ready for a sample to perform the test."

Noah wheeled himself down the hall to an elevator. After arriving on Elisabeth's floor, he noticed the door was closed. Noah knocked and Mary opened the door.

"We're ready when you are."

Elisabeth was sitting in a nearby chair sipping some tea. The aroma and calming effects of hot tea made her feel better.

Elisabeth smiled and said, "Thank you Noah."

Mary said, "We'll be there in a few minutes."

Noah was always a gentleman, "Take your time, the test can wait until Elisabeth's ready."

Noah wheeled himself back down the hall to the

elevator. As Mary stood in the doorway of Elisabeth's room, she thought about how much she liked Matt's friend from Delta Defense. Even though Noah was the oldest passenger on the ship, he was wise beyond his years. There was something mysterious about Noah that Mary couldn't grasp, something about his compassion that transcended everyday relationships. Noah really cared about people and their wellbeing. He worked tirelessly with Talan to calibrate the probe for a successful test, to put Elisabeth's mind at ease.

Elisabeth and Mary showed up at a cabin that had been converted into an office for Noah and Talan.

Noah handed a cup to Elisabeth, "If you could give us a sample up to the line marked on the cup."

Elisabeth took the cup into a nearby bathroom. She reemerged after a minute and brought the sample to Noah. The men went to work and began to measure the content of Elisabeth's urine sample. In some respects, they were looking for unique changes that were different from the readings of Mary, Cering, and Kimi. If Elisabeth was pregnant, the probe should give high readings of a hormone that wasn't present with earlier tests. A group was lingering in the area, waiting with anticipation.

Talan punched some keys on the laptop that was connected to a smart phone, which was connected to a probe in the cup. The men kept a close watch on the computer screen as the smart phone measured elements in the cup and transmitted results. Talan was overlaying the graphs of the women on top of each other.

Noah said, "Let me dial up the doctor's private line."

The phone rang a few times before it was answered, "This is Joseph."

"Dr. Schwartz, it's Noah Webster from the Excalibur. Results are coming in and I was wondering if you could review the graphs compiled from the tests. We have three controls and our test female. If you have time, we'd like you to verify what we're doing is correct."

Dr. Schwartz replied, "Let me get to my office and login. You have my email address correct?"

"Yes we do."

"Once the results have been transmitted in full from your smart phone, send me a screen shot and I'll take a look. Be right back."

The doctor muted his phone and finished up with a nurse. He went to his office and logged into his email.

"I'm back Noah, let me find your message." The doctor tapped away on the keyboard and pulled up an email from Talan Serin. He opened the attachment, which revealed the results from four females.

"Noah, along the grid you will see a spike between 12 and 15 on the x-axis."

Noah replied, "Yes, Talan and I noticed that when the results were being populated."

"The y-axis shows a reading of about 27 for the points between 12 and 15 on the x-axis."

"We see that as well," Noah was pointing to the computer screen. Mary was biting her nails at the doorway as she listened to one side of the conversation. Elisabeth was waiting nervously with her.

"Based on the probe you used, the smart phone

application and test results, the graphs clearly indicate that your test subject will be dining for two later on."

Noah was relieved. He looked at Talan and gave him a wink. "Thank you for your time Doctor Schwartz."

The doctor was happy the test confirmed what the men were hoping to find. "Think nothing of it. Let me know if you need to schedule a few follow-up appointments before she delivers."

"Will do." Noah hung up the connection and turned to the women.

"Elisabeth," Noah had a serious tone in his voice.

Elisabeth sheepishly answered, "Yes Noah."

"Looks like you're dining for two this evening." Noah smiled and began to clap his hands.

Mary immediately hugged her sister-in-law. She couldn't believe that her little brother was going to be a father. Elisabeth began to weep with joy. After her abortion, she never knew if she'd carry a child again. She didn't know if God would bless her with another opportunity to bring life into the world. God had not only forgiven Elisabeth, He sent individuals to protect her and love her like family. Because God had blessed humanity with free will and its inherent flaws, He sent Matthew Hiatt to father Elisabeth's child and protect her from future harm. Her womb was blessed, and she would carry one of the most important children since His son, Jesus Christ.

Cering and Kimi held each other's hands and began to pray. They prayed for continued blessings, Elisabeth's health, and the safe journey and return of Matt and Mike. Everyone congratulated Elisabeth. Each of them offered up anything she needed to be comfortable, safe, and secure on the ship. John was navigating the ship and sounded the horn three times when he heard the news. After everyone celebrated Elisabeth's news, Talan and Noah shared some more information with her.

Talan revealed, "Just so you know, the PH tests can be a good indication of sex for the child. While not certain, until an ultrasound is performed, there is a good chance you will give life to a girl."

Elisabeth wiped tears away from her eyes, "Matt said that we would have a girl and her name would be Ariel. Ariel Hiatt. The name was revealed to him through a dream."

Talan laughed, "So it is settled. We shall celebrate the day we welcome Ariel Hiatt into the world."

Mary looked at Elisabeth, "Ariel is a beautiful name."

Elisabeth said, "Let's go get some sun and fresh air, I could use it. Cering and Kimi, you want to join us?"

Cering replied, "Absolutely. The weather is beautiful today."

The women went to the forecastle, which was now equipped with lounge chairs and end tables that were secured to the deck. If it wasn't for several spinning radar antennas, large caliber anti-aircraft guns, and Israeli Defense sailors keeping watch, the Excalibur had the appearances of a modern day cruise ship. Cering had poured millions of dollars into fortifying Captain Phil's ship. Sesom had always favored traveling by boat over airplanes, trains, and automobiles. The oceans were vast and provided great protection from the confines of traveling by land or air. The Israeli Defense Force helped the Excalibur monitor military vessels and cargo ships close to the ship's position. As the Excalibur crossed the Atlantic to sweep the western coast of Africa, the sun hovered lower on the horizon and the temperature dropped ever so slightly.

****

Sawyer's phone vibrated. He excused himself from a meeting and took the call as he exited a conference room.

"Are we still on?"

Morgan replied, "Yes, we will meet at the Capitol in 3 hours. I've reserved the Reagan Room for us."

"What about Gilmore and Lash?"

"They will be there. Just the four of us."

Sawyer seemed pleased, "Very well. The clock is ticking, I'm curious about the briefing."

Morgan said, "See you in three," and hung up the phone. The Capitol was one of the best places to keep a secret. Lawmakers were always meeting with Pentagon officials, lobbyists, advocates, and other groups to map out a plan for future liberty or corruption, more of the latter. Morgan didn't even call the meeting at the Capitol building. General Gilmore contacted Vice President Morgan shortly after his return from Canada. Gilmore knew the Colonists were putting pressure on the White House staff to step down, or step aside to establish a new government. Colonists firmly believed the current system of government must be dissolved in order to advance the country. Washington had too much control and too many laws had been bolted onto a bureaucratic system of power and greed. The Colonists wanted change, and they insisted that Thomas Sawyer lead the charge to change Washington from the inside out; he was planning to do just that.

****

Matt and Mike made the trip to Egypt and were holed up in Dahab. They would wait until Cering and Sallah arrived to carry on with their mission to locate Ahri. The first thing they did was open up a laptop and contact the Excalibur. Elisabeth and Mary were waiting for their video call. The women were excited to share the news about Elisabeth's pregnancy. They dialed in and saw their men; neither of them had been shaving.

Mary smiled, "You guys look rough. Long trip?"

Mike laughed, "Long trip on a C-130. Plenty of turbulence and the plane was packed with gear. I love you honey."

"I love you too Mookie. I miss you, so do the kids."

Mike asked, "Where are they?"

"Hanging with Jonas, Cering, and Kimi. I believe they were taking the kids for a swim."

"Bummer, sounds more fun than a call with dad anyway."

Mary continued, "I wanted Elisabeth to join me and not have distractions."

Matt asked, "Is everything okay?"

Elisabeth smiled and said, "I miss you."

There was still awkwardness in the style with which Matt and Elisabeth explored their romantic feelings.

Matt responded, "I miss you too," and then repeated himself, "Is everything okay?"

Elisabeth was glowing. She smiled and looked at Mary. Mary returned the smile.

"I'm pregnant Matt."

Mike got out of the chair and yelled, "Yeeesssss. My little bro is having a little baby." Mike began dancing his own version of Gangnam Style in the background.

A bit in shock, Matt smiled and said, "Really? You're pregnant?"

Elisabeth was happy to see that her husband was smiling and surprised at the same time. "Talan and Noah ran tests. They compared the results against tests taken by Mary, Kimi, and Cering and had a doctor look at them. They are 99.7% certain that I'm pregnant. We will know for sure when I go for an ultrasound."

Matt wiped his face and whispered, "Wow. I'm going to be a dad."

Mike would occasionally come over and squeeze Matt's shoulders as he danced around the room. Matt couldn't take his eyes off of Elisabeth. For whatever reason, she had become more beautiful than she was before. Mary put her arm around Elisabeth and the group shared their excitement.

Elisabeth looked into the camera, "There's one more thing Matt."

Mike quit dancing around the room. Matt asked, "What is it?"

"According to the ph tests conducted by Talan and Noah, they are fairly certain we're having a girl."

Matt was amazed. He remembered his dream with Elisabeth's aborted daughter Lisa. She had foretold of Matt and Elisabeth's daughter, and her name would be Ariel.

Matt smiled widely and said, "Ariel. Ariel Hiatt."

Any doubt of Matt's calling and journey with the Disciples was removed immediately.

Mike came up behind his brother-in-law and gave him a bear hug. "It's a girl too! Where are my cigars?" Mike went from dancing around the room to rifling through bags looking for his cigar case.

Mary congratulated her little brother. The group continued to chat about Elisabeth's health, traveling on the Excalibur, and Cering and Sallah meeting up with Matt and Mike in a few days to track Ahri. Mike lit up a cigar for Matt and gave it to him.

Matt said, "Probably a good idea that I'm smoking this a few thousand miles away from you."

The group signed off the call. Similar excitement was felt on the Excalibur and a small hotel suite in Dahab. The hotel suite backed up to a beautiful view on the Gulf of Aqaba. Matt and Mike took their cigars on the back porch and watched fisherman and divers a few hundred yards from the shore. Even though temperatures dropped during the winter months in Dahab, diving remained popular year-round because of the coral reefs and tropical sea life.

****

Morgan shook the General's hand and said, "Gil."

General Gilmore replied, "Hello Morgan."

The General took Thomas Sawyer's hand, "Good afternoon Thomas, nice to see you again."

"You too General Gilmore."

Colonel Lash followed behind Gilmore and shook hands with Morgan and Sawdog. The men took seats at a large rectangular table meant for more people.

General Gilmore opened up the meeting, "Thanks for your time this afternoon. If there is any doubt, I'm the one who called this meeting. I understand the Colonist party is putting pressure on the White House and House of Representatives to resign their positions to pave the way for a restructured government." He looked at Thomas Sawyer, whom nodded in affirmation.

Gilmore continued and looked at Morgan, "I understand that you've been given a timetable to exit the White House and are less than 21 days away from a confrontation with The Colonist party over the future of our government." Morgan nodded and continued to listen.

"Gentlemen, I ask for your patience and understanding. I believe that we can come to a resolution without having Americans coming to blows on our own soil."

Sawyer was curious and incredulous at the same time, "How do you propose we accomplish that?"

Gilmore revealed, "Before the end of this month, President Crevan will be removed from office. People with access to government intelligence, including you, understand that a group of self-proclaimed Disciples made an attempt on the President's life in Los Angeles. While the media has spun the story in several different directions, tight circles understand what really happened and how close Crevan was from meeting his maker."

Gilmore stood up and went to a nearby table, poured himself a glass of water, and continued to pace around the room. "Lash and I have been in touch with two decorated servicemen close to the Disciples, Michael Barnes and Matthew Hiatt. They are family through marriage and committed to working with the Disciples and assisting them with their goals and missions. They are unwavering in their support of the Disciples and understand their actions are interpreted as treason against the government of the United States. In short, they could care less."

Morgan interrupted, "Why are they so interested in removing the President from office?"

"Plain and simple, they believe President Crevan serves his own purpose and has little interest in the future of the United States. They point to several times in the past when Crevan aligned himself with evil people to undermine the goals of the United States' government and the American people. Many of my own regimens from the 1st Marine Division sent to the Middle East reported they were fighting the same rebels they were training for security detail. Some, including me, believed that Crevan was funding rebels for his own agenda and personal gain. Others believed that he was funneling millions of dollars through the State Department to fund terror camps in the region. Crevan and I had words over the matter and haven't trusted each other since."

Sawdog began connecting the dots, "When I was working with Congress to consider the ways and means of maintaining a strong military while cutting funding for outdated programs, Crevan's name would come up occasionally. Many people shared their frustrations over Crevan's inability to account for tens of millions of dollars that ended up in rebels' hands. Every time we asked for details, we were told the information was classified and we couldn't review Crevan's spending because of its sensitive nature."

Colonel Lash provided further detail, "Barnes and Hiatt believe that Crevan is working with a group called Samil. They are well funded and organized all over the world. Samil has utilized terror camps, in the name of radical Islam, to train people interested in destroying western civilization. Their leaders are master manipulators and call their missions jihads and terror campaigns against the west to bring power and dignity back to the Middle East. At the end of the day, Samil could care less about Islam or jihadists; they want to pit religions against each other as a means to conquer territory. In some respects, they are masterminding crusades to topple all religions worldwide. Once they have leadership in place at all corners of the earth, they will burn churches to the ground and commit genocide against anybody who supports organized religion. They are behind the dirty bomb attacks in the United States, the invasion of China by the Russians and Mongolians, the uprising in Indonesia, and several hotspots in the Middle East."

Morgan asked, "What does Samil want?"

Gilmore answered, "They want power, control, and wealth. For those who believe in the Bible and the end of times, they want to prevent a Second Coming of the Messiah. The Disciples believe that an important child will be delivered into the world to prepare everyone for the final days of our planet, at least the physical planet as we know it today. With the decline in spirituality, religion, morals, values, and everything else you learned in Sunday School, the Disciples believe, I mean know, that the Second Coming is upon us. According to the Disciples, God has always warned us of imminent doom before plagues, floods, Sodom and Gomorrah, you name it; the chosen one will prepare the world for our prophesized end. The only concept preventing God from taking the world back right now is free will. God gave us the choice to follow His gospel to the Kingdom during our lives. People will still have a choice, but this time it's good versus evil, God versus the devil, and all of the other Biblical metaphors you can think of. Samil is doing everything in its power to prevent the child from being born; they believe that will prevent the Second Coming from happening."

Sawyer asked, "What do you think?"

General Gilmore smiled as he continued to pace the private meeting room. "I have had much time to think about what's happening in the world. God, Country, Corps, Family, and Self; the Marines have a long tradition of putting God first. Therefore, I am here to support Mike and Matt with whatever they need. Whatever respect I had for President Crevan was left in the Middle East. At this point in my life, I want to make sure that my conscience is clear and I'm leaving a better country for my grandchildren. With a Third World War in full force, I will turn to those that support God in this fight of good versus evil. I'm not sure how else to approach the issues at hand. I am a man of faith and tired of playing politics. The Disciples have my full support."

Morgan knew General Gilmore very well. Gilmore put others before himself and he wasn't surprised the General would put his faith in the hands of a few. Matt and Mike were special Marines and Gilmore had great admiration for their dedication to service and protecting their country, he knew the men personally. Gilmore and

Lash had agreed to support Matt and Mike in their mission to restore power to the people of the United States. If Samil didn't control the west, they would struggle to maintain worldwide power and dominance. They would also have less chance of preventing an essential birth from taking place.

Sawdog asked, "What about the child?"

Lash said, "The Disciples have been sent, or selected, to protect the child. That's all we know. According to Hiatt and Barnes, Samil is pursuing the woman that will give birth to the child. All of the Disciples are well trained and masters of modern warfare and hand-to-hand combat. To protect us, Hiatt and Barnes didn't share much information. They share just enough, so we understood their intentions."

Sawdog persisted, "So why have you called us to this meeting? What do you need from us?"

Gilmore said, "Lash and I aren't politicians. With that said, we understand that our government has outlived its usefulness, at least in its current structure. Seeing as the Colonist party intends to change the government by any means necessary, we may be able to accomplish a number of goals without much bloodshed."

Sawdog was interested, "Do tell."

Gilmore took a seat across from Morgan and Sawyer, "Lash and I are proposing that when the Disciples take Crevan out, you will need to be the voice of reason to conduct a coup d'état against the United States' government. Because Morgan is the successor to the President's office, and I don't believe Lance has any interest in the position, now is a great time to move forward with the Colonist party and eliminate an outdated two-party system. Sawyer can help transition the government peacefully with the support of Morgan. Largely, the people of the United States will support you."

Sawyer commented, "And if we fail?"

Lash chuckled, "We don't think like that in the Marines."

Gilmore expounded, "Have you ever climbed a mountain over 14,000 feet?"

Sawyer answered, "Yes."

"You know how when you reach the precipice and can see in any direction? North, south, east and west?"

"Yes."

"And you can go in any direction from the top of the mountain without much difficulty, thought, or consideration?"

Sawyer nodded his head.

"The choice you make is more important than the direction you take. If you don't study the weather patterns, wind, sun, and position on the mountain before taking a step, you can make a fatal error. In my estimations, making the right choice is more important now than any other time in your life, political and otherwise."

Morgan wanted clarification, "You said by the end of this month?"

Gilmore nodded, "Yes, therefore Sawyer can call off the dogs in his Colonist party. They will need to develop a plan, albeit secretly, to transition the government away from a two-party system. Seeing as Morgan will be in charge, at least from a Constitutional standpoint, to assist with setting up a government that makes sense to the people of the United States. If we can all agree that a change needs to take place, a coup d'état must happen in order to restructure the government. The military will support the change."

Sawyer asked, "How can you be so sure?"

Colonel Lash laughed, "Most of us can't stand politicians. We'd rather work for a Commander-in-chief. Based on the platform of the Colonist party and current support from active military, you'll have the strength you need to make a change to the structure of the US government."

Morgan and Sawyer didn't need much more convincing. Approval ratings of Congress had been single digits for a decade. President Palmer had improved the tarnished image of the highest office in the United States, but Crevan lacked popularity in his own circles and came off as insincere with the American people. People were nervous in the United States and had good reason to be so.

Morgan asked, "When?"

Gilmore answered, "We have reason to believe the Disciples will strike during Thanksgiving. As we've seen in previous years, the President will travel overseas to visit military bases throughout the Middle East before he meets privately with leaders in the territory. After Desert Storm started several years ago, Presidents would make surprise visits to the Middle East for the troops. What used to be a surprise trip has become an expectation for some Presidents; Crevan will make the trip because President Palmer didn't miss a chance to honor the troops in the Middle East during a

Thanksgiving holiday. Crevan understands that his popularity is low and continuing to drop. While I don't think Crevan cares much about his popularity, he must maintain some level of confidence with the troops. When the Disciples make their move, you must be ready to step in and take charge of the government. I have made arrangements to move troops from the 2nd Marine Division at Camp Lejeune to participate in security exercises and detail in Washington, DC over Thanksgiving. What people don't know is that they will be providing security and detail for the government during your transition. Colonel Lash and I will remain in Washington during the holiday for your protection." Gilmore smiled as he finished up the sentence.

****

Sallah and Cering made the trip to Dahab, Egypt without incident. Matt and Mike hadn't conducted any research or surveillance on Ahriman Abraxas. They spent the downtime diving and fishing in the Gulf of Aqaba. They would videoconference Mary and Elisabeth a couple times a day to share stories and chat with other Disciples on the ship. The men were growing beards for the month of November and looked rugged. Once Sallah and Cering arrived, the group got down to business and began working with Talan and Noah to narrow down possible locations for Ahri.

Ahri was always on the move and traveled with an extensive security team. He had six decoys that looked and dressed just like him. Whenever Ahri would leave a location, the six decoys would leave at the same time in different cars for different locations.

In a hotel room overlooking the Gulf, Sallah revealed an important piece of information, "A cousin of mine roomed with one of Ahri's decoys at a university in Saudi Arabia. I spent some time with them several years ago."

Matt looked shocked, "Really?"

"Oh yes. I believe that I have him as a contact in one of my social feeds. Very few people know that he is part of Ahri's entourage."

"Why didn't you say something?"

Sallah was puzzled, "I didn't know you wanted me to say something."

Mike reminded Sallah, "You're part of our group now. Anything you can add to the insights and details of a mission must be shared. Not only to improve the chances of a mission's success, but to protect us against someone recognizing you and blowing our cover."

Sallah thought for a moment, "You're right Mike. I apologize for not sharing the information earlier. I didn't think anything of the relationship. The decoy is not the one we want anyway."

Matt smiled, "The decoy is exactly who we want."

Sallah asked, "Why?"

"He will know Ahri's travel schedule. The decoy may have little knowledge of what Ahri's destination will be, but he will know where Ahri is leaving from and at what time."

Cering added, "Security detail is usually controlled by tight circles, many family members and close friends. Obviously your cousin's friend has earned the confidence of Ahri and his colleagues. He probably knows a great deal of information about Samil and other important leaders in the group. Decoys are nothing new to the Middle East. Al Qaeda has been inserting peaceful decoys into the United States since before 9/11. How close is your cousin to the decoy?"

Sallah answered, "My cousin spent two years living with Habib in the dorms. I got busy selling sugar and was recruited by the CIA. I lost track of what happened to Habib until my cousin, Musa, told me that Habib was working for a very powerful man with great wealth and resources. I didn't think much of it, until now. I believe they are still pretty close. As you say in the United States, small world."

Matt gave Sallah a kiss on the cheek. He knew that Habib was a huge lead to determine when and where

Ahri would be positioned.

Matt insisted, "We'd like to meet with your cousin at his earliest convenience."

Sallah asked, "Should I tell him why?"

Matt, Mike, and Cering answered Sallah emphatically and simultaneously, "No!"

Matt instructed him, "Just tell him you need to meet with him as soon as possible. Where is he?"

"He is living in Mecca."

Matt turned to Cering, "Have Suzie make arrangements for four different flights from the King Hussein International Airport to Mecca. We will travel independently. Sallah will fly out last."

Cering smiled, "Mecca is not accessible to non-Muslims. We will need to travel on official business for the Olive Branch. Because of Mecca's size, plenty of international trade takes place in the city. Glad you're growing beards, you won't stand out as much. We won't be able to visit areas around holy sites in the city, it's too risky. In my opinion, Sallah should fly out first; he should also have his cousin meet us at the airport. The three of us should fly out together and meet up with Sallah and Musa at the airport on a later flight. Musa can serve as our escort."

Sallah showed some concern, "I have no identification, no passport, nothing."

Cering smiled, "Papers will be here this afternoon. You will travel with an alias as certain bad people and governments are looking for you. We all travel with aliases. Just study your paperwork and everything will check through customs."

Sallah said, "This is a little more involved than a few wire taps and riding on a motorcycle."

Mike laughed, "Welcome to the big leagues my old friend."

****

*Abraham lived for 175 years, and he died at a ripe old age, having lived a long and satisfying life. He breathed his last and joined his ancestors in death. His sons **Isaac** and **Ishmael** buried him in the cave of Machpelah, near Mamre, in the field of Ephron son of Zohar the Hittite.*

Genesis 25:7-9

Mecca is a city of rich tradition and historical significance. Matt and Mike couldn't believe they had spent time at the Western Wall in Jerusalem and were on their way to Mecca. Having Sallah travel first and explain the nature of the trip to his cousin was risky. If Musa didn't understand what Sallah was part of, or if Musa felt threatened by meeting with an Egyptian businesswoman and some westerners, Cering, Matt, and Mike could be in the wrong place at the wrong time. Saudi Arabia stayed safely on the sidelines as Israel, the United States, and Muslim countries engaged in bloodshed. Saudi Arabia allowed the United States to use military bases for wartime operations to keep Iran, Syria, Afghanistan, Yemen, and parts of Iraq in check. While several neutral countries benefitted from the military protection of warring countries, many of them preferred that the warring countries destroy each other and leave the pieces to the countries that remained neutral. Saudi Arabia had distanced itself from hard-line Islamists by supporting the west with military bases. Drone missions flown by the US from Saudi Arabia were critical to gathering intelligence and striking targets; a majority of the Muslim population in Saudi Arabia was critical of allowing the United States to support their military from Arab soil.

Matt, Mike, and Cering landed early afternoon at the King Abdulaziz International Airport, a couple hours after Sallah's flight had arrived. The airport had huge

terminals to accommodate travelers making the
pilgrimage to Mecca for Hajj once a year. Cering visited
a bathroom and wrapped her face and covered her body
with an abaya. When she came out of the bathroom,
Matt and Mike didn't even recognize her.

Cering said, "Let's go, we will need to pass through
Customs."

Matt looked at the woman walking away, "Was that
Cering?"

Mike grabbed a bag, "I think so, let's go."

The men caught up with her and Matt said, "All of the
women are dressed the same, don't get too far out front
or we might lose you."

Cering said, "If everything goes as planned, Sallah and
Musa will be waiting for us at Customs. Because of
gender parity in Saudi Arabia, I must be escorted by a
male."

Mike asked, "Gender Parity?"

"Yes. Women must be escorted by a male at all times."

Matt said, "What about us?"

"You are visitors too. Visitors from the west
nonetheless."

Mike laughed and looked at Matt, "Gender Parity?"

Matt said, "Gender Parity."

Cering kept walking; she had traveled to several parts of
Saudi Arabia in the past. Once the group arrived at
Customs, Cering did all of the talking. She explained

how they were meeting up with warehouses shipping wool to India and the two Americans were purchasing inventory for a large textile corporation. Cering was smooth in her presentation and extremely believable. The paperwork checked out, their itineraries were legitimate, and Sallah and Musa were waiting for them at the checkpoint.

One of the Custom agents called out for Musa, "Musa al Dossari."

Musa stepped forward and answered the agent's questions. Sallah had obviously coached Musa to help Matt, Mike, and Cering pass through Customs. He explained that he was acting as a chaperone for the Olive Branch company and would escort the group until they left from the airport later that evening. The agent reviewed their paperwork while occasionally looking up to verify descriptions of the travelers. After a few seconds, the Custom's agent waved them through. After watching Musa in action with Customs, Cering had no doubt that Musa was Sallah's cousin. Musa was very dynamic and animated in his discussion with the Agent, enough so that the agent became irritated after a few seconds with him.

As the group was walking away, Cering said, "Well done Mr. Al Dossari."

"Thank you Ms. Kadesh. I received honors in a few acting classes that I took at the university."

"I can't imagine why. Please call me Cering."

Sallah said, "You hungry?"

Mike replied, "You know me by now Sallah. I'll never pass up an opportunity for food."

Musa was excited, "We will dine at one of my favorite restaurants across town and enjoy Ruz Kabli and dates. You will love the food."

Mike asked Sallah, "Who is Ruz Kabli?"

Sallah began laughing, "Kabli is a very tasty dish. You will enjoy it."

Mecca is a very tightly controlled city with several checkpoints. Non-Muslims must have very specific reasons for visiting the city. Cering's company, The Olive Branch, was well known in business circles around the community. Mecca was only 40 miles from the Red Sea and cargo ships contracted by The Olive Branch made several deliveries on a weekly basis. After a ten-minute car ride and passing through one security checkpoint, the group arrived at a restaurant called Salam Saudi. The restaurant was busy and loud, perfect for an afternoon meeting with some Disciples. Cering kept her head covered and removed the veil from her face. Musa was stunned by Cering's beauty.

Cering said, "Thank you for taking the time to meet with us."

Musa replied, "Anything for Sallah. He told me that you are a good group of people."

A waiter came over and took drink orders from the group. Matt and Mike followed suit and ordered Mecca Colas.

Matt addressed Musa; "Sallah informed us that you attended the university with a man named Habib."

"I did. We roomed together for two years. Habib is a good man."

Matt stated, "Based on what Sallah shared with us, Habib may be part of Ahriman Abraxas' security detail and serving as a decoy."

Musa looked at Sallah and answered, "Not many people know, but he is working for Ahri."

The waiter delivered beverages and Sallah ordered different types of Kabli and some fresh dates.

Mike said, "We will guarantee his safety, but we need his help."

Cering removed a case from underneath her garments. Talan and Noah had programmed a small tracking device that was black, extremely thin, with an adhesive backing for attaching to a cell phone battery. She pushed the case and device across the table to Musa.

Matt explained, "We need you to meet with Habib and have him attach the device to the battery of his cell phone."

Musa asked, "Why?"

Mike said, "To guarantee his survival and ensure that we kill Ahri along with the decoys."

Musa was nervous and excited at the same time. Ahri had a reputation for being a ruthless and callous leader; Habib had witnessed Ahri's temperament firsthand while working for him.

Musa was curious, "Has Habib done anything wrong?"

"No. Unfortunately, his job comes with a number of occupational hazards, including us. We have reason to believe his boss is networked with some of the most dangerous and evil men in the world, including the current President of the United States. We will find Ahri and we will kill him. Because your friend is protecting Samil leadership, he will be in harm's way. The easiest way to take out a target with six decoys is to kill everyone. That's what we plan to do."

Cering took over, "As long as your friend agrees to help us, he will have a win-win situation. He will be the only decoy that escapes with his life and we will reward him handsomely for the assistance. You and Habib will never have to work again."

Musa looked at Sallah, "What about my cousin?"

Mike smiled, "He is one of us. Even though he won't have the luxury of never working again, we will take care of Sallah. Sallah and I have known each other for years." Mike raised his Mecca Cola and toasted Sallah.

Sallah said, "Habib, you can trust these people. They will do what they say, nothing will stand between them and a mission."

Musa said, "I have heard stories about Samil, or the group that represents the Angel of Death. In these parts, they seem to be a division of radical Islam. They have had some success recruiting young jihadists interested in bringing down the west."

Matt responded, "Samil has only one goal, spreading evil to every corner of the earth. Once they have achieved their goal, they will abandon any group or faction that has supported them. While young and impressionable, those following Samil have no idea about their true intentions."

Musa said, "And what if my friend doesn't believe me?"

Cering answered, "He will die with the others. We have

a team of trained operators coming to hunt down Ahri and kill him. They will not stop until they complete the mission. Because your friend is a decoy, he will be killed with the others. Decoys are treated just like primary targets."

Mike asked, "Can you meet with him in the very near future?"

Musa looked at Sallah, "I can."

At that point the waiter brought their meal to the table.

Matt wrapped up the business part of the lunch. "Meet with Habib, let him know we will take care of his personal safety and financial future. Instruct him not to share any of the details. If anything else, he can flee Ahri and disappear. His assistance would improve the success of our mission though. Enough about business, let's enjoy this great meal." Cering said a short prayer and the group enjoyed an authentic Arabian meal.

****

Scratches must have sensed that Elisabeth was pregnant. The cat wouldn't leave her side and Elisabeth had adopted Scratches as her companion. Little John and Rebecca enjoyed having a furry friend on the ship. Most nights, Elisabeth, John, Rebecca, and Scratches would sleep together by pulling three twin beds together. They would set up forts and read with flashlights.

Captain Phil helped Elisabeth fight off morning sickness with several of the same panaceas used for motion sickness. A regimen of herbs, teas, and oils helped Elisabeth reduce the symptoms of nausea. Several of the Disciples and a few of the IDF Sailors were really good cooks, and they would prepare a la carte meals for Elisabeth. The first trimester was the most critical to a child's development. At Suzie's request, Dr. Schwartz sent some instructions and nutritional supplements to the IDF in anticipation of the Excalibur's arrival off the coast of Israel. The good doctor would maintain communication with Elisabeth to discuss diet and exercise programs.

Everyone on the ship was happy to reach the Mediterranean again. The seas of the Atlantic had become very rough, a typical predictor of a harsh winter in the northern hemisphere. With less tides and warmer waters than the Atlantic, the Mediterranean wasn't as difficult to navigate for the Excalibur. The ship was only two days away from reaching its location off the coast of Israel. Around the globe, the war was intensifying in China, to the north of Israel, and in the Middle East. With multiple countries attacking China, Russia shifted its focus on advancing the military through Georgia and meeting up with Iranian troops in eastern Turkey. Syria began attacking Turkey to the north in preparation for the Russo-Iranian advance to the Holy Land. Russia believed that Israel was a misfit country in a territory surrounded by Muslim leadership. To prepare for a new world order, Russia had agreed to assist radical Islam with an attack on the Holy Land, as long as the territory remained neutral and served no spiritual or religious purposes. Mosques and Temples would have to be destroyed in the Holy Land if Russia lent support to their Muslim neighbors.

****

An Israeli Super Dvora II class patrol boat was racing toward the Excalibur. Matt, Mike, Cering, and Sallah had traveled safely back to Ashdod and were being ferried by the IDF to the ship. Captain Phil sounded the horn and everyone began to gather at the stern of the ship. Matt and Mike hadn't shaved for three weeks and looked rugged. The Dvora pulled up along the starboard side of the Excalibur. Aaron and John tossed ropes and a ladder down to the Dvora for tying off and climbing up the ship. The captain of the vessel boarded the Excalibur and met briefly with Amen. Amen thanked the captain for the escort and wished him well.

Mike and Mary kissed as John tugged on his father's pant leg. He brought the kids a few gifts from his trip to Mecca; John was obviously more interested in the souvenirs than Rebecca. Matt and Elisabeth were kissing each other as the sun reflected off the water and warmed their faces. Matt's hair was wet with ocean spray as he smiled, knelt down, and spoke to Elisabeth's stomach. Mary noticed her brother closing his eyes and speaking to his unborn daughter.

Mary said, "Well look at that."

Mike took note, "He'll be a great father."

Everyone on the ship welcomed Matt, Mike, Cering, and Sallah back home. Sallah was walking with confidence as he'd served the Disciples well in Mecca. Matt asked for everyone to meet at the gym in an hour. There were plenty of situations and issues to discuss. Matt walked up to Noah and called Talan over.

"Can you guys update us with information on President Crevan. When he plans to travel? What bases he will visit? What leaders he will meet with over the

Thanksgiving holiday?"

Noah said, "You bet. Very interesting following the conversations and extracurricular activities of the President."

****

Matt was happy to take a warm shower. The past several weeks had been a whirlwind of risk, relationships, and reconnaissance. He missed Scratches, the Disciples, his sister, niece and nephew, but most of all, he missed his wife. The transformation Matt had undergone was not much different than others called by God, Allah, Yahweh, Jehovah, and other variants of His name. Faith is led by decisions of chance, and rewarded with the sacrifice of doing great deeds for others. Matt fell hard for Elisabeth and was attracted to her faith, beauty, sense of humor, and motherly mannerisms. She was great with little John and Rebecca and he knew that she would become a wonderful mother to their daughter, Ariel Mary Hiatt. Elisabeth and Matt determined Ariel would carry the middle name of his sister.

Matt and Elisabeth caught up on events in the time leading up to the meeting. Elisabeth was feeling better and was excited to be working with Dr. Schwartz, albeit electronically, to care for Ariel. Dr. Schwartz was a unique doctor. He was more concerned about a patient's wellbeing over anything else. While the medical community had become more focused on quantity than quality with government mandates on healthcare, Dr. Schwartz truly focused on the quality of a patient's experience. Elisabeth felt safe. Elisabeth was also amazed by the caring nature of the Disciples, IDF sailors, and Captain Phil.

The couple went downstairs to the gym and everyone was waiting and eager for Matt to kick off the meeting. In some respects, the Disciples knew that time was running out and the war was favoring the nations overrun with Samil leadership.

Matt stood in front of the group as their elected leader. "Before I begin, I would like Noah and Talan to give us an update on POTUS."

A screen, projector, and audio equipment were set up in the gym. Li dimmed some of the lights in the area of the electronics.

Talan showed a few slides and said, "As many of us predicted, Crevan will be traveling to parts of the Middle East and Saudi Arabia during the Thanksgiving holiday. He has instructed the Deputy Director of the Secret Service to plan for travel to the Balad Air Base in Iraq and the Ali Al Salem Air Base in Kuwait. From there he will fly to Saudi Arabia and meet the Saudi king and leaders from Russia, India, and Taiwan. Crevan has decreased diplomatic relationships with China and Israel as Samil leadership isolates the two countries."

Matt said, "From a strategic perspective, our best chances with Crevan will be in Kuwait. Because of the decoys in Ahri's entourage, Cering and Lucas will be moved from Team 1 to Team 2. Instead of Dorje remaining with the Excalibur, we will need him to suit up for Team 2. With Sallah's help," Sallah smiled from ear-to-ear as Matt brought up his name, "we have recruited a decoy from inside Ahri's security detail to work with us."

Noah brought up a slide that showed a small piece of pliable plastic. "The GPS device was installed this morning in a cell phone. We are working with the IDF sailors to gather satellite images to confirm the decoy installed the device. After we confirm the decoy's phone has been tapped, we will be able to isolate Ahri's location before President Crevan arrives in Kuwait."

Matt was pleased. "Please continue to gather intelligence through the taps placed in Crevan's jaw and Habib's phone. Talan, can you bring up a slide of the Air Base in Kuwait?" Talan did as instructed and showed a satellite image of Ali Al Salem.

Matt used a laser to point, "South of the base, there is a road called Sabah Al Salem Al Sabah. Suzie will make arrangements for us to take a van into this small town to the southeast. Because prevailing winds are typically from the northwest in Kuwait, and Air Force One will be approaching from the southeast, the flight plan of Air Force One will come very close, if not directly over, Al-Jahra." Scratches quietly entered the gym and became interested in the laser pointer. She sat beneath the screen and her head began to rapidly follow the laser, until Matt pointed the red dot on the floor and Scratches started to chase it. Everyone in the group became amused with Scratches persistence and speed. She watched patiently as the red dot returned to the projector screen

Matt showed several different slides of the Air Base, the small town of Al-Jahra, and two runways utilized by aircraft at the base.

"A few years ago Noah worked on a very portable shoulder deployed surface-to-air missile (SAM) weapon. Even though the details of the project were classified, and remain classified, Israel received a dozen weapons to protect against rogue planes and missile attacks. Will you brief us Noah?"

Noah wheeled around Matt and closer to the screen. He brought up a slide that showed a Delta Defense SAM unit. "While this may look like any other SAM weapon, this one is unique. When we developed the weapon at Delta Defense, we employed the use of artificial intelligence to have separate operating systems analyze each other. One of the operating systems controls heat-seeking capabilities, while the other focuses on the properties of acquired targets. The beauty of this missile is that it transmits important information back to the operator about targets that have been locked. Heat is a very simple target to lock for any missile, but acquiring a target and locking in can be quite difficult for SAMs. Planes, helicopters, and other missiles can deploy countermeasures to detonate and draw heat-seeking missiles into their blasts. Many times the heat seeking SAM will lose its target with deployed countermeasures. With the Delta Defense SAM, once the missile has a heat lock, it begins to process millions of algorithms about the shape, speed, structure, and a whole host of other characteristics about a target. The missile can determine what type of target it's pursuing, possible evasive actions, and how many people are on board. If people evacuate or eject from an aircraft, the missile can deploy secondary measures to take out the passengers. During testing, we called the weapon the Black Widow because of its properties. The missile would leave plenty of widows behind." Noah showed of video of the DD SAM during a test.

Lucas admitted, "That's nasty."

Noah continued, "The program remained classified because of its use and function. The United Nations wouldn't approve of deploying secondary measures to kill passengers that escaped an aircraft with parachutes or by ejection seats."

Amen said, "We have used the weapons in the field. They are precise and every bit as deadly as the video shows."

"Team 1 will utilized two SAMS in the field to bring down Air Force One." Noah found the words he was saying hard to grasp.

Noah shifted his focus to Team 2 while bringing up another slide. "Team 2 will need to rely on these highly sophisticated infrared optics for surveillance. Because they are very sensitive to animate and inanimate objects, they can show the exact location of people in rooms, closets, basements, whatever. With a few adjustments, they work well day or night. Mike, Amen, Cering, Lucas, Dorje, and Kimi will carry sniper rifles and rocket propelled grenades. Sallah will be the spotter and call out targeted positions through headsets. Our mole has placed a tracking device inside his phone. Talan and I will program the optics to isolate the mole's location in Ahri's entourage; everyone else will be expendable. Because Ahri's group moves quickly, in some respects too quickly, simultaneous acquisition and execution of targets is plausible. Because most of you have carried out missions like this in the past, you understand the importance of doing this right the first time. Talan and I will support the missions through your video feeds. The IDF will be dropping off the SAMs and optics tonight under the cover of darkness. Talan and I will scrub the equipment and ensure its dependability and accuracy. Any questions?" Noah looked around the room. The Disciples understood what needed to be done and how the missions should unfold.

Matt stood up, "Thank you Noah and Talan for the information. Teams 1 and 2 will engage at the same time and leave a lasting impression on Samil. We have met with key people of the United States' government to take full advantage of our mission to eliminate Crevan and Ahriman. Many events will be set in motion once we act. Our success will pave the way for future success. We will receive intelligence about our mole tonight from the IDF. At that point we will have a clear idea if he's on board and willing to support us. Because Thanksgiving is in three days, we will need to leave tomorrow evening for our destinations. Amen will lead Team 2 and I will lead Team 1. The IDF will handle transportation of our two teams. No paperwork or passports necessary for these missions. The IDF will evacuate us from safe spots once we have completed our goals. Captain Phil will maintain a safe distance from the shores of Israel." The

Captain gave Matt a nod.

Matt motioned for Li to turn the lights back on, "Any questions?"

The room was quiet. Everyone was excited to take the fight to Samil. The Disciples had lost Liam, Trevor, and their leader Sesom. Samil had killed thousands with dirty bomb attacks in the United States and inserted cells of their leadership in several unstable countries. On a global perspective, Samil was gaining ground and winning the war of terror. Operation Thanksgiving would involve missions for the Disciples to change the dynamics of leadership in the United States and eliminate a key leader of Samil.

****

Late in the evening, a Super Dvora II patrol boat pulled alongside the Excalibur. Matt, Amen, Jonas, Talan, Noah, Phil, and Mike met with the Captain and a few of his crew. The boat delivered two Delta Defense SAMS, the specialized set of optics, and intelligence about Musa's cousin, Habib. As predicted, he was with Ahriman and his GPS device was working according to plan. Nobody, not even Sallah, had communicated with Musa or Habib since the meeting in Mecca. According to intelligence, Ahri would be traveling to Armenia during Thanksgiving. Because of the distances involved to Kuwait and Armenia, the IDF would utilize helicopters for transport to specific airbases and fly the groups by small stealth planes to their destinations. Low altitude drops would be necessary to avoid radar detection. With hot spots everywhere in the Middle East, transportation would be tricky. However, Saudi Arabia, Iraq, and Turkey were allowing the Israeli Air Force to use parts of their airspace.

As Russia and Iran teamed up to the north of Israel, the prognosis looked bad for the Holy Land. IDF intelligence showed massive brigades of Russian troops, equipment, and missiles being mobilized in western Russia. Troops from Iran were meeting up with the Russian brigades in Georgia. Even though Russia declared the move defensive, Israel had enough intelligence to seriously consider an attack from the north as imminent. The military and citizens of Israel were nervous for good reasons.

Matt thanked the Captain and his crew for delivering the weapons and optic device. He requested that the Captain thank the IDF for their continued support with surveillance and use of the Israeli sailors. The Israeli sailors were crucial to the Excalibur's cover and navigation. In the event of an attack, the sailors were trained to utilize the antiaircraft guns and other countermeasures installed on the ship for defense. The IDF and Italians, at the Vatican's request, had pledged to support the Excalibur from the air. They were willing to provide air support if the ship was attacked.

As the Dvora pulled away from the ship, Matt experienced a feeling of emptiness.

"Everything alright Matt?" Jonas sensed Matt was struggling with his emotions.

Matt replied, "Yeah, I think so. You ever get one of those feelings?"

Jonas smiled, "All the time. Don't forget whom I work for on a daily basis. What specific feelings are you experiencing?"

Matt looked out into the darkness, "That we will be successful, but our success will come at a price. That's about as specific as I can be right now."

Jonas knew the feeling well. "As leader of the Disciples, and inspiration to the others, your job is to provide us the best possible chance of success. Based on the teams you've put together, and the missions we have in front of us, you've done your job. Much like when God created man and woman, and gave us the best chance to have a good life while helping each other, He left many of the details up to us. God knew that, given a choice, several would stray and deny His very existence. He also knew that the time would come for a Revelation in order to reclaim the earth and take souls with Him into salvation. Not everyone will make the journey, not everyone will succeed when the time comes."

The men stepped to the rail of the ship as Jonas continued, "The people in this group, on this ship, have been chosen for good reason. They give you the best chance of success."

Matt looked at Jonas, "So, how do you explain Sesom?"

Jonas had thought about an answer already. "It was your time to lead."

****

As the Philistine moved closer to attack him,
David ran quickly toward the battle line to meet him.
Reaching into his bag and taking out a stone,
He slung it and struck the Philistine on the forehead.
The stone sank into his forehead,
and he fell facedown on the ground.

So David triumphed over the Philistine with a sling and
a stone;
Without a sword in his hand he struck down the
Philistine
and killed him.

1 Samuel 17:49-50

Mary and Elisabeth were nervous. Because of the Excalibur's proximity to the war on several fronts, death was in the air. Everyone could sense it. As the women said goodbye to their husbands, the Disciples, Jonas, and Sallah were all business. The IDF helicopters airlifted Teams 1 and 2 from the stern of the ship. Amen and Matt would have a day of surveillance before they executed the missions. All of the air travel and a low altitude drop would need to happen at nightfall. Talan and Noah would monitor the teams' positions, communications, and vital signs. For any mission, communication was the key. Everyone knew Air Force Once would be flying into Kuwait under the cover of darkness. The SAM weapons of Team 1 had modified night vision viewers. They could detect movement and heat up to 80 miles in the night sky.

Team 2 would be dropped near the city of Yerevan in Armenia. Several Russian and Iranian leaders were convening in Yerevan to discuss operations and movement of the battalions. Amen and Cering were fairly certain that Ahri would join the generals in

Yerevan; Talan and Noah would know for certain once the mole landed with Ahri's entourage in Yerevan.

****

Now the word of the Lord came to me, saying, "Son of man, set your face against Gog, of the land of Magog, the prince of Rosh, Meshech, and Tubal, and prophesy against him, and say, 'Thus says the Lord God: Behold, I am against you, O Gog, the prince of Rosh, Meshech, and Tubal. I will turn you around, put hooks into your jaws, and lead you out, with all your army, horses, and horsemen, all splendidly clothed, a great company with bucklers and shields, all of them handling swords. Persia, Ethiopia, and Libya are with them, all of them with shield and helmet; Gomer and all its troops; the house of Togarmah from the far north and all its troops—many people are with you.'"

Ezekiel 38: 1-6

Matt, Jonas, Ethan, and Li sat in a van near a convenience store in the city of Al-Jahra as the sun began to set to the west.

Matt said, "Ethan and I will fire the SAMs. We have one shot at this, so let's make it count. Jonas and Li will provide cover with the Tavor assault rifles. No need to fire at citizens unless they're hostiles. Don't let anybody video you with a smart phone or camera. We will wear masks just in case. Jonas will handle communications with any curiosity seekers."

Ethan spoke into his headset, "How long Talan?"

Talan and Noah were in the control room set up for the IDF sailors. "According to Crevan's tracking device, he should be coming from the south, by way of the Indian Ocean and up through the Persian Gulf. He's flying over Africa right now. Based on his speed and our calculations, POTUS should be in your neighborhood in a little over four hours."

Noah mentioned, "Considering the speed and altitude of Air Force One when they fly over, the likelihood of countermeasures being deployed when SAMs are launched will be minimal. Even though AFO will detect and launch countermeasures automatically, the missiles will be at their back door before they are effective."

Noah switched his focus to Team 2, "Amen, are you in position and ready?"

"Yes. Sallah is on the second floor in a vacant office facing an Armenian government building. I am south and can see his location to the west and Dorje's to the east. Mike and Kimi are in the same office building as Sallah, but situated on the floor above him; I have a visual of their positions as well. Cering is covering the north exit from a rooftop. Once the shooting starts, IDF Special Forces will drop Lucas to the northwest of the building. Lucas will be our runner and meet up with Habib. Security is visible and predictable."

Talan said, "Sallah, we have a good read on Habib's location through your video feed. How are the optics working?"

"Very well. Counting Habib, we have sixteen people in the building. The infrared locator is working well. Looks like the group is meeting for drinks before dinner. Habib is coming up red and everyone else is green." Those listening to the radio feed could tell that Sallah was excited. Noah and Talan had a clear signal for their video feed of Team 2.

Matt was a little concerned, "Amen, I'm not sure if the group will remain at the location for four hours. If they begin to leave before POTUS arrives in Kuwait, execute the operation."

"Will do. Mike?"

Mike answered, "Yes, Amen."

"You focus on targets in the building and Kimi will engage the security detail. Sallah will call out targets for Mike at the front of the building."

"10-4"

Amen's team had RPGs in case they were needed. With all of the exits covered, and crossfire raining from above, RPGs would be a last resort for Team 2's mission. As with many other missions, the game of hurry up and wait seemed like a lifetime. The Disciples, Mike, Sallah, and Jonas would maintain complete radio silence to focus on the task at hand. Occasionally, Sallah would update Team 2 with locations of people in the Armenian government building. Drinks and dinner took a little over two hours and Ahri appeared to be presenting information to the generals, decoys, and other military leaders. Even though Sallah, Talan, and Noah couldn't hear what was being said in the room, the teams could only imagine that Ahri was treating the Iranian and Russian leaders to an unforgettable meal; one that was accompanied with a large payout and specific instructions about when to attack Israel and Turkey from the northeast.

Military operations, for most countries around the globe, had become a game of corruption and power. While governments used to represent the ideals of individual rights, monarchies, dictatorships, liberty, and religion, money had paved the way for corruption and use of military leadership for selfish purposes. Several years prior, Syria had changed the way people viewed dictators. A ruthless tyrant had elected to kill any citizen in opposition to his government. Samil watched with amazement as western civilization allowed Syria to indiscriminately butcher its citizens. Even though Syrians called out for help and support, the calls fell on the deaf ears of ineffective bureaucracies.

****

"Matt, we are beginning to see movement from the security detail positioned in front of the government building. Looks like the military leaders and Ahri are getting ready for departure." Amen continued to look though his riflescope to the north.

Matt answered, "The operation is a go Amen. POTUS is due to arrive in 40 minutes. Execute according to plan. Sallah has the call." The others listened to the radio feed as Team 2 loaded and locked their weapons.

Amen said, "Lucas, standby. We aren't certain of whom will be departing first."

"Standing by."

Sallah said, "Four vehicles pulling up to the main entrance of the building; eight people making their way to the front of the building. Mole is still in the dining area. Security detail exiting vehicles with automatic weapons."

Sallah continued, "People dressed in military uniforms exiting the building."

Amen said, "Standby. Any visual of decoys?"

"Negative. Eight remaining in the dining area; decoy one of them."

Amen ordered, "Do not engage the military convoy! Stand down until Sallah's call." The military leaders loaded into armored vehicles and drove away quickly.

A moment later, more armored vehicles made their way to the front of the government building and split up. Two parked in front, two to the north, two to the south, and one to the east.

Sallah verified, "We have seven vehicles parked at all exits of the government building. Two in front, two to the north, two to the south, and one to the east, security has exited the vehicles with automatic weapons. Eight remaining occupants shaking hands and hugging each other, departure imminent."

Amen asked, "Is security detail in uniform?"

"Yes. Button down tops and khakis, all the same color. Color appears to be beige based on what I can see."

Amen called out to the team. "One shot to Ahri, then use RPGs for security vehicles. Cering and I will reload and take out second vehicle from our positions. Mike and Kimi, take out vehicles according to your position; left-to-left, right-to-right."

Kimi replied, "10-4."

Sallah said, "We have movement. Mole is heading toward the main entrance. One hanging back in the dining area."

Amen continued, "Roll Lucas. Mike and Kimi standby, everyone else is a go. Fire when ready."

Sallah focused in on the two men heading to the front of the building. "Target in front, friendly in back. Maybe 15 meters from the entrance."

Mike responded, "10-4. On your mark Sallah."

"5 meters, friendly in the back. Here they come." As Sallah finished his sentence, Amen, Cering, and Dorje took out the targets and security detail. The sniper rifles were high powered and equipped with silencers. Sallah could hear bullets nearby whizzing through the air.

Mike said, "Target is heading for lead car. Kimi take out security."

Mike hit his target and began shooting security detail with Kimi. The mole went to the ground and covered his head. Lucas rolled up in a German sport's car and hopped out of the backseat. He was carrying a Tavor assault rifle. Lucas went around the armored cars and called out for the mole.

"Habib. Let's go." Mike, Cering, and Dorje were destroying armored vehicles with RPGs.

Sallah said, "Remaining person heading for entrance. You're about to have company Lucas."

Lucas turned as the remaining occupant came through a large wooden door. He unloaded three rounds, two to the chest and one to the head. Lucas grabbed Habib and rushed him to the vehicle waiting in the street. The men disappeared into the backseat as the car sped away. Mike and Kimi destroyed the armored cars parked at the front of the government building.

Lucas called out to Habib, "Good work, keep your head down."

Amen called out, "Time to go." Talan, Noah, Captain Phil, John, Aaron, and the IDF sailors began high-fiving each other in the control room.

Dorje headed south to meet up with Amen. Three more high performance vehicles were waiting to pick up Cering, Amen and Dorje, and Sallah, Mike, and Kimi. Lucas was on his way to the rendezvous point with an Israeli stealth helicopter.

Amen looked at his watch, "Three minutes until lift off. Destroy all vehicles, retain all weapons."

Three minutes felt like an eternity when racing toward evacuation. Four IDF drivers escorted Team 2 to a nearby helicopter that landed seconds earlier. After the teams exited the vehicles, IDF Special Operations tossed timed C4 explosives in the front seat of the high performance autos; each of the vehicles had a full tank of gas. The IDF had scrubbed the vehicles and scratched out VIN and serial numbers. Team 2 could hear emergency vehicles responding to the carnage nearby. Everyone, including the drivers, piled into the helicopter and the pilot was in the air in a matter of seconds.

Amen reported to Matt, "Targets eliminated, bird in the air, everyone accounted for, including our mole."

Mike came over the radio, "Your turn."

Matt said, "Well done Team 2. T-30 minutes until Air Force One is overhead. This one is for Sesom."

****

Noah broke radio silence, "Matty, AFO is less than 100 miles from your position. Plane is coming up the Persian Gulf from the southeast. Looks like one escort, an F-15."

Matt said, "Thanks Noah."

The van had been moved to Entertainment City west of Kuwait City. Jonas was driving and Li was in the passenger seat next to him. Matt and Ethan were in the back readying the gear. An IDF stealth helicopter had departed from Israel, flown over Jordan, and refueled at the border of Saudi Arabia and Iraq. They would rendezvous with Team 1 in a neighborhood with an adjacent field.

Noah updated Team 1, "AFO is approximately 70 miles from the airfield. The plane will go dark before it reaches the coast of Kuwait."

Ethan responded, "10-4."

"Shut down the lights." Matt was ready for one of the most important missions of his life. Ironically, the operation was against the country he had fought for, spilled blood for, and taken an oath to protect. Jonas stopped the van on the side of a street in a neighborhood that was almost pitch. Between the front seats sat 10 pounds of C4 explosive. Jonas set the detonator for 15 minutes and depressed a red button. The bomb began counting down for detonation.

Jonas said, "Bomb is armed."

Matt asked, "You have the remote?"

"I do." Jonas had a remote that could detonate or disarm the bomb within a distance of 400 yards.

"Let's roll." Team 1 left the van behind. Matt and Ethan carried the RPGs on their backs. Jonas and Li carried Tavor assault rifles equipped with flashlights and laser sights. In less than a minute, Team 1 was positioned in an open field. Ethan set the RPG on his shoulder and began to search to southeastern sky; Matt did the same.

Ethan asked, "Noah, can you show us the global positioning of AFO through our viewers?"

Noah punched the keyboard and sent a signal to the RPGs. "You should have the target in your view finders. Arrows pointing to the target will help acquisition if it's not in your sites. Don't lock until the target is overhead; AFO will detect someone has locked on the plane with radar."

Matt said, "10-4. I see the plane. Making a roll to the west for final approach.

"I see the target too. Thanks for the feed Noah."

Noah responded, "You bet. Let me know if you need anything else."

"How is the neighborhood doing Li?" Matt didn't want to take his eyes off the target.

"Quiet. A few lights on, but no disturbances." Li was monitoring the southwest and Jonas was surveying the southeast.

Matt said, "Computer showing AFO is nine minutes away, standby. Don't worry about the escort plane. He won't even know what hit AFO. The F-15 will be looking for enemy aircraft."

The IDF control room on the Excalibur was still. Aside

from a few beeps and flashes, nobody moved or said a word. Captain Phil, Aaron, John, Mary, and Elisabeth were sitting against a wall listening to communications. Noah, Talan, and the sailors had several overhead computer screens monitoring global positions in front of them. Team 2 was traveling over the Black Sea and on their way to Romania.

Matt came over the radio, "Two minutes and counting, plane is completely dark. Target lock when bird is overhead."

Ethan was looking through the viewfinder, "10-4."

Matt said, "Once we lock, I'll give the command to fire."

"Fire on your command." Ethan was controlling his breathing. The adrenaline flowing through his body was initiating a fight-or-flight response. He was able to control the hormones with rhythmic breathing that was slow and steady.

Matt was equally excited. With two good shots, the Disciples would deliver a hard blow to Samil and evil leadership gaining power across the globe. Matt slowed his breathing and thought about the dirty bomb attacks, Noah and Jonas being shipped to Gitmo, and the death of his friend and leader Sesom.

Matt began the countdown, "Ten, nine, eight, seven, six, five, four, three, two, one, lock on target."

AFO was at 3500 feet and descending. Because of the low altitude and slow speed, the RPG computers finished their algorithms in less than two seconds. The escort plane was slightly behind the left wing of Air Force One.

"Fire." The RPGs launched and reached AFO's wings in a flash. The pilot must have noticed the lock because he began to turn the plane hard to the right as two missiles struck it. President Crevan's plane exploded into a giant fireball that lit up the sky and neighborhood. The F-15 escort had to take evasive action to not be engulfed by the explosion. Matt depressed a GPS tracking device on his vest and the men started dropping flares.

"Let's move north. Bird will be here in seconds. Blow the van Jonas!" Matt slung the RPG over his shoulder and began to race through the field with the others. Jonas pushed a button on the remote and a large explosion occurred behind them a few hundred yards away that shook the ground. The F-15 became interested in the explosion and radioed for ground support from the air base and Kuwaiti military.

Ethan said, "I hope the Iraqi Republican Guard didn't set mines in this field during the Gulf War."

Jonas replied, "All the more reason to run faster," as he ran by Ethan.

Air Force One debris began falling from the sky well short of the airfield. Pieces of the plane crashed down on Sixth Ring Road on the west side of Al-Jahra. The IDF stealth helicopter had been positioned over Kuwait Bay for Team 1's signal.

The Commander of Ali Al Salem Air Base picked up a phone tied directly to the Pentagon.

"Commander Paul, this is Vice President Morgan. Please patch me through to the escort of Air Force One."

The Commander was shocked the Vice President phoned the base so quickly after the explosion. "Yes sir." Commander Paul spoke over an intercom and ordered the command center to patch the Pentagon line through to the F-15.

"The line is yours Vice President Morgan."

Morgan called out to the F-15 surveying the neighborhood, flares in the field, and remains of a van that was still burning. "Alpha Charlie 1-7-7-6, this is Vice President Morgan. I order you to stand down and land your F-15 at Ali Al Salem immediately."

The pilot didn't believe the order at first, "Vice President Morgan, hostiles are in the area and have destroyed Air Force One and all souls on board."

Morgan said, "Captain Marshall. Return the plane to base and that's an order. Let me remind you that you're speaking to the acting Commander-in-chief. If you fail to follow my order, I will guarantee that the only thing you fly for the rest of your career is a kite."

Marshall peeled off his route and replied, "Copy and returning to base."

Morgan said, "Commander Paul, send emergency responders to the wreckage and work with the Kuwaiti people to put out fires. Secure the area and we'll send a response team to investigate the crash site. With regard to military operations, stand down. Information and orders will be coming soon."

The Commander was even more confused, "I understand sir." The phone hung up. Everyone at the base was in a state of disbelief. Some began shedding tears, as they couldn't comprehend the magnitude of what just happened. Standing down and not responding seemed very unnatural during wartime operations.

Cabinet members at the White House, including the

Joint Chiefs of Staff and Secretary of State Watt, were beginning to assemble in the Presidential Emergency Operations Center below the East Wing. General Gilmore and Vice President Morgan were coming from the Pentagon to the White House to meet with Cabinet members that were available; others would join by a satellite feed. Colonel Lash was at the nation's Capitol with Thomas Sawyer. Gilmore had decided to accompany Morgan to the Pentagon and join him in the Presidential Emergency Operations Center to share news of the coup d'état; Lash was fine with the change in plans. As congressmen and women were made aware of the news, they immediately began assembling in their respective chambers. The time was 3:16 pm in Washington DC.

As Gilmore and Morgan entered the White House, much of the administration and White House staff were in panic mode. Gilmore and Morgan maintained their composure as they went to the East Wing and took an elevator down to the situation room. When they arrived, people in the Cabinet were trying to determine who was responsible, when to strike, how could this have happened, and all of the other obvious questions that would be asked in a situation room. Vice President Morgan asked everyone to be seated, as he would begin the briefing to bring everyone up to speed. Other members had dialed in via satellite.

"General Gilmore and I came from the Pentagon and we're well aware of the circumstances surrounding leadership and the United States' government right now."

Joint Chiefs of Staff Richards interrupted Vice President Morgan, "Is it true that you gave specific orders for Commander Paul to stand down in Kuwait after Air Force One was attacked from the ground?"

"Yes."

Richards was irritated by Morgan's quick response, "And how can you justify ordering our military to stand down when the President of the United States is under attack?"

Morgan looked Richards directly in the eyes. "If you'd shut your mouth for a few seconds, I'll let you know exactly what's happening in Kuwait and with our government."

Once Morgan mentioned "government", people understood the downing of Air Force One was a little more involved than a well-executed terrorist attack.

"While unfortunate, the destruction of Air Force One is part of a bigger operation. This is a coup d'état to unseat President Crevan and restructure the government of the United States of America. We know that Crevan was involved in dirty politics and shady military operations while he was serving as Secretary of State. He was shuffling money, ordering assassinations, and working with a group called Samil to unseat President Palmer and coordinate attacks on the homeland with dirty bombs in four of our major cities. After Crevan assumed the office of Vice President, Secretary of State Watt continued to finance suspicious operations in the Middle East and Indonesia. Crevan and Watt had the perfect plan to help Russia gain territory and control in eastern Asia. Samil was counting on Crevan to run operations in the west and Russia to control the east."

Secretary of Defense Drake asked, "Why? What were they looking to accomplish?"

Morgan responded, "On the surface, they wanted to control the world with evil dictatorships to wipe out religion and prevent any chance of a 2nd Coming of a

Messiah. They wanted complete control of all financial and natural resources of the planet. Samil is very determined and has ties to several governments involved in the current war."

Watt said, "That's absurd. You're trying to draw on people's emotions and these self-proclaimed Disciples to take over the government. You've never liked Crevan and devised your own plan to remove him from office."

Joint Chiefs Richards said, "I agree. Without the military, you won't be able to rally boy scouts to support a coup."

Gilmore smiled, "That's where I come in. Vice President Morgan has the full support of Marines from Camp Lejeune conducting training exercises in DC at this moment. He's also acting as the CIC for the United States military right now. Morgan pulls rank on you Richards."

"And don't forget who you are speaking with Gilmore. I have a little more brass than you and I don't have to acknowledge anything until congress recognizes Vice President Morgan as the President and Commander-in-chief." Richards was obviously angered by Gilmore's insinuation.

"That's just it Richards, I don't want to run the country. I'm not here for my own power or position. On my orders, Colonel Lash and Thomas Sawyer are meeting with Congress to inform them of what will happen over the next 30 days. The House will be dissolved and the Senate will remain intact. We will continue to reduce the size of government and focus on returning liberties and money to the American people."

Secretary of Defense Drake said, "Thomas Sawyer, why Thomas Sawyer?"

Morgan said, "The Colonist party provided the government notice to dissolve the House of Representatives and restructure the Executive Branch weeks ago. According to Sawyer, and confirmed by the FBI, the Colonist party was planning an attack on Washington, the Pentagon, and several key sites across the nation. Because many of the members of the Colonist party are military, I felt that an attack on Washington, DC and other Federal buildings across the nation would lead to a Civil War that would spill into the streets and claim tens of thousands, if not hundreds of thousands, of lives. The Disciples were going to assassinate President Crevan because of his ties to Samil and his evil nature. Because two worlds were colliding at the same time, we leveraged the acts of one to propel another. Thomas Sawyer was part of those conversations because of his power within the Colonist party. He has been called on to help us restructure the government, with one unified party. I don't have all of the details, but a new government must be established in order for the United States to move forward."

Secretary of State Watt began to leave his chair when Morgan stopped him. "Not so fast Mickey, you're under arrest for embezzlement, supporting terrorist organizations, and conspiring to torture and kill Americans." General Gilmore stood behind Mickey Watt's chair.

A phone began ringing in the middle of the table and Secretary of Defense Drake picked it up. Morgan asked, "What is it?"

Drake hung up the phone and said, "Turn on the television, any news channel."

Morgan turned on a TV nearby that was already set to a news station. Reports were coming in from Saudi Arabia that Israel had been attacked with several short-range nuclear missiles. According to several satellite images and eyewitness accounts, the IDF had destroyed a few missiles in the atmosphere, but six missiles struck Jerusalem, Haifa, Tel Aviv, and Ashdod. A coordinated attack was launched by Lebanon, Syria, Iran, Russia, and the West Bank at the same time. Even though several missile defense systems were successful, hundreds of thousands of Israeli citizens were presumed dead and thousands more injured.

Israel launched a counterattack and emptied their silos of nuclear warheads that wiped out the West Bank, Lebanon, southern Syria, western Russia, and all of Iran. Israel had warned of severe retaliation for any nuclear attacks against their country. Unfortunately, the largest cities of Jerusalem and West Jerusalem were completely destroyed. The Holy Land was wiped from the face of the earth.

Morgan dismissed the Cabinet members and walked to the Capitol building. Secret Service was leery of Vice President Morgan making a 1-½ mile journey on foot, but he wanted to walk the mall. Gilmore had the Marines from Camp Lejeune provide additional security for Morgan's stroll. Once he arrived on Capitol Hill, he found Sawyer addressing the House of Representatives. While news was pouring in from all over the world, the representatives in the lower house of Congress knew that change was necessary in order to move the nation forward. Thomas Sawyer had earned the trust and respect of both houses for many years. His dream of a new government was coming to fruition.

Morgan spoke to both houses well into the evening. He described how he had no desire to pursue the Oval Office and would return to the state of Texas and consider the future of public service. Based on Sawyer's outline for a government overhaul, Lance Morgan would

be out of a job in 90 days. Morgan lent support to
Sawyer and described how difficult the journey would
be. Above anything else, the nation needed to come
together.

****

When the war intensified in the Middle East, Captain Phil moved the Excalibur hundreds of miles from the coast of Israel to the north of Egypt. Elisabeth was devastated by the news of what happened in Israel, the West Bank, and countries to the north and east. Based on the magnitude of Israel's counterattack, Elisabeth's parents were probably dead.

Cering made arrangements for the Excalibur to dock at Alexandria in Egypt. Team's 1 and 2 were being escorted by the IDF to meet up with the others in Alexandria. Captain Phil excused the IDF sailors from the ship to return home and help with rescue efforts. He told the sailors they were always welcome to return to the ship and sail with him in the future. Phil felt terrible about the tremendous loss of life and devastation to the most Holy place on earth.

Captain Phil saw Mary and Elisabeth on the dock with little John and Rebecca. He thought about Sesom and said a prayer for his African friend. Sesom had a vision, a vision of a better world. One that would be prepared for the 2nd Coming of the Messiah and understand the significant differences between good and evil. The End of Alpha would pave the way for a better future, one that reconciled the past and embraced prophecy, the Beginning of Omega.

****

Matt was sitting in front of makeup lights at a television studio in Alexandria. Everyone was there to support Matt and stood behind the stage production. A makeup artist was applying base and teasing Matt's hair.

"Is this really necessary?" The peanut gallery in the back of the room began to smirk and giggle.

The director asked, "Do you need a teleprompter?"

Matt replied, "No. I know exactly what I want to say."

"Don't forget that this will be a live broadcast covered by much of the world."

Matt laughed, "I'm at my best when the pressure cooker's on high." The peanut gallery began smirking and giggling even more.

"Can we do something about those people in the back of the room?"

The director looked at Lucas and said, "You handle your own security."

"Good idea," Lucas made a fist and punched his left hand. Everyone kept up the laughter as Matt prepared for his primetime debut.

A producer came over the intercom, "We go live in 30 seconds. The makeup artist finished up and the production team took their positions.

"How do I look honey?" Matt smiled at his wife.

"Inner beauty is what God seeks." Elisabeth quoted a verse from the Bible and shrugged her shoulders.

The producer counted down from ten seconds until the red light illuminated on the top of the camera.

As major networks interrupted their regular programming, Matt looked straight into the camera.

"I am the Twelfth Disciple; twelve of us were called, nine of us remain. We are responsible for the downing of Air Force One and assassination of Ahriman Abraxas. Media outlets may spin the story in several directions and have you believe something that isn't true. The reasons for our actions are too complicated to list in a television broadcast. Therefore, I ask for your trust and understanding.

As you can see by the military uniform, I've served in the United States Marine Corp and Special Operations. I love my country and the opportunity to serve when called. My calling has taken me beyond the military and now I serve a greater purpose. The Disciples will prepare the earth for its return to God.

The world is currently divided between those fighting for good and those who fight for darkness. President Crevan and Ahriman Abraxas represented the wickedness that plagues our world today. They have successfully set up a network of evil that rivals the German empire of the 1930s, and they have an abundance of followers. They call themselves Samil and they are powerful in the United States, Russia, Indonesia, and the Middle East. They will employ any means necessary to establish dictatorships with unstable governments. They prey upon weak government structures, those with radical religious beliefs, cultural differences, and any other divisive means they can use to their advantage. Samil's sole purpose is to prevent the 2nd Coming of the Messiah. We are here to usher in our period of Revelation, a renewal of spirit and mankind.

I'm not here to convince you of anything. Most of you won't believe me, even though what I'm sharing was prophesized 2000 years ago. You have a choice to consider because the final battle won't be fought over politics, religion, or money, but your soul. Make sure your house is in order for God did not send His Son into the world to condemn this place, but to save the world through Him. For you truly know that the day of our Lord comes as a thief in the night, and so will his Disciples."